BW

Virgin Soul

Virgin Soul

Judy Juanita

VIKING

VIKING
Published by the Penguin Group
Penguin Group (USA) Inc., 375 Hudson Street,
New York, New York 10014, USA

USA | Canada | UK | Ireland | Australia | New Zealand | India | South Africa | China
Penguin Books Ltd, Registered Offices: 80 Strand, London WC2R 0RL, England
For more information about the Penguin Group visit penguin.com

First published in 2013 by Viking Penguin, a member of Penguin Group (USA) Inc.

ISBN 978-0-670-02658-6

Printed in the United States of America
10 9 8 7 6 5 4 3 2 1

Designed by Carla Bolte

PUBLISHER'S NOTE
This is a work of fiction. Names, characters, places, and incidents either are the product of the author's imagination
or are used fictitiously, and any resemblance to actual persons, living or dead, business establishments, events, or
locales is entirely coincidental.

In loving memory of my parents

Marguerite Juanita and Albert Haywood Hart Jr.

For their enduring union

and

for teaching me the meaning of commitment

Freshman

1

Uncle Boy-Boy was a dentist and Aunt Ola Ray was his wife and I was not their adored child—I was more obligation than kin, their dark-skinned orphan-in-residence. I had gotten accepted into SF State as a freshman, but my "financial resources" amounted to my seventy-two-dollar monthly Social Security check. I wasn't about to ask them to support me. It was 1964 in Oakland, California, and the Monday after I graduated high school I hotfooted over to Oakland City College and registered. Very soon thereafter, I moved to the Berkeley YWCA for $12.50 a week and kept my head attached to a Dictaphone at the Alameda County Welfare Department twenty hours a week to earn my way through school.

Thus, one month out of high school, July 1964, I hit Oakland City College's summer session. The powers that be had changed the name to Merritt College and were building a hills campus. But we called it City, a raggedy, in-the-flatlands, couldn't-pass-the-earthquake-code, stimulating, politically popping repository of blacks who couldn't get to college any other way, whites who had flunked out of the University of California, and anybody else shrewd enough to go free for two years and transfer to Berkeley, prereqs zapped. Other colleges may have been places where one and all rushed to finish, but at City, guys stayed on, growing not necessarily wiser but hipper. If women stayed longer than two, two and a half years, they were old meat. I learned fast what I wanted to be.

When I got there, Huey Newton had been there a few, old as salt. His girlfriend's locker was next to mine. She and I took tennis and French together and traded notes for Western Civ. I didn't know diddly about the Greeks being invaded by the Romans, but Margaret, whose parents were Greek, knew it like the back of her hand. Our lockers were right next to my journalism classroom, where I was always dashing out of the newsroom fancying myself a kind of cub reporter on a mission around the school. Journalism was exciting where English 1A was stifling. I got used to Huey's high-pitched voice asking me, "Have you seen Margaret?" He was always looking for her. She and I practiced often, lobbing shots on the court and using our mot du jour. Sometimes we walked to her parents' house, a colonial three-story on nearby College Avenue, talking French all the way. They made a strange couple. Margaret was white, tall, and husky-voiced, and had dark hair down to her waist and gushed upper middle class. Huey was short and cute but street. With his pop-out-of-nowhere demeanor and pointy-toe shoes, he fit my image of a crazy nigger. What I loved was listening to the black intellectuals and white boys from the W. E. B. Du Bois Club talk; my friends lumped all of them together as Communists. On hot afternoons we sat for hours on the front lawn, cutting class or coming back after class to see if they had fainted from heat prostration. I was there as often as I was in class. Their language made no sense to me—Fair Play for Cuba sounded like U.S. volleyball teams going to Havana.

Summer session at City was the most exciting time, because everybody was there hanging out: the black Greeks from San Francisco State and San Jose State picking up the free six credits; the students from the black colleges home for the summer; and the grads fresh out of high school. To see, be seen, and catch. Everybody ragged down. I had never seen so many fine dudes in my life. My friends and I had a rating system: the X-ray guys—they were the ones who looked clean through your clothes; the bifocals—they studied you to see if you measured up; the four-eyes—they studied, period; and the 20-20s—just right. Not fresh but willing, not snobbish but particular, and so sure they were going to be somebody.

The 20-20s were rare. One wanted to be an accountant, not just a bookkeeper, but a certified public accountant. We were impressed. I saw him years later collecting tolls at the Bay Bridge. Another one never specified what he wanted to be but was earnest, polite, and neat, the trappings of aspiration as essential as aspiration itself at that stage.

And *seddity, siddity, sedid*, the word hasn't gotten to *Webster's* dictionary yet. The uppity, light-skinned sedids went to Snookie's for lunch; Snookie's was all plate-glass windows and striped candy colors. The sedids possessed money or, in lieu of that, yellow, high yellow, sandy yellow, mellow yellow, sandy, mariney, light brown, peach, or caramel skin; the line stopped there. Money for Snookie's regulars meant living in the hills or, for dudes, driving a dick car—the Stingray or the Jaguar—in red, silver, or white. An MG was okay too. If they didn't have the car, money, or name that signified daddy was a judge, Realtor, doctor, or lawyer, or that mother was a schoolteacher, and if they weren't cute, i.e., keen featured, didn't dress sharp—blue cotton slacks with the madras belt and shirt to match, gray gabardine slacks with jeff shirt and pullover sweater, uh, sleeves very full, if you please—the guys had to have a rap, a line that wouldn't quit: *You rocking, baby, from the front, the side, and all the way back.* Thank goodness for equalizers, for *x*, the unknown factor that makes for resiliency.

The get-down place to go was not seddity Snookie's but dark and dusty Jo Ethel's, the greasy spoon where Percy Mayfield blew the blues and the doughnuts were as fresh as the milk was sour. I saw Huey occasionally at Jo Ethel's, never on the makeshift podiums with the intellectuals. I didn't hang much anywhere and didn't get around. The first time I heard someone call Mary Jane an aphrodisiac, I imagined that black patent leather shoes were a kind of kinky turn-on. The students talked sex like medical practitioners. Clothes hangers, quinine, horseback riding, liver pills, 1,001 ways to get unpregnant, and the corresponding 1,001 ways to get knocked up all over again. If I had taken their word as gospel, I would have thought the plumbing of every student apartment in the vicinity of City was clogged with fetuses. Good grief.

Whenever the conversation or eyeballs rolled my way, I, biting my cinnamon roll or, better yet, getting up to go to class, assiduously hid my virginity.

Even though I had left my aunt and uncle's house, their home training echoed in my head: "We want you to be a virgin until you graduate from college. If you're not a virgin, you won't graduate. Once you have sex, you can't think about anything else."

One night, when it was too late to leave the Y, I ran out of sanitary napkins. I asked at the desk. No one had any. Another resident offered me a tampon.

"I can't. I'm a virgin."

She looked at me like I was crazy. "Seriously, you can't use tampons?"

"Won't they break my hymen?" I said. She laughed uproariously.

"Have you ridden a bicycle, honey? Your hymen's in the wind. Anyway, in anthro we learned that *virgin* originally meant an independent woman who didn't answer to anybody. Man or child. Nothing to do with sex, baby. Ever hear of the Virgin Mary?"

I wanted to choke her. *Honey. Baby.* Give me a Kotex, not a lecture. I was desperate to become part of the 3 percent at City who transferred to a four-year institution. I had to keep my nose to the grindstone and make it out of there.

And anyway, I knew I had a hymen because I could still feel it, honey.

2

Because of the 10:00 P.M. curfew at the YWCA, I loved going dancing Friday afternoons at the Whisky a Go Go in San Francisco. It was a hip scene where everybody black and alive in the Financial District connected, set up the weekend, the deejay playing "Out of Sight" and talking ultracrap in the background:

I'm playing the hardest working man in showbiz both sides number one and number two. Stop thinking Vietnam. Ain't no burning draft cards up in here. Up in heah! That's against the law. LBJ says it's illegal. We 'bout having fun. Vietcong'll kill a black boonie-rat as quick as they kill a white boy. Don't be fooled. War is the ultimate get-over. War makes the world go round.

But back at the Alameda County Welfare Department, 401 Broadway, in downtown Oakland, I kept my nose to the grindstone and ears to the Dictaphone, except for Julie, whose desk faced mine. She couldn't keep her nose out of a paperback, head tilted, straight Dutch Boy hair a cover for her face except for her lips. I had never seen such large lips on a white person; hers were naturally the color of chewed bubble gum.

"Juliegirl, fake it," I whispered. Her lip color varied with the weather; when it was cold they registered the deeper pink of pencil erasers. "Put your earphones on." She was reading our copy of William Goldman's *Boys and Girls Together*, and looked up as if I had yanked her right out of the Brooklyn in the book. Her vow was to live in every one of the fifty states. Her dream was for us to run off into the world and live by our wits.

"Girl hoboes, Julie?"

"Geniece, it's called adventure."

"My folks would call it living pillar to post. How would we eat?"

"Lettuce and tomato salad, fruit, day-old bread." She walked me one lunch break to the back of the Safeway and showed me how much food the store threw away.

"More food in one night than we could eat in a month." Even if I tried to feel hostility against her as a white person, I couldn't. She gave each state its own nickname. Wyoming was Why-owe-me and Illinois was Ill-wind-and-lotsa-noise. She seemed capable of hurting only herself, not me. Even a man could see right through her. She said so herself. And she blushed easily. California was Can-you-afford-ah? She didn't care about a college degree or becoming a big bubba-tubba. Oregon was Oregano, Arizona was the Arid-zone. She was a resolute nobody. She looked up sharply when she heard a big word, as if explaining it to herself phonetically. Julie, the last white girl on the face of the earth. Another coworker had been at 401 Broadway for eighteen years.

"Imagine, Geniece," she said more than once. "Only twelve more years until I retire at fifty-five." The idea made me shudder. But where else was I going with no degree and sixty wpm? I could only start a new tape:

Client was seen on February 8, 1964. All six of the children were at home running around the front steps. Some were half clad but they did have shoes on. I called her Miss Jones when I entered the residence. Client insisted I call her Queen Barbara. I told Client I would call her Miss Jones until she showed me a marriage license or a legal name change. She demanded that I call her Queen Barbara or step back out the door. I reminded Client that her next check was dependent on the report of this inspection. Client shut her mouth. I proceeded to the kitchen where I checked the contents of the cabinets. Canned goods were mostly pork and beans, Spam, and tuna. I saw a can of salmon. Told Client that was a relatively expensive purchase for a family of seven on a recipient's income. Client told me it was and I quote "none of your damn business" what she fed her kids. Does she

really think Harold Petioff cares? Let them eat pigs' tails and pig in-
nards for breakfast, lunch, and midnight snack—

I shut off the transcription tape and took my foot off the Dictaphone
pedal. Damn it, I had signed on already which was too bad. Enough of
Harold Petioff, the social worker everyone in the pool hated to transcribe. We hated him but not because he was prejudiced. Which social workers weren't prejudiced? I hated Harold Petioff because his
prejudiced comments were longer than anyone else's.

> Client is pregnant with her fourth child. Maybe she'll get lucky and
> have triplets so she can save herself and the doctor two more trips to
> the hospital. . . . I told my client who listens to T-Bone Walker and
> John Lee Hooker all day long that buying blues records was a com-
> plete waste of her discretionary income.

Day in, day out, I was breathing in noxious contempt.

My special treat was to cross the San Francisco Bay and leave my Oakland with the beautiful man-made Lake Merritt plopped in its middle,
feeling like Lot only if I looked back. I was a daughter of a multitude of
colored folk who came from the South before and during WW II to get
defense-industry jobs and a taste of freedom which allowed them to
live in projects called Codornices Village, Encinal Projects, Harbor
Homes, or Parchester Village in Albany, Alameda, West Oakland, or
Richmond, the only places bloods lived then unless they were the
funeral-home or beauty-parlor folk, or high yellas whose paler-shaded
countenances magically procured them homes, put their kids in Catholic schools, opened charge accounts at uptown stores like Capwell's
and I. Magnin.

The one and only time I went into I. Magnin in San Francisco I left
behind me something better than money. I had gotten my first check

from 401 Broadway and tripped on framing it. In small lettering, some government board had decreed: VOID IF NOT CASHED WITHIN SIX MONTHS OF DATE HEREON. Who in the hell kept checks for six months? I cashed it, bought Uncle Boy-Boy a pack of his favorite cigars ("They must have gotten these out of Cuba before Castro took over"), and walked past the marble facade of I. Magnin. The light was dim. I took off my sunglasses and saw fabulous scarves blemished with names of famous designers. *What good can his name do me?* I felt like a million bucks. In a voice the charm school people would call well modulated, a girdled saleslady addressed me: "May we help you?"

We! She thought she owned a part of this store? "Just looking." I couldn't remember skin so white since my sixth-grade teacher. And the satin pillow hairdo. No bedtime bouncing around with a hairdo like that to protect. She lifted an arched eyebrow. I turned to look at my profile in the spacious, floor-to-ceiling mirrors. Just as I threw my head even farther back, I noticed a white man looking me up and down. He had on a plain navy suit with a red tie. A dick, just a store dick, but a dick all the same. *They always think a Negro's about stealing.* I would if I wanted to, I wished I could tell him, although the thought of stealing made me queasy.

Rolling my eyes at him, I stepped inside the elevator with a middle-aged couple, the woman wearing a sable coat and hat, gloves, alligator shoes, and a square bag to match. I stood quiet, not pushing any buttons, not doing anything but being. Let the machine do it all. This elevator ought to take me anywhere. To Africa, if I want, right now. Home—to get that cold piece of chicken. When the doors opened on the third floor, a tiny white poodle spilled out of her arms. I hadn't even seen it. As I stepped out I wondered if it had been inside the sable, on her arm, in her bosom, where?

Another pale saleslady stepped forward to greet us—the mismatched trio. She looked at me, glanced at my bulgy, rough leather bag and my Army-Navy store wool peacoat, and smiled at them.

"May we show you something today?" she asked them, smiling at the poodle. So much for me. She could see I wasn't in the market for gators and fur. Looking around, I noticed a scarcity of racks. *Damn!*

Where are all the clothes? The clothes weren't interesting. They were like Sunday morning church clothes for the Realtors' wives in Aunt Ola Ray's church. Bored, I walked around a bit, looking at myself in the mirrors. When I came back to Mister and Missus Gators 'n' Fur sitting on velvet Victorian chairs, the saleslady came out of a stockroom with pastel gowns that swished on satin hangers.

"This is a Ceil Chapman." She began displaying them. The husband nodded approval; the wife stroked and murmured to the dog on her lap. An ultraordinary A-line shift of yellow wool crepe with a narrow belt elicited enthusiasm from them.

"We have a cape to match."

The wife said, "I like it very much." Even the dog yapped approval.

Her old man—like it really didn't even matter—asked, "How much?"

The saleslady said eight-ninety-five, but I knew she wasn't saying $8.95.

My bottom lip dropped, my throat went dry. I put the dress I had been looking at back in place and began walking toward the elevator. Maybe they were just saying that to astound me. Nine hundred dollars for a simple-ass yellow dress. I was in the wrong place. Even if I could, I wouldn't have paid that much for something I wouldn't force a dog to wear. I began to get mad, then madder. Is this what this crap is all about? Is this what the high yellas and preachers' wives have been do-ing all this time? Sashaying into I. Magnin and the like, paying all of the Sunday services' four collections and who knows what else so some washed-out, wrinkled-up white lady will think we got class, which she wouldn't know if it slapped her. Which is what I needed to do to myself for even thinking of bringing my high behind in this mir-rored contradiction. For the first time in my life I really did want to take something that didn't belong to me. The voices inside said: *Thou shall not steal. . . . If you take even one grape from the grocer, God will see that. . . . Uncle Boy-Boy said people who steal have inferiority complexes.* I looked around and realized it was an impossibility—too few clothes and too many mirrors. And, dammit, I needed to go to the bathroom, knowing instantly that I could not stand the idea of any more time in this store than I had already wasted. Bathroom be damned. I got back on the elevator, thought for a minute, and pushed the top-floor button. The elevator started going up, and I reached under my skirt and pulled down my panties. *Why not? Heck, it's not against the law.* I stood with my panties at midthigh as the door opened at the sixth floor and a young woman and child got on. Dammit. They got off at the fifth floor. As soon as they stepped out, I pushed the "Door Close" and "Mezzanine" buttons, pulled up my skirt, and crouched down. It came running out like water from a free faucet. *Can't drip-dry now.* I pulled up my panties, felt the crotch of them slightly wet as I straightened my skirt.

First floor. All out, colored peoples. All in, white people. I glided slowly across the floor. When I met the bright sunlight of Union Square I turned back to look and, to my utter surprise, my grandma Goosey's face was up on a billboard next to the marble entrance, big as Texas, smiling ugly at me. My heart jumped and I broke out in a sweat. Then I realized it was only my conscience, not my real grandmother, who bought her household appliances with Blue Chip Stamps. I walked on through the square, scattering fat gray pigeons to my left and my right.

3

When my grades from first semester came back, I was happy:

- English 1A, [B–];
- Introduction to Western Civilization, [C+];
- French 1, [B];
- Journalism, Basic Principles, [A];
- Journalism, News Production, [A];
- Tennis, [A].

....

I enrolled in Engl. 1B, French 2, the second half of West. Civ., and Journalism: News Writing, for spring. I was ready to write for *The Tower*, the college paper, and added three additional units in psychology. I was making headway on getting my chocolate buns out of City in two years flat, so I wouldn't be old meat. I sent off for applications from Negro colleges. Some evenings I recited the names of the colleges, singing them like a spell to invoke a full scholarship somehow: *Howard/Spelman/MorrisBrown/Talladega/Alcorn A&M/Philander Smith/ Wilberforce/Hampton/Xavier/Wiley/ BethuneCookman.* But the magic only produced my family, which kept crowding into the picture I had made into flesh. Bushy unpressed hair, leather sandals, jeans, one-of-a-kind earrings from my favorite hole-in-the-wall shop in Berkeley, and eyes ringed with Maybelline black eye pencil. I had started in high school with eyeliner because it made my eyes pop. We couldn't wear pants in high school, so it was liberating to wear jeans seven days a week. All I had to buy were cute tops to complete my wardrobe. When I started shopping, I found the earring shop that pierced ears for nothing if you bought three pairs for ten dollars. So I got my ears pierced right after I moved out of Boy-Boy's. The hair was the biggest change. I couldn't take the smell of chemical relaxer, even though I knew I looked like a wild thing. I tried to change when I went around family. They hated my hair, the eyes, and my jeans. They wanted pedal pushers and pert hair, like when we were girls. My solution was simple to imagine, harder to act on: Don't go around them.

I had been the broken-home baby, as Aunt Ola Ray called it. In my father's family, we were all raised together. Two of his brothers had big, stable Montgomery Ward and J. C. Penney families; Uncle Boy-Boy and Aunt Ola Ray had Buddy and Corliss; and the oldest son had me. Grandma Goosey called children like me the all-by-theyself babies.

Broken-home baby. All-by-theyself babies. Both terms irritated me tremendously, whether it was Aunt Ola Ray's pitying voice as she neatly folded yet another Butterick-Vogue-McCall's pattern and stuck pins in the red tomato pincushion or my grandmother's muttered cursing of wayward mens, one of them being her son, my very own flesh-and-blood father.

"No count, pissantsy boots. Leaving these all-by-theyself babies for the family to raise." As harsh as Goosey's rant was, I didn't feel as bad as when Ola Ray, who wasn't blood, said it. In the interest of the entire family they threw us in one pot, called us all The Cousins, the boy-cousins and girlcousins. Even when we reached the age of consent, we remained the boycousins and the girlcousins.

Corliss and Buddy, her brother, were my favorites. The two of them together looked like the mocha plastic bride and groom on the top of the cake. Cute. Smart. Personable. Striving their asses off. College-bound from the first day of kindergarten. Buddy was the genius who did ROTC, Reserve Officers Training Corps, all through high school. Uncle Boy-Boy said ROTC would look good on his transcript and get him into a military medical college. Corliss was held up as a role model for the rest of us, the perfect person, straight A over straight A, junior to senior high, every single course. That had to have been like some kind of fate not humanly possible. It seemed like everyone thought Corliss had no flaws and that the rest of the cousins must have had terrible complexes because we weren't her. Personally, I didn't think the zebras in the back of the pack worried if their stripes were crooked or if their black and white needed touching up. They kept zigzagging with the pack.

It was one thing to have the talented tenth at home and know Corliss and Buddy without their guards up. But at Oakland City I saw that constant striving to look like an up-and-coming black bourgie as constant straining. When I started I thought matriculation was clear-cut: Get sixty units and get out of there. When I started I thought dressing sharp was a simple carryover from high school. The Snookie's regulars had nice clothes; the girls wore cashmere cardigans and plaid tartan Pendleton skirts. But I took university transfer classes, and the regulars in there with me didn't come to class and didn't finish the semester, part of a pattern. School would be jam-packed the first few weeks of the semester, everybody hanging out. Then, at midterms, fewer and fewer students. By the end of the semester, City looked like it had been evacuated. Tuition was free and the student ID card cost two dollars. That's why I was there. Maybe the guys who stayed on were there because they couldn't transfer. Not after two years, not after ten years. The guys who looked so hip when I was seventeen began to look like they were stranded at a way station. It puzzled me that the bourgie students looked so confident and secure inside Snookie's, inside their no-browner-than-a-paper-bag cosmos. They assimilated the look of the white middle class but not the academic go-getting. But it didn't get under my skin that they weren't as smart as the radicals. Only family could get under my skin.

No matter how much my family irritated me, though, I loved cousin Buddy. As a matter of fact, Buddy, if he could have, would have painted me up even more, tightened my jeans, added second hoops to my ears, and sprinkled stardust on my eyelids. Corliss may have been goody-goody but Buddy was good. Just plain good. People liked Buddy. With Corliss, it was the she-can-do-no-wrong bit. With Buddy, it was whatever he did, right or wrong, was so much fun, so outrageous, nobody minded. Of course, he was smart, smarter than anyone, so that was his first qualification. Then, he was cool.

For his high school graduation party in 1961, Corliss and I dressed up so I could help Aunt Ola Ray serve Buddy's friends and their dates. But Buddy banished us from the living room and the patio. Such power. Aunt Ola Ray, meek as a lamb with her genius son, obeyed. Corliss and I spent the whole evening on tiptoe watching the partygoers from the catwalk near her room. I ached somewhere deep below my stomach listening to Johnny Mathis (of course Buddy had all twenty-six albums), sang along with "Chances Are," and stared at his friends' lithe and perfect bodies as they leaned into each other, doing the dip and snapping their fingers. I wanted to be like them—cute hip smart and going off to college. Going across the bay to State was going away. Hardly any of Buddy's friends were going to Berkeley, and the ones that were—Herbie, Phillip, and Reid—didn't impress me. They looked neurasthenic, like they had asthma and would cough in your face if they kissed you. I noticed they didn't arch when they danced. They looked as stiff as their slide rules.

In his second year of med school in the navy, Buddy got engaged to Andrea, an old-line bourgie born with her father's stethoscope around her high-yellow neck. Forget the silver spoon—the child of the black bourgeoisie comes equipped with the tools of her father's labor. Andrea and I knew each other from being candy stripers at the hospital in high school. I knew she was very sincere, if a bit dull, as happens when you hit the child over the head from infancy on with status, money, and keeping up with the next-best Negro.

As it turned out, being the only black candy stripers there, we became friends. Not boon coons, but friendly enough to share dreams, to unfold with each other.

I want to go to Fisk, pledge my second year, meet a Meharry man in my junior year, and get married the summer after I graduate, she'd told me. This didn't sound like a dream, more like a plan, nothing of the ethereal in it. But her face looked dreamy when she said it. I wanted to get as far away from Oakland as I possibly could and fall in love as many times as I had fingers and toes. Maybe my stuff didn't sound so ethereal to her either. I was not surprised to hear of Andrea and Buddy in love. He hadn't gone to Meharry Medical School in Nashville, the mecca for young mocha women wanting the mocha groom and the mocha life. But he had gone to medical school in the Navy and was interning at Oak Knoll Naval Hospital in the Oakland Hills. Andrea wanted the cousins who were the right age to be in the wedding. So she called me up and asked me.

....

I had gone to Aunt Ola's, who had started in on my hair, dragging me to the coffee table in her front room, opening up *Ebony*, her etiquette book. Aunt Ola Ray had paper-clipped a section on fancy hairdos called "Baubles, Bangles, and Bangs," which had the three variations Aunt Ola Ray wanted the bridesmaids to wear:

1. *The Bun of Fun, 2. The Holiday Gamin, or 3. The Holiday Temptress*

All three of these hairdos were for women who pressed their hair. I hadn't gone back to pressing mine, and it had grown long and bushy. People reacted like they didn't know if I was on my way to the beauty shop or I was just country and didn't know better than to walk the city streets with unpressed hair.

"Oh, Geniece, I've been thinking of you," she said, turning the pages. "You can wear one. Aren't they beautiful?" Beneath a picture of a woman putting on a black beehive wig were the words: *If you are a woman, you need a wig.*

"This is typical *Ebony* assimilation advertising, Aunt Ola."

"Wait till you see how it looks." Aunt Ola left the room. I looked at myself in the gold leaf mirror above her mahogany server.

I leafed through the magazine. An ad for Nadinola bleaching crème caught my eye: "Nadinola brightens your opportunities for romance just as swiftly and surely as it brightens and lightens your skin."

Aunt Ola Ray came back in with a black wig, a silky straight pageboy. Despite my frown and my pulling back, she settled the monstrosity over my bushy hair, as deftly as she used to get me to take the laxative Black Draught. She just did it. She pulled me in front of the mirror. The wig sat there like a top hat on a shelf.

"It doesn't fit."

"We'll make it fit."

"No, Aunt Ola. My hair is my hair. If it's all right with Buddy and Andrea, it should be all right with you."

"Buddy and Andrea! What do they know? I'm in charge of this." For a few minutes she bunched up my hair underneath that hat. Hot and wanting to scratch my scalp, I broke loose.

"Aunt Ola Ray, how can you read a book like *Crisis in Black and White*"—I picked up the book that was on her coffee table next to the *Saturday Evening Post*—"and not understand that this wig is yesterday?"

I hadn't read *The Crisis in Black and White*, or anything else by its author, Charles Silberman. But I had seen it boldly displayed in bookstores in Berkeley and assumed it was hip. Opening it up to a section Aunt Ola Ray or Uncle Boy-Boy had penciled, I read it back to her, dodging her attempts to make the top hat fit. Reading the first few passages, however, I realized quickly that I had assumed wrong.

> The lower-class child, moreover, tends to have poor attention span and to have great difficulty following the teacher's orders. The reason is that he generally comes from a nonverbal household. Adults speak in short sentences, if indeed they speak at all.

"Aunt Ola Ray, this is insulting."

"I think he has something."

"He has something, all right," I said. "An allergy to colored people." I continued aloud for the sake of my own amazement.

> And when they give orders to the child, it is usually in monosyllables— get this, bring that. The child has never been obliged to listen to several lengthy sentences spoken consecutively. And the speech he does hear tends to be of a very simple sort from the standpoint of grammar

and syntax. In school, the class teacher who rambles on for several sentences might just as well be talking another language.

"Oh, we can't talk English, can we?"

"Now, Geniece, he's talking about a certain kind of child, from a certain kind of home."

"He is not. He's talking about black children. The book isn't titled *Crisis in a Certain Kind of Black and White*." I tore the wig off and set it down. "How much did you and Uncle Boy-Boy pay for this book?"

"Five ninety-five."

"You paid to be insulted. Listen to this."

Lower-class children have a limited perception of the world about them: they do not know that objects have names (table, wall, book) or that the same object may have several names (an apple is fruit, red, round, juicy). . . . The slum child's home is characterized by a general scarcity of objects: there are few toys, few pictures, few books, few magazines, few of anything except people and noise.

"This is absolutely ridiculous. Why did you underline it? Do you want to believe it?"

"That's the way it is. You don't know. You've never had to live like that."

"Aunt Ola Ray, I'm lower class. My father left me. My grandmother raised me."

"We all raised you and we aren't lower class."

"Technically speaking, aren't I an orphan?"

"You never had to go through what this man is talking about."

"Sometimes I felt like Cinderella, like a discard."

"Niecy," Aunt Ola came at me with an imploring look. "You're exaggerating. What did you lack for? Nothing. Not a thing."

"Only my father and my mother. The people who made me up in the first place."

"We're your people. You have people."

"Who'll love me for who I am and not try to make me into an *Ebony* magazine model?"

"Geniece, you are overidentifying with the poor. It's mental indulgence and a way of feeling sorry for yourself."

"And, Auntie, you are overidentifying with Mr. Silberman and his theories." I handed her the wig. "I don't want to be in the wedding if I have to wear this."

My aunt took it and fluffed it out, first the bangs, then the rolled-up sides.

"It fits you. You should wear it, not me," I said.

She beamed at herself in her gold leaf mirror. Then she put the wig on, turned around, and beamed at me.

4

I kept candy striping at the hospital with Andrea after high school, and that's where I met Wish. He was the only boy candy striper, but nobody minded, because he was so sweet and careful with the patients. Wish was the nearest to a boyfriend I had come, though petting was as far as we had gone. He took classes all over the Bay Area, because he was learning carpentry and studying architecture. When he showed me a magazine photo of a Buddhist nun who had set herself on fire in South Vietnam, I didn't know what to say. I thought it would give me nightmares, so I didn't look long. Wish cried when he folded it up. With his thick glasses, sandals, and carpenter's tool bag, he reminded me of Jesus. He was always helping me out, and I thought he would be the first one. I gave him the name Wish Woodie, because he was such a whiz with wood and stuff. But his name was Aloysius, which I thought insane for some black person to have named some tiny brown-balled baby. Then I found out he was adopted by white folks when he was eighteen months. To know that explained everything about Wish Woodie. He was like-white except he was born-black.

"Did you know that the Cadillac has tail fins sharp enough to slice a child's hand off?" he asked me one afternoon as we walked down University Avenue in Berkeley. We always met up at the post office.

It was a fog-free day, and I could see the gunmetal gray of the Bay Bridge and the rust red Golden Gate as if each bridge had been painted on a powder blue canvas.

"Wish," I said, "why would a kid, even a pure Aborigine, take his hand and pull it like a slab of baloney against the tail fin of a Caddie?"

"Geniece, can you hear yourself? Why would you say 'a pure Aborigine'?"

"It's a figure of speech." Aunt Ola used it all the time.

"Don't you know Aborigines are the oppressed indigenous people of Australia? They have to live apart from society."

"Like lepers?"

"Segregated, cast off." Wish Woodie had full-body squareness— square shoulders, square hips, square right on down to his large square toenails.

"Okay. I won't use it anymore."

His shoulders were wide. His jawbone was wide. He almost looked like a put-together person, with sticks, blocks, and two-by-fours— except for his color. His skin was a rich caramel shade that made me want to touch him and be touched by him all the time. Made me, ordered me to touch it. I loved being hugged by him, being enveloped in his arms. Human ropes. His other softening element in all that angularity was his hair. Wish Woodie never combed it. And he never cut it. He just washed it and let Mother Nature dry it. I loved it. It was soft as cat fur and black as velvet.

I asked him once, "Are you a *blippie*?"

"What's that?"

"A black hippie." He thought that was so funny, but I wanted to know.

"Do you want me to be a blippie? I'll be one. But you have to be one too," he said.

"I can't be a blippie. I comb my hair every day. And I work. At jobs where I punch in and punch out."

"Hippies work."

"Not at 401 Broadway. They march outside. They apply for welfare. But hippies don't work for the welfare department."

"So quit," he said.

That's what I liked about him. Of course I would never, in a life of Thursdays, be like Wish Woodie, who could do his carpentry and survive forever. I liked so much about Wish Woodie. I admired that Wish Woodie was comfortable anywhere and honest all the time. I felt out of place often and could tell the truth only in certain places. If I spoke my mind, I figured, I'd end up with no friends, no relatives, and definitely no guys. And he was thorough. We spent a whole weekend talking about moving to San Francisco.

"Move to the city? With you?" I said. We had come to the Copper Penny restaurant on University Avenue, where we bought little tin pans of cinnamon bread for a quarter, and got chocolate milk and an orange for our lunch.

He shrugged. "Well, with or without me, you need to move to the city."

"How would I support myself?"

"All kinds of things to do in a city." As often as not, Rocky Road candy bars dipped in hot chocolate were dinner.

"Well, Oakland's a city. What's the diff?"

"The Haight."

"Well, Oakland has a . . ." I sputtered for a minute. I couldn't think of where hippies lived in Oakland except for the spillover from Telegraph in North Oakland.

"What if, Wish, I got over there and couldn't do anything?" *What if I didn't make it?* I asked myself.

"I'm trying to tell you. That's a city for you. Always something to do. That's why people go to cities."

That night we drove to the city, to the Haight-Ashbury, to Stanyan Street, to a garage behind a sienna-trimmed white apartment building. We pressed a buzzer and the garage door opened. As its triple panels folded into the ceiling of the garage, I saw a whole wall of pressure cookers. One that looked like it was a twenty-quarter, enough to feed a platoon at Fort Ord. Lots of two- and three-quarters. A tall skinny pressure cooker that looked like a stainless steel stovepipe. Pressure cookers, tops and bottoms, Wish Woodie, a white boy who looked about fifteen, and me.

"What is this?" I said.

"This is Michael. He fixes pressure cookers," Wish said by way of introduction. "Is this how you make your living?" I asked Michael.

"Sure. I don't need much. As a matter of fact, I have to turn away work." Michael pulled out a shoe box full of carefully bagged marijuana.

A bag and a five-dollar bill changed hands. I could hear my folks: *Don't be no educated fool.* A pressure-cooker fixer with a pot business on the side?

"Mind if we smoke one here?" Wish Woodie began to roll a joint.

"Yes, I do. I never let people do that here. I don't smoke anything, not even cigarettes."

I looked at Michael closely. His cheeks were the pink of salmon. I could smell his breath—slightly sweet, like baby saliva. He was sexless, like a lamb.

"Do you live here?" I pointed to the apartment building overhead.

"I live wherever I find myself when my body decides to rest."

When we got on the freeway back to Oakland, I couldn't get out of my mind the little garage stuffed to its gills with shiny and unshiny pressure cookers, Michael's salmon pink cheeks bent over them, his polishing bare arms, him singing to himself as we left, the garage door closing him off from the outside. With deep breaths I took in the San Francisco fog scented with his baby-saliva breath. I was an Oakland girl, nothing more, nothing less, born in Berkeley, steeped in Oakland like sassafras in a pot of boiling water. Across the bay was the Orient. Frisco.

5

I was accumulating transfer credits and hanging on to my virginity
while Martin Luther King was vowing to talk to the Vietcong himself
to end the war if LBJ wouldn't. Good grief. I can imagine how that was
going down in the Oval Office. Guys were getting drafted left and
right, the bombers were killing poor people and Buddhist monks, and
accidents kept happening over there like in the movies. A B-57 loaded
with bombs crashed into a South Vietnamese village and killed twelve
villagers, but our crew survived miraculously, just like in the movies.
My coworkers refused to read the front page of the *Oakland Tribune*.
The names—Mekong, Danang, Vinh Binh—had a poetic ring to me,
and it wasn't all bombs; we dropped toys and supplies over towns in
South Vietnam. No matter. I had to concentrate on transferring or be a
transcriptionist for the rest of my life.

I convinced *The Tower* editor that the guys on the lawn, the black
intellectuals, were a new breed, incredibly smart, deep, heavy hitters,
a step beyond the New Negro. He mumbled that they were just a
bunch of rabble-rousers but gave me the assignment. "Out of curiosity," he said. I approached one of the guys on the lawn, the one who
was always introduced with the reminder that he had attended Harvard, like they were saying, he's that smart so you have to take his
word for it.

I didn't know how to address him: guy, man, brother with the Albert Einstein mustache, splib—nothing was appropriate. I fell back on
journalism.

"I'm writing a story for *The Tower* on the students who speak out
here on the lawn. Can I get some info from you?"

He nodded. I went further. "Can I get your name?"

"Freed Man."

I wrote down Friedman and he pointed a long bony yellow finger at the name in my notebook. "You got it wrong. I'm a free man. And I freed myself. First name: Freed; last name: Man. Dig it?"

I wrote it down like he said, but I knew this wasn't going anywhere with my editor.

"Anyway," he said, like he was peeping my hole card off the bat, "I'm not a student here. You need to talk to this cat Allwood."

I needed to meet someone who was enrolled, and Allwood, a physics major, worked at the branch library near campus. He said that Allwood had dropped out of school for a year to read a thousand books. That he was a heavyweight and wanted to get even heavier. So I shanghaied this Allwood guy at the tiny branch library shelving books.

"Can you find me a really good novel?" I said, staring at his angry black pupils with as much sophistication as I could muster and thinking what a pretty beard he had. Allwood was light and I wasn't too keen on light dudes on account of my father supposing to be light and curly haired. And on account of my being dark skinned. There are always howevers. And Allwood was exceptionally good looking, tall and skinny, and came across as pissed at having to file so many books. I completely forgot my prepared questions.

"Have you ever heard of James Baldwin?" It was a question he put to me simply, but I had about a teaspoon of simplicity to my name.

"I might have," I said. "I have this thing of remembering everything I read but I forget the names unless they're really odd, you know."

He knew all right and laughed, which I thought was my accomplishment.

"Here." He shoved *Another Country* at me. "Read this," he said, and pointed to the teenage bookshelves. "And don't get any more books from that section."

I read it that night, the next day, and half that night. Reading it made the inside of my body stretch into a taut muscle. Rufus and his sister made me feel stronger, earthbound and sky-swept at the same time. The only things that mattered after I finished the book were love and hate, living and dying. My specialty, my major in life, i.e., newspaper reading and books, was tragedy. I couldn't keep away from it.

Another Country felt like the world of love and hate and living and dying compressed between my hands.

....

I needed to see Allwood again for the story. He told me he had read three hundred books during his self-imposed exile. I'd already written that he'd read a thousand books but changed it. Three hundred, a thousand, what was the diff to me? I read two books a month. He said he had become an expert on black history, world history, and revolution. He and I walked back and forth across Grove Street to the lawn, to Jo Ethel's. With his sandy skin he could have walked into Snookie's with ease, but he had nothing but snide remarks for bourgies.

"They learned their manners from cleaning Miss Ann's tables and polishing her silverware. Then they made her manners their values, their whole way of life."

When we were walking past Snookie's, he said, "You're real, they're not."

I knew he meant the light-skinned line of demarcation that meant I would have been stared at if I walked in and sat down. Like *Darkie, who told you we wanted you in here?* Even if I'd been with him.

I poured my heart into the article for *The Tower*. Allwood's picture and the interview got good space—top half of the front page—and a lot of comment. Allwood liked it; the Grove Street orator from Harvard acknowledged me one afternoon as "the together sister from the paper." I got a sunburst from being called "together." Even Huey said something besides, where's Margaret? He said the article showed I had my head screwed on right.

Emboldened by my little rep, I asked to cover Tracy Simms. She was brought to campus by the W. E. B. Du Bois Club, *da boys club*. She was one of two hundred historic civil rights demonstrators who had gotten arrested protesting an all-white sales force at the Sheraton-Palace in San Francisco. My cousins and I, thrill-seeking high school students, had gotten on the bus to San Francisco and sat in the lobby of the Sheraton during the sit-ins on Auto Row, gawking at the demonstrators and rich people trying to slip by the protesters. I probably laughed at Tracy Simms in my ignorance.

As soon as I got to the small auditorium and sat in the back row I felt the thoughtlessness of my participation at the Sheraton. Tracy Simms, who had chaired the Ad Hoc Committee to End Discrimination, was speaking as if she was fresh from Auto Row. Something was incongruous from the jump. Her shirt was sloppy, not the movement uniform of overalls and chambray shirt, not the good girl pressed jeans look. And her hair was half straight, half nappy, like she had chemically straightened it but rinsed it before the nappy part got straight. And her hair wasn't like mine. I had stopped straightening it at all. She looked like she couldn't decide to be a bourgie education major or a straight-out hell-raiser. The auditorium was packed with regular students, plus the entire Cuba–Castroists–*da boys club* who normally held sway over Grove Street. Only she was the one behind the podium.

When she opened her mouth, I could tell she didn't have the lingo down. Her first mistake was using the word *Negro*; people booed her. Her second mistake was being bewildered enough to use the word *integrationist*. Students interrupted her, talked over her. I felt for her. Her comeback was along the lines of *"I'm a nice colored girl who fell in deep dukey, and I just happened to be a leader because that was my way back out of dukey."* Not on the money, honey, the audience informed her with catcalls and hisses.

I reported on the speech, and then asked my editor if I could write an editorial on the people who wouldn't let her finish her speech because she wasn't together like the street orators. He worked with me on it. I focused on their intolerance, on how they heckled her off the podium. Yes, I admitted, she was a walking inventory of political naïveté, neither a Marxist nor a socialist, but simply a black girl from Berkeley High who wound up leading a two-day sit-in, lie-down-in, sleep-in at the Sheraton-Palace Hotel in the city. Because she turned up ordinary instead of glorious, folks got huffy.

When *The Tower* came out, you'd think I'd stripped in public. All hell broke loose. A guy everybody liked named Abner admonished me in front of the cafeteria crowd like I was a child.

"Did you write that editorial yourself or did the editor make you take the other side?"

"I have a mind of my own, thank you," I said. The insufferably cute, insufferably fashionable, golden brown MacNair twins and their chic briefcases were attached to him.

He said, "The next time we want to see it before it's printed."

"And who is 'we'—the word patrol?" I replied, munching on my cinnamon roll and orange juice. "I'm an I, not a we."

He walked off with his fashion models, glancing back like I was a fly. I was shocked to stand up to him, but more shocked that I had crossed a line and hadn't known it. All I had said was, mind your manners. Not earthshaking.

Allwood told me to keep writing.

He said, "Bourgies don't want to understand the process of social change. It upsets the pecking order." And I'd thought Abner was chastising me for being reactionary. I hadn't thought I was the social changer. I liked that Allwood was fearless. He made it seem like I was shaking the status quo. Some energy was moving from me to him or from him to me. Whichever it was, we were connecting.

6

Allwood and I went out for hamburgers and movies at the Fox Oakland. We walked down Telegraph Avenue in Berkeley, checking out the free-speech orators, soapbox evangelists, and secondhand bookstores. Then we'd go back to City, to the street orators rapping rapid-fire about Cuba, black history, the man. The Harvard guy loved to rant on LBJ's participation in the Kennedy assassination: "The man is out to get you, the man is out to get you, brothers and sisters, wake up, the man is out to get you." With utmost authority he talked about Johnson being in on the assassination and jacking off in Kennedy's neck wound on Air Force One. It was hard for me to picture that with Mrs. Kennedy in the bloodstained pink Chanel in the front of the plane. But I had a boyfriend, and he was cute.

I thought we would have our first fight over sex, not the intellect. It didn't matter to me. We went for pizza and bowling, for spaghetti and peewee golf. But all that wasn't enough for Allwood. Not nearly enough. This one Friday night, when I had made him drag us to the miniature golf range in San Leandro, right as we were about to begin the second of nine holes, he gave me a list. A reading list.

"What is this for?" I asked.

"This is your real education. Read these ten books. The revolution starts in your mind."

I didn't know revolution from Adam, but I knew that F. Scott Fitzgerald had given Sheilah Graham a reading list of the classics—my Western Civ instructor had talked about it with a big smirk. If Allwood wanted to play it that way, I was not game. But I listened to the list out of curiosity. *Muntu* by Janheinz Jahn, *David Walker's Appeal*, never heard of them.

Black Boy by Richard Wright.

"I read that in high school, brotherman," I said, driving the ball to the green.

"You need to read it again," Allwood said. "You have a different head now."

He read on, trailing behind me, my caddie with his list.

"*The Rebirth of African Civilization* by Chancellor Williams, *Illusion and Reality* by Caldwell."

Never heard of them, couldn't even front it off. But I wanted to have read them. I wanted to know everything that Allwood and the Harvard soapbox orator and all the rest knew. If it was all info in a book, why couldn't I know it? I was a reader. I was a student. I wanted to be smart, not the smart of the white kids transferring to Berkeley, not the pseudosmart of the black bourgies coasting on their skin color, but the smart of the radicals who I respected because they weren't cowed by anybody, least of all the passersby on Grove Street throwing insults and soda cans at them. Allwood's list was unrelenting.

The Wretched of the Earth by F. Fanon.

"Allwood, that's only the bible. How many midday rallies have I watched? I have eyes." I handed him the club so I could see the list for myself.

Hadn't heard of the next two, *Black Nationalism: A Search for an Identity in America* by E. U. Essien-Udom, and *Return to My Native Land* by Aimé Césaire, but the ninth one on the list, *The Souls of Black Folk* by W. E. B. Du Bois, was very familiar.

"There's a copy of this in Uncle Boy-Boy and Aunt Ola Ray's library, for heaven's sake."

"Well, I know you know the last one on the list," Allwood said, lining up the club head with the ball as if he was Jack Nicklaus. "But I put it there so you could reread it after you've tackled the rest." It was *The Fire Next Time* by James Baldwin.

"Well, thanks for some credit." I didn't know how Sheilah had felt with F. Scott, but I was too through. "Do you think you're dealing with an illiterate? I know some things. Okay, maybe I don't read as much as you, maybe not even a tenth, but I'm in—"

I sputtered. I wanted to say intelligent but Allwood was an intellectual. I was neither.

When we went up to my room at the Y—we could have day guests—Allwood walked over to my bookcase and pointed at the middle shelf, the eye-level shelf. It was my spot; I could go there blindfolded and pick up my favorites. He sneered as he began yanking titles off the shelf.

"Yes, Mr. Intellect, I love Taylor Caldwell and William Goldman."

Calm down, I had to tell myself, as I began thinking about plowing through the books I hadn't read. He took all Cal-transfer courses, could speed-read nine or ten books a week, went through the *Chronicle*, the *Trib*, the *Wall Street Journal*, and then some. I respected his intelligence.

Allwood said, "Paperback books have given the petty bourgeoisie an inflated ego problem. I read therefore I am."

He pulled out my copy of Philip Roth's *Letting Go*, my all-time favorite. Allwood snatched out a couple of pages at random. I didn't believe I was seeing him do that or that I was sitting there waiting to see how much more he would do. I sat there, half shell-shocked, half alert. What was this Negro going to do with my motley paper crew? He continued tearing out pages at random. A hard head makes a sore back, I heard Grandma Goosey's scratchy voice from somewhere, but his back looked perfectly straight. Maybe I was the one. Sitting there like I had lockjaw. I managed to tear my locked jaws open.

"What are you doing, you crazy-ass motherfucker? Those are mine. Did I tell you to even touch them? Fool!"

Allwood continued, going from Roth to Bellow to Mailer to Malamud to Moravia. He threw all the pages he had torn out into the wastebasket and then he struck a match.

"Oh, no, are you absolutely and totally gone?" I leaped up. He set the fire with one movement of his hand.

"What did you call me?" he said, looking devilish, enjoying himself while I beat out flames and rushed to open a window.

"Now go back and read those books and see if you missed anything. See if you missed a beat," he said. "They ain't gotta write tight. Uncle

Sam said, Jew boy, you can write all night as long as that's all you do. Write till you ain't got words left to write with. That's how I want to keep you occupied. And you think the Jew boys' bibles are sacred."

"Moravia is Italian," I said, tearing from the smoke, my own uncertain outrage and the sight of my paperback books burning.

"The Jew boys are a bunch of crybabies and jerk offs," he said. "Don't cry for them. Do you think they bother to cry when we go down in flames?"

Allwood stood next to me as particles of soot drifted out the window. "Do you honestly think they cried at their desks when Watts went down?"

I didn't care what they did at their desks. All I wanted was to read what was left of my books to see if Allwood was right. Would I miss anything? Was *Letting Go* overwritten? I grabbed it and pages fell from my fingers, smudging them. A part that had been torn out but not burned was about e. e. cummings, or E. E. Cunningham, as the Gruber character called him. I remembered Gruber saying, "What is that stuff supposed to be anyway? A poem?" I remembered the phrase "Culture is everywhere" on one page and Sarah Vaughan singing on the next page, which was now dust to dust. The smoke that twisted into my nostrils had a scent not unlike a row of hot combs. My tears fell on my torn-up paperbacks, a muddle of print and soot, and I pictured Philip Roth standing side by side with Earleatha, Aunt Ola Ray's beautician. Earleatha had hot-combed my hair every two weeks from the time I was eleven until I left home. I could see Philip Roth, standing in sweaty-hot Our Beauty Shoppe on Eighty-fifth Avenue and East 14th Street, Earleatha telling him in her impatient, fast-talking way, "Oh, no, we don't need any of that in here. Maybe you want to go on up to Bancroft or MacArthur, where white folks do hair." Telling him that as she directed traffic, the back-and-forth between her beauticians, clientele, all in various stages of unpressed and undressed hair, the slick Ricks bringing in hot clothes and hot watches, the churchy women scurrying in with the brown paper bags from Safeway with the oil and steam stains coming from the fried chicken dinners inside them.

"But you don't understand," Roth would say, holding my restored, intact copy of *Letting Go* in hand. "Jews are not white."

"Well, what color are they?" Earleatha would ask, resting the straightening iron on the burner, her hand on her hip. "You look white to me."

"Everybody makes that mistake. I'm telling you, everybody," he would reply.

"White is as white does," Earleatha would tell him, looking at his book with disdain. "The only way you can prove it is for you to tell me something that ain't white people. Can you write about colored people?"

"We call them *shvartzahs*."

"No, no, no. Can you write people like this?" Earleatha would have gestured to the people in the shop, the people orbiting around her as if having hair like white folks, which they neither wake up with nor come out of the shower with, is the sole objective of colored existence. That world I grew up in was just like the one phrase I remembered perfectly from the novel: "a world full of people pushing and pulling at each other with absolutely clear conscience."

"I can try." I put those words into Philip Roth's mouth. Why was it so important at that moment for my favorite author to have written about people like me? So I could justify reading Roth to Allwood? So that I could begin to understand why Allwood's books and the world they contained gave me more of a sense of awareness than my own supposedly lightweight book reading and apparently insignificant life heretofore had? So I could hold onto that world in my head even as I felt it disappearing? Going up in smoke every time I heard it cut down to size by Allwood's logically incessant rhetoric. It was Allwood who had the final word and not my apparitions of Philip Roth and Earleatha.

"Geniece, check out Chancellor Williams for your Jew boy fixation. He runs it down how the Ten Commandments came out of the African Constitution way before Moses went up Mount Sinai. Which was in Africa."

Whenever Allwood insisted, I resisted, but only to a point. I wanted to know what he knew, feel what he felt inside that righteousness. The only way in was to surrender, and I was willing. I had plenty of motivation and a demonstrated interest, but I needed a catalyst. Allwood was the reason I became black.

7

Not long after he mutilated my copy of *Letting Go*, Allwood stood with me as we breathed in the exhaust fumes on the landing from the sooty Cypress Freeway in West Oakland, a stone's throw from the Oakland Army Base. We were at my grandma's place in the projects. I took Allwood to Goosey's because I wanted her to screen him. Good ole Goosey, my little grandma the color of peanut shells. She didn't come to the family get-togethers anymore, said all the babies made her nervous. But Goosey would tell a body the rough stuff. When the family fussed about my unpressed hair, she had muttered, "Ola pitched a shit fit about your hair," then fixed my plate of stewed chicken, rice, and turnip greens.

To bring this bristling black knight of mine on his black horse of militancy to meet the one who sheltered me—from the world as much as from Ola's niggling ways right next door to us for that long spell of childhood—was as right as putting filé in gumbo. As I waited for her to walk her little old lady steps from rocking chair to door, her cane thumping, I heard her as she had been, firm and watchful. Goosey kept care of the little girl me and the adolescent me, took me over after my father vanished from sight when I was barely in walking shoes. I often wondered if my father's family fully supported my adoption by Goosey because they were ashamed of her son's behavior or because I was too pitiful to ignore—motherless, talking a strange gibberish at four that no one could understand.

"I'm too old to be surprised, Niecy," she said, taking a look at my bushier-than-ever hair. Goosey made me turn around and bend my head so she could run her finger along the nape of my neck. All the nights of her braiding, combing, brushing my hair, and greasing my scalp came back. "Your kitchen never grow like the rest of your head," she said, fingering the tightly curled naps at the nape of my neck. *Kinkabugs*, she called them.

I accepted that she too saw the past in what I was trying to make the future. "Don't want me to smile ugly, so I won't," she said, beckoning us into her tiny kitchen to smell her dinner. Aunt Ola and Goosey had their differences, but each was a past master of the silent insult, the smiling ugly.

I could tell by the way she looked at Allwood sniffing her shrimp-fried okra, her corn bread, and her fresh apple cobbler that she liked him. If she hadn't, Goosey would have slammed the pots shut and showed us the door. He couldn't get over her okra. She complimented him on his teeth, acting dumbstruck that they were so white and even.

"I've never tasted okra without the slime. Where did it go?" he asked her after the first plate. Goosey fixed him more. Allwood ate four plates, which I thought was disgusting. But they seemed to enjoy each other and his gluttony.

"You got to stir-fry your chopped okra for forty-five minutes first," she told him, glancing at me as if to say, boy worth something if he can ask about okra.

"You mean, Mrs. Goosby," he said, calling her as he'd been introduced, "you stood over a hot stove for forty-five minutes stirring this okra?" I couldn't believe it, Allwood and Goosey. When he got to politics, I waited for this affinity to evaporate. Allwood started in on his concentration camp rhetoric; I started scraping plates. At one point, he even called Goosey *sistuh* Goosby. And she said, "Uh-huh." I hated being referred to as a sistuh, as though these men had become some new breed revolutionary deacons. I had seen the deacons in church get free feelsies when sisters got happy and fell out, and I was suspicious. Same position, different condition.

But Goosey listened intently. "Last month, there were protesters marching all down in here," Goosey said.

"That was International Day of Protest," Allwood said.

"Didn't look much international," Goosey said. "Wasn't a colored in the bunch."

"They want those ships headed to Vietnam empty," Allwood said.

"War's good for colored. Only time they use us for all we're worth," Goosey muttered.

"Don't believe it," Allwood said.

She kept on, "I hear they're building us a new post office, the biggest PO in the Bay Area."

"Don't believe it," Allwood said. "It's nothing but a holding cell for nigguhs." I flinched at the word, even though Allwood used it purely as political discourse, but Goosey didn't bat an eyelash. "The man always uses your tax dollars, your land, your neighborhood, and your labor to enslave you. You vote him in to do it. That's true brilliance. You don't let him do it, you ask him to do it."

I had heard the rhetoric before. Interesting the first time, numbing once I knew the argument by heart. I listened for what usually came next: That's what they did in Germany to the Jews. He didn't say it. But I'd forgotten: He eliminated that one after he got the Volkswagen. Goosey listened patiently, then sent in her fastball, her final word on politics. I knew this by heart too.

"I don't believe nothing no politician says. On Election Day, from 'fore time they gave us the vote, I goes out of town. Catches me a Greyhound and goes right on up to Sacramento. Yes I do. They might could call here wanting to take me to the polls. But you know what I tell them? And I can be packing my bag, cool as a cucumber, know what I say?"

She caught him there, with the same low ball on the inside that she threw the canvassers; Allwood was speechless.

"I tell them they can kiss it where it's red and bitter. Ain't no problem getting off the phone after that."

Allwood let out a hearty laugh, far from his snide whistle. He continued laughing while he spread his long legs out in her tiny living room. He didn't realize what a different signal he was sending her. When the cousins came, we did hit and run: hit the kitchen; run some green under the sugar bowl; split. But Allwood and Goosey hit it off like a ball and bat. Knowing Allwood was there to swing the bat, she threw more curveballs.

"Ola say you two keeping company," she said, with more of a question mark on her face than in her voice.

"We've been seeing a little bit of each other, yes I'd say," Allwood said.

"Do you live at home with your parents?"

He nodded vigorously. "Home, nowhere else," he said, slapping his knee. "I like my own bed, my own bedroom, in fact, my own house."

"Well, there you go. You know they used to call me a nervous Nellie, I was such a hard one to sleep next to."

I started to say that's not what he meant but had to consider maybe that was exactly what he meant.

"Nobody sleeps in my bed but me so nobody to please but me." Goosey got up and started toward the bedroom, laughing. "A bird don't dirty his own nest. Why should I?"

Allwood started looking at the pictures on her mantel.

"Are you looking for me?" I asked.

"I saw you when I first sat down," he said, pointing to my high school graduation picture. "I want to see what you looked like when you were little."

"I got you some here." Goosey hobbled back in with pictures and her letters.

She showed him the one with me howling my head off. The boy was getting RBIs without even looking.

"That Niecy's like a cat: hates to get her feet muddy and don't like rain." Allwood studied the picture and turned to me. "Why didn't you tell me that?"

"You couldn't tell?" I was surprised.

He shook his head.

For Goosey this illustrated everything about men. She started clapping her hands and sat on the sofa between us, too through.

"Didn't I tell you? Boys get hog wild and pigtail crazy. Can't see but one thing. I was a girl, few years older than Niecy in that picture, and there was this boy lived down the way from me. We couldn't been but twelve and thirteen. He used to tell me he had a frog in his bedroom and didn't I want to see his frog. Well, after he had gone on bout this frog every day, I wanted to see it. But I never went to his house, even though he come play at mine. Folks strict like that back then about girls.

"One day, he came up to me in the school yard and said he had the frog. But he couldn't take it out or else somebody might try to kill it. He said if I promised not to tell anybody about it, I could feel it. So I put my hand in his pocket and, sure enough, I felt his frog jump when I touched it. After that, every day, he would call me over and let me touch it."

Goosey edged up on the sofa cushion.

"It happened this one afternoon, we were walking home from school and we stopped by the creek. I told him he needed to let that frog go. I didn't think I could keep the secret any longer, and I didn't want the frog to get kilt. That's when he told me, 'Lindella, you got a little frog too.' And he pressed my underdrawers till he found my little frog, and showed me how to make it jump. So then we played frog every day until he asked me, 'Lindella, can my little frog come over and visit with your little frog?' I didn't see it was any different from plain visiting. Then my grannie saw one day that my stomach was hard and poked out and she said, 'Come here, Lindella June, let me examine you.' They found out that I was pregnant. But I hadn't been kissing no boys, and that's what they told us could get you a baby. 'Don't be kissing no boys, that get you pregnant.' So there I was, not even developed, didn't know bottoms up—pregnant."

"Don't worry, Goosey. I know about protection."

"Poppycock. If you make music, you make babies. I wanted to tell your young man how your father came into the world."

She turned away from me and spoke directly to Allwood.

"We called him Brotherboy, because it felt more like he was my baby brother than my baby. I was thirteen. Then I had Boy-Boy at fifteen from my first husband, Mr. Hightower, who was nice enough to give Niecy's father his name too and raise him along with Boy-Boy. But Mr. Hightower died on me, bless his big heart. I was sixteen and alone with two small ones."

I got money out to put under the sugar bowl, but Goosey wasn't through yet.

"I get low-sick, chill fever, I pulls out these letters my mama wrote me."

Goosey had her brown, tattered letters from when Boy-Boy's grandmother had helped her get back on her feet after Boy-Boy's father died. She had read them all to me when I was young. Every few years she had me go to the variety store and buy a new red ribbon to tie around them.

Goosey patted the letters and untied the red ribbon. I let out a sigh. I was ready to go. My grandma handed us each a letter from the top of the pile. I couldn't bring myself to open the one I had, but Allwood opened his right away. He started to read but she stopped him.

"Let Niecy read it since she bout a Lindella June if I ever."

That was what she was getting at, don't make her mistakes. I wasn't going to make her mistakes. I couldn't; they didn't have the pill then. I put the letter back on the pile and crossed my arms and shifted my impatience from foot to foot.

The brat in me came out around Goosey, the only person in the world who loved me as I was, not all gussied up. Allwood was looking at me, his eyes all wide like he was seeing me up close. Just to stop that gooey look, I took the letter and breathed hard. "Okay, I'll read it, for heaven's sake."

> *To Mrs. Lindella Goosby, 18th and Fondulac, Muskogee, Oklahoma*
> *From Mrs. Florence Stapleton, Columbus, Georgia*
> *On the date of the fourth of June*
> *In the year of our Lord nineteen hundred and twelve*
>
> *Dear Lindella June*
> *Please give Ma Goosby my kindest regard—She is not as you say*
> *Adding salt to the wound—This blow has hit you an her equally hard*
> *But I hear your heart bleating like a lost sheep across the windy plains*
> *As to this so-called Rev Cleophus—Ma Goosby did write*

Accusing you—Of taking an improper liking to him
Trust her in this matter—Circuit preachers can preach the gospel
Good as any man in a pulpit—But roaming is their habit
A womans heart an the prairie—Near bout equal to them
The very fact of him saying to Ma Goosby—What he never say to you
She a little piece of leather but she well put-together
Show he have less on his mind—An more round his holster
Than is good for him or yall—He sound like a dip over here
Dip over there type—Iffen I read Ma Goosby right
You still young even with death—Having sat down
Inside your heart—Trust Ma Goosby as I do
For these two God honest reasons—She is blood to your child
She been through an through the storms of life
She can also iron up a petticoat stiff as you please
An thats an accomplishment Lindella darling
Men be like found money—Iffen you find a shiny dollar on the street
Spend it dont depend on it—And dont be expecting to find it
Again—Sometime colored women happen up on mens
Like found money—You know what Poppa John used to say
White folks do business Negroes make rangements
Sometime what else can we do? Anybody you decide to get
A hold of Lindella—please remember
Here for the day gone for the morrow
We trying hard as bees in a bonnet to keep
Your heart from breaking again—A body can only take so much
Our preacher said death is a natural necessity
It must come to pass—MUST MEANS MUST
Keep the Good lord in your heart—Heep start but few goes
I am planning a late summer visit.
    Love, Mama
P.S. Preacher men is the hardest mens of all to live with
Has to keep his natural devil cooped up inside him
Let it out onliest in front of his wife and children
Even men with vices easier than a man of God~

. . . .

We drove back from Goosey's past the Oakland Army Base, Allwood jabbering on about Vietnam, something about the count up to a million in North and South Vietnam. I was thinking about Goosey's letter, not the main part, the postscript about preacher men . . . "the hardest mens of all to live with." I was involved with someone trying to live up to an ideal.

"Allwood, what're you talking about? There couldn't possibly be a million soldiers dead."

"I said the U.S. dropped that many bombs on 'nam. North and South."

"Where did a million bombs land? I thought it was a small country. Good grief, Charlie Brown."

"You wish it was a cartoon. Once the Senate and the House passed the Gulf of Tonkin Resolution, it's like giving LBJ a blank check to fight the war in Vietnam."

My head hurt at the thought of all the bombs bursting in air.

"Hope that can be seen is not hope," Goosey used to say. I had hoped for these two people who accepted my dark skin and nappy hair to meet. And my hope had manifested. I had such a compact world in my heart that was somehow completely undwarfed by the tumultuous world outside of my head.

8

I wanted to clue Allwood into the rest of my people gradually. My family was a circle of all kinds of people—educators, high school dropouts, drop-dead beauties, a dentist, a mechanic, party-hearties, the serious ones, the quiet ones, talkers, gamblers, some in the main-stream, others who lived right on the edge, some who had gone over the edge. A crazy family, but Allwood was crazy too. Wouldn't crazy people recognize each other?

Whenever the family got together, my aunts called it a get. We used Uncle Pink and Aunt Patsy's big ranch-style house in East Oakland behind Castlemont High School's pool. We kids never tired of playing hide-and-go-seek, mother-may-I, and running around and around that brick-and-redwood house. When the adults got busy playing bid whist and poker we forgot about eating until they got hungry. We stopped dead in our tracks when Uncle Pink pulled up from his seat like a snorting bull and shouted "Boston, baby, bos-tun."

That sprawling house fit my family. Pink, a gym teacher at Castle-mont and assistant coach of the track team, was the unofficial wel-coming committee of the family. If you got past Pink, you had a good shot at survival. Pink came in the family "with my chest out," as he told it when he got a little tight, and, after a while, he seemed like fam-ily and Patsy, the blood relative, like the in-law. Pink presided over the weddings, funerals, and gets. He played cards the best. He raised five daughters, none of whom got pregnant before marriage, as he took pride in saying.

As we drove up, I could see my clan was out in full force for Pink's fifty-third birthday. Right in front of the driveway sat Zenobia's blush pink 1957 Studebaker.

"That belongs to my aunt Zenobia. She bought it to celebrate the in-tegration of Central High in Little Rock," I told Allwood.

"It looks brand new," Allwood said, as we parked behind the Stude-baker and got out. In dusk, it gleamed like Zenobia, the beauty of the family, high yellow with a straight nose and peach-colored hair. I knew she'd be the first to look Allwood over, inch by inch, right down to the roots of his not-so-kinky hair. I rang Pink's doorbell. I looked at Allwood as we stood outside the country I had grown up in and saw him anew, not a stranger, but still a foreigner to my life.

I should have been protecting Allwood from the occupying army. But all I wanted was some of Patsy's gumbo before it ran out, at which point, instead of cracking legs and sucking crabmeat, I'd be sopping juices at the bottom of the pot with a dinner roll.

Pink opened the door. Families are found people. Mine spilled from the stone-and-rock fireplace at the end of the room—relatives, babies, children, some at the long table, others at card tables, some in chairs balancing plates. Allwood looked lost. My heart started to sink; did they leave me any gumbo?

"Now, Niecy, I've heard of CP time," Pink said. "But this is outrageous." He lifted me off my feet.

"Oh, we had to go to San Francisco first," I said.

"And what's in Frisco that you can't get in Oakland?" Pink said. I started to tell him, but he talked right over me. "Is that where you got this fella from?"

Pink stood back, blocking the doorway, arms folded over his chest. I was in; Allwood was out. I introduced them.

"You know we gotta see your birth certificate right off the bat," Pink said to Allwood. Behind me, I heard the noise of forks and knives clinking on china. The smell of giblet gravy pulled at me.

Allwood, sweet that he was, actually scrounged in his pockets as if he'd find a birth certificate. Pink laughed and let him in.

"Young blood, that's our way of saying, *where the hell you from?*"

Uncle Al, Pink's baby brother, told him, "Ordinarily we don't open the door unless you have your birth certificate." Allwood didn't get it.

It was a crazy statement, not a question, even if it came out like one. Being dumbfounded was the best response. Anger meant the boy was too many generations removed from the country. If they joked back or matched it—that never happened. They don't make them like that anymore, as my uncles said. Pink and Uncle Boy-Boy said a different kind of water in the soil sends a different kind of blood to the brain—young blood.

From across the room, Uncle Boy-Boy took one look at Allwood and began moving toward us. He asked in that voice that carried thirty feet, "This your new potato head?"

I didn't find it offensive, but Allwood sent Uncle Boy-Boy live voltage, which did not penetrate.

"I thought your father was long gone," Allwood said, looking at my uncle. Uncle Boy-Boy and I have the same straight line of eyebrow that I tweezed out, the same red tint to our dark brown skin, and the same fifty-two-tooth smile.

I introduced them. "This is my father's younger brother. He and my aunt raised me."

"Go get your young man a plate before it's all gone," Uncle Boy-Boy said, as he shook Allwood's hand. That was all I needed.

"And don't forget my sweet potato bread," Zenobia called after me. Zenobia made more delicacies from the sweet potato than George Washington Carver dreamed for the peanut. I headed for the kitchen, but I could hear them starting in on Allwood. I heard someone ask him if he was a hippie. I looked back to see how much discomfort was showing on his face. He was smiling. Wait, just wait.

Clovese, Aunt Ola's sister, stood guard over the food. "Where you pick up that heiny man?"

"Did you guys leave some gumbo in the pot for me?" was all I could answer.

"You fucking him?" She ladled out a serving of the thick brown stew over rice, put it aside, and began to ladle out a second one.

"How you wake up your shoe-shine face next to some yellow dog?"

I couldn't wait. I added filé to one of the bowls and took a bite. The shrimp and rice in my mouth made me delirious.

"Not me," Clovese said.

"Clovese," I said, going next for the smothered chicken and ignoring her comments. "Is the chow-chow hot or is it hot?"

"It's steaming. What else is chow-chow supposed to be?" she said, spooning a taste next to the spot of black-eyed peas and neck bones over rice. I could taste the cold and spicy chow-chow of cabbage-carrots-tomatoes-peppers next to the heat of the peas and neck bones already. I needed ice water for the thought of it.

"I wouldn't want to wake my black face up next to a yellow man. No, lordie," Clovese said, pouring ice water for me. We were the darkest women in the family. Had been allies since I came into the world when she was a teenager. She used her mouth to defy the taunt: *If you're white, you're all right; if you're yellow, it's mellow; if you're brown, stick around; but if you're black, get back.*

"I'm fixing a plate for him," I said to her. Clovese drew back.

"You into this Negro?" she asked me.

When I shrugged, she said, "Well, excuse me, Niecy."

It's not a crime, I wanted to shout. Instead I put down my plate and began fixing Allwood's. "He doesn't eat pork, Clovese," I said.

"He young. What does it matter?" She ladled the turnip and mustard greens from the pot onto his plate.

"A lot of people don't eat pork anymore. You know. The teachings of Elijah Muhammad. The Honorable Elijah Muhammad?"

"You mean that Muslim shit?"

"Clovese, come on."

"Come on nothing. Negroes jump on any bandwagon going by. What if he tell you to stop eating? Period? You gon do that? All because of some little old man in Timbuktu? Negroes got to use common sense. If your grandpeople hadn't eaten that pig, ain't a one of us be alive today. Did the honorable Mr. So-and-So tell you that?" As she talked, she loaded Allwood's plate with red beans and rice, greens, piccalilli, smothered chicken, creamed cauliflower, salad, and homemade rolls, everything that was on my plate except the peas.

She started to put that on but I stopped her. "No pork. For real."

"This is beef neck bones. From the cow. You ain't the only one into something better," she said. She came from behind the table for her hug. As she embraced me, I held my head back.

"Clovese, are you going to bite me?"

"Are you my niece?" She bit my cheek, holding it between her lips for a warm second. That was Clovese's trademark. "Don't let no man use you for a piss pot, hear me?"

I headed back for Allwood, passing dessert on my way: pineapple upside-down cake, pecan pie, and fried apple turnovers. Next to the desserts was a roll of wax paper for carrying a plate home instead of trying to make it into the Guinness right there.

"Give in and get up," Pink was saying. He was telling Allwood and everybody around him about his stroke. I handed Allwood his plate, assuring him there was no pork on it. Pink never ran out of ways to tell his story. Tonight he was telling it third person.

"Pink had fallen, with his big fat black self, on the kitchen floor and having a hard time getting up. So hard that I thought he couldn't. So my dear wife Patsy called for help, but the ambulance never come. Now here I am living in this house that a white man used to own, working a job that the white man says a Negro is not supposed to do. So why I think he'd send me an ambulance? But I did. And it never came. And there I am on the floor and can't get back up."

I looked at Allwood, to see if he liked the food. He was giving Pink a look that said he thought he was ignorant. But he was eating more than he had ever eaten of anything I had cooked for him, which wasn't saying much. I relaxed and started to grease.

"So Pink," Pink continued, "hungry for Aunt Pat's Sunday dinner, asked Pat to serve him his dinner on the floor. And you know what my wife told me? As sure as you born, Pat said, 'Absolutely not. Give in and get up.'"

This was the cue for anybody with two cents to jump in. Aunt Ola Ray gave it a religious slant, "And, hallelujah, Pat said, 'Give in and get up.'" Zenobia flavored hers with self-respect: "Patsy couldn't do it. She told Pink 'Give in and get up.'" Uncle Boy-Boy said, "Off your knees, brotherman."

Allwood muttered under his breath to me, as I showed him where the bathroom was, "Your family is so bourgie." To me, bourgie means straining up to be bourgeois. "My family," I growled, "who have all worked very hard to get what they have are, for your information, fun loving, loud, argumentative, boastful, food loving, proud, and," as an addendum, "they don't like to eat at restaurants. The women cook." I don't know where that came from; they ate out on occasion.

When I got back in the room, everybody was beginning to line up next to the phone for Buddy's call. We each got to shout at Boy-Boy's pride, his son the doctor.

"My son Buddy is serving in the Philippines right now," Aunt Ola said to Allwood.

Pink corrected her without condescension. "Not the Philippines, Ola. Vietnam."

"Well, over there," Aunt Ola said. "On a ship. A duty ship."

"Boy's not on a ship or we couldn't talk with him," Pink said.

"Well, where is he, then?"

"Danang." Pink repeated it, as if he saw it.

Allwood repeated the word as if it was unbelievable, *Danang, Danang.* "Your cousin's in Danang, and you didn't tell me?"

I said, "I thought he went to Hawaii."

Uncle Boy-Boy talked from the phone. "He's in the trenches."

"I don't think so," Allwood said, his voice low but clear in the excitement. It was the first time all evening that he didn't look uneasy. "Medical doctors can't carry weapons. Geneva Convention." Pink had heard him.

"How's he going to protect himself if he don't have a weapon?" Pink said.

I began to help with the cleanup when Uncle Boy-Boy announced, "Buddy wants to speak to Ruby Boogers."

"Ruby Boogers, Ruby Boogers," the kids began to chant. When I got my nose pierced, I bought a ruby nose ring, and my nose had gotten infected. Buddy had instructed me on what to do and named me Ruby Boogers. By the time I healed I had lost interest in wearing it. The family never let me live it down.

"Ruby Boogers with rings in her nose and bells on her toes," the kids sang louder.

I took the phone. "Dr. Bud?"

"Yeah. Is this the booger queen?" he said, laughing in his Bugs Bunny–Bela Lugosi way. "Still raising hell, Ruby Boogers?"

Me, the hell-raiser? Buddy was wicked: "I'll pass gas on your pillow if you don't give me your Popsicle." Many nights I slept without a pillow. When I took the phone, my voice cracked.

"Come back soon, you hear me, Buddy?" I said. When I handed the receiver to Uncle Al, I felt something strange and tight in my throat. I looked out the picture window. Somewhere between gets I had become a grown-up.

As I sat with the adults, I noticed the army green canvas strips on Allwood's combat boots from the Army-Navy store. They looked rough next to the flats, pumps, Oxfords, Florsheims, and slip-ons from Monkie Ward's, Karl's, and J. C. Penney's. All evening I had wavered, thinking Allwood wouldn't fit in and hoping he might, no way would he like my people and maybe he would. Art Linkletter settled it. I never knew how Ola would get into Art Linkletter, but she took great pleasure in finding a way to put this story into any conversation with someone new. And since she couldn't cook, Art Linkletter was her way of redeeming herself, of contributing to everyone's edification.

She'd use whatever lead-in she could—the television, a child saying a curse word, the latest crime in the neighborhood. I was gorging on upside-down cake when she started.

"Did you watch Art Linkletter's show *Kids Say the Darndest Things*, where he called little children from the audience to the microphone?"

Allwood nodded. He didn't know where she was going. The rest of us did.

"He asked them, 'What would you like to be when you grow up?' And each little one said very plain and clear, 'I want to be an engineer. . . . I want to be a spaceman. . . . I want to be a this or a that.'" Each time she told it Aunt Ola interchanged the professions. Stockbroker, nuclear scientist, the president, anything unattainable for a black man. But she always finished with "a this or a that."

"Mr. Linkletter called a little black boy up to the microphone, 'And what would *you* like to be?'"

"The little black boy didn't hesitate a bit. 'I want to be a white man.' So Mr. Linkletter said, 'Well, why would you want to be a white man when you grow up?' And the little black boy said, 'Cuz my momma said niggers ain't shit.'"

As usual the adults hooted. The kids, who had filtered back in, laughed at the laughter. The adolescents shrugged, because the whole routine was so old.

Aunt Ola Ray continued as always. "The little boy couldn't understand why the crowd was going mad. The network cut Art Linkletter off the air. Cut him off." She sliced the air with her hand to show how fast. "When they came back on, they had changed the subject. But millions of people had seen it. Millions."

Aunt Ola paused. It was pause-worthy. Millions had heard colored folk speak our piece through the mouth of this one little boy. Forget Roy Wilkins and Thurgood Marshall and Marian Anderson. All the struggles for equality, justice, and redress of grievances. My family might have been absurdly profound or profoundly absurd, but bourgie? Never.

Allwood didn't laugh, but nobody noticed. They were laughing too hard. Why was it so appealing? Was it like an inoculation? You'd never get it once they stuck the joke in your bloodstream? Was it so ludicrous as to be a basic untruth? Was it comforting to the adults that children took them so literally? Was it assuring to the adolescents that adults were not to be taken literally? Did Allwood lack humor?

As we sat there and the evening wound down and folks started to leave, Uncle Al, Pink's youngest brother, started talking to Allwood and suddenly said, "You have a brother drive an AC Transit?"

"That's my father," Allwood answered.

Allwood's father a city bus driver? I had never asked him about his father's job.

"You swear, man? You and him, you look like brothers," Al said, holding his youngest, Renee, barely four years old.

Uncle Al turned to her. "This here is Shakespeare's son. Shakespeare is his daddy. Remember Shakespeare, our bus driver?"

She nodded her head shyly, looking at Allwood with recognition.

"Man, I have listened to that cat blow for days. Your poppa is a heavy dude. The college kids on that route nicknamed him Shake-speare." The more Uncle Al talked, the more some kind of light came into Allwood's face.

"Yeah, he's a Shakespeare nut. Goes to all the plays in the park and the little theaters," Allwood said, as he rubbed and stroked his beard. "He dragged us when we were kids."

"You know something?" Uncle Al said. "When finals and midterms come up, them college kids be asking him all kinda questions about Shakespeare. They make your old man late on his run. I seen 'em, man, they be writing what he's saying."

Uncle Al shook his head and turned to put Renee down.

"And that's your old man." Uncle Al kept shaking his head and smil-ing as he shook Allwood's hand. Allwood looked at ease for the first time all night.

Renee, clinging to her father, kept looking at Allwood as Uncle Al started walking away, his back to us. "Who him name?" Renee said shyly to me, pointing to Allwood. I repeated his name clearly, over-enunciating.

"Who him name, who him name?" Uncle Al hushed her but it be-came a litany.

When we got ready to leave, we passed Renee and Uncle Al. As soon as she spotted Allwood, Renee started to say something. Then she put her thumb in her mouth and started sucking furiously.

Who-him-name was right.

I finished my first year with thirty-three units, a GPA of 3.2, and a boyfriend.

We were finished connecting. We were connected.

Sophomore

9

Allwood and I had to be the only two beings on earth crossing the Bay Bridge in a silver Beetle rehearsing phrases in Arabic in March of 1965. The radio was blaring that two Marine battalions had arrived the day before on China Beach at Danang.

"Malcolm's assassinated February twenty-fifth, and LBJ approves troops to go to 'nam on February twenty-sixth. No coincidence," Allwood said.

As we came out of the Treasure Island tunnel onto the San Francisco side of the bridge, I could tell Allwood was pushing his buttocks down into the seat by the way he was gripping the handle on the dashboard. I pushed the four one-dollar bills that the toll collector had given me into my jeans pocket. We were headed for the Black House in the Fillmore.

"Allwood, do you think pushing your ass into the seat is going to stop the bridge from swaying?"

"You're driving too fast, Geniece," he said, craning his neck to check my speed. He was right. "As-salaam-alaikum." Allwood said it for the umpteenth time, enunciating every syllable.

"Wa-alaikum-as-salaam," I said, trying unsuccessfully not to say, "Wall, the lake um's a salami, brother sister baloney, and most high potentate."

Allwood shook his head.

"I'm sorry, I'm sorry. I take it back." I made grabbing motions into the tight space of air around us. "I put it all back in my mouth."

The San Francisco skyline, the offices full of yellow light and reflected dusk, glittered. Allwood sighed. I drove to Fell Street and went up the hill, practicing and being corrected until we reached Divisadero Street, where I broke.

"They will not allow me in if I don't say this exactly right? Kick me into the street if I say it wrong? Who is the boss of Salaam and

Sa-laikam, anyway? Tell me. It sounds like Abbott and Costello meeting up as sheiks on the street."

"Believe it or not," Allwood said, "you're going to like it." We finally parked at Hayes and Broderick.

"I don't see a black house," I said.

"It's not painted black," Allwood said, steering me. Behind the wheel of the VW, the gearshift in my palm, I was in charge, since Allwood couldn't drive a stick. But outside that cooped-up space, I waited for his arm to tell me which was the right house. It was a two-story Victorian with a low-angled roof jammed between two other old houses. It looked no different from the others except it was a light green between celery and vomit, which I felt like I might do.

God, San Francisco was such a thief. A lady of the night, a sorceress with her hands out. Every time, all my years as a child, that we crossed the bridge, we had to pay to get in, pay to get out, pay for every little thing. Oakland was free, San Francisco was not. Pay me, pay me. Pay for the Pacific Ocean and the beach. I am expensive, the city always said, so pay me for my wonderful dark treats like the Steinhart Aquarium, with its dark wide hall lit up by tank after tank of bright gold green blue sharks dolphins whales stinger fish, cold-eyed still-as-a-corpse fish that didn't blink or budge when we tapped the thick glass with our fingernails. Pay, the voice said, to whomever took us on Sunday to the Fleischacker Zoo, Goosey, Boy-Boy, Uncle Pink, the hand of San Francisco reaches out to grab your stupid little nickels and dimes. Pay. Even as I stood in front of the Fat Lady, whose cackling gap-toothed twelve-feet-high, three-feet-wide body made me laugh for a solid hour, even as I collapsed in tears driven out of my eyes by laughter, I understood that the other name for San Francisco wasn't Frisco; it was pay you dumb jerks from Oakland pay. I could hear the fat lady cackling at the Pacific Ocean, at the stream of frazzled parents, rowdy teenagers, noisy kids, and little colored me with braids and pedal pushers. God, would I ever grow up?

"As-salaam-alaikum," I said, as we walked up the balustraded stairway.

"Wa-alaikum-salaam," he said back and rang the bell.

The front door had leaded stained-glass windows on each side. I peered through one and saw a man with skin the color of a Hershey bar and teeth a stunning white. Even though I saw him, when he opened the door, he startled me. Allwood gave the Muslim greeting.

"Wa-alaikum-salaam, Brother Allwood!" The man's tone was so deep it rumbled. He took my coat from me. Inside I saw San Francisco once again in the dense, narrow, vertical interior. I was almost dizzy with expectation.

"Is this the sister's first time here?" he said to Allwood. I couldn't let him not talk to me.

"As-salaam-a-laikum," I said proudly. His bushy eyebrows raised.

"I'm Geniece Hightower. I've never been here before." I extended my hand to him. He looked at it and laughed. More rumbling. Inside me.

"You niggas from Oakland is quaint." *Niggas from Oakland.* Did he sing that? Did his voice go up on *niggas* and back down on *Oakland*? Whatever was coming from his dark neck was like a boat bobbing on an ocean. I couldn't take my eyes from it.

"This is our fortress against the wolf," he said, leading up the stairs. A hand-lettered sign hung between the sconces: IN THE BEGINNING, ALL THE WORLD WAS BLACKNESS. They changed a quote I immediately remembered from Western Civ and John Locke: In the beginning all the world was America. It was of a piece with the Grove Street orators, so smart, so seemingly University of California–bound yet not, so Harvard yet not, and here I was in this grand Victorian transformed by blackness. Not blackness, Blackness.

"The wolf?" I felt the quivery knot in my stomach. He laughed so hard I thought I should stop asking questions.

"Everybody. The system, the world, the city." He stopped and leaned on the mahogany banister. "The garbage in the streets, the past, the present, maybe the future."

He raised coal black eyebrows. "Street niggas come up with a lot of existential rhetoric too."

"Bibo," Allwood addressed him.

"Your name is Bibo?" What a crazy-sounding name.

"Wanna check my birth certificate?" he said. He and my kinfolk shared the same odd birth certificate pun. I felt like I was bobbing alongside him.

"Bibo, what time does it start?" Allwood's voice grounded me.

"The music or the speeches?"

"The speeches."

"Speeches for the good brother Allwood right in the Malcolm X door." The brother pointed to a closed door. Allwood squeezed my arm. I watched wordless as Allwood walked in and the door closed behind him. I heard a familiar-sounding high-pitched male voice inside. But it was overpowered by the rumbling intonations of the man next to me.

"You belong in here." Bibo steered me toward a kitchen where a woman was stirring something that smelled like lamb and garlic in a pan. He disappeared down the hall.

He meant to direct me to the kitchen, and I do know about manners, but from the other side of the house I heard drums, vibrations, thumping, somebody blowing poetry like a saxophonist was inside his throat. I followed the sounds to another house connected by a passageway. I bobbed along, dealing with a ferocious conga beat. That was when I saw dancers. The first thing I noticed was dark, dark sisters, their hair trimmed and moving with their bodies like fitted caps. It was a dark world and I fit, or so I thought until I looked in the mirror where their torsos twisted around me like serpents. I looked like a Tarzan native on a Hollywood movie set. I looked wild and untamed, countrified. The dancers had sculpted Afros. I had hair all over the place. The dancers had African print draped around them. I had on frayed jeans. The sheer exertion of their bodies pounding, feet stomping, and hands tapping brought up images of my family, the side where light people, the high-yellow side, just had to be light. That's all, be light and that's all. The women who were light didn't even have to know how to dance, just be light, which made them pretty. I knew the browner people in the family could be smart as hell. It was never enough. If you were brown, you better know how to do something and do it well. Even then, you didn't get slack. Clovese had her picture in her paper at work. I could tell she was real proud of it because she made copies and gave them around. But I heard my aunt say, "So dark you can hardly see her."

I headed for the kitchen. The woman there was slight with kumquat-smooth dark skin, an ankle-length skirt draped on her. Her back formed a graceful arch over the pan, her head wrapped in a purple silk scarf with pencil-thin green stripes. She didn't see me and I didn't want her to turn around and catch me staring at her. The smell of what she was cooking taken together with her appearance was enough. I was hearing the words *Ali Baba and the Forty Thieves* and *as-salaam-alaikum* in a jumble in my head. If I saw her from the front a snake might spring from the top of her head and twist over and grab me from myself. *No!* I wanted to shout out at her. *No!* You can't have it. I own it.

I wanted to take in this Blackness but I didn't want to drown in it. People who were radical and black or part of the resistance to the man and the system had confidence oozing out of them. They seemed to never doubt themselves. I wasn't like that.

I turned and walked down the hall to find Allwood, my security blanket. I couldn't find the door. I got stuck in the hall. Where was Allwood who had gotten me into this? I had to go into one of the rooms. What if I walked in on somebody doing it? House parties always had a bedroom upstairs where somebody dumb would happen on somebody not so dumb. But this wasn't a house party. I took a deep breath and opened a door with a poster of Malcolm X on it.

"Some people think this is paradise. California. We're free. The South is behind us. Jim Crow is behind us. The ocean is our frontier now. We're a part of the wild, wild West. . . . Don't believe it."

The speaker's voice was high-pitched and familiar. It was Freed Man, with his Albert Einstein mustache, at a podium, two chairs on each side of him. The room had four rows of wooden folding chairs, with an aisle about a foot wide. But the room was lopsided because everybody was sitting on one side. The men looked alike, unsmiling with big Afros. I was escorted to the empty side. I became aware of my jeans that were tight and frayed on the inside of my thigh. "You're not a part of paradise. For you—" the speaker said. Seated, I recognized everything about him, his tallness, his gangliness, his light complexion, like a faded yellow. "For you," he repeated, with the same rhetorical flourish he used on Grove Street in Oakland in front of City College, "California is paradise with rules, a paradise for fools. And the main rule for Negroes, that is, the unschooled fools who still call themselves Negroes, the main rule is . . ."

He broke off there and started laughing. In all those lunchtimes I had watched him with the Grove Street orators and taken leaflets for Fair Play for Cuba from him, I had never seen him look jive or relaxed. But he was laughing a deep, hearty laugh, shaking his entire torso. How could he shake and bellow like that here in this foggy black heart of San Francisco and never have seemed at ease even once in the sunshine and touch-me-I'm-blue skies of Oakland?

"Wait!" The word hit the room like a thunderclap. I started in my seat. I needed to go to the bathroom, but even more urgently needed to get his point. I was following Freed Man like I'd followed preachers' interminable sermons on Sunday afternoons. Only then I'd waited for the preachers, who as a class Uncle Boy-Boy labeled ignorant, to say something ungrammatical or simple so I could dismiss the whole sermon. But the Grove Street orators were different. They were book smart.

"That's what the man insists that you do. Wait for justice. Wait for equality. Wait until he gets ready to give you freedom. To give you justice. To hand out equality on a silver platter."

The men started clapping. I clapped with them. They stopped. I put my hands back on my lap. Freed cleared his throat like a reverend. Did God awaken him in the night with the next day's sermon? A God like Malcolm X or Marcus Garvey or Elijah Muhammad or maybe Nat Turner? His God was definitely a black man who wore owly glasses and Big Ben Davis coveralls and carried a briefcase, like he did.

"And then he concocts a rationale for why you have to wait. Not why you should wait, why you gonna wait. Dig it. He gets some Irish cracker—who's probably been to Harlem twice in his whole life—to put together a report and put his name on it. Yeah, the Moynihan Report."

This was Allwood's turf. I was on familiar territory here.

"Yeah, the Moynihan Report, which just means some potato farmer's great-grandson is getting over on you, making his name, his rep, paying for his wife to hire your mama to make her dinner and wash her underwear out by hand—yeah, your mother, we know why sistahs' hands be so rough—and sending his kids to a college you couldn't get in if you had straight As and perfect SATs. I know because I was one of the first Negroes at Harvard. Went in a Negro, invisible and all that shit, came out a black man. Had to. It was either break through to my blackness or die. And you see me standing here."

The men clapped in unison. When I clapped, I broke the oneness.

"Yeah. Moynihan . . . the very name makes me want to take somebody out. Moynihan says the Negro community has been forced into a matriarchal structure which, because it's so out of line with the rest of American society—Dig that, you-outta-line Negroes—he says we seriously retard the progress of the group as a whole."

I still needed to pee. The walls were lettuce green semigloss; somebody had done a nice job on the trim and the windowsills . . . alabaster. Nice. I still wanted to find Allwood. But the speaker was up to the clincher here in this bedroom auditorium.

"I don't know bout you, but I got a daddy. Fo your ass," he said. *Yeah, but do you know where he is*, I asked with my eyes, *cuz I don't know where mine is.*

"This looney-tune white man is the USA, your Uncle Sam. And the same mothers and fathers he's disparaging—which is a fancy white man's term for putting your ass down—those same black people are paying his salary, slaving, paying taxes so the man can write this bullshit, get a PhD off of it, and keep you down where you can't even get up and fight cuz you busy trying to prove to him that what he's saying ain't so, which he knows already and that's why he puts it out there. So you'll spend the next twenty-five years trying so hard to disprove a lie that it begins to sound like the truth and Moynihan, some potato farmer's great-grandson, gets called a prophet."

Freed Man was through. I had attended enough church to know that. The men began clapping.

"We don't need no hand clapping."

They stopped. "And we don't need no more Jesuses. One was enough to keep us under the yoke for four hundred years." Well, I didn't see a collection plate, so I got up and slithered out so I wouldn't have to shake hands with the right reverend. But he called my name before I could get to the door.

"Sistuh Hightower," he said. I nodded. He remembered my byline.

"Is this your first time at the Black House?" *How could he tell?* "Are you reporting on this?"

"No, no, no, I came with Allwood."

"Don't be embarrassed," he said. *Oh, shit, he could read my mind.* "You're not dressed the way the sisters dress here."

He pointed me with his hand on my elbow back to the kitchen. "Fatimah will give you the word. She's a Nubian sister. Queens speak a language only other queens can understand. Dig?"

"Nubian?" I asked.

"Yeah. New Being. Nu-bi-an. That's the word here."

I had no choice, it seemed, but to return.

Fatimah stood in the kitchen, smiling at me as if she had been waiting for me all night. I touched my hair. It felt wiry and woolly. She smiled again.

"You are a queen. Beautiful," she said. I didn't know what to say. *Beautiful.* What kind of word was that to be connected with me? I had been called cute and dark, sexy and dark, long-legged and dark. Beautiful?

"You've never been called that, have you? A queen?" she asked, her voice soft and rich.

"No, never," I said. *Napoleon nose* had been one of my nicknames from the cousins. I had a small waist and pretty feet, my one physically perfect feature. Men had singled out parts, as if the whole was worth very little but the parts could be worth something at auction. I never believed men who said I was fine because I thought they used the word interchangeably with the thought of wanting to fuck me. The brother who had called her a Nubian came to the kitchen.

"Tightening her up?" he said.

"Harris." Fatimah's large brown eyes seemed to pour the word out to him. She had been cooking for him, I was sure. He turned to talk to someone down the hall. "Let the white kids lead a palace revolt. Let the white man be divided. Divided he falls, united we stand. When the man closes ranks is when we should be alarmed. That's when he's at his deadliest."

He turned back to me and said to Fatimah, "Lumumba, Patrice Lumumba. She's got that same steady look in her eyes. She's got a chilling thing going down in her eyes. Yeah."

My only frame of reference for anybody's Lumumba was a dark-as-night boy in high school with very African features. From the South, he wore Big Ben overalls and clunky workingman's shoes, and kids called him Lumumba. He had a crush on me and my friends had made fun of me because of it. They had called me Lumumba's wife, which I had hated.

When Harris walked away, I felt free to ask Fatimah. "Am I seeing things wrong or do I just happen to see a lot of light-skinned brothers in the movement with darker-skinned sisters?"

She laughed a tinkly crystal laugh. I wondered what her hair was like under her scarf.

"You picked up on that, huh? These brothers have an elevated consciousness and, yes, they're trying to prove something. Allwood is your man, right?"

I shrugged. She smiled like she knew something I didn't.

"Harris, Allwood, our light-skinned men in the movement, they feel deeply about us as sisters, as beautiful black women."

"But is it overcompensation?"

"Maybe you see it as overcompensation. When you look outwardly, unless you look in a mirror, you can't see yourself. You can't see if you're skinny or fat or white or black. You see the people around you. Whatever they are, that's what you are. When you wake up in the morning, you wake up human, no age, no color, and no sex until your eye hits either a mirror or another person. Then it's instant. That's who you are—who you sleep with, who you eat with. So I think these brothers have grown to resent being categorized, put down because of their light skin. They're trying to prove who they are inside so they won't be judged by the outside."

I felt a sense of alarm. "Will they dump the dark-skinned sister once they've made their point?"

She laughed again. "Did Malcolm leave Betty?"

"Malcolm X's wife was dark-skinned?"

Fatimah got a book from a stack on the table and showed me Betty Shabazz's picture. "Brother Malcolm's overcompensation benefited us all. He became as powerful as we are. He exposed us to our power and that was his power. That's why they had to kill him."

She put the book back and walked behind me. "Let me show you something."

With one deft movement of her hands, she twisted my hair, tighter than I had ever twisted it, into a ponytail. She pulled me up and we went to the mirror in the hall. I looked at her hands, at her long smooth fingers, with their white half-moons. They told me my mother had strong fingers with beautiful half-moons.

"Do you see how different you look with your hair off your face?" she asked me.

For so long, I had used my hair as my shield. To see myself in front of her as I saw myself in the morning was a shock.

"You are a beautiful woman." She turned my chin from side to side. "Look at your face, your jaw, those beautiful planes. Look at the light picking them out. You're a thousand years old. They couldn't beat the African out of you. They couldn't fuck it out."

She wouldn't let go of my head. One hand held my hair tight from my scalp, and her other hand, satin soft and cool, cupped my chin. "You have to say it," she said.

"Say what?"

"I am such a beautiful woman."

I said it quickly.

"No, say it slowly looking at yourself, not me."

I said it again, but it was hard not to look at her. She was beautiful.

"Look at you. No man can make you unbeautiful. Say it as if it meant all the gold in creation was inside your beauty. Inside you."

I looked at that mirror and saw the Geniece she saw. I wasn't only parts put together. She let go of my hair; it went back all over the place. But it didn't matter. I was not my hair or my pretty feet that no one ever saw first, or any other part, not even my mind. I was a whole new being that this woman had showed me. Bibo came sauntering down the hall and grabbed my arm, pulling me away. Fatimah smiled and watched as we walked away. He wasn't so overpowering. He wasn't overcompensating either. We went to another part of the house, but he kept pouring poetic shit into my ear.

"Elvis ripped off Big Mama Thornton . . . The hound dog . . . Jughead was an agent provocateur for the FBI. . . . Millie the Model had silicone implants, but we didn't want to hear it. . . . Yeah . . . *True Romance* tears stop where the real ones start. . . . Ike was a colored man. . . . Dinah Shore's a fugitive from the Negro race. . . . Sammy Davis Jr. got that empty eye socket from the mob. . . . Little Lotta's fat comes from the diethylstilbestrol in all those hamburgers she stuffs down her fat white gut. . . . Even if we heard it, it would have gone in one ear and out the other. . . . Archie and Veronica freaked on her daddy's bed. . . . You gotta use your imagination, otherwise you'll just be thinking some guy is peeing inside you. . . . Richie Rich made his money from black sugar workers in rural Cuba. . . . Louie Louie was a flasher. . . . Nkrumah has led Ghana into the future fabulous."

He walked toward Allwood, who was waiting with his coat on and looked strange, as if I had gone away and we were connecting after a long absence.

"Are you ready?" Allwood asked, one hand on the door. When we got outside, the cold night air fell right on the spots where Fatimah had held my chin.

"Yeah, finally," I said.

The next day I went to the barbershop and had my hair cut into a natural.

Sleek, short, very African.

10

Allwood and I had been more than friends but less than going all the way for almost a year. I had forty-five units and wanted to go to a black school, but who was I fooling? No moolah, no black college. But my life was changing anyway, thank goodness. I had moved to a one-bedroom apartment in South Berkeley for eighty-eight dollars a month, and I was no longer bound by the Y curfew. I put away the silver circle pin I had worn since high school to show that I was a virgin. I wasn't ashamed, but to be a sophomore and a virgin was not something to brag about, especially when you had a boyfriend.

I liked Allwood as a person. I respected his intelligence and always will. I might have been a little bit in love with him, but Allwood's idea of a good time was to debate the merits of W. E. B. Du Bois versus Booker T. Washington, for starters. Then he'd switch to the Harlem Renaissance and black literature, do a stretch on Paul Robeson and the radical connection between theater and socialism, do a spiel on the Pullman porters and the sociological impact of trains on black folks, jump from Jean-Paul Sartre on the language of domination imposed by the French colonialists on Algiers and end up with an analysis that connected Little Rock, Arkansas, to the Algerian war. And, of course, the Mekong Delta and the Vietcong and the war spreading into Laos and Cambodia. That swamp containing guns, soldiers, generals, and names like Westmoreland, McNamara, and Hershey was never far away. Very educational, mind you, but on any given Friday night, my cultural conditioning got the best of my intellectual affinities.

I began to see astride his lanky shoulders hung in his loden green car coat two huge globes filled with seawater. The one on his right shoulder was the American continent and the left shoulder globe was the African continent. Allwood would say *what's up?* or *you got it*, but he was giving me a globe. Then I would be equally weighted down. I got so irritated one Friday night when he started in on his Cuba-socialism-Afro-American-capitalism jazz, I exploded.

"Allwood, I have a corn on my left baby toe. I am not in the mood. Life does not begin and end with the problems of the world. Fuck Cuba. Fuck the United States too. Fuck everything troublesome for at least an hour of every day. Particularly when we're together. I will not be indoctrinated into fucking you."

I didn't mean for the last part to come out. But I was tired of the spiel and didn't like not being able to stand him, because I wanted him to be the first. But things had to be right. I wanted to be in control of that much of my destiny. I was in essence negotiating when, where, how, but not why. We had settled the why wordlessly.

This particular Friday night, we had gone to the party house on Alcatraz Avenue right above Adeline in Berkeley. In all the times I had partied there, I never scrutinized the apartment, never cared who lived there. It was just a bunch of Sigmas who gave parties. Splibs crowded into a smoky room doing the shotgun to Junior Walker & the All-Stars. Now the front room was bare except for the radiators, a dining room chair with a faded rose velvet seat, an old brass lamp, and a brand-new stereo. The box was long and shiny and belonged somewhere else, like behind a plate-glass display window. Allwood led me through a hall to the back. I was squiggling, but he was solemn. The back room into which Allwood led me contained a single, solitary daybed, soiled and gray, with no sheet, no nothing. The thought of my bare brown bottom on a strange bed without even a clean sheet was beyond me.

I thought of the room I had imagined walking into, one with polished parquet floors and bookshelves all around. Huge yellow and brown wide-wale corduroy pillows. The bedroom was rather small for the huge bed but that was okay, because the bedspread was all gold puff, the huge window had a beautiful view of the Berkeley Hills, and the sheets were clean and creased. Into this we floated and landed, facing each other. Then Allwood glided into me effortlessly and began to climax. I told him to stop and wait for me, and he did, and we began to really feel each other, to feel sensual and come together. It was supposed to be breezy.

"Allwood." I began to seethe. "Are you crazy. I only have one cherry. Do you think you're going to pop it on that?"

He looked embarrassed but he didn't say anything.

"You know what this reminds me of?" It brought to my mind a whorehouse.

He shook his head.

"Would you eat off that sofa, Allwood? The guys take fast girls here to do it. I can't believe this. When you said a friend's apartment, you know what I thought?"

"I know, I know. I'm sorry. Let's go."

When we got outside and started walking toward the bus stop, Allwood looked depressed. "What are we going to do?" he said.

Allwood counted his change carefully. He had gotten us a motel room at Motel 6. He stood at the window of the motel room watching the freeway construction near MacArthur Boulevard.

"Pretend the money is for a good cause." I was softening. Anger was not the proper accompaniment for the First Time. The daybed in my apartment would have been suitable if we were going to be mad. I wanted glorious. We fiddled around. I checked the bedclothes, looked in the closet for a ghost of romance; Allwood read the Gideon Bible.

"Anything you like in there?"

He looked at me, a little sad. He sat on the bed. I felt this enormous warmth move me. I had won the Battle of the Motel Room.

"Allwood," I began so softly I surprised myself. "I'm sorry for acting shitty. Let's just relax."

We lay there for a few minutes, Allwood fully dressed except for his loden green car coat, which he had hung with no small amount of care in the empty closet. Then we began to kiss. Routine, routine. Off with my blouse. Not so routine, but not so different either. The hands on the thigh bit. Routine, routine. His lips on my breasts. The norm lately.

Only more exciting now. His shirt came off. Out of the ordinary. Thin Allwood had a set of dark nipples like buoys on the yellow sea of his chest. I touched them; they got hard just like mine. Really nice. I kissed them. He started laughing. Then he got up and began to unzip. Allwood's Big Moment. I stared. He wore white briefs.

Hair black and curled—I probably would have fainted if it had been anything else—from his navel down to his penis. I had never seen one not in a photo or on a statue or a baby boy. It looked like it had been planted there, with all that hair for soil, just dangling there amid his beige-colored balls.

"Allwood, this is rather nice." I began to take my clothes off. I hung them over the chair. When I looked back, Allwood was staring at me, lying down, his penis standing straight up, well, maybe a forty-five-degree angle. I felt a tension in my thighs.

"Allwood, where did you get that yellow missile?"

"Huh?"

"God, Allwood, is all that supposed to be inside me?"

"Yeah, but not at first."

"When? What happens now?"

"You can either hop on it or I can hop on you."

"It's going to hurt?"

"Not too much."

He laughed. It was okay for him to feel humorous. A nuclear submarine with destroyer force wasn't aiming for his gut.

"Are you serious?"

"C'mon, Geniece. It's just like when we kiss and feelsies. Only more."

So we did some kissing and touching. Only I was thinking, *Kid Geniece, this is the real thing, a real live loud moan, a real live hard penis, a real body moving against me instead of the thought bubble above my head.* My pelvic area went into its own orbit. How easy, nothing complicated about this. Follow the circle, Geniece. Allwood sat back on his knees again, rubbing the yellow missile. It had a new face, bloodied.

"It has blood on it. . . . What happened? . . . How come I didn't feel it? . . . I'm not a virgin anymore, Allwood."

He laughed. The torpedo shook. It had a new face, bloodied.

"You're still a virgin. But not for long."

It finally happened. I felt it inside me again. It didn't hurt so much as it felt so darn pointed.

"Darn, why is it so sharp, Allwood?"

I really didn't know where to put my legs. Straight up, I was told. That's ridiculous. I tried it, Allwood moaned and the torpedo moved in a little more. Oh, now that hurt.

"When is it going to feel good?"

"Give it a few minutes."

I felt stupid with my legs up in the air. Suddenly and partly to keep my mind off the hurt, the painful feeling, I started thinking about the window and if anyone with binoculars had caught sight of two brown legs with feet on the end sticking straight up.

"My legs are tired, Allwood."

"All right, baby."

Then it was like buckshot exploding inside me. Unbelievable. I felt this person exploding inside me. Allwood started moving faster. What was I supposed to do with my legs? I put them alongside his back. That was more comfortable for me, but I didn't think it was for him.

"Wrap your legs around me."

"Like this?"

"Yeah." His face looked like nothing I'd seen before, like he lost control of the muscles around his mouth.

It still hurt, but I was thinking, *It's over, the pain is over, finally I'm not a virgin anymore, I'm a full-fledged member of the society of people who do it. I was doing it. No. I had done it.* Entry is act.

"I'm gonna come."

"What does that mean?"

"It means it feels real good, babe."

"Oh, Allwood, does it? What's gonna happen?"

"Watch." Famous last word.

Allwood's body tightened. He got real rigid. Oh my goodness, his balls flapped against my behind. Allwood moved fast and I grinded. It still hurt, but I was so curious to see what would happen. He started shuddering. I couldn't recall seeing anyone not in a horror movie shudder before, especially on top of me. Oh my goodness, was Allwood in pain too? Everything felt so tight, like we'd locked into each other. Of all things to remember, I saw *Pit and the Pendulum*, the last scene where the cage closes on the lady who did Vincent Price wrong. I bit his neck.

"Geniece Geniece," Allwood shouted. The next thing I knew his tongue went all the way down my throat. For about thirty seconds, I thought I was going to die of suffocation.

"Did you come?"

"Did I!"

"Was it the way it's supposed to be?" My legs were wrapped around his back.

"Yeah exactly."

"Did you like it?" Everything felt gooey.

"Be quiet for a minute. Stop fucking with me."

I count to sixty.

"Why is it still hard, Allwood?"

"Because I'm ready to go again."

"What does that mean?"

"This is just a rest period."

"You're kidding." All of a sudden I feel sore.

"No, I'm not."

"You're going to repeat the whole thing?" I wanted to get up and see how much blood I lost. I shifted around.

"Don't do that."

"I have to go to the bathroom, Allwood."

"Okay, okay, get up." It came right out like a greased pole. Allwood yawned and stretched. My legs felt like they'd been stretched apart for hours.

"How long did it take, Allwood?"

"I thought you had to use the bathroom." Allwood looked at his watch. "About half an hour."

"That's all? I feel like a jockey." I was afraid to look, so I didn't even lift up.

"You can close your legs."

"Okay, don't rush me."

I rolled over. It felt sticky. The sheet had a spot not bigger than a fifty-cent piece. Oh crap.

"Is that it, Allwood?" I was disappointed.

"Is that what?" he laughed.

"My cherry."

"Yeah, you want to take it home for a souvenir."

This was a big letdown, a really big letdown.

"I'm glad this is not my wedding night. I would want a divorce, or at the very least a good explanation."

"Next time," he said, slapping my fanny, "it'll be better. For you."

"Allwood," I said on my way to the bathroom, "was I good?"

"Fair. C+." I didn't know if he was kidding. What was I supposed to do? Stand on my head?

Allwood walked into the shower. For the first time since we stepped into the motel room I remembered that everything had been very mellow and that we'd been relating like ordinary people the entire night. No politics, no heavy rap.

"You get an A. No kidding. You handled yourself like a pro." Allwood laughed, but it made me feel funny. Now that I wasn't a virgin, that could be insulting.

I wondered what Allwood would think if he could have seen inside my mind. He probably wouldn't have cared. Maybe he would. Then again he couldn't see inside mine and I couldn't see in his, other than all the bookshelves. Maybe ignorance is bliss, maybe it's plain ignorant.

"Allwood, I don't think I want to do it again," I told him after we cleaned up.

"I know," he said. "You got up."

"You mean ordinarily you start right back up and don't clean it up or anything?"

"It depends." Allwood started putting his clothes on. I knew he was getting lonesome for his car coat.

"Do you get any of the six dollars back, since you only stayed an hour?"

"No. Let's hurry up. I'm hungry."

. . . .

Amid this frenzy, I got my semester grades:

- Poli Sci, [A];
- French 3, [A];
- Journalism, [A], of course;
- Physiology 1-1 Lab, [D]. This really hurt my GPA, because it was a five-unit course.

I couldn't figure out if this being almost in love was hurting or helping my GPA.

11

I was almost in love. It would be interesting to find out what it takes to be in love. That little word—*in*—is so stupidly crucial. Does it mean you have to be *inside* the love or *into* this love or *inserted* or *in between* it? I worked myself into a frenzy over this two-letter word.

It felt like a little room was inside my body, and I had the key and I gave it to Allwood, who fumbled and got the key in the lock and pushed the door open, and the hinges kind of squeaked and Allwood went in and made himself at home. In my room. Inside my life in a room that's a part of my body, a room I never see, a room that was so inviting to him and so mysterious to me. Where in the confines of that room was the *in* in in love? What was the connection between that room and my feeling for Allwood? I think when I finally made that connection something not clear became all too clear.

Inside my room, while I was outside, he walked around in it, opening and closing the windows. In my little godforsaken, me-forsaken room. Once he was comfortable, Allwood talked a lot. He did this all the time. It threw me off at first. I never seemed to recall hearing or reading about men talking a lot when they're in the throes of passion. The image I had was they talked you into bed, and after that was accomplished, it was all grunt and groan.

What a shock to find out that Allwood, the real Allwood, the questioning Allwood instead of the statemental Allwood, came alive as he began to come.

"Do you like me because I'm light?" This was a shocker when he came up with it. He was only the most black-identified guy I'd ever known. But I was learning to let Allwood talk when he was inside the room. By not answering out loud, we got to a different kind of conversation, one we never had if I had to use my voice.

What do you mean, because you're light-skinned? I answered him in my mind. And, as if he'd heard me, Allwood said, "Or do you like me because I'm lighter than you?" *What difference does it make at this point?*, one part of me wanted to say, the part that the talking Geniece would have said. But the other part, the part of me that liked that bodily way of exchanging information, did things I would never have said.

Out loud, I said, "Allwood, I like you because you're so smart." That's what I thought. I never told Allwood I liked him initially because of his meanness, which I found dangerously exciting. After I got to know him, I realized he wasn't mean at all. So then, I had to think of what I thought he was to reproduce the dangerous feeling, which was how I got into my feeling for Allwood and my feeling, limited, incomplete, or not in love, such as it was for him in the first place.

. . . .

I found out Allwood was not mean in between our first and second time. We were sitting on the bench outside on Grove Street. The Fair Play for Cuba guys had stopped stopping traffic; I guess they met their quota of cars coming from Berkeley into Oakland. Or maybe they had to go to class. Allwood told me some of them did matriculate to Berkeley and some just stayed at City, where they could be radical for years on end.

Abner, who was neither radical nor bourgeois, mostly a species of generalized irritant, stopped to talk to us. They greeted each other like long-losts, hugging even. Allwood never hugged the Fair Play guys. They usually nodded and grunted, no hugging.

"Man, tell your ole lady why we hang so tight. Man, tell her we ain't no fags," Abner said. Why he would think that was beyond me, but I was curious by then.

"Aw, man, I'll get around to it," Allwood said, and then the two of them went into a powwow right there in front of me. They started talking as if in a foreign language—one with a lot of laughing and hand slapping. When they were through, Abner went on into the building. Allwood sat there, chuckling to himself. I shook his shoulder.

"Don't just sit there. Tell me why." He began to tell me about their church's senior class outing, when he and Abner and the other kids, most of whom attended Oakland's only all-black high school, Mc-Clymonds, had gone up to the snow near Lake Tahoe for a two-day trip. I had read about it in the *Oakland Tribune*. And even better, my best friend's friend from the same church had been there too, so I knew details: the pond that wasn't frozen solid; the sign that they ignored; the break in the ice; the kids who had fallen through; the three who drowned; the teary funerals; the sadness when the ones who didn't die graduated. I had heard those details.

"I'll never forget. I thought I was going to die. . . . There were feet kicking me in the head and it was cold, Geniece. That water was so cold. But it was a strange thing. It was very clear down there. I didn't open my eyes for the first few seconds after I fell. But when I opened them, I could see my friends, my classmates. It was so clear. But it was too cold to think. All I could do was kick and be kicked. Then I saw a girl jerk her head back and her body went limp and then horizontal."

Allwood stood up in the broad North Oakland daylight and I believed him, because he went into position, turning, jerking, kicking, and paddling.

"I grabbed her."

"Why did you grab her?" I asked. "She was a goner."

"Instinct, I guess," Allwood replied. "And I went up with her. Her body, which should have been a deadweight, carried me up to the surface."

"I don't believe it," I told him, even though I believed every word of it.

"She actually wasn't dead. She hadn't drowned. I never figured out if she saved me or I saved her. But we both got out alive." Allwood sat, his face even lighter with this energy of nearly dying. I sat closer to him, as close as I could, in the middle of the day. The cold of the pond went through me.

"Abner knew, because he was the one kicking his way up, he knew. But the church gave me a special award for bravery." Allwood buried his face in my neck.

"Like a plaque." I couldn't understand Allwood's face in my neck at all. This was so uncharacteristic. He didn't even hug until after we had gone to bed.

I heard him say one hundred dollars. "They gave you, you got one hundred dollars for it?" He shook his head against my shoulder.

"But what did Abner know?"

"He knew that I didn't do shit. At least, if I did, it was by mistake." Allwood straightened up. "Do you think they gave her one hundred dollars?"

"She's alive. Maybe that was her reward," I said.

"I gave her half the money, but her mother made her give it back. Her mother said I saved her daughter's life. That's what everyone thinks. Except for Abner." He went on, in his way, repeating, formulating this question-and-answer hypothesis over and over. Who saved whom? How did he save her? Abner knows.

He never talked about it after that time. It was like a birthmark that he had shown me and never needed to explain again. I thought about it every time he kissed my neck, which was how he began to come. Allwood, my talky, dense Allwood, so hot and sweated up, yet so cold and confused underneath the surface of that pond. I followed him as he fell through the ice, his eyes shut against the cold, the boots of his classmates and Abner kicking his eyes open. The colder the pond, the hotter my body temperature. As he paddled and pushed to the surface, dragging her limp, inert body to the surface, Allwood pulled me sweating and shivering into the room. I could not seem to enter any other way. When he broke through and gasped the air for the first time, I gasped too, coming as hard as I could. When he and the girl, now breathing and gasping too, were rescued, I could rest and open my eyes. Then Allwood came. And we could surround each other like lovers. Before we got up, sometimes I'd think, *If only I knew what it takes to be in love.*

....

One night, when he insisted we make love first to Cecil Taylor, then Coltrane, I told Allwood, "Don't make me paint myself black."

We had worked out a trade-off. Since I had gone to the Black House, he'd come to my family get-together. Neither of us wanted to go at first. We had that in common. It had taken time, but we were pulling together.

"The Black House. Why is there so much fuss over black? Black this, black that. Five years ago, you couldn't pay people to say the word. Now they want to lie down and die in it."

He sighed, and from the shelf in his head picked up a book—yet another bible full of new commandments. (1. Think Black. 2. Feel Black. 3. Look Black. 4. Buy Black. 5. Learn Black. 6. Love Black. 7. Talk Black. 8. Fuck Black. 9. Act Black. 10. Be Black.) As Allwood hunted down his citation, I listened to myself. To my dismay, I sounded like my family. If I were arguing the same point with my family, I'd be Allwood and they'd be Geniece. I'd be schooling them and telling them to be black. It happened every time I visited home. My cousin called me a Stokely Carmichael windup doll. Yet here, with Allwood, I acted in direct opposition to that. I wanted the music off.

"I only want to hear us. The music will drive me crazy."

"That," Allwood said with the authority of a kindergarten teacher, "is just what you need."

"No," I said. We stopped midfuck, and I got up and lifted the needle. "I don't want craziness. I want my nice orgasm the way I'm used to it. I want my own explosion. I want your hip bone rubbing against mine, that's all that it takes."

I had been coming on my own since I was five, when I picked up the idea that I was a mermaid. In my sleep I became one every night, a blond one with nippleless titties. Coming was nothing unusual for me. Maybe finding out right before my period started that what I did to myself after the rest of the world quieted was called sex, maybe that was unusual. It held the same amount of pleasure for me as sneezing, which I did a lot because I was allergic to pollen. Coming itself was no big deal. Why did I have to do this the black way?

I picked up the album covers. "I don't want Trane going up my vagina. It's so simple. Let's fuck, let's roll, let's come."

"You're too practical, even about sex," Allwood said. "You're like a man." We argued this in the middle of sex, started it up, got it going, and, Boom! our own version of coitus interruptus. It made for a bigger climax.

"I'm not greedy, I don't want more. I want the same."

"It's never the same, even if you think it is."

He stood up naked, his skin the color of a Lorna Doone shortbread cookie, his penis very hard and insistent, almost an exclamation point. Allwood was the exclamatory voice; I meant to put an end to things with my once-and-for-all declarative. The music went on. I got back in bed but needed a little more arguing down to heat back up.

"I think sometimes," he said, following McCoy Tyner's bang-a-bang-banging up and down my spine, "you would have been better off if you had never learned how to masturbate."

Now how was he going to work in burning in hell, pimples, and the Black Thang? The music went on, Cecil Taylor thwacking his ivories right into my eardrums and Allwood following close behind with his tongue. He came out for breath but Cecil held his ground.

"Don't look so defiant, Geniece. It just would have been nice," his voice had begun to slur and soften, "if your first orgasm had been with me."

"But, Allwood," I said, now on top of him, "I come with you because I came with me over and over first."

"This is different. You'll never forget this," he said. Famous last words, I thought.

He came. I came. And, glory be, as the old folks say, you learn something new every day. It was better with the music. Bigger. Creamier. Harder. Softer. Faster. Slower. So black was beautiful, and I was a believer in—if nothing else—the eighth commandment.

12

Having roaches in my place was embarrassing when we first saw them; worse was becoming pals with them. Allwood sprayed my mattress for roach eggs outside next to the brick incinerator. I sprayed the whole place, and after two days Allwood carried the mattress back inside. We sat there like it was a luxurious feather bed. I wasn't sure how he was feeling, but I was feeling sweet, sweet, sweet. I decided to thank him with my special tamale pie. After all, how many people fumigate for you?

I bought Red's Tamales ("Tuesday is Red's Tamales day," their TV ad said), six to a package, two cans of Hormel chili with meat, chopped green onions, and grated a cup of cheddar. I layered the tamales and chili with the green onions, topped it off with the cheese, and popped it in the oven. I also bought a package of frozen sliced strawberries and two packs of Hostess Twinkies.

The tamale pie aroma was chasing away the last of the roach spray, we had *The Supremes Live at the Copa* on the box, Diana Ross was belting out, "You're nobody till somebody loves you," Allwood had rolled a couple of bombs, and the doorbell rang. I opened the door to Wish Woodie all in my face. I was stunned. *Wish Woodie Allwood Allwood. my boyfriend my friendboy.* I was used to each by himself. I hadn't anticipated a juncture of the two.

"Geniece, it's Smoky Joe's café out back," Wish said. My landlord had burned trash in the incinerator. "And I'm getting a contact high standing here. Damn, let me in."

I leaned against the door in the middle of a sammich, a sandwich that had gotten smooshed. I let Wish in and introduced him. He pulled his hand out of his Windbreaker but pushed it back in the nylon pocket when Allwood didn't extend his.

"Have I seen you at the poor boys' hall?" Allwood asked Wish.

"What's that?" Wish asked, turning to me.

"It's like a dorm for brothers across from City," Allwood said, rolling a joint.

"Nah, I never hang around City," Wish said.

"I remember your face. You hang around Telegraph?"

"You mean up at Berkeley?"

"*Up* at Berkeley? I'm talking about the Avenue. Those four blocks from Bancroft Way to Dwight Way. Maybe Sproul Plaza."

"The Ave, yeah. I'm always up on Telegraph." Wish's toes looked like Brazil nuts in his leather sandals.

"The rest of the campus is off-limits." Allwood's toes looked pale in comparison. "Haven't you seen that sign on Sproul Hall: COLORED PEOPLE NOT ALLOWED EXCEPT JANITORS?"

"They don't welcome Communists either, but it's not quite Ole Miss." Wish looked out at the incinerator. "I guess I didn't see you at Cinema Psychedelica."

"Don't have the leisure to take LSD," Allwood said. He'd sized up Wish as an acidhead. I felt bad for Wish.

Allwood kept going like he was drilling for oil. "The Avenue's your playroom?"

Wish shook his head. "I wouldn't say so. I'm a watcher."

"Uh, watching life go by with the beatniks in Cafe Mediterranean?"

"It's Caffe Mediterraneum," Wish said. We had walked by the coffeehouse often, zonked, and I knew Wish didn't even go there. Up and down Telegraph, in and out of Pepe's Pizza, Moe's Books, Sather Gate Bookstore, the bakery, record stores—Allwood and I spent the most time at the folding card tables, matching the ism to the schisms—Ban the Bomb, Young Socialist Alliance, W. E. B. Du Bois Club, Progressive Socialist Party, Berkeley CORE, Young People's Socialist League, Campaign for Nuclear Disarmament.

Wish asked, "Were you up there Vietnam Day?"

"That's the first time I saw Bob Moses from SNCC. If I was into heroes, he would be it," Allwood said.

I'd never heard Allwood use the word *hero*. I wondered if he had blacked out the *non* on his SNCC button before or after seeing Bob Moses. "Norman Mailer was drunk. What a gas. Did you see that?"

Wish shook his head and said, "Norman Thomas, the socialist, the mime troupe from the City . . . Berzerkeley. Mario Savio called being at Berkeley sucking at the breast of the holy mother university." They started slapping hands and laughing.

"Yeah, the knowledge factory," Allwood said.

"Man, were you at Sproul Hall in sixty-four?" Wish looked at him, half in awe. Allwood shook his head.

"I wasn't there when Savio climbed on the police car during the thirty-two-hour sit-in. But I was there when he compared the university to an odious machine and told the crowd at Sproul to put their bodies on the wheels and the levers and halt it completely."

"We saw from the City portables the sheriff's brigade riding on motorcycles to Sproul Hall," I popped in. "The *Trib* said they had more police going down Telegraph Ave to get those students than when President Kennedy came in sixty-three."

"I heard Mario Savio on KPFA," Allwood said. "They play the tape over and over."

"You have to admit Berkeley's different from a lot of places," Wish said.

"It's still not nirvana. The white man's heaven is the black man's hell," Allwood said.

"I was born in Berkeley." I wanted to lighten things.

"For real?" Wish said. "That makes you a berserk baby."

"I'm the only one in my family. Everyone else's born in the South or Oakland." Their intensity turned from each other.

"My father and mother lived on Acton Street in Berkeley," I said.

They sat back, Allwood relaxing instead of being on the defense.

Wish said, "Acton. That's the other side of Sacramento?" Allwood nodded.

"My father, according to my family, gambled away the mortgage in an all-night poker party. We had to move to government housing, the projects. That's how we ended up in Codornices Village on the other side of San Pablo Avenue where Berkeley Farms dairy stands now."

Wish said he'd heard of a Codornices Village for UC student housing in Albany, the town next door to Berkeley.

"Owned by the university," Allwood said. "Emergency federal housing. Three-quarters black, the rest students and Japanese relocated from the concentration camps. Codornices Village was their first stop. Blacks rioted in the fifties when they closed it. That's where we lived when I was a kid."

I remembered being on the floor of our unit in Codornices crawling under the wringer washer, oil dripping onto my plaits, getting spanked.

"What if we played together, Geniece?"

I saw myself eating mud pies in the dirt with Asian children, watching the big kids play Old Maid in the grass, being scared stiff of the tall albino boy with the tuft of blond hair that looked like a horse's mane. The fear that he was a man-horse had given me nightmares.

"We were allowed to occupy every square foot between Sacramento Street and the Bayshore Freeway," Allwood said. "It's not as though we haven't made any progress."

"Don't venture off the plantation, even in Berkeley," I said.

Allwood turned to Wish. "You've gone to Rumford's Pharmacy around the corner?"

Wish turned to me. "Is that where you sent me for stockings that time?"

Allwood shined that on. "Byron Rumford, the owner, was the first black elected official in Northern California. He established the Fair Employment Practices Commission and then the Fair Housing Act of 1963."

Wish looked puzzled again and Allwood was reveling again, as he always did in ignorance. It was just a relief to me that for once I wasn't the ignorant one.

"FEPC from the Fair Employment Practices Act," Allwood said.

I added, "Rumford passed the act, then C. L. Dellums from the Brotherhood of Sleeping Car Porters chaired the commission."

"We had to start getting blacks elected," Allwood said. "The Okie fi-nokees wanted the black migration to disappear once World War II was over. It took us until 1959."

"Wasn't good old Berkeley the base for all this?" Wish said.

"Yeah," Allwood said. "Liberal Berkeley, which passed and then re-scinded its own fair housing ordinance in 1963."

"So I didn't die and go to heaven in 1964 when I moved here," Wish said.

I piped up, "That's the year the school board was nearly recalled be-cause of desegregation."

"The white folks you have to watch real close are the liberals, in their own backyards," Allwood said, and, finally, we all laughed together.

"My father and his whole church participated in a boycott of Berke-ley downtown," Allwood said. "*Don't buy where you can't work.* Those friendly black cashiers at Woolworth's?"

"I know. Zorro put them there," Wish said. "Black Zorro."

That's what I loved about Wish. He knew Zorro like I knew Zorro, the masked freedom fighter from the comic book, not the Disney hero in a wimp's body. Wish was parrying with Allwood. By coming back with black Zorro, Wish was being sarcastic, like he knew that black people fought for their rights in Berkeley, and no one galloped in on a charger and gave them rights. But Allwood was too serious for the irony. Instead he had his I'm-going-to-figure-this-one-out look.

"White folks don't want to deal with a lot of this stuff they created. They have a reason to want to blow their minds with LSD," Allwood said. "We don't." And then we smoked two more joints before they started retracing their footsteps.

"What about the Afro-American Association?" Allwood said to Wish.

Wish shrugged his shoulders. "What's that?"

"Don Warden's organization. They have the Sunday meetings." All-wood still had the I'm-going-to-figure-this-one-out look.

"Beats me. I never heard of Don Warden," Wish said. Allwood sniffed the trail like a police dog.

"You never heard of Don Warden, the most prominent black attorney in the Bay Area, the man Huey Newton calls the most dangerous brother in America?" I said. I thought everybody knew Don Warden.

"He's a rite of passage for brothers," Allwood said. "The Afro-American Association—his group—hipped us to the reality that we don't need more laws for justice, we need more justice. But after that, the association's all about Don Warden."

We smoked the last of the rolled joints.

Wish produced a doobie from his pocket. I asked if he wanted some tamale pie. He looked at my kitchen walls. "What happened to your roaches, Geniece?"

"Sprayed them into the beyond," I said.

"Let's hope," Wish said, before taking a plate.

"Now I know where I've seen you. West Campus, Berkeley High," Allwood said.

The whole room settled down. Even the incinerator calmed. We'd found it.

"I do carpentry there," Wish said.

Allwood reacted as if that was impossible. "You're an employee of the district?"

"No, man, you know it's hard as hell to get on with Berkeley Unified."

"Tell me. They don't let splibs swim in the pool except on Friday nights. Unwritten rule."

"What do you do there?" Wish asked.

Allwood, holding, took a big drag and forced it into his lungs, then passed it to me. "I tutor history, physics, calculus . . . you know, white kids on the way to Stanford, Cal Tech, Reed."

I went over to the kitchen drawer. I wanted to share my black college brochures from down south with Wish and Allwood. I stumbled a little because of my buzz. When I opened the drawer underneath the kitchen counter, my eyes weren't completely focused. Wish started pointing to me like I had the cooties, and Allwood started laughing, and I looked at my arm to see what was up.

Roaches were leaping out of my drawer, flying out, as if they'd been waiting for me to open that drawer for weeks. The three of us began swatting and slapping with the brochures. As we pounced on them and they pounced on us, I could almost hear them breeding, hatching, and listening to me and Allwood talk black, learn black, love black, fuck black all semester, hatching and scheming to scare the black out of me right at that moment. We pounced for a while, until Wish said we'd got them all.

"The last of them?" Allwood asked him.

"I hope so," I said.

"I'm still suspicious," Wish said. He went back to the drawer and carried it outside. Allwood followed him out. I swept up the mess and went outside. Wish had dumped the remaining contents into the trash. "They probably laid their eggs inside Geniece's black college brochures."

He looked back to the apartment. "What's in the other drawers?"

"Silverware," I said. "That was the only drawer with papers in it."

"Let's put the trash in the incinerator," Allwood said, "to be sure."

My gibberish started. I heard it, heard myself, still high, murmuring to the flame: *Howard/Spelman/MorrisBrown/Talledega/PhilanderSmith/Wilberforce/Xavier/Hampton/Wiley/BethuneCookman.*

"The talented-tenth factories," Allwood said, tossing the brochures in the incinerator. "They nurture reactionary tendencies in the race. Not what Du Bois had in mind."

He turned to Wish. "Don't some of the kids call you Black Jesus?"

Wish nodded and shrugged. "It's the hair."

We stood there in a trance watching the heat ripple the air. I spoke. "When I was three, my father took me to a doctor in Berkeley, a specialist. I was talking like I just was now. I made sense to me, I guess, but no one else. The doctor told my father I was retarded. Before we left Codornices Village, a UC doctoral student worked with me, changing my speech pattern. I was her dissertation."

The heat rippled through the chill in my body, a chill from the San Francisco Bay that settled in about 4:00 P.M. no matter the day's temperature.

"But they say my dad grabbed me up, shouted, '*Is this what you get paid fair money for?*' And stomped out of there."

It came to me as I spoke that Allwood had scooped me up, the same way my father must have done in the doctor's office, with indignation and love. When we went back in, we scarfed the rest of the pie. While Wish and Allwood were eating the corners, zeroing in on the crust and sauce and shreds of roasted cheese left, I made dessert. We sang along to "Put on a Happy Face."

"Here's how to have your whipped cream on top," I said, slicing the Twinkie lengthwise and inserting the sliced strawberries, one by one, between the cake and the white cream.

"Where did you get this recipe?" Allwood asked, and that got us going, cracking up. I was the first one to keel over, passed out—like a light. They must have put my legs up. When I woke up they were out, on the floor, on the pillows from the daybed. I sat up in the dark, listening to them breathe. How strange to feel so comfortable with two men sleeping at my feet. I tried to pick it apart. When I colored as a kid I had a hard time staying in the lines. I'd color the wolf periwinkle along with the sky, or give the wolf a carnation pink tongue pink teeth pink legs pink forest. In this unlikely, unexpected cocoon, I felt safe.

I knew I was becoming militant. I just didn't know if I wanted to become *a* militant. Malcolm X, Betty Shabazz, the protesters, the sit-in demonstrators down south were my heroes. I loved them from a distance and on paper. But the militants I met, mostly the guys on the soapbox on Grove Street, were harsh and abrasive and condescending to everyone, not just white people. And they made people do things. They had the power to make people quit school and read a thousand books. They could make someone go cut her hair off. They stopped traffic on busy city streets and directed willing souls to go to Cuba, to Africa, to the Deep South, to dangerous places where they might not make it back. I didn't want that kind of power over people. I just wanted it over myself.

13

Once I got rid of my roaches, I let Allwood hold political education classes in my apartment. We went through Chairman Mao's little red book, Chairman Frantz Fanon, Chairmen Marx and Engels, Chairman W. E. B. Du Bois, Chairman Herbert Aptheker, Chairman Carter G. Woodson, chairman, chairman, chairman, so many chairmen and I only had a few chairs. My job was grand poobah of the bathroom, the vacuum, the seating arrangements, bringing kitchen chairs into the living room if my beat-up sofa wasn't enough.

I made myself another job: cook. Every Tuesday morning I figured out something to cook for the four to six people who showed up, or sometimes only Allwood and the cook. Tamale pie, red beans and rice, stewed chicken over rice, macaroni and cheese with canned tuna. Once only the cook herself showed her face. So I ate all by myself. But most of the time, somebody came knocking on the door around 7:00 P.M.

One of the last Tuesdays of the whole semester I was unprepared for what happened except that, imitating Goosey, I had filled a ten-quart stew pot with black-eyed peas, neck bones, and rice. At least it looked like Goosey's. I did my best to get it looking like it was supposed to. People showed up by 7:30, CP time. Cool. We dialogued until 7:45, when who should come strutting in like he owned the place but Abner. I barely spoke. He sidled up to me like he had never threatened me in the cafeteria.

But I was in no way prepared then for who came in after snaky Abner: Michelle Stubbs. She and I had graduated Castlemont High School together. She was a superbourgie. What was she doing at a PE class? I thought she was away at a black school like Howard or Fisk. Instead, here she was with Abner, practically bound to his wrist.

I couldn't see it unless he was hustling her. I simply couldn't see the two of them together. She was Miss Ultra Bourgie. She had everything—a daddy with a title (Dr. Stubbs), parents with a home in the hills, long straight white people hair—everything except she was dark. Not dark like me, not that dark, but darker than a paper bag. In her world, she was dark. I knew she hadn't turned into a black militant simply because she was darker than what was allowable in her social circle. Not Michelle, who drove a T-Bird like Natalie Wood in high school. Some things just don't happen. Allwood began to pass around a new pamphlet that everybody examined with great curiosity.

By 8:00, everybody was engrossed in the pamphlet, Allwood was lecturing on it, and I couldn't concentrate because Michelle and Abner were sending each other eyeball telegrams. What was going on with them? I finally saw the pamphlet. I looked at the first page not really thinking about it. Then my eyes focused and I had to keep myself from screaming, *This scares me to death.* A salty, spitty fear rushed into my mouth. The picture was frightening.

"The good brother Williams was run out of North Carolina by the KKK," Allwood was saying. "And you know why?"

"Yeah," Abner said. How did he know? Had he studied this pamphlet already? He annoyed me every time he opened his mouth.

"No, tell me why," I said.

Allwood looked at me like he was telling me that nouns are people, places, and things. "Because he armed himself."

Oh. Elementary. I should have figured that one out. At the bottom of the pamphlet was the legend PUBLISHED IN CUBA AS A PRIVATE PUBLICATION. Above that was a poem from Robert F. Williams, one line of which struck me: "a soulful dream exploded at the end of a lyncher's rope."

"Why does it seem like we have to avow violence? It seems like we should disavow violence." Michelle talked for the first time but the same way she did in high school, adding a whine to the last syllable of her words.

"It doesn't seem like it," Allwood said. "We do."

"But whyyyyyy?" she asked, dragging out *why* till kingdom come.

"This is whyyyy," he said, pointing to the pamphlet, mimicking her voice. He had her read aloud from it.

Not only do we support the righttttt of our brothers of Vietnam to defend themselves against the armed aggressionnnnn, repressionnnnn and tyranny of US imperialism and its running doooogs, but we wish to thank our brothers for the splendid examples they are giving us.

The whine was killing Allwood.
He stopped her and read it himself.

After almost 200 years of inhuman bondage and shameful dehumanization under the present US Government, our meek and passive people, like our brothers of Vietnam, Cuba, the Congo, Mozambique and throughout Asia, Africa and Latin America, are beginning to cast off the imperialist-inspired curse of turn-the-other-cheekism. Yes, on the very mainland of Neo-colonialism our oppressed people are turning the streets of racist and imperialist America into battlegrounds of resistance. More than any other people in the world, our people understand the savage and beastly nature of barbaric Yankeeism. We know the hypocrisy and inhumanity of the evil government of our beloved country.

The words inspired the males greatly. They cheered and repeated the catchphrases—"turn-the-other-cheekism," "battlegrounds of resistance," "barbaric Yankeeism"—as if they were the equivalent of "Go team!"

"Is the brother talking about West Oakland or is he not?" Abner said.

"No, he's not. He's talking bout the Fillmore, if I'm not mistaken," Allwood said.

"Hold up. He's talking about East Palo Alto, ain't he?"

"I don't think the downtrodden and oppressed people in Richmond would agree. I don't think they would agree with you one bit."

I knew they were starting on a riff that could go up and down the state. I got up and added my bit. "I can see Brother Williams is talking about downtrodden and oppressed people everywhere." It being 8:15, I went to the kitchen to heat up the food. Michelle came in to talk. She pulled in close and whispered without the whine.

"We've been going together for two weeks."

I was so shocked I dropped my spoon in the pot. In her regular voice she said, "You better get the spoon before it melts away-ay."

I fished and she went back to the whisper. "I am in love with him."

I stirred briskly. She went on with her whispering. "I know. It's out there. A friend who is his friend introduced us at Black Friday."

She went to Week of the Angry Arts–West? Poetry, a LeRoi Jones play, music, dance. And I missed it because of work. Shit.

"I didn't know if I would like him. Then we got to talking, and he told me about the drowning." My ears perked up.

"What drowning?"

"You know, when those students fell through the ice on the senior outing. When we were in high school." I stopped stirring.

"Oh, that." What could he have told her that would have popped the cork off the bottle? I mean, all he did was save his own ass.

"He told me about Allwood and him being down there. And how Allwood made it up to the top first. But Abner, my baby, was almost a goner. But he managed to pull himself up along with this girl who was nearly dead."

"Believe half of what you see and none of what you hear." I said this to the pot, because she wasn't even listening. She was pouring this fiction in my ear, I mean pouring, like out of a box of Morton's salt.

"They tried to make him a hero and give him an award but he wouldn't let them. He said he wanted to forget it, it was too scary."

She stopped whispering. "That man got me, girl-ll." She took the spoon and tasted for me.

I was speechless. Not thoughtless or mindless, just devoid of the power of speech. Niggas! I could kill them both. Cockhounds! And cockhounds too lazy to make up their own line. Deliver my black ass.

"It needs some salt. And do you have any garlic powder?" I showed her my spice shelf. She proceeded, with her bourgie ass, to intervene. A little vinegar. Some cayenne. A little thickening with flour. Between us, we put our foot off into some black-eyed peas.

Later, I couldn't decide whether to tell Allwood and mess up my come fantasy. I decided not to. While we were doing it, I saw the girl floating, like a buoy, toward the surface of the lake. Only her eyes were open and blinking as she struggled and kicked her own way up. I felt strong when I fixed it like that, like I controlled the borders, the way into and out of the room, all by myself. I came even bigger.

14

I had missed angry arts week because of work, and I had to study for zoology. But I wasn't going to miss Stokely Carmichael. My cousin Corliss met me in downtown Berkeley, and we caught the UC shuttle to the Greek Theatre. Walking up the steep ramp, we could hear Stokely's distinctive West Indian accent broadcasting across the stadium:

> It's a privilege and an honor to be in the white intellectual ghetto of the West.

We were perspiring our asses off to get inside. They had to hold a Black Power conference on the hottest day of 1966. Even so, it was mostly white students and hippies. I didn't care. I had been reading about Stokely and the Student Nonviolent Coordinating Committee for weeks. SNCC. You had to squinch your nose just to say it—"Snick." When we got in, we saw Students for a Democratic Society banners and flyers all around. SDS, SDS, SDS all around, no SNCC. The sign on the podium he stood behind read BLACK POWER AND ITS CHALLENGES in big bold letters.

"Why is SDS sponsoring this?" Corliss asked.

"Maybe they're paying! Shut the jabber, Corliss. He's talking."

> In 1968 I'm going to run for president of the United States. I just can't make it 'cause I wasn't born in the United States. That's the only thing holding me back.

He kept calling us the Pepsi generation, even though the vendor was sold out of Pepsi. All anybody was drinking was orange Nehi. He was as intellectual as the Fair Play for Cuba orators on Grove Street. But there was a violent thrill floating through the stadium like lightning even though the skies were powder blue and the white clouds seemed suspended. I couldn't figure if the thrill was Stokely Carmichael or my imagination.

> The question is, how can you build political institutions that will begin to meet the needs of Oakland, California? And the needs of Oakland, California, are not one thousand policemen with submachine guns.

He was giving Oakland a nod, like when the famous gospel singer inserts the local church's name in the song. I was shouting *Pow-uh* a lot. It was fun. A girl on the other side of the stadium kept shouting back *Black Power, Black Power*, real proper but still a black voice. We started answering each other. Then other voices in the crowd would answer both of us. Stokely started recognizing our two black voices in the crowd, pushing his black fist my way, then her way. Some people were getting irritated at this call-and-response, I could tell, but it felt good.

> The question is, Can we find white people who are going to have the courage to go into white communities and start organizing them? Can we find them? Are they here and are they willing to do that?

He was spanking the crowd with the Black Power paddle. It was thrilling but scary, like he was creating Frankensteins. Three hours zipped by like twenty minutes. It took forever to get out of the stadium. I was still chanting *Pow-uh* when Corliss spotted the girl who had been chanting with me.

"There's your twin, Niecy," she said with sarcasm.

I was shocked. My call-and-response was a high-yellow regular from Snookie's, an ultrabourgie who had never looked my way, much less spoken. She had let her hair go back. She waved and kept chanting with me until we got lost in the crowd.

15

I had long since evicted my roaches when Corliss came to see my apartment. She looked around it. "This is cute. I thought it would look like a motel. It's not bad."

Something inside me pleaded with Corliss not to talk like Aunt Ola with the don'ts: "Don't wear red; you're too dark." "Don't date until you're finished with your formal education." "Don't let a man use you for a piss pot." "Purse your lips when you're not talking to make them smaller." How Buddy came from Aunt Ola is one of the world's great mysteries.

"Put nice underwear on, Niecy," Corliss said. "Mother sent me to get you to San Leandro to get our bridesmaids' dresses. You're in Bud's wedding."

"But Aunt Ola doesn't like my hair."

"She'll never change. It's the way she was raised."

. . . .

We parked near the stores on East 14th Street in downtown San Leandro; the shopkeepers came out to watch us, their stares like spotlights. We had crossed a forbidden zone.

"Do they think it's an NAACP protest?" I said. Corliss glanced at them and kept on going. She was used to it, being the only black at Lone Mountain College on the hill in the city.

"Forget them," she said.

"Corliss, I can't believe you said that."

"Crackers don't intimidate me anymore," Corliss said.

Anymore? The first time I visited her, her dorm room was down the hall from Bob Hope's daughter and across from some maharaja's niece. Corliss's hair had looked like she had washed it and forgotten to straighten it. Her white roomies had given her a Toni Home Perm, which white girls used to get a permanent wave. It wasn't for our kinky hair. It had burned her scalp and messed up her hair. "Nothing's wrong, it'll grow back," she said when she showed me her burned scalp before we saw a movie on campus, *Last Year at Marienbad*, which I hated, especially when she and her friends discussed it afterward in French. Worse than not understanding it at all, my three semesters of French allowed me to understand snatches of the movie and the conversation. Corliss wanting to be what she wasn't infuriated me even more.

"Why didn't you hot-comb their hair? See how they'd like their hair all burned to a crisp."

She had cried. "I thought, *It can't hurt, my hair's not that bad.* Now I'm imprisoned by my hair."

In San Leandro, Corliss and I walked into the bridal shop, past the rude stares. It was mirror, mirror, everywhere; the salesladies' made-up faces the color of starch, the gowns and mannequins like so many frosted white wedding cakes. And there we were, in those mirrors, with our beige, brown, and very brown selves, making the mirrors go mocha mad. The salesladies looked asphyxiated, as if breathing around us might make them mocha too.

The two mothers, Andrea's mother and Aunt Ola Ray, were making a big fuss over gowns. There were six bridesmaids, all of us different body types. When Andrea came out in her wedding gown, everyone hushed. She walked out where we could see the train behind her. As they all began to ooh and aah, I had the funniest feeling, like I was going to throw up. I kept trying to look at Andrea and my stomach kept turning. I looked instead at the mirrored Andrea and I saw all of us in a jumble: me, orphan me, the darkest one there as usual; the white ladies; my aunt; the mannequins staring frostily at the invisible men for whom all this was done; the bride in her everyday bra with the straps showing where her gown went off her shoulders; the tan line on Andrea's yellow chest and her peachier-colored arms. I thought of the earnest, hardworking, dirt-poor colored people in the South getting hosed and beaten up and chased by dogs in the pictures in *Life* and *Time* and *Newsweek* so that we could do this. Every single black man who had gotten lynched and every woman who had been raped by Mister Charlie had caused the white bitch of justice to finally tip her scales in our favor. For this.

I was sickened. I felt defeated, but inside of this feeling of defeat, I felt something else. A snap like a rubber band. At that moment, when Andrea walked around in her gown, a door flew open. All of a sudden I felt like I was walking above all of these people. Something changed all over—my feet, head, and solar plexus. I felt like Buddy. Like the way he could walk past Aunt Ola fussing at Uncle Boy-Boy for cleaning his eyeglasses in her dishwater, as if they were kids and he was the parent. I felt that cool, at that moment, unbound.

We began to try on our gowns, raspberry sheaths. When I looked in the mirror, I saw myself, the others, and burst out laughing. The pinched-in waist made my small bust look like it was swimming in the top of the sheath. Corliss with her long straightened hair and big bosoms also looked ridiculous. We couldn't even get hers zipped up the back.

"These dresses are made for white women, with no bazooms and no behinds," Corliss muttered. "Stop laughing at me, Niecy. You look like a Zulu warrior stuck in Queen Elizabeth's garden frock."

"This whole wedding is for whites. Colored people not allowed except for janitors," I muttered back at her. The other girls were fussing over their gowns like they liked them, which was tomfoolery as far as I was concerned. Aunt Ola Ray came over to us, mad as she could be. She started poking her fingers around our waists and talking low and hard.

"I want you girls to stop laughing like hyenas. Stop showing your color. We may be the first Negroes to spend this kind of money here. We're the ones who have to make the good first impression so they'll treat the rest like human beings. So straighten up and fly right. Both of you."

She walked away. I straightened up dramatically and made a flying motion with my arms. Corliss tried to keep a straight face, but couldn't. We howled. Aunt Ola Ray turned around and gave us a long look.

The six of us marched in front of the mirrors, and the ladies, black and white, looked at us, and I got the exact door-flying-open feeling again. The dresses and the colors of our skins made for a raspberry and brown and white sundae in the mirrors. I saw myself peeing in the I. Magnin elevator. I heard Stokely in his SNCC overalls at the Greek Theatre calling the crowd the Pepsi generation. I saw myself jumping up and down shouting and him saying grandly, "It's a privilege and an honor to be in the white intellectual ghetto of the West." And I stood there in San Leandro, in a raspberry sheath made for an expectant and entitled white woman with a flat tush and small tits, understanding that this place was my Deep South. We didn't have Bull Connor's attack dogs coming at our throats or his minions hosing us down. We weren't being beaten by the KKK in plain sight of his police officers. But we were breaking barriers just the same. Our six inches of progress moved us all closer to the finish line.

Without trying, I had found out how to be cool. Stand still, show up, and be out of your body and into your mind at the same time. Thank you, Corliss. Thank you, Aunt Ola Ray. Thank you, Andrea. Thank you, white salesladies. Thank you, I. Magnin. Thank you, *Time*, *Life*, and *Newsweek*. Thank you, Stokely. And thanks to the lynched and the lynchers and the marchers and the marched on. I had the answer.

16

Cool carried me all the way through the wedding, with Aunt Ola Ray promenading every ounce of her doctor's mother status. From the front of the church, I saw Ola fluttering in her seat, dabbing at her silk lace hanky like she was grieving a heavy loss. A body would've thought she was losing her Jesus instead of her only son. But I could forgive Aunt Ola Ray her whole bag of airs when she sang. And she sang magnificently for Buddy and Andrea. She got to that line—*He's wonderful/wonderful/wonderful/wonderfulwonderful/wonderful/wonderful/wonderful*—and before she let it go, Aunt Ola Ray could have turned out the Cow Palace. I didn't know what Reverend White had planned for his "Meditation," which was how the wedding program printed it:

Solo . . . Mrs. Ola Ray Hightower
Meditation . . . Officiating Elder

He couldn't ignore "Wonderful," though. It was ringing throughout the entire sanctuary, floor to ceiling, stained-glass wall to stained-glass wall. My scalp tingled, as much from the tightness of my hair drawn back as from Aunt Ola Ray's contralto oscillations.

Reverend White's deep voice took over:

What God hath put together, let no man put asunder. Don't let no woman other than your to-be-wife tickle your fancy.

I looked over at Buddy, my big brother of a cousin. I caught his eye, and he twitched his ears like a puppy's, something he'd taught me to do.

Don't pick up the telephone and call your father.

With everyone else I looked at Uncle Boy-Boy beaming.

No offense to Dr. Hightower, but please don't call your father. Neither your mother. You are a team now. Hold on to each other.

Andrea looked like she'd stepped out of a pre-Raphaelite painting, daisies garlanding her hair. In the sanctuary, Reverend White's voice echoed from the rafters.

When gray skies open up and fill up your cup, turn to God. If you keep Jesus at the head of your companionship, you will never lose this sacredness.

As I stood there, my stomach rumbled, empty as a washed pot. I hoped no one heard, although as clear as "Wonderful" I could hear Zenobia fussing at Aunt Ola Ray the night before at the wedding dinner that Zenobia had catered at her house.

"Somebody gonna have to get up off some money," Zenobia had said, sitting in her blue brocade Louis-the-umpteenth chair. "Colored folks need to learn etiquette. The bride's people supposed to pay for the whole show. Doctors and dentists on both sides, Buddy's and Andrea's. Somebody need to show Miss Zenobia some appreciation."

"Now, Zenobia, don't get so out of sorts," Aunt Ola Ray had said.

"I'm not sick. I'm mad." Zenobia wanted money. Uncle Boy-Boy grumbled as he left to go get the greenbacks she wanted to see slapping her palm.

Reverend White's stentorian voice reaching to the rafters kept pulling my thoughts back to the church.

Don't hug your mother. Don't call your other counselors. When gray skies open up and fall upon your cap, turn to the counselor above all.

I'd worn my own hair but let Earleatha straighten it to a fare-thee-well and pull it back into a chignon, my gift that felt like a brick on my neck. I thought of Allwood. If he had come, would he have worn those combat boots?

At the wedding dinner Zenobia cornered me. I had gone outside on her front porch with Buddy and his old friends, Herbie and Phillip, who were holding: *Man, who's got the weed. . . . I ain't holding nothing but my pride. . . . And your dick forever, man. . . . Aw, man, you walk around with a joint in your wallet. . . . Don't hold out on us, not at a moment like this. . . . Yeah, I need to be high to be here.* Flicking ashes into Zenobia's thigh-high blue vase, the one she put out in front so we could find her house whenever she moved, we got high as kites. I went back in. Zenobia sat down and started on me, about as high off her J&B as I was off my stuff.

"Now see, if your father was here, wouldn't be no running out of here and paying for her share. Her folks have money. Jimmy would have called up the doctor proper and said it real nice, now, but he would've said it."

Said what? What would my father have said, the great absentee? Would people talk about me like this if I up and left? *The great Geniece, we could always count on little Niecy when we couldn't see shit from shinola.* Even high as a kite, I didn't hold illusions about my father. Gone is gone.

"Zenobia, whatever you say, I'm going to attribute it to the occasion, the scotch, and your hard work in laying out this magnificent dinner."

Reverend White's voice boomed through, "You are a team, hold on to each other," but Zenobia's hand on my arm dragged me out of the wedding. Our pressed skins looked like vanilla fudge and dark chocolate fudge. She squeezed my arm that night before the wedding as if she thought I was about to pull away, holding me between her plump fingers the way I'd hold a chicken leg to bite into the juiciest part.

"You know your father had to leave."

"Oh yeah, Zenobia. White folks ran him out of Oakland. Out of California on a rail, right?" I started to laugh. She tightened her grip.

"He had to leave once your mother died. He did everything that a man was expected to do for a woman."

Reverend White's voice pulled me into the present, into the room full of people in fancy dresses and suits: "A man shall leave his father and mother and cleave . . ." But Zenobia's voice with its cigarette rasp held my head as tight as her grip on my arm. It held me at the dinner as tightly as Reverend White's held me in the church.

"Jimmy Hightower was a dutiful, faithful, attentive husband. And father," she said.

I saw Buddy grinning at Andrea. I had tears in my eyes. *Dammit, was I crying?*

"My big brother worked hard, he brought his money home, he remembered all the special occasions, the birthdays." *Shut up, Zenobia.*

Standing in the church, feeling my satiny underwear and slip—my present from Aunt Ola—I glanced over pews until I found the back of Zenobia's head. She always wore her hair up to show her wispy-like-white-folks nape. I'd left her side at the dinner to refill my plate, but Zenobia was tenacious. She clutched me by the arm.

"When your poor mother got sick and died, he lost the will to live."

The reverend was going on like he was in church, which we were, but it wasn't Sunday. It was a wedding, for heaven's sake: "Lean not on thine own understanding."

Zenobia looked at me as if she were seeing one of my baby pictures. "You looked so much like her, even as a baby. Your mother was so precious to him that when she died he couldn't bear to look at you."

I knew I looked like my mother's side of the family, but Zenobia, tipsy with the wedding hullabaloo, was exaggerating—a family trait, lying for emphasis, no malice intended. Reverend White's voice cut through: "You are held to fulfill the perfect circle of trust." I tried to imagine a perfect circle of trust. The wedding ring symbolized a perfect circle of trust. Was the family the perfect circle all gathered around the new couple? The family, blood tight and hungry for the big meal, the cake, the festivities, partying, the *Hey man, I ain't seen you since way back.* The oak pews were a family tree all decked out in satin and silk and Sunday-go-to-meeting. I wanted to rest against Zenobia's neck and breathe some of her exactitude.

"The way that man left, he had to. Jimmy would have wasted into a heap of a man. Working on the waterfront, pulling down that long green, unloading all kinds of stuff. Shipments of toilet paper. Can you see that, a ship full of toilet paper? But they always called him in when they had a shipment for the zoo. Your father loved him some animals. That's why he loved the track. The horses."

She let go of my hand, and smiled as she talked. But it was a smile for something in her. "You know, if somebody had ever helped him the way he helped us, he would have been a vegetarian." She was strong and drunk, all over the place.

"Veterinarian, Zenobia?" She looked at me like I had slapped her.

"You never did call me Aunt, did you, Niecy?" I never had. "They get a shipment for Fleischacker Zoo, they call up Jimmy Hightower." Fleischacker came out of Zenobia's throat sounding like fly-swacker instead of fly-shacker.

"They said your father and the other men tried, for hours, to get this one elephant off the ship. It was pregnant." Zenobia got up and demonstrated. "A pregnant elephant in a corral and some longshoremen trying to lift her up from the ship to the truck. They tried everything and they almost made it."

"Were you there, Zenobia? How did you hear about it?"

"It was payday and your father called me to meet him in Frisco and get my money he owed me. That's the way he was; he owed you, he paid you, right out his check. Ain't no thief up in this family."

Reverend White clutched the microphone at the pulpit with a flourish befitting a minister of his long standing and spoke with finality: "If you keep Jesus at the head of your companionship you will never lose this sacredness."

Zenobia's voice deepened. "The men finally got the elephant up off the ship. But the poor thing was just too big to reach the dock. I think it was the corral or a railing on the corral." She looked like she was about to drift right into the past.

"Zenobia, what happened?"

"They couldn't hold on to her. The railing broke and the corral dropped. The elephant fell into the harbor. The whole thing sank. If you could see the look on his face. Sadder than a saint."

No one had told me this one.

"I worried if he had to bear any more. Next thing Jimmy's gone. That's all."

"I wish he was here," I said.

"You will never be Andrea or Corliss. And you can't strut Black Power down the aisle. Leave it alone."

There it was again: Stay in my place, dark girl. "Leave what alone? Black Power, drunk Auntie?"

She grabbed my shoulder. "I'm not that drunk. Be who you is cuz you ain't who you isn't. We all have our limits. Our natural limits."

"Unnatural limits, I'd say."

"No, no, no." Her painted talons dug into my bare arm. "How you born is God's way of setting limits. You think you'd carry on this way if you weren't that dark-skinned baby, so dark you shocked everybody?"

Parents are supposed to nurture their children, not the old drunk auntie. Zenobia let go of my arm and snarled. "You just like me. Too dark, too light. Same difference. I came in high yellow calling my own tune. It's why I never married. No man got to rule over me because he worshipped my skin color. Nothing you do surprises me, Niecy. Not Black Power. Not nothing."

Zenobia sat down with an inexorable cross of her legs, like she might sit forever. "You not walking this aisle. You have a whole world else to go."

Be who you is cuz you ain't who you isn't.

It was a license to push away from it all. My license. Drunk Auntie gave it to me.

17

I went to have my natural shaped at Original Bros. Hairstyling Salon on San Pablo Ave. The young barber, with his sculpted beard and Afro, kept to the task, commenting on my hair just above a whisper:

you need to come every week to keep your fro up

There were brothers in the shop who had googobs of hair. I knew they weren't coming every week. Barbershop orators, they held forth. Ladies, cool and silent, flipped through *EBONY* and *Jet*.

your hair grows fast so you know you have to keep it trimmed

Someone asked a loud-talking brother in army green fatigues if he had gotten his clothes at a thrift shop. "This is what I wore in 'nam, before they dishonorably discharged me," he said.

"Yeah, but you ain't in 'nam. You in Oakland, bro," someone said.

"'Nam. People need to look this in the face. Yeah," he said.

"Mack," someone said, "I catch it on the box."

"TV! White folk world," he said, sucking his teeth.

keep it neat keep it trimmed

"So what's the real deal, Mack?" someone said.

They looked at him scornfully. His hair was unkempt, and he didn't have that Grove Street Marxist rhetoric down.

"I wore this for three months in 'nam, didn't bathe or shave, rinsed my teeth with water from a fucking stream."

One of the women customers frowned and flipped even faster through *EBONY*. He noticed.

"That's the way it was, sweetheart."

"You ain't hitting on nothing," one man said. "Sound like *Hogan's Heroes* to me." Everyone cracked up, even the *EBONY* reader. My barber kept talking low:

you got that African bump back here, your hair would look good real short

The vet spoke. "How many brothers you know coming back in boxes?"

People started murmuring: "Alphonse . . ." "Terence . . ." "Yeah, man, Larry ran the 440. . . ." "Couldn't outrun the 'cong, could he?"

"That's just it. Splibs being put on the front lines. Only they ain't getting shot by the 'cong. They getting it right in the back from white paddies from Georgia and Texas."

"Aw, man, that's ridiculous," a brother in a front chair said.

Another said, "Do the Vietnamese got prostitutes with razor blades in their pussies only for brothers? Like in Germany in World War II when they said we had tails."

even if you don't get a cut, keep your line together

The vet lowered his voice. People paid more attention once he lowered his voice.

"It's different, I'm telling you. We got more in common with the yellow man than your so-called fellow white Americans."

He looked around and picked up a coffee cup.

"It's all different and we can't even see it. With our eyes wide open. Man, Dow Chemical makes this stuff—polystyrene. This shit you drinking from makes napalm stick to the skin when the bomb explodes. 'Nam's strictly business for Dow. This shit ain't about no democracy. Napalm is some terrifying shit."

His voice got loud. "Man, going in there was terrifying. Would you like your baby sister roasted alive? To make a big corporation bigger? Fuck that. Not with God as my witness. Uncle Sam gave me a dishonorable discharge. Shit, give me another one. Hit me two times. Hit me three times."

keep the shape that's what you want

My barber raised his voice and directly addressed the vet. "That's why your broke self needs a j-o-b."

"Wake up, wake the fuck up," the vet said, easing in the front chair. For the next twenty minutes I looked at the floor watching his black tufts build in piles, then hills, then rows of hills, until it all became a landscape of hair.

———

The Original Bros. barbershop and Earleatha's beauty shop were two of a kind. Because my hair grew so fast and I was used to Goosey or Earleatha doing it, I found having a natural took just as much time as a perm or press. But it was a black halo of flowers that had burst open atop my head after a long freezing winter. It stopped traffic and I loved that.

18

The one course Allwood and I took together was summer session Cal-transfer American History. By then, Allwood had gotten his acceptance letter from Cal Tech, which didn't mean much without a scholarship. The thought of another class at City made me sick. But Allwood and I pitched together and bought one set of texts, *The Peculiar Institution* by Kenneth Stampp and *Lay My Burden Down: A Folk History of Slavery*, and read to each other. When Allwood read, walking around, crouching, or reading matter-of-factly, the voices of the yoked slaves were right with us in Oakland, as far from the antebellum South as one could get without falling in the Pacific. I heard their voices alongside echoes of Goosey, Uncle Boy-Boy, Aunt Ola Ray, and Pink.

> *She'd get the doctor iffen she think they real bad off. . . . I sells milk and makes my living. . . . It seem like the white people can't get over us being free and they do everything to hold us down all the time. . . . You's a fool, you is.*

I liked that the men and women in the books made their own perfume, balling up their clothes in rose leaves, jasmine, and sweet basil for days. *Lay My Burden Down* was published before I was born, but their ways sounded familiar. They poured buttermilk over greens and crumbled bread in pot liquor the same way I sopped up the last of the gumbo with the ends of bread. They took care of all the children regardless of origin. They talked about poor white trash the same way my aunts and uncles did.

Oakland even had its own version of paterollers, overseers for the massa—the oh-pee-dee, the Oakland Police Department. It even recruited in the Deep South, placing posters in Army and Marine recruiting stations. Reddy, a good friend of the family who didn't look black, called it the oh-pee-dee after he got on as a dispatcher by passing in the fifties. He told us how oh-pee-dee called us every name under the sun but the child of God—*niggers, apes, jungle bunnies, bastards, nincompoops, idiots*, but mostly nigger. They'd come to work on Fridays raring to go get them some jungle bunnies, but Reddy never let out a peep about who he really was—until retirement. Then he took Helen, his very brown-skinned wife, and Wayne, his brown-skinned son, to his retirement party. Wayne was Reddy's spitting image except for his skin. At the party Reddy told them not only he was black but how happy he was that he wasn't white. And that his greatest accomplishment was getting Wayne through Stanford with the help of a Police Athletic League scholarship. Reddy going to work for the man for twenty years, smiling ugly all the while.

The folks during slavery did a whole lot of smiling ugly too, instance after grim instance of it. I identified with them, especially when, happy but bewildered, they first tasted freedom. One said: "Even the best masters in slavery couldn't be so good as the worst person in freedom." Those two books got inside me, deeper and gutsier than any I'd read, more than Allwood's ten books. I was like them, exhilarated and bewildered.

Allwood and I looked at newscasts about air raids in Vietnam and the escalation of the war; Hanoi, Haiphong, Ho Chi Minh swam in my head with visions of the earth blowing up and my never having children. Allwood outlined the Radical Reconstruction and wrote his scholarship essay for Cal Tech, "The Pen or the Sword." The Admissions brochure requested a timely topic.

It was a Tuesday when the phone rang. We were listening to President Johnson announce that twenty-two hundred Americans had been killed in Vietnam and nearly twice as many South Vietnamese. Allwood's father, sounding exactly like Allwood, asked for him. Allwood listened for a minute, said uh-huh over and over, and, once, before he hung up, "Don't worry, I'm not going to."

"Cal Tech called my house," Allwood said. The school wanted to interview him in person that weekend at the Hotel Leamington in downtown Oakland.

"A coat-and-tie interview?" I asked. He nodded. "I'm impressed, All-wood."

He couldn't allow himself 100 percent of a smile. That would have been contrary to the posture he needed to hear Stokely Carmichael speak at a school in West Berkeley. I couldn't go because I had to work. Before I left the house, I sat for a few minutes and thought about us. *He's going away. I'm staying right here.* I had never broken up with a boy-friend because I'd never had a boyfriend to break up with. I thought of Uncle Boy-Boy, who used to say about all the friend-boys who came to the house, "Don't put all your eggs in one basket." Allwood had started out more like a friend-boy than a boyfriend. But he'd become my boy-friend and our basket of blackness didn't come with moonlight decla-rations of undying love or red hearts. Had the brush that painted me black sloshed my heart too? What if I left everything and went with Julie hoboing across the country? The postcards that I would send from Ill-wind-and-lotsa-noise or Why-owe-me—who would miss me?

After work Allwood came by to watch Stokely on the late news. Pia Lindstrom, the blond Channel 7 anchor who was Ingrid Bergman's daughter, articulated the phrase "Black Power" like it was a new dis-ease. Stokely's eyes danced in his face inside a little square at the side of her head. Allwood looked like he was going to grab her by the neck.

"Still trying to make like we don't exist."

"What else did Stokely say?" I asked.

"We're not going to play Jew if the white man wants to play Nazi."

"He said that? I can see them trying to paraphrase that."

We turned on KDIA black radio, turned off the TV sound, fired up, and got in the groove. I combed Allwood's hair. He hated to comb his thick, coal black hair. More often than not he picked it out with a cake cutter, patted it, and that was the extent of it. About once a week, sometimes twice if we were getting along good, I'd shampoo it in the sink. Then, with him sitting on the floor between my thighs, me on the chair, I'd comb out his hair, brush it, oil it, and braid it while we watched old movies on the black-and-white.

The night before the interview we saw an old movie where the guy who was fourteenth in line to the throne plotted and killed off everyone to get his inheritance. Then his wife did him in once he was in line. As Maceo, James Brown's saxophonist, would say, cold-blooded. Allwood said power corrupts, absolute power corrupts absolutely. Power entranced me, but I didn't see it as corrupting, especially not the power of intellect.

....

Allwood walked in after the interview, sport coat on and tie loosened like a character from *Father Knows Best* if the son had had a Negro friend. When Allwood sat on the daybed, he looked faintly like a husband who'd had a big day at work.

"Honey, can I get your slippers? Is baby wiped out by the men in the gray flannel suits?" He didn't laugh.

"Not to worry. Taste this delicious pot roast. . . . *Pot* roast? A little pot in the roast."

He still wasn't laughing, although he was watching my every move. Something had happened at the interview, something shaming. I waited.

"Did they take back your admission?"

He shook his head. "Everything went fine."

"Did you get militant on them?"

We had practiced appropriate answers to difficult questions. One in particular we role-played several times: "What is the best way for the Negro race to make progress? A: Education, the surefire path to improved opportunities for all citizens in a democracy."

"I said black. A lot."

"Did they react?"

"No. As a matter of fact, they wanted to talk about the marchers in Mississippi, and Martin Luther King and Stokely marching arm in arm."

"How did you handle it?"

"I quoted Adam Clayton Powell when he called Black Power a working philosophy for the new breed." He relaxed a bit as he got into Grove Street oratorical position. "Proud young Negroes who categorically refuse to compromise or negotiate for their rights."

"Then it's just a matter of them deciding on the amount of your scholarship?"

He didn't say anything.

"You're getting a scholarship?" Tuition alone was the cost of a new Volkswagen.

"They're giving me a full tuition scholarship, and partial room and board." Allwood hugged me so tight I couldn't see his face. I felt the artery in his throat pulse.

"I have to leave Monday."

I felt the word *leave* in his throat, a glottal thump. My ear lay against the cord of muscle crossing his neck. It took a minute to sink in. All I could say was, "Leave how?"

"The train."

I saw a train leaving a station, me watching it go. I held tight, as if we were drowning in a boat in a gusty wind. I felt moisture on my cheek and let go of him. Both of his cheeks glistened, and in his tears all my pictures of him appeared: Allwood pacing the apartment, holding forth, lecturing; reading, his uncombed head bent over as he savored his books, especially his black books, opening each one as methodically as peeling an orange; setting my paperbacks on fire, explaining they were trash and me telling him it was my trash and he better replace it. I had accustomed myself to his moods: arrogant, thoughtful, harried, studious, joking, sleepy, passionate. He said *I love you* but only in bed, never after, never before, and never outside of the apartment. I must have said what I was thinking, *You never came with roses*, because he looked sad and said, "I could go get roses now."

"It wouldn't be a surprise."

Allwood sad, Allwood intuitive was surprising. As comfort, I repeated how much I wanted to go to a black college, all the better to absorb all the wondrous information in the world of black thought.

This ordinarily made him laugh, but he wasn't laughing. That night, before he left, while we were going at it, full strength, he whispered, *You are a black college unto yourself.* My Allwood.

············

Monday morning we talked on the phone, but from the train station with noise, people, and space between us. Allwood had to begin immediately as a math lab assistant. "I barely had time to pack, especially my books," he grumbled, asking if I'd drop him from the course that we were in together. I had a warm flood of all the places he had touched—the radio dial, the front doorknob, the light switch in the bedroom, and especially his car coat, his long sandy fingers and walnut-looking knuckles fumbling with the dangling buttons. He left the Bug but not the pink slip for the car, and I didn't have any money to buy it. All week Allwood's face came at me. Even the class seemed different. The instructor, Mr. Carlisle, young, blond, and white, with a thick head of hair and a head-in-the-clouds presentation, reminded me of Allwood, mainly the thick hair. I tried not to picture us having sex.

············

One afternoon the instructor announced that the Soul Students Advisory Council would be paying the class a visit. The two SSAC students, Huey Newton and Bobby Seale, posted themselves at opposite sides of the classroom. My warm thoughts of Allwood came up accidentally. Huey gave me a little nod, but neither of them spoke; they stood, their torsos as stiff as bayonets. I thought of the warmth of Allwood's palms pressing my back. *Look at their mugs,* the student behind me whispered. *They're not cracking a smile.* I thought of the scowl on Allwood's face when he stood on the shelving ladder in the branch library. Mr. Carlisle, so pale and slight, as if his degree from Harvard had kept him out of the sun and stunted his growth, talked as though our textbook author Stampp was a colleague. "Stampp and I concur that slavery became 'untenable' economically." When he used finger quotes he reminded me of Allwood. Something about that made me ache and see myself braiding Allwood's hair. After about ten minutes, Bobby Seale said, "We came to make sure the curriculum of black history is being taught." The chalk in Mr. Carlisle's hand shook as he wrote on the board; he looked smaller in their presence. Bobby said we'd been brainwashed long enough. The room became a political education class. *Who-him-name?* Mr. Carlisle nodded after every sentence Bobby spoke, unlike any teacher I'd ever seen. It hit me with every nod of his head—I had been in love. In love. I had been in love and hadn't even known it. Every nod felt like a tremor inside the room. I looked around, but no one was registering the same quake. Huey and Bobby left after a while, but Mr. Carlisle kept nodding. In fact, once they left he nodded after any of us spoke. I wanted to shake him and make him stop. All the fluid in my body gorged in my throat. Why was he nodding so much? Allwood had never taken me to meet his folks. Was I only acceptable in the new black world? *Who-him-name?* Some students had begun the nod too, but unlike his nervous gesture, theirs was begrudging. Allwood's soft voice gurgled against my neck, *You are a black college unto yourself a black college unto yourself*, and I saw the curve of his earlobe, his way of holding the phone receiver between his shoulder and his jaw, his shoulder blades and the long, narrow hollow between them that I had patted dry a few times. He hadn't bathed at my house much. I tried to count the times. It started to drive me crazy trying to figure out how many times. I saw him bending to dry his calves first, then his torso, odd since I did the opposite. I blinked and felt teardrops on my hand.

What had the ex-slaves experienced in the midst of struggle, bewilderment, joy, oppression, freedom, death, liberty, injustice, hope, and terror? Mr. Carlisle was asking us. I shouted, but no sound came out, Love. Black love. He was nodding before any of us talked—if we looked like we were going to talk. Each insane nod hurt me, and I couldn't say a word to anybody. Oh my, I wasn't different from Andrea with her mocha dreams. Love hadn't shown up with chocolates wrapped in passion red foil. Yet here I was, the thought of Allwood making everything as black as a field of scorpions, a black rose blooming inside me pinned beneath a black heart. *Who-him-name?* Malcolm

Betty Lumumba Bobby Huey their bayonet bodies PE classes the Black House his loden green car coat Fair Play for Cuba the Grove Street orators my hair going from straight to bushy to sleek to bushy being swooped up by him coming as hard as I could whether or not the drowning girl opened her eyes my skull filling with the fluid it was peculiar like Marvin Gaye said and all of it was his name.

19

I couldn't bear the thought of staying at City one more minute. I started calling State's Admissions Office incessantly. I loathed pinheads who hung around the State and Berkeley extensions, taking a class and calling themselves students, picking up coeds, plastering the Cal or State decal on their car windows or wearing school sweats at the tennis courts like they really belonged. But once Allwood left, I understood. Whatever it took—whatever—I was out, even without my AA. Too bad if ten thousand other people wanted to get into San Francisco State. I had done six semesters at City, including summer sessions— seventy units, the maximum transferable. I was through with City. I was getting into State if it killed me.

I decided to go over to State and see if showing up would make a difference. I couldn't just keep calling Admissions. I had to put my body in motion.

I crossed the bay on the transbay bus. For the long ride down Market Street through downtown San Francisco, I took the M streetcar, a scowling brother at the wheel. At Macy's, a slew of people and students boarded. A SF State binder pushed against my earlobe. By the Twin Peaks tunnel, everyone was so jammed I couldn't turn my head. The train went into the tunnel, the lights went out, and the car seemed to glide on momentum. No one but me seemed startled that we were traveling through the belly of the city. *What if we're trapped? What if this is a dream and I never leave City and the Dictaphone?* When we came to daylight, the wedged Victorians with bay windows like buckteeth had disappeared. Manor houses with manicured lawns came into view. As we pulled past the Stonestown shopping mall, swarms of students walked toward State like bees around a hive. I got scared for a minute.

Everyone poured off the back exit of the streetcar. I got up slowly and stepped down. The door started to close on my foot. I heaved my purse through the door, which closed.

"My purse is stuck," I shouted. The conductor glanced back; the car lurched forward. He barked, "NEXT STOP." I stood in the well as the car wheels rumbled over the tracks, passing San Francisco State and the swarms of students. I tugged at my purse. At the next light, the conductor, smiling ugly, signaled me out. I stepped out and stumbled on a heap of gravel in the middle of Nineteenth Avenue. The streetcar moved on, cars sped by.

Another streetcar approached from the opposite direction. Several white girls, waist-length hair flying, ran across the track in front of it, laughing, their flared bell-bottoms flapping. They stopped next to me at the curb and teetered. The oncoming cars half a block away were gaining speed after the light. I started to cross, walking fast.

"Come on," one of them said. She caught up with me. "They can only kill us."

"What's your major?" she said, her dark blond hair plaited in one long thick braid. Like propeller blades, we whirred our way to the sidewalk.

"Journalism," I said, adding, "I think."

"I thought I saw you before. I'm in French."

"This is my first semester." I wasn't lying. It would be my first semester once I got in.

"Ever?"

"No, here."

"And you're just registering today?"

I nodded as her friends pulled toward the southern border of the campus. They were a few yards away when she looked back at me. She began singing Roy Rogers's song: "Happy trails to you, until we meet again / Happy trails to you, keep smiling until then, . . ." and they joined in. And then they disappeared into the swarm. I could hear their lilting, silly voices over the crowd, birds tweeting, cars in third gear, and motorcycles gunning.

I had set foot on campus.

....

Twisting spaghetti lines of students were everywhere. Student vendors, Army recruiters, sorority and fraternity insignia tables. Students for a Democratic Society pamphlets, SDS flyers pasted on top of SDS posters, Progressive Labor Party buttons on the SDS tables, Young Socialist Alliance mimeographed handouts, exasperatingly talkative, inquisitive, long-haired, short-haired, blond-haired-blue-eyed students. I looked for friendly, inquisitive, talkative blacks, or the few faces I might have known from City. No such. Instead, an Experimental College flyer caught my eye.

enroll in 70+ courses   the college within the college   the free U
change your life   change dead curricula   learning is a free country

many courses credited as instructor-approved special study 177s for 1–3 units

anyone can teach a course

The small print described it as "the Free University that began as student-initiated courses not in the traditional curriculum. The Council of Academic Deans has approved Experimental College courses for credit toward the General Education requirements."

Like a bird-watcher, I spotted the black students in multihued array, in spiff versions of Sunday-go-to-meeting clothes. I prepared my tentative, cool smile, shifted my purse so my opposite hand would be free to give a little wave. A girl in a suede suit glanced at me as her girlfriends fussed over her outfit. I smiled. She glanced away. I concentrated on my packet, wondering how to get on a friendly basis if no one spoke to me. I passed a table, the school paper, the *Gator*, stacked on it. Keeping my visual perimeter open, I scanned the headlines: ASSOCIATED STUDENTS, ACADEMIC SENATE, SELECTIVE SERVICE, STUDENT ENROLLMENT UP, VIETNAM DEMONSTRATION, ANTI-VIETNAM DEMONSTRATION. It all started to blur. The headlines, flyers, brochures, antiwar posters plastering every inch of open space, even the big sloping middle of the campus was rubbing at me, a mind bend, an optical illusion. **Growing Up Absurd** and **Compulsory Mis-Education With Paul Goodman** topped the list of courses. Below this, someone had scribbled a Goodman line:

students are the most exploited class in american society

The courses included:

revolution: pure and simple
the holiness of herman hesse
schizophrenia
violence vs. non-violence
lsd: an introduction
che guevara
the maharishi mahesh yogi
free love, nudity, masturbation and bisexuality
angel eyes: poetry from the beats
beat zen, square zen, zen.

I worked down the list. When I saw **black nationalism** and **black psychology**, I ripped the pull-offs and carried them to the next registration step. I kept reading:

miseducation of the negro
the history and social significance of black power
lsd: the psychedelic experience based on timothy leary's
   manual

When I presented my list to the registration assistant, she pointed out that I had signed up for twenty-seven units, an impossibility. She showed me how my Experimental College courses would become academic units once I was officially admitted. I ended up with eighteen units, six EC courses. I bought an SF State binder of my own and went to check on my status at the Admissions Office. After an interminable wait, a student clerk told me my folder was still in evaluation. I hated the thought of being a pinhead that hung around State or UC Extension hoping to get in.

But I had done my best for the time being. By the time I finished, the air had cooled and students were headed in droves to the Muni streetcar stop at Nineteenth Avenue. I stood on the narrow platform until the M came. On board I stood in a throng so dense I couldn't reach the steel rings. Sweat, tobacco breath, Juicy Fruit gum, hair, the sharp edges of books and notebooks, the feel of buttocks, the long lean slant of a back on mine, a breast perhaps not a breast pushing into me—in a blur it all became San Francisco State and I was swallowed like Jonah, whole and standing in its gut.

20

Aunt Ola called me up on a Sunday out of the clear blue.

"Your uncle and I will be so proud of you when you get your BA degree. That's what really counts in this world, you know." I was already on the path toward my BA. I knew an AA in language arts, not that I had one yet anyway, didn't mean squat.

"We got this postcard notice in the mail from Merritt College. Are you thinking about nursing, Niecy?" Samuel Merritt was the name of a school of nursing in Oakland. "It's talking about your graduation day."

"Merritt College is the new name for Oakland City College, Aunt Ola. They built the new hill campus and renamed it that."

"You must be part of what they're calling the last AA class from the old college then. And they want you there, even though an AA isn't much more than a high school diploma." Ola went on about how a social worker or a probation officer needed a bachelor's. I was focused on getting into State officially. All I needed was Ola getting huffy with me about not having the same amount of education Buddy and Corliss had.

"We'll help with the costs," Ola said. "It says here you need to pay thirty-five dollars for the cap and gown and the diploma."

I knew they would have paid for my freshman tuition—forty-eight bucks a semester—at State if I had asked, but why would I have asked? Right then I decided to pick up my AA degree and graduate. I worked for it—it was mine, even if Oakland City College was history.

I entered the auditorium on Grove Street, shocked that the whole school looked so raggedy. I was even more shocked when the program began and I was ushered onto the stage. I thought I was up there for a prize, which I couldn't believe. My average was 2.7-something, a B–. As I began to recognize faces, I realized about fifty of us onstage were the ones getting the AA degrees. The printed program had 170 names of graduates. *At least I'm not the only splib up here.* Abner was onstage too. My party-friend Layla, whose father was Richmond's first black policeman, was sitting across from me.

She slipped me a note: "Can you believe what it took to make it out of this rattrap?"

I mouthed, *No I can't, yes I can, where are the parties?*

Layla motioned to the back of the auditorium. Like yesterday, if I ever saw a carbon copy of Oakland City College's front steps, the welcoming committee stood: Virgil, Cootie, Tony, and Reynard. They were the opposite of the radicals, the Free Cuba brigade. Virgil was the ringleader, a dark-skinned, clean-headed, long-limbed dude who knew from creation where all the parties were. Tony was second in command. They were North Oakland guys. While the president of the college droned on, I thought maybe it was the turf advantage, because Oakland City sat in North Oakland. They were all cockhounds—I knew that from the cafeteria—but North Oakland had top dogs.

"Of our total student body, the students you see here today represent the three percent that transfer annually to the four-year institutions," the president was saying. "They have fulfilled our mandate from the master plan for education. The California legislature determined back in 1950 that any person in this great state would be entitled to the highest education, right on up to the University of California, provided he had but the capacity and the will."

I saw Huey at the back of the room talking loud and gesticulating to the Virgil-Abner contingent. Huey was political but always at the haps. I wondered what he was saying. The first time I had gone to a party up in Berkeley where there was no music playing, and there were white kids (I could tell they were UC students because the guys wore creased khaki pants and twill shirts) sitting on the floor by the wall smoking marijuana, Huey had come in and mixed as if they were his next-door neighbors.

"And these students have shown the capacity and the will to make it this far. Only time will spell the next steps. Some are going on to Berkeley and research or professorial careers. Others are transferring to the state college system to train to become teachers; others are transferring from here to specialized schools. . . ."

"And some are going to stay here and party forever," I whispered to Layla.

"But only if they have a wang dang doodle," she whispered back. "If all you have is a pussy you have to move on."

I found my name in the list of graduates. They spelled it right. Good. Layla's name was there and underneath hers was Huey's. Layla Nelson. Huey Newton. I stared at his name, Huey P. Newton. The nerve! Old as salt—he had to be twenty-three or twenty-four—graduating with me from Oakland City College. When it came time to march and pick up our diplomas, I noticed the guys in the back ready to scope us all out. I wondered if they were trying to figure out which women they had a chance with. I was so busy scoping them back that I almost didn't hear my name. As I walked around the room and tried to style in front of the guys I was so glad I hadn't invited Uncle Boy-Boy and Aunt Ola. I saw Layla and then Huey pick up their diplomas. During the cheese-and-crackers reception, I tried to eavesdrop casually, so I could find out where the parties were. Instead I found out what the guys were so hot and bothered about.

"Man, I'm telling you," Virgil was saying, "we need citizen alert patrols up here."

"Man, people from CORE and even the NAACP tune in the police on the short-wave radio in South Central. They studying the cops," Cootie said. He was little and had big eyes.

"Why for?" Tony said with a stammer.

"After Watts, you have to ask why?" Virgil said, with scorn. "You know, that's when the OPD started carrying shotguns and riding fo deep. After Watts they say we keeping a watch on you stand-up Negroes."

"Dirty dogs." Cootie slit his eyes and looked at the podium as if evil was up there.

"The police are worse than dogs," Huey said, springing to life. "Dog is too good a name for them. They're swine. They wallow in the slop of oppression."

I was caught between two rushing rivers. Huey, so street yet so smart, was going on and on about the patrols. Layla was blocking moves from Virgil. She never went with dark guys. She had gotten in San Jose State and started yakking about how she was going to pledge Delta Sigma Theta. While Huey talked, the guys were mesmerized. Virgil told Layla she was light enough to make AKA. Layla said her boyfriend was a Kappa. Under her breath Layla whispered to me but loud enough for Virgil to hear, "I heard Huey got arrested for trying to pass off a five-dollar bill for a twenty."

"What do you mean?" I said. The fellas were enthralled by Huey, except for Virgil.

"You know," she said, "he gave the clerk a five and then acted like it was a twenty. My daddy said he's known for shortchanging, and then if he gets caught, he gets all up in court and gives the jury a first-class runaround."

"You mean larceny?" I said and she nodded.

"Aw, man," Virgil said, "Huey's petitioning the United States Supreme Court." He turned to me. "You ever heard of William O. Douglas?"

"Of course."

"That's who Huey appealed to, Justice Douglas, but the form he originally submitted it to was the United States Supreme Court of California." He laughed. "Ain't no such court. Even I know that."

Huey looked offended. "That's not why they turned my petition back. I didn't attach the order of the Supreme Court of California, which had denied me a hearing and an affidavit of service."

Layla had her light-skinned girl's sneer on. She asked Huey, "Where did you get your legal knowledge?"

"I took a course in criminal law from the deputy DA of Alameda County."

"From whom?" Layla clearly did not believe him.

"Ed Meese." She rolled her eyes at me. But I didn't roll back because I remembered the name from the *Trib*. I had been fascinated by the Stephanie Bryan murder, opening up the *Oakland Tribune* every afternoon after school, imagining with Corliss how a girl like us could be murdered. She had been fourteen, walking home from school, and had disappeared from sight. First her purse turned up. Then her body was found beneath a woodsy cabin belonging to a Clark Kent type. They executed him in San Quentin five minutes before the governor called with a reprieve.

"Four days ago," Reynard broke into my freethinking. He was cute too but standoffish, like he was judging everybody. "The Supreme Court ruled that a person's confession can't be used against him in a court of law because the police never advised him of his right to any attorney or the fact that anything he said could have been used against him. *Miranda*."

He wasn't jiving around. Huey wasn't either. I wanted to ask if Ed Meese had anything to do with it. But I didn't want to sound stupid.

"Where did you take a course from Ed Moose?" Layla asked.

"Meese," I corrected her. It connected right then. He was the DA when the police busted the free-speech students at Berkeley. And then I saw my uncle Reddy talking about the "oh-pee-dee," the Oakland Police Department. He had said being a DA was a white man's stepping-stone to the governorship. And that Earl Warren was proof positive.

"Meese, moose, mouse. What's the diff?" Layla said.

"I took the course right here," Huey replied in a matter-of-fact tone. "And I've taken courses at San Francisco Law School." He was not at all intimidated.

"Isn't a fool his own lawyer?" she said.

Virgil jumped in. "A fool would not have had two hung juries and gotten dismissals of misdemeanors and parking tickets."

Layla could talk fast too. "Who but a fool would live his life in front of judges?"

I asked Huey, "Why are you petitioning the Supreme Court?"

"To erase this felony conviction from my record. I didn't commit a felony. I'm not a felon."

"What did you do to get in trouble in the first place?" I asked. I expected him to give me some song and dance. Instead Tony started talking about some house party they had been to, on Fifty-seventh and Genoa in North Oakland some time ago. A guy there had started bugging Huey while Huey was trying to eat.

"Man, this blood grabbed Huey's arm, and Huey stabbed his countrified ass."

Huey said, "I was convicted of assault with a deadly weapon."

Ooh. I got real still. Layla got still. We looked at each other. I was out of my element and Layla's face said she was too. I started thinking John Lee Hooker, Big Mama Thornton, juke joints, pigs' feet; *roundhouse negroes*, I could hear Goosey saying. The fellas started playing it, taking positions, jabbing, stabbing, and duking it out.

"Aw, man, Huey was talking race," Virgil said. "He told this dude he was an Afro-American. And that set the dude off. Completely off."

"Man," Tony said, "he say, man, the dude say it just like this, 'How do you know I'm an Afro-American?'"

They hooted, all except for Reynard, who was slick and tall and always carried a Pan Am flight bag. He was the only one dressed up, in a tie and sport coat. He said, "The guy should have known. By looking in the mirror of Huey's face."

Tony went on. "Then Huey say, 'I got twenty-twenty vision and I see your black face just like mine, and you got kinky hair, just like mine. So you must be who I am. An Afro-American.'"

Reynard spoke quietly. "Huey said, '*Therefore* you must be *what* I am.'"

Tony, excited, talked over him. "That's when Huey made his mistake. He turned his back on the blood."

Huey said to Layla and me, "I wasn't mistaken. It was logical. My steak was getting cold." I wanted to laugh at this vision of him sitting down at some crowded house party eating a piece of steak and probably a side of potato salad on a paper plate.

"And that's when the Negro got angry," Tony said. "And he said to Huey, 'Nigger, don't turn your back on me.'"

"Oh, so that was you on the 88 bus," Layla said to Huey. "You're that one who started that riot when somebody stepped on your shoe. Fool ain't know he committed a cardinal sin: Never step on a Negro's shoe."

I laughed with my mouth closed, but Huey looked at her like her skin was transparent.

Huey said, "This Negro goes for something in his left pocket. And he grabs my arm."

Cootie, blocking out all the moves, said, "That fool say, 'You must don't know who you talking to.' Huh! He the one. Brother stabbed him. In the temple, with the steak knife."

"Is this a classic case of overreacting?" Layla's voice dripped scorn. "I mean, stabbing somebody because they grabbed your arm?"

I asked Huey, "He didn't have a knife, did he?"

Huey shrugged and said, "I didn't know."

"Huey told the court that fool coulda had a hand grenade or the atomic bomb in his pocket," Cootie said, cracking up like he had been there instead of just signifying.

"Huey also said it could've been a handkerchief," Reynard added.

"Why did you do it?" I asked Huey.

He replied in a deliberate voice, as if he had said it before. "Because he was angry. Because he grabbed me in a firm grip; because when he put his hand in his pocket I heard something rattling; because his face looked mad. And." Huey paused. "Because he had a scar."

Layla hooted on that. She said, "Uh-oh. Scar means he stepped on toes before."

We were, all of us, ready to leave City and meet at Kwik Way Hamburgers at 21st and Telegraph, except Huey, who kept on. "Self-defense requires a double showing. You have to have been in fear of your life or serious bodily injury."

He wasn't just a hood. But Virgil was producing addresses for house parties like rabbits out of a hat. I wanted to hear what Huey had to say.

"And the conduct of the other party has to have been such that it would produce that state of mind in a reasonable person." He had memorized it all.

As he was talking, Layla crossed in front of Huey, her face to me, and mouthed, "Street, street. Hood, hood."

No sexual bells were ringing, but his skill at spewing facts was interesting. He was urgent and political like the Fair Play for Cuba guys, only without the weight. He was lithe like the god of eloquence and theft, the one who wore winged shoes, Hermes. I stopped myself from looking to see if he had on bourgie wingtips or street brothers' pointy-toe Stacy Adams. I didn't want to feel sorry for him if he was wearing pointy toes. He was who he was.

Virgil, the house party chief of North Oakland, wanted to make sure we got the locations of the grad-night parties written down: Snake Road; Dwight Way; Fifty-ninth and Racine; Grizzly Peak Boulevard. Layla ate parties. Her face, calculating which one to hit first, lit up. Too bad the color line was so strict; she and Virgil were two of a kind.

The night was in motion. I had made it out of City College officially.

21

It never took less than an hour to get through to Admissions at State on the pay phone at 401. I stole time from transcribing; Julie watched for me; and I was prepared with *I have cramps* if the sup questioned me. After fifteen minutes Julie came out; I started to hang up.

"Don't hang up. Sup's in a meeting about the pickets. Coast is clear," she said. Pickets were carrying signs outside 401 protesting poverty-level payments. Julie fiddled with the folding glass door to the phone booth, then got a serious look on.

"I want you to be the first to know."

"What? Are you pregnant?"

"Heavens no!" Julie looked like she had swallowed a whale and was about to spit it out.

"What happened?"

"I'm hitting the road. The south first, then Central America."

"You're going?" She bobbed her Dutch boy. I imagined a doll with blond hair in a toy car tooling across the plains. "Good for you, Juliegirl."

I hung up and started out of the booth. But something pulled me back in. One more try. "When are you giving your notice?" The number starting ringing on *giving your notice*.

"I wanted to see when you wanted to give it."

"Me? Giving notice?"

"Yeah," she said, as if it was as easy as finishing one of our paperbacks. "You can't stay at 401 forever, you know? I'll sell the Corvair. The VW engine's air-cooled, doesn't need water."

"Julie, it's not my car, it's Allwood's." I heard a woman's voice on the other end of the receiver. "Did I get through? I can't believe it." I gave her my name.

Julie said, "We can start in the Southwest, work for a few weeks, take off when we feel like it, hit the road, maybe even drive to Honduras."

"Julie, even if I don't get in, I can't just jump in a car and take off." I was picturing the toy car with blond and brown dolls tooling toward the Gulf of Mexico.

"Why not?"

I couldn't say.

"Allwood is gone, so you don't have a boyfriend. No dependents, house, nothing."

"I don't have an education."

"Neither do I."

A voice came on the line. The voice said, "Geniece Hightower?"

"Yes," I answered. I confirmed I was an applicant for admission as a junior.

"Neither do lots of people," Julie said. "They survive."

"Wait a minute," the voice said, putting me on hold.

I spoke to Julie. "I don't have parents either." I saw Goosey fanning herself on her slipcovered couch: How could I leave without even saying good-bye?

"Nobody does once they reach the age of consent."

"Julie, you're white, you can go anywhere." She kept on like that wasn't so.

"Venezuela, *señorita Geniece. Muchas gracias.* You took Spanish."

"French."

"French, Spanish, *que sera, sera,* we can do it, Geniece."

The voice came back on the line. "Brace yourself; we accepted seventy units from Oakland City, you've been admitted. Your letter's in the mail."

I gasped and Julie patted my back like I was choking, and I managed a thank-you before I hung up and hugged Julie close to keep from floating away.

"I'm in."

"Geniece . . . we could go all the way to South America in the VW. It's air-cooled."

Uncle Boy-Boy's voice came to me: *Don't tell white folks your business; they'll always try to change your plans.*

"Julie, I got accepted. I have my own trip."

This was the point that I knew for sure everything was going to change.

22

Allwood came back from Cal Tech the week after I officially got admitted. I got a jolt when he walked in the front door, but he looked odd. His car coat didn't fit anymore.

"Allwood, your wrists are sticking out of your coat. Have you grown?"

"I grew almost an inch."

"In three months?" I couldn't believe it.

"Even my shirt size went up a half inch."

I still dug him. That hit me. I wasn't expecting old times. We'd only talked on the phone. The soul sister and the intellectual, the two clouds no longer one behind the other. When he suggested we drive to State so I'd know the way, I didn't say I knew it by heart. Before we left, he asked if I had gotten rid of his dashiki.

"Of course not. Do you still want it?"

"I want to wear it." He put it on in front of me. It felt strange to see his underarm hair and his arms paler than his face.

"Are you spending a lot of time in the math lab?"

"Like a big dog."

He put his car coat over the dashiki.

"You need to dump your car coat in the Goodwill bin."

"Just don't forget your sweater," he said.

"I don't need it." I had on my pink Levi's, my flat-ribbed poor boy top, and clogs. "It's sunny."

Allwood grabbed my sweater on the way out. "It gets cold in Frisco. The ocean."

"I know the city."

It was misting when we came out on the Treasure Island side of the Bay Bridge. We drove past downtown San Francisco and switched freeways after Army Street. When we headed west we hit the fog. The rusted windshield wiper blades began to squeak against the glass, which ordinarily got on my nerves. But I was wound up. When I saw the signs pointing us to the zoo and San Francisco State, something started to vibrate in my gut. We rolled through the fog on Nineteenth Avenue alongside a Muni streetcar. My heart jumped in my chest as the campus, my campus, sloped into view. It was deserted except for a cadre of gray-and-white seagulls poking through the gusts of fog. A marble block stood at the entrance, a message from the ages carved on it. I twisted my neck to read it, rolling down the window. But the cold rushed in.

"Put your sweater on, Gee," Allwood said.

I yanked it off the backseat and put it on.

"Were you excited when you enrolled at Cal Tech?"

Allwood nodded. For a few minutes we sat in the VW next to the four-story library. I started babbling and wasn't paying close attention as I started the drive back.

"Transferring is out there. So much stuff to get straight." Allwood pointed us down the Bayshore Freeway toward the San Francisco airport.

"Where are we going?" I asked.

"To see Betty Shabazz." I didn't know what he was talking about.

"We're going to see Betty Shabazz at the San Francisco airport. She's the main speaker at a program for Malcolm X tomorrow. She's arriving from back East around one-thirty."

Betty Shabazz in the flesh. I couldn't believe it. We left the city, passed Brisbane and the homes cascading across the hills of South San Francisco in pastel stucco lines. Little boxes made of ticky-tacky.

We had passed the bare brown hills with waving grasses, chaparral, and wildflowers when Allwood said, "My dad signed the pink slip over to you. He knew we were sharing it anyway."

He pulled it out of his coat pocket. I didn't know what to say. I hadn't paid a penny for it. I took the pink slip.

"Thanks, Allwood." I didn't mention that the Bug needed a new carburetor. Nobody had given me anything since high school graduation, when Zenobia sent me three dozen yellow roses. My ears had gotten warm then, and they warmed as I held the pink slip between my thumb and the steering wheel. They got burning hot. I thought of the word *beneficiary*. I was his beneficiary, like he had died and gone to heaven and left me a used Volkswagen. It felt good.

I turned my mind toward Betty Shabazz. Would she look sorrowful? Fierce? Happy? Proud? I wondered if she'd have on all black. I pictured what she'd worn to Malcolm X's funeral. I pictured the draped black veil on Mrs. Kennedy. I wanted Betty Shabazz's veil to be blacker, heavier, more profound. Mx wasn't in the Nation when he died. Had she followed him out, faithful wife? Did she still pray five times a day? I thought of how I would look if I joined the Nation, wearing those long skirts all day. Geniece X. I couldn't picture it.

....

Allwood and I went into the airport terminal. Another brother in a dashiki, squinting at the late afternoon sun, stepped between Allwood and me. I thought he was an African tourist until I saw him slap Allwood's hand.

"Escort the sister back to the car, brother Allwood."

I was geared up to see Betty Shabazz, the closest I'd ever get to see Mx, the man himself.

"She's cool," Allwood told him.

"No, she's not," the brother said, walking backward, one hand on a rifle, the other held up between us. "Stuff just went down. The brothers from the Black Panthers in Oakland almost got into it with the pigs."

All three of us seemed to be going in different directions.

"What's happening?" I asked, trying to move toward Allwood.

"The sister should be at home, taking care of her business."

He stepped in front of me, blocking me. I walked around him.

"Sister, I'm sorry, but you're out of line."

Allwood turned, impatient with the brother, I thought. Instead, he said, "Geniece, go back and wait in the car."

"Wait for what? I want to meet Betty Shabazz."

"Sister, this is not a tea party. This is life and death."

"I'm together."

"No. You're holding your man up and you're holding me up. And that's reactionary." He patted his side like he had a gun there too. "We're ready to protect the lady."

I looked up at Allwood, but he was acting like I was something that had dropped out of his nose. I grabbed hold of his sleeve. "Tell me this doesn't mean I can't see Betty Shabazz."

He shrugged and the brother said, "This ain't the time."

"Oh, I get it," I said.

"No, if you got it," the brother said, "you would've got to stepping."

He turned to leave and Allwood started walking with him. I stood there fuming, my lips poked out to the air controller's tower. It occurred to me that if I were anybody but Geniece Hightower, black girl from East Oakland, I would have been able to see her. Joe Blow from Kokomo rides on a plane for eight hours NYC to SF and never recognizes her or the legacy she's carrying right next to him. I started after Allwood. I knew he was listening to me even if the other brother was a stone wall.

"Allwood, if I was an ordinary passenger from Sebastopol or Colma, coming in on her flight, then I would get to see her. To them she's a colored woman on a plane. They don't see Betty Shabazz. And he's gonna tell me I'm not important enough to see her?"

"See you at the car," Allwood said.

"Allwood, he's telling you I'm not important at all. Am I numb or dumb? Not me, sweetheart." I felt ripped off. Big-time. But I was beginning to lose my cool. I looked around and saw more brothers, with rifles, lined up in twos. A gang of policemen walked briskly past me. I walked behind them, the police and the brothers giving each other the evil eye. No one tried to stop me. In the waiting area, brothers lined up near the gate, police and two sisters with big bowl Afros and African wraps behind them. I smiled; one nodded grimly. The other pointed to the tarmac and said, "Sister Betty's plane is here." I got excited; the sister who had nodded touched my arm, as if to calm me.

An old cop, a Broderick Crawford type, walked up to the brothers with a camera. The next thing I knew, Huey Newton stepped up to him, as bold and as straight-backed as he had stood in my history class, and said, "Don't take any pictures."

A knot formed in my stomach. Bobby Seale moved in front of the camera, with his knock-kneed self. The cop acted like he was going to take pictures anyway. For an instant, everyone stood there, transfixed.

Huey said, "We're going to smash it," and I remembered his high-pitched voice; then I heard him call out, "Jive racist cop."

Huey started talking as if he was lecturing the whole airport: "If he takes any pictures, he's going to provoke something. That's where it's going to start at." *You're not supposed to end a sentence with a preposition*, I said silently.

"Right now," Huey said with finality. The police began talking as if they were persuading the one with the camera to back off. *He can't shoot pictures and people at the same time*, I thought. I flashed on all the times I had seen boys and men, always colored, always in East Oakland, always spread-eagled against patrol cars or wrists manacled in the small of their backs, lying on the ground like trash. Never face-to-face. Never.

A stealthy calm settled in, like a kind of truce that everyone had agreed to invisibly as the plane taxied in. I spotted Allwood up real close to the gate and wanted to shout, *Allwood, you're a bystander! This is where it's at!* I'd have to tell him everything that had happened on the way back.

Passengers streamed off the plane, an unbroken line of white people, one after another. I wondered if we'd all come here merely to confront each other. Then I saw her. I recognized her straightened hairdo with the deep bangs, her smile between a grimace and smiling ugly. She extended her arm in greeting, and a circle of brothers and sisters and then cops formed around her like rings on a tree. Everyone looked so serious, but when she looked my way I gave her fifty-two-tooth. She acknowledged me. My fear and resentment fell away as if she'd sheared them off. Then the phalanx of men with cops motored her through the airport like a Rose Bowl float. I was so giddy.

Outside the terminal Allwood and I met up. I was euphoric, but he looked just the opposite. He told me to drive, because he had to go with the brothers. He told me where everyone was headed—the *Ramparts* magazine office downtown. I got a little lost, but I got there.

I parked the Bug, got out, and saw Allwood standing across the street listening to a brother who, I could see from the back, had on countrified wide-cuffed jeans and a black leather coat. He was sounding on Allwood something ferocious.

"If you going to be for real, then be for real," he was saying. "Petty bullshit cultural nationalist bullshit is bullshit, dig?"

Allwood didn't say anything, didn't nod his head, and didn't acknowledge me when I came up to them. Mute.

"I waited for you," I said to him.

"Shut up," the brother in the coat said to me without even looking at me. That pissed me off. I thought I'd left that at the airport.

"What's the deal here?"

"The deal is your man ain't got no gun," he said, finally turning to face me. I saw he was the brother from the Black House named Bibo. He didn't look like he remembered me at all.

"You ain't packing?" he said to Allwood like I wasn't there. "How was you supposed to defend her? With your fists? A dictionary? Chairman Mao says power comes from the barrel of a gun."

"And Jimmy Baldwin said—"

"Don't quote that faggotty bullshit from Martin Luther Queen. That intellectual bullshit ain't playing here. Either you willing to die for the people or you bullshitting."

Allwood spoke. "I know what my duty to the masses is."

"No, you don't. You think the masses are asses."

"I love my people," Allwood said.

"Enough to die for them? Don't lie. Don't front. You couldn't front in there." Bibo pointed to the building. "So don't try to front me off. I know you going to school to get your GNP degree. Your Good Negro Papers. So you can dictate to the masses and eat crumbs from the massa. I got your number, brother Allwood, and it don't even add up to one. Your mind is revolutionary, but your heart is bourgeois."

"You're the one," Allwood said, "making a big mistake, writing off brothers with skills."

"The Vietcong ain't got nothing but rice, man, and they kicking ass. Degree is your excuse."

"When the revolution takes place," Allwood said, "and shit goes down, believe me, brother, the people will need engineers, doctors, lawyers, social scientists, scientists, nuclear physicists."

"You can wear all the Malcolm X sweatshirts and SNCC buttons you want. Brother, your shit is not deep. If you ain't willing to give the imperialist an ass kicking when it counts, how you going to walk up to the victory table and say what? You was too busy studying to fight?" He shook his head. "We can train the people."

"Not that fast. Look at Guinea. They're struggling, man. Yeah, man, after they chase out the colonialists, the British, the French, they have to deal with rebuilding. Skills. Do you realize that only ten percent of adult Africans can read and write? Ten percent!"

"All I know is this," Bibo said, pointing to the *Ramparts* building. "Those brothers in there from Oakland pulled some coattail today."

"I'm from Oakland, man. I grew up in Oakland," Allwood said.

I piped in. "And I'm from Oakland, and I know Huey and Bobby from City."

Bibo stared at me and said, "Sister, it's not who you know, it's how you know them."

He continued to talk to Allwood. "Those brothers in there. They're the real deal, man. Huey had a shotgun, Bobby was carrying a gun, the young dudes were loaded with guns, man, loaded. The Black Panther Party of Northern California looked like fools! Man, they calling them paper panthers, I ain't a paper nothing. Is that what you want to go down as?"

For a minute, they didn't talk, just stared eyeball to eyeball. I had helped Allwood fill out his application to Cal Tech. I knew what he wanted *to go down as* because I had typed it: physicist.

"You know what's the most important thing you can do?" Bibo asked Allwood. "Quit school for a year and struggle for the people, day and night. Can you do that?"

Allwood stood mute. I could hear Uncle Boy-Boy drilling at the root of the matter:

And have these young men gone to college?
And do they have good jobs?
Do they even have jobs?
Do they have records?
Have they been to jail?
Are they married?
Where do you think they're going?
Are you even thinking about going with them?

. . . .

"I'm not quitting school," Allwood spoke with a tone of finality. "I have to get my degree or I'm useless."

"Your parents drilled that into your head," Bibo said.

"There's nothing worse than a smart black man without an education," Allwood said.

"How about smart without a conscience?" Bibo said.

I got back in. "What about all the sacrifices our parents and grandparents made to get us to this point? All their struggles were fought so we *could* become educated."

"This is a movement from the bottom up, not the top down. It's not about being better than somebody else," Bibo said.

"Not better than," I said. "As good as, and able to help other people as well."

"Allwood, give the people one year. Even white boys go to Africa for the Peace Corps for two years," Bibo said.

"My scholarship's open this year. I have to finish, and then help my people."

"Scholarship!" The utmost scorn filled Bibo's face.

Inside I screamed, *If I had been offered one, I would have jumped on it, baby cakes.*

"Huey says cultural nationalism is irrelevant and romantic," Bibo said, walking away, shaking his head. "Wearing a dashiki ain't a solution, brother."

....

I drove Allwood back to Berkeley in complete silence. Keeping an eye on the Bay Bridge traffic, I glanced at the ships coming into port, the seagulls, Alcatraz, Treasure Island, the Port of Oakland, the Naval Supply Center, the mudflats in Emeryville that ran along the shoreline. I got off the Nimitz Freeway where it began stretching toward Sacramento and the American West, at Ashby Avenue, the south end of Berkeley, my hometown, my city, home. I pulled up next to the incinerator and yanked the emergency brake.

"Allwood, why didn't you tell me this Betty Shabazz thing was about guarding her? I thought we were going to see her. All you had to do was hip me to the fact that at least some of the brothers would have guns."

He didn't say anything.

"Bodyguards and guns go together."

"I wasn't thinking about it."

"Allwood, that's fucked. . . . Who else had guns?"

"Just the brothers with Huey and Bobby. The group talked it out last night. The ones who came brought unloaded guns."

"Unloaded guns?" I shrieked. "That's some stand-up outlaws."

He didn't say anything for a few long seconds. He didn't want to talk about it with me.

"Students are the oppressed," he said as we went inside. "When you understand that, you know that you struggle against the system wherever you go. Wherever that is. For me, it's Cal Tech."

Allwood's a teacher, not a social changer. That hit me so hard I had to brace myself against the door as he changed out of his dashiki and talked. "The study of our history, our struggle, our oppression is all preparation for service to the community."

When we got inside, Allwood folded the dashiki carefully. Suddenly he shook it all out, rolled it in a ball, put on his car coat, and stuffed it in a pocket.

"It looks like an abscess growing out of your rib," I said.

"It doesn't matter," he said. He shifted it to the other pocket, then looked at me. "I guess we should say good-bye?" he said. I wasn't used to a sheepish Allwood.

"Hasn't it been nice knowing me?"

He smiled. "Not nice. Deep." We kissed, but it wasn't mush-mush. Sweet but no mush. "Your lips are still soft."

"What was so deep about it?" I asked.

"Everything. And then some."

"No, be for real," I prodded. "After all this time, was it for real?"

"Of course, it was for real."

"Then what about it was most for real?"

"You can't quantify it like that."

"You're a scientist, aren't you?"

A smile spread across his seriousness. "You know the Model T Ford?"

I nodded. "Of course I know it."

"But can you name the cars that came after it?"

"Chrysler, Plymouth?" I shook my head. "I don't know."

"That's because you always remember the first one."

"That's the deep, that I won't forget you?"

I stood as he nodded and walked down the driveway to the street. The bunched-up dashiki made his coat protrude on one side. He turned and gave me a wave.

"I didn't want to get corny on you," he yelled back at me.

"I know," I yelled. *I know* reverberated until I couldn't see him anymore.

"I know," I murmured. "I know."

I started to shiver. When I clasped my doorknob, it sent an even colder current through my palm.

Junior

. . . .

23

The incident with Betty Shabazz marked a point of departure for everybody. The Black Panther Party of Northern California had started after the Lowndes County Freedom Organization in Alabama made the panther its symbol to counter the segregationist Alabama Democratic Party, which had a rooster as its logo. A small group of brothers, including Allwood, inspired by the Alabama freedom fighters, chose the panther as its symbol. It had all started around Oakland City College and the Soul Students Advisory Council. But when Huey and Bobby insisted on revolutionary struggle, the intelligentsia and artists went one way, and the Black Panther Party for Self-Defense took the harsher route of integrating the gun for self-defense with politics. Each group inspired me to read and to learn.

I showed up for my first day of classes at State with hordes of students on the floors and windowsills, lining the walls and standing three-deep at the doors, seemingly eighteen thousand pleas for the same mercy: more classes.

"If you're trying to avoid the draft, consider the Experimental College." The psychology statistics prof refused to hand mimeographed syllabi to everyone. "You can get your student deferment with EC units too."

When no one budged he said, "Don't take up space if you don't have to."

A chorus of voices told him, "We have to."

I didn't know quite what to do. I was officially a junior at the hippest college in California. I had paid my forty-eight-dollar-a-semester tuition and gotten my student body card. I didn't want to drop the EC courses I had signed up for and risk not getting any classes. I walked back outside. The fog had cleared. I sat on the grass and flapped out my peacoat. The grassy rectangle at the heart of the campus sloped downward to the Commons, the student cafeteria, and the bookstore. Students milled about, stretched out, sleeping, eating lunch, playing Frisbee, talking. My stomach grumbled; I'd saved three hundred dollars to tide me over until I found part-time work. But it was going fast. I had a work-study job interview. A clump of black girls passed by, ebullient, spiff. I half smiled; they were wrapped up in each other. They were the Andreas, the Corlisses, who had never heard of Frantz Fanon or Robert Williams. I crossed over the rectangle to the Administration building and went up the steps. I had tried so hard to get into State, swimming upstream, Allwood by my side. It was different from what I had envisioned.

But the interview was a snap. The work-study interviewer gave me a choice of on-campus work sites. I chose Admissions. The Admissions Office administrator barely looked at me, asking if I could handle the window for the next hour. I was shocked that they didn't care if I knew anything. What if I talked crazy? Student requests for admission status, transcript evaluators poring over grades, test scores, recommendations—someone brought me a soda, which I barely had time to sip. The students were confused, anxious, upset, lost, and waiting to get in. They wanted information. I learned where all the major buildings were. The person who brought me the soda said, "Admissions is the only work-study overtime on campus. Twenty-five hours a week isn't unusual." My hunger subsided. The thought of quitting 401 Broadway was daunting, but I worked the window for the next two weeks nonstop. I date-stamped application entries from all over the world, scanned essays and personal information, and filed transcripts. Lives came out of the words: how little money one's father made; the off-the-wall place one had traveled to; family crises; serious illness defeated; political activity noted like a badge of honor—"I belong to the W. E. B. Du Bois Club." They weren't afraid: "I participated in the freedom rides." Stuff I never mentioned: "The protest changed my whole life." State was a destination for radical students: "I'm a child of a union family." Dissidents.

The streets of Berkeley were the pull for people bucking the system. Nonconformists. State was pulling students like me. I was not an in-between. I was a junior facing a cast of thousands wanting to be right where I was, a part of something big, essential, swimming in the big ocean.

24

Allwood had been my guide, but he had moved on. I could too. I started my third week wearing my burgundy pantsuit from Roos Atkins and my hair in a woolly bun. I ventured to the cafeteria, ordered pea soup, and took my tray to the edge of the pool. The black pool.

"You must be new," a guy next to me said. "Nobody eats that cheesy soup."

"I started last week." I didn't mention my EC units.

"It shows. You paid grand theft for that suit."

"Not really."

"Oh, what then? You got it hot?"

A girl next to him said, "Don't be so mean." Then she spoke to me. "Forget Marcus. Your suit is sharp."

I lost my taste for the soup. "I'm Geniece."

"Where you from?" Marcus asked.

"Oakland."

"Figures."

"Why?" He was getting on my nerves.

"I'm from LA. I got cousins in Oakland. Humbug shit, humbug parties. Oakland is either seddity niggas or Negroes ready to fight at the drop of a hat."

"Maybe your cousins were lame," the girl said.

He shook his head. "Only good thing about Oakland is the scrunch. Party in Oakland and you will scrunch, sweethearts." I thought that closer-than-close slow dance with a rub and a dip was exclusive to East Oakland.

A much older brother in a baggy suit, white shirt, and bow tie, carrying *Muhammad Speaks* newspapers, approached.

"*Muhammad Speaks*," he said, in a voice loud enough to reach beyond the tables. "The true word. The last word. The truth of the Honorable Elijah Muhammad."

Lowering his voice slightly, he pointed to Marcus's ham-and-cheese sandwich. "Still eating that pork, bro?"

"And gonna keep on till the day I die, William-fifty-seven-varieties-of-Heinz X." Marcus defiantly bit into the grilled sandwich. I wanted one.

"William 12X," he said, veered back a table, and sold a paper. I motioned to him.

"Thank you, sister with the natural hair; I should've come to you first."

"What do the twelve Xs mean?" I asked.

Someone laughed, a laugh of derision that didn't faze William 12X.

"X stands for the unknown. We discard the names our slave masters gave us and use X. It's the mathematical symbol for the unknown. Our last names, our real last names, are unknown. There were eleven Williams who applied for their Xs before me."

"And where do you apply for an X?" the person who laughed asked.

"Nation of Islam headquarters on Cottage Grove in Chicago, Illinois, my sister. Paper's a quarter." I paid for it, and William 12X offered one to Marcus.

"Not on your life," Marcus said.

"I bet you subscribe to the *San Francisco Chronicle.*"

"Yeah, and it's only a dime."

"You can read the devil's rag sheet for an hour, can't you?"

"So what if I do?"

"The devil makes you think being smart is the key to life. But Allah teaches—"

"William Triple X. I heard your spiel already. You say the same thing over and over like a tape recording."

"If you've been brainwashed, as our people have, you need to hear the truth over and over again, and over some more, until it sinks in and dislodges everything negative and harmful you've learned about yourself."

"Next time," Marcus said, getting up and leaving.

"One day there won't be a next time," William shouted after him. "And you'll be too lost to find your way back."

. . . .

At work I witnessed students stream in and out of the dean of admissions's office. These appointments were listed as DD in the big appointment book. I tried to figure out what DD stood for without asking: Done Deal, Diplomatic Denial, Doubtful Decision, Dedicated Drone. I studied their expectant faces as they came in like white lemmings. All but one that I saw were white kids. Some were clearly jocks, big hunky guys, but the females looked about my age. They all looked earnest, and they all showed up on time for their appointments. When I asked Fannie, the black transcript evaluator, she crinkled her nose and told the others the names I had come up with. Big laughs.

"Whatever our total enrollment figure is, we waive the regular requirements for two percent of that figure and admit the exceptions to the rule. Most of them are jocks coming in on athletic scholarships. It stands for Dumb Deb. Dumb debutantes. The two percent quota. Mr. Somebody's daughter or son."

"The not-so-smart kids of important people?" I thought of all the times I had applied.

"Don't have to be important. Just know somebody important," Fannie said.

. . . .

In spite of my statistics professor droning on about factor analysis and covariance, I didn't fall asleep. After class I went into the Gallery Lounge. People were casually milling about an interview area blocked by a screen. A Peace Corps sign was out. Students were browsing through the literature near a pile of luggage and knapsacks. A curly-haired man in rumpled corduroy short sleeves loosened his nubby knit tie and walked up to me.

"Are you interested in the Peace Corps?" He seemed tired. "Have you seen our brochure? Would you like to sign up for an interview?"

I nodded, an effort not to exhaust him further.

"Maybe you'd like to talk with our rep." He pointed me toward a young black woman sitting near the luggage. She smiled and extended her hand to me.

"I've been on my way to Tanzania for three months," she said with a Southern accent. She walked me to the last set of chairs. In front of her ears, she had glued her spit curls. Behind her ears, her chin-length hair had been straightened so stringently she had lost some hair at her temples. Without thinking, I said, "Who's going to do your hair in Tanzania?"

When she laughed she was real. "I'll fake it for as long as I can. Then go all the way back."

"Who knows? Maybe they have hot combs over there?"

"In the city, I'm sure. But I'm going way past Tanganyika. I'm going to the bush country to set up a school."

She was from Tallahassee and had majored in psychology at Florida A&M. A black college graduate. I was immediately in awe. "I'm a psych major too."

"Oh, the useless degree," she said. "Without a master's, that is."

"I might switch."

"To what?"

"Education or French or maybe English." An outright lie. I'd major in English in a hundred years. "Do you need a degree to get into the Peace Corps?"

"Yes, or a skill. Where would you like to go? It's a big continent."

I couldn't even make up an answer. She seemed to sense I was dumbfounded. Go where? I didn't have an African country on the tip of my tongue. I looked down at her snakeskin go-go boots. I decided to be honest.

"I stumbled on this. The Peace Corps sounds interesting, but I've never been out of California."

"And you don't know what you want your life to be?" she said.

"I'd like to be a probation officer or a social worker." I went back to fabrication.

"That's what you want to do. Not what you want to be."

Was she waiting for me to say something stupid? To do, to be. Two of the simplest infinitives in the book.

"Don't think so hard. I'm not trying to trick you."

"How old are you?"

"I'm only twenty-three. And yourself?"

Twenty-three. Light-years away. I'd be a college graduate by then, taking a civil service test, wearing dresses and stockings and pumps every day. Yes, Sir, no, Sir, yes, Ma'am, no, Ma'am. The report is on your desk.

"I'm twenty, almost."

"When I come back from the Peace Corps, I plan to get my master's in international relations here at State." She beamed. "And then join the State Department and travel until I'm thirty."

"So that's what you want to be in life."

"No, that's still what I want to *do*. I want to *be* a God-fearing, loving wife and mother."

"You sound so clear. When I think of the future, it looks crystal-ball cloudy."

"It settles down. Give it a couple of years."

We exchanged numbers, but I knew I'd never see her again. I felt this odd suspension of my body, like it was a liquid poured in another liquid, a chemical poured into this vast space between Oakland City College and SF State, in between what I knew for sure and what was unknown. Niecy X. Niecy 57X. Niecy Who? All that unit counting at City to land in between again.

25

"Discretion. That is the heart and soul of the process of public policy." My public administration professor had thick maroon-tinged lips. "And no one is more important, more discreet, more fundamentally trust-bound than the secretary. In the delicate pads of her fingertips are your secrets, and in her ears, in the inner sanctum of her brain are your confidential deliberations. The secretaries are the nervous system of any business or office."

I raised my hand. The way he looked at me I understood instantly I wasn't supposed to interrupt.

"If they're that important, why aren't they paid more?"

He lifted his bushy, black, caterpillar eyebrows until they stood out over his horn-rims and ran his hand over his crew cut.

"Salaries in the public sector are set by educational level, by training, and by experience. Show me a secretary with a BA, management courses on her précis, and management, or even management trainee, experience, and, voilà, you'll see a comparable salary."

"Voilà" came with an arm gesture that said *simpleton*. A male voice behind me broke in. "That's not the point she's making."

I turned. He didn't look like a protester, his hair wasn't long, and his shirt was laundered. But he spoke with as much authority as the professor. "Secretaries are donkeys in the office, beasts of burden. They're paid thirty-five hundred to ten thousand dollars tops, because if you pay donkeys good money, they might get the idea that they're not donkeys at all."

The professor cut through it all. "My wife's a highly competent secretary right here in the Econ Department. She'd be highly insulted if she thought her job description was jackass." Students, laughing, began to pack up. Class ended.

I thought of him as I got a grilled-ham-and-cheese and went to the Gallery Lounge. In the middle of the room, at the podium, moving like her body was aching, a small snappy woman kept opening her mouth wide—Aunt Ola would have called her "unladylike." But the voice coming out of her sounded like Joe E. Lewis. I was concentrating so intently on the cheesy, buttery taste, and crunch of my sandwich that I only saw her mouth opening rhythmically. She had people stretching their necks to pick up her rhythm. I couldn't pick it up until I finished eating. She stopped and stood still, as if she was picturing something that brought her pleasure, smiling ugly.

"You know, don't you, that the entire internal structure of the black male-female relationship changed when Aretha Franklin took on Otis Redding's 'Respect'? She changed what had been a man's plea for the love of a good woman into a woman's absolute and nonnegotiable right to a serviceable relationship, including—"

She looked around, making sure everyone was listening before she finished: "—penis, but not restricted to it, dig?"

Not many blacks hung out in the lounge. There were none to see this but me. The white students were getting off on her. I shrank, waiting for something smiling ugly to come out. She started humming and swaying. They seemed mesmerized. She was so little to have that much command. Then she looked at me and spread her arms out, whispering directly at me and smiled ugly, like my thoughts had irradiated. *Nigger.* She said it softly, as if she were calling to me right in front of all the white people. *Nigger.* She repeated it even softer. Then again, until it seemed she was weeping. But she was saying it with warmth, not hatred and accusation. *Nigger, nigger, nigger.* Like a lullaby, she whispered it. Then she was silent. She bowed her head and someone started to clap. But she threw her head back and shrieked so loud everyone jumped.

"NIGGER!!!"

She kept shrieking, saying it four or five times at that unbearable pitch. Then she grabbed herself and stood with her legs apart, like she was in the middle of sex. I was embarrassed and intrigued. She talked so fast the words jammed together.

Nigger, the one-word country, the foreign language anyone can learn in an instant, the muscle on your tongue, licorice music, *nigger* shit, *nigger* please, *niggers* and she's, *niggers* drive me up a wall, *niggers* never learn, no *niggers* allowed, *niggers, niggers, niggers,* eenie meenie minie moe catch a *nigger* by the toe, *nigger*-lover

She turned her black marble eyes on me and bowed. They applauded. I just stared, her voice reverberating inside my head. Someone got up to the mike and said, "Mali is the last of Poetry at Noon. Give her a hand. And if you're interested in taking an EC class with Mali, sign up today."

I went over to her. The other students crowded her, but she pulled me in, her hand soft inside mine.

"Did I shock you?" Everyone looked at me.

"Not in the least," I lied. I was lying a lot at State. "I hear you loud and clear. Putting it out there so people have to deal with it."

"You looked shocked."

"It was a barrage." She patted me big sisterly on my shoulder. Up close, she looked to be in her late twenties.

"What's your major?" As soon as I asked, I knew she wasn't a student.

"I'm from LA. Up for a poetry seminar. I might teach a course next semester. Are you an English major?"

"No way. But I'd love to take a course from you."

"Well, look for Poetry with Mali."

"Mali what."

"Just Mali."

The next day I skimmed the *Gator* to see if anyone had by chance covered it. On the next-to-the-last page, in a column called "observed," someone had written:

Once again, the EC has taken its overly generous funding and clubbed us over the head with it, this time under the guise of culture. A

Southern California Negro poet billed as Mali harangued and pontificated in the Gallery Lounge noontime happening. Thank heavens the students had the good sense to ignore thoroughly Modern Mali's unprintable imprecations, remaining polite and silent until she finished. Would that the Malis of the world proliferate but not here at our expense.

The *Gator* made journalism look like a joke, an insult. It shut down all ambitions I had to go into journalism.

26

By my third week in Admissions I'd gotten the hang of it—filing apps, scheduling Dumb Debs, sorting mail, getting the scuttlebutt from Fannie, manning the information window. A steady stream of anxious, frustrated, lost students searched my face for answers. The black faces gave the cursory nod, the pinched hello that said we were descended from the same folk down South who had raised us with good morning, how y'all doing, peace be with you. Some spat out the obligatories. A scent of pipe tobacco filled the space between one black man and me. I got his record.

"I thought window duty was for whites only. Kept all the Negroes behind closed doors. You're the first spook they let give out information. You know that, don't you?"

He talked like Edward R. Murrow, staccato, breathless, in a hurry to get the syllables off his tongue. But he wasn't in a hurry to move.

"No, I didn't." His form showed a 1943 birth year. The people behind him were getting irritated, clearing throats, shifting books arm to arm.

"How long have you been here?" he barked. "I need the health plan brochure."

"At the window?" I gave him the health plan brochure.

"No, at State?"

"A few weeks."

"That explains all this smiling." He glanced over his shoulder. "Let them wait. I've been waiting all my life."

He leaned in as if my face was his echo chamber. "White paddy, white paddy, you don't shine; white paddy, white paddy, kiss my behind."

He picked up his books and flounced off. I was so flustered I wanted to close my eyes and make the whole exchange disappear. Instead, I had to help all the people he'd shown his ass. They addressed me curtly, as if he and I were one and the same. It took about fifteen minutes for the line to reformulate. I was mad because he was mad at white folks in general and they were pissed at me in particular. Fannie pulled my coattail.

"Don't ever let Horace stick his big ears through the window. Nobody, not even your mother, sticks their face past the window."

"How could I have stopped him?"

"Closed it on his motherfucking face." And lose the job. I didn't think so.

"Horace is crazy. Do you know how long he's been going to State?" Fannie had her hand on her hip and her chin on her chest. "Wearing those same Perma Press hopsack slacks and square-bottomed Rooster ties?"

Another evaluator chimed in. "Isn't he the guy who smokes Peach Brandy cigarillos? I think his cigars are mellow."

"You would," Fannie said.

"So what if he's been here since Ike? He's cool."

"It's not cool to have been here long enough to get three bachelors," Fannie said, as she went back to her cubicle.

"He's been here twelve years?" I asked.

"No, dummy," Fannie said. "And he is not the norm. He is the exception."

The other evaluator shouted over the wall. "All kinds of students take years and years to get their degrees. That's the beauty of State."

Fannie made an ugly face, crunching her freckles into a mass. She whispered, "For white people. Not for splibs. If a boot stay, it's because he's stupid. Horace is case in point. Negroes have to get in, graduate, and get out. Shit. White folks have"—she raised her voice—"all the time in the world . . . la de dah."

She put her hands on me. "Come here, tall girl."

We went into her cubicle. Lined up, shelf upon shelf, were college catalogs: Berkeley, UCLA, University of Oregon, Ohio State, Colgate. She turned on her calculator and sat down.

"How many units are you going to transfer with?"

"Seventy from Oakland City."

"And how many are you taking this semester."

I was embarrassed to tell her eighteen EC.

She raised her eyebrows and pulled her glasses down her nose. "Eighteen Mickey Mouse. All the same on paper. All you need is 120 to pick up your sheepskin. That's all you consider. Every semester you ask yourself, How close am I to 120 units?"

She ripped off the tape from the adding machine and handed it to me.

"Not with the sequence of courses I have to take as a psych major."

"Then switch."

"Switch?"

"Switch majors, dummy. Take social science, the easiest way to get out. This ain't no playground. It's an institution, dig? Like San Quentin. Don't stay here longer than you have to. You might can't get out."

"I haven't even started, really."

"Who's supporting you? Mommy? Daddy?" I shook my head. "If the Dumb Debs can do it, so can you. I'm just saying, don't act like you got all the time in the world. I'm divorced with two kids in Catholic school. I do it by myself. Colored women can't depend on Prince Charming. I came from junior college too and whipped through in four semesters without Experimental Disneyland. You can do it. Horace is here because he wants someplace to bullshit. He could've had his degree. I know his wife. His kids play in the same league with mine; she's carrying the weight. You know what kind of car he drives? A Corvair! Perfect, looks the same from the back and the front. Ditto Horace. Asshole to asshole."

I thought of City, the street-corner orators who were in their mid- to late twenties. "College is Horace's game?"

"Exactly. He's in engineering, which I grant you can take a while. But that hammerhead's been here long enough to grow rust."

"Horace is a dud?"

"Actually, Horace is smart. As long as wifey's content that he's working on his degree, he got it made in the shade."

Fannie marched me out of her cubicle. "You can do this. Here's what you need to do. I know you're commuting from the East Bay. Move into the dorms. You can't take all those units, work twenty-five hours here, and go back and forth."

"I can't move in the dorms. I can't afford dorm housing."

"Not the dorms, dummy, IH."

Interim Housing. IH. I had referred several people there. Emergency housing.

When I rode home I felt quivers in my gut as I crossed the Bay Bridge. Not horny quivery or having to pee quivery. A high-frequency oscillation, like when I knew Allwood was going to be the one, like when I saw Cicely Tyson on TV with George C. Scott in *East Side, West Side*, and it was the first time people weren't seeing the white-looking Lena Horne or mulatto-sexy Dorothy Dandridge but an African-dark woman. Checking out the San Francisco roller-coaster skyline of buildings and lights, brooding Mount Tamalpais darker than the night, I thought about Fannie in her thirties, already flopped at marriage, raising two kids on her own. I didn't want to end up like that. Who was she to criticize Horace? Maybe she envied him. Horace had someone. I could smell Horace's sweetish tobacco, see him driving his Corvair assbackward, giving drivers the finger. What would I do if I graduated so soon? Take the probation officer exam for Alameda County. The social worker exam. Be an evaluator at State. Calculator, cubicle, confinement. I wasn't even all the way in, and she wanted me to rush out.

....

I parked the Bug behind my apartment, breathing in the Berkeley air cooled by the San Francisco Bay. When I moved there I bought a new serape from the back of a truck, paying a man from Mexico in crisp bills that he folded into tattered, sweated-over ones. Now everything looked old, the serape threadbare, cabinets as if from a Sears Roebuck catalog. I didn't want to turn on the lights. I put my books and purse down in the dark kitchen, groping for the kettle, the faucet, prepping my mug with a tea bag. I fingered the abstract design on the mug and blew into it, making sure a bug hadn't gone to bug heaven on me.

When I heard the kettle whistle, I turned on the light. When I poured, I saw something black, fingernail-size, float to the rim. A roach that had eluded my roach hunt floated in its coffin, my mug. I started to pour it down the drain. But first I went to the drawer where all the roaches had hidden before. Grabbing a spatula, I cursed the entire species and yanked the drawer open. No roaches jumped out. I went through the drawers, cabinets, sink, and refrigerator.

Fannie was right; it was time.

27

Interim Housing, the tough-shit place for students who had no place or no money, was boot camp—showers with no curtains or walls. When I finished showering the second night, I was relieved to see no one but the other black woman on my floor. I didn't have to parry funny looks. I had noticed her long straight hair the day before. It looked like somebody had chopped it all off. Her face was round and sweet, almost defenseless looking.

"What happened to your hair?" I asked.

"I cut it off." She stepped closer, as if to give me a good look.

"What style did you want?" I asked. "A Mia Farrow?"

"I was tired of it." She was reet petite, with serious black eyes like watchtowers.

"Why didn't you go to a beautician?" She bent her head for me to see, then motioned for me to touch it.

"Believe it or not, I want a natural."

"Do you have a perm, or is your hair straight like this?" I touched her warm scalp.

"Lustrasilk, but it's pretty straight anyway." Ola had used Lustrasilk for years.

I pulled her hair lightly at angles from the roots. "You can get a natural. It would just take time for your hair to go back."

You could forget you had nappy hair if you Lustrasilked continuously.

"I stopped treatments about a year ago, when I came here," she said.

"You're a sophomore?"

"Second semester junior. Nursing. My name is Xavi."

"Zayvee, like Jay Vee?" She nodded. "I'm Geniece. Psych."

"Xavi is short for Xavier. I was supposed to be a boy."

"What's so special about boys?" I was trying for funny and got there. She cracked up. "Do you really want a natural?"

"I must if I cut off all my hair."

"You could put Tide on it. That would strip it."

"You must be kidding. Tide? I can't shampoo my hair with laundry detergent."

"You'd get your natural quick."

....

Xavi's Tide-treated hair took a week to revert to a soft limp natural, with straight strands sticking out. We decided to try to room together off campus and began checking the listings at the housing office. The lady behind the desk gave us a hard time.

"How do you girls know there's even an apartment available?"

Xavi was polite. "If one's not posted, we want it before it gets posted."

"Any unoccupied apartments are posted on the bulletin board," she said, barely looking at us. I'd had it with barrack green. I couldn't sleep surrounded by ugliness.

"If we were white, would an apartment be available?" I asked.

"I don't know what you're implying."

"C'mon," I said to Xavi. "She'll never give us a break."

The lady's face turned bright pink. "I don't make the rules."

As we walked out, Xavi turned around, grabbed the room reservation list, and threw it on the desk. "This is what I think of your rules."

Outside the office, Xavi was shaking; when she opened her mouth her lips moved, but no sound came out. The woman called Xavi back in and gave her a housing referral and me a dirty look.

28

Xavi became my first off-campus friend in the city. She got a studio on Parnassus near UCSF for $105 a month. I wasn't jealous, because I figured Xavi deserved it. She stood up to the housing office lady. I was beginning to see that defiance got results, made the rules bend at State. But Xavi and I didn't have the same political understanding. Xavi didn't see anything wrong with Ronald Reagan being governor. The idea of it made me ill.

"He's an actor. He's used to having a director for a brain. Remember *Death Valley Days*?"

"We're not old enough to vote anyway."

"I don't care. It's like having Donald Duck or Mickey Mouse running things."

"My parents voted for Pat Brown. Did yours?"

Mine. Did mine? I didn't have parents. "I don't have parents." My throat got so dry I got a crick in it. She didn't say anything. We were sitting on her bed trying on sample tubes of lipstick. I tissued off the Orange Jujube and dabbed on Carnaby Coral.

"They all are too bright for me. When are they ever going to make lipsticks for dark lips?"

We kept trying them on anyway—Pink Paisley, Naughty Iridescent Violette, Nectaringo, Great Granny Red—and wiping them off.

"We look like the low-rent Supremes," Xavi said. "You're Diana."

"Because I'm the gorgeous and talented one?"

"No, just the smile. I'm Flo."

Xavi dug into her jewelry hatbox and pulled out crepe paper fans in a rainbow of color. "The Supremes don't use fans," I said.

"These aren't fans, Geniece. They're froo-froos," she said.

She began manipulating the crepe paper, folding and unfolding it like origami, until it fanned out into geometric shapes.

"Froo-froo paper earrings—you never saw them?"

"On models, not real people."

"They're for pierced or unpierced," she said, handing me a pair. She put a flap of purple and pink on one ear and a white carnation on the other. She gave me a set of blue cubes with Egyptian eyes. We turned her transistor radio on and started dancing to the mirror and the Isley Brothers' "Twist and Shout," a solid hour. Xavi could Mashed Potatoes up a breeze; I showed her how to Watusi. When the deejay got mushy, we were ready to tune him out. But he put on Ruby and the Romantics' "Our Day Will Come," so we did cha-cha-cha and then tuned him out.

"Open the window, Xavi. It's funky in here."

We squeezed our heads into the window frame and hung out, our faces suspended. The night breezes were heavenly.

"What happened to them?" Xavi said. "Did they die?"

She meant my parents. I sighed.

"My mother died when I was three. And my father left. I mean, he left Oakland."

"He's still alive, though?"

"I don't know."

"He went out for a pack of cigarettes and left?"

"No, he prepared. He just didn't tell anybody where he was headed. The family took over." My voice got quivery. "It's not like who am I. I know stuff. I have family. But it is like, am I a nobody?"

"Because you have to ask?"

"Yeah, it's not a given." My jumble, my puzzle, was registering with her.

"Do you keep it a secret?"

I couldn't answer right away. "Everyone assumes I have parents."

"Who do you tell that you don't?"

"No one, I guess. Those who know don't ask. Those who don't know don't ask."

"Geniece, a secret is something you keep hidden on purpose. You never told anyone?"

"I told my boyfriend."

"Anybody else?"

I scrounged around in my head. Julie. "Somebody I used to work with."

"Why tell me?"

Because you have a face like a wishing well. I didn't say that. "My cheeks are as cold as Popsicles, Xavi. Are yours?"

"Why me?"

"I trust you, I guess. You're nice."

"I know."

"Let's hang our faces until they freeze," I said. "Then come in, and the air in the room will feel like needles hitting our skin."

"Have you ever heard of sadomasochism? We are bringing our choc-olate faces in now." I liked that about her, that she only went so far. We felt prickles anyway. We lay on her bed, side by side, and rubbed our faces.

"Now my body's getting cold," I said.

"The cold has to go somewhere." She threw her leg across mine and I bumped it off and she bumped it back and we rubbed the outside of our calves, my left one, her right one, together.

"I feel your stubble," I said.

"And you don't have any. Your legs are so smooth."

"I'm the hairless wonder."

"You never grow hair on your legs?"

"Never. Look at my arms."

She ran her hand up and down my arm, then over my fingers.

"You're hairless. That's unusual for somebody with so much hair on the head."

We were silent for a while. I felt the hairs on her leg brush my leg each time she inhaled. "This is like sex."

"I know. But it's not."

"I know. But it's like it. I'm feeling the tingles."

"I think we're close enough for me to tell you my secret."

I held my breath.

"It's shameful," Xavi whispered.

I couldn't believe it. I was lying in bed with a lesbian. A colored lesbian. I blurted, "You're a lesbian?"

Like the corpse in a Hollywood movie that lies in the coffin one moment and pops up wide-eyed the next, Xavi sprung to sitting position.

"No. Not on your life."

What could be more secret than that? I thought.

She turned to me with this ultraserious look. "It's kind of shocking."

"You don't have to tell a secret to match mine," I said. "I consider my stuff a fact of life anyway, not a big dark secret."

But I wondered what hers was. It had to do with sex. *What else involved shame, secrecy, and shock?*

"I had a baby two summers ago."

"You're a mother?" I was shocked shitless. Xavi kept on like she was purging.

"I wasn't showing during the semester. I had it at a home for unwed mothers, but everybody found out anyway. I felt like an outcast."

The way she said *it* made me shiver. "How did people find out if you gave birth during summer?"

"They found out when I was pledging. I was the laughingstock of the whole school. And my mother had me go through pledging knowing everybody had found it out. The big sisters treated me like poop, on top of the pledging crap."

"But how did they find out?" Xavi was talking to her mother, not me.

"My mother said, 'You're not the first pledge with a baby off somewhere. . . . There's no record of this, no birth certificate, no proof.' I was going to be a soror if she had to shake up the Supreme Court. The social worker at the home told my mother I needed counseling at school, because I gave it away."

"Oh, that's sad. You had to give your baby away?" She nodded.

"I couldn't keep it and I couldn't give it up. It was a struggle."

"So what happened?"

"I let them take the baby. My mother wrote the dean of girls a letter and sent me a copy. It was all strictly confidential. But it got out. The big sisters found out."

"Secretaries read mail. I read confidential stuff in Admissions every day."

"I know. That's what I told my mother. She said the dean called and said it wouldn't go on my record." Xavi went to the bathroom but didn't shut the door.

"So now you're an AKA, and you're not a mother, and it's all cool?"

"I never went to another sorority function. And I pray for my baby girl every night."

A girl. Xavi came back in the room drying her hands. "She looked like me. A replica."

"Babies change, you know?"

"All I know is those first two weeks."

....

A few days later we caught a bus to the old opera house in Bayview Hunters Point. Sisters on campus had organized a community black-is-beautiful program. When we walked in, I saw what the deal was right away: an African emporium. Money changing hands. Business. An African boutique owner had display tables full of material, African cloth for your body and head, baskets overflowing with fabulous amber beads, shell necklaces, cowrie shells, African wood carvings, drums, stools, tin masks, delicate earrings and bracelets from horsehair. People were buying left and right. Xavi bought a pair of earrings that looked like elongated drums and went to put them on in the bathroom. The sister who seemed in charge came over and asked me my name. After we got acquainted—her name was Li-an—she asked if I wanted to be in the show that night.

"Um, what do I have to do?" I thought I'd have to buy something.

"Just show up," she said.

"When?"

"Tonight. Seven. Show starts at eight. We have to rehearse, mainly the order we come in."

"Rehearse what?"

"You pick an African wrap from the sellers and a record you dance to."

"Dance?"

"Yeah, each sister comes in like this." She handed me her clipboard and then twirled around, popping her fingers and dancing. When she turned she cocked her head, more friendly than conceited. She walked to a table and put on a record. Bo Diddley's nasal voice and guitar-twanging backbeat filled the room. Xavi was buying material for an African gele head wrap, the earrings swinging already from her lobes, her hair, in spite of the Tide, more beatnik than anything else.

I tried my turn, knowing I wasn't brave until the dance floor was full and I got ideas. I was better at running my mouth, but the backbeat, twanging to the rafters, made me try.

"You're all right," Li-an said. "Come on, all we need is one more person."

"Okay, but what about my friend?" I motioned to Xavi to come over.

Li-an added my name to the bottom of a list, telling me I was the last one. Her complexion was ruby brown, different from all the other shades of brown I had become expert at categorizing. Each of us was a wholly different shade of brown, and a different style of natural hair.

When I told Xavi about the show, as I expected, she said, "I want to do it, too."

Li-an went to change the music.

"You can take my place. I'm not that good a dancer."

"Be for real," Xavi said.

"I don't want to be in front of an audience. Somebody else can floor-show while I check out the spotlight. Take my place, please."

"Only if you're sure," Xavi said, beaming.

We walked over to the turntable and I asked the person who was holding the clipboard list with my name to substitute Xavi's.

She shook her head. "She can't be in it. She has straight hair."

"What's the deal?" I popped back. Xavi looked like she had been shunned. "Are you for real?"

"This is for sisters," she said, finished with the matter, and walked off.

My natural glare yanked at its leash. "This is not happening," I said, looking around for Li-an.

"It's all right. I don't want to bogart," Xavi said.

"Oh, I'll be queen bogart," I said. "This don't sound very African. More like bringing out the nigger in me."

I spotted Li-an, who was coming toward us with the sister clutching the clipboard in her hand.

"What's your name?" Li-an said to Xavi.

Xavi spelled her full name, then said, "It comes from Xavier."

"Are you a student at State?"

Xavi nodded, her eyes working like wheels.

"What's with this she's-not-a-sister stuff?" I asked.

"I'm sorry, that keeps coming up," Li-an said. "This started out as a natural show, so everybody could see all the ways sisters are getting the natural hairdo. And then, you know, it just grew."

My leash started to slacken. Li-an kept on. "Initially somebody thought only sisters with naturals should be in it. No sisters who wear their hair straight."

"This is her natural, as natural as she can get it. We even tried Tide," I said.

"Really?" the sister with the clipboard said, looking at Xavi's hair the way I did the first time I saw it cut.

At the show, Li-an put Xavi, the African wraps, and "Hey Bo Diddley" together. While Xavi strutted, Li-an whispered, "I need a roomie to split my rent. Half of $125. Know anyone?"

29

Li-an had found a large high-ceilinged studio in the Fillmore. My half came to seventy-eight dollars for everything including utilities, a bargain even after paying forty-eight dollars for tuition. When Li-an said she would need my help to sneak out of her parents' house, it was still a bargain. I helped her sneak out of her house in the Bayview District. I had moved out at eighteen on the nose with Uncle Boy-Boy's help. No one had been delirious that I was shoving off into my brave new world, but no one begged me to stay either. In contrast, Li-an was afraid her parents would get the police in Bayview to issue an all-points bulletin for her.

When we got to her house in the Bayview section and went up to her bedroom, it took us three hours to pack her clothes, unicorns, books, stereo, her Catholic school cheerleader outfit, memorabilia. Three hours. When we got ready to go, her bedroom looked bereft. She left behind hot combs and straightening combs all over the kitchen, bathroom, and bedroom.

Every hill we drove down, her overloaded suitcases hit my head. The suitcase we'd placed on top of her boxes felt like it was loaded with cement. When we drove level, I'd get a break and feel the pounding. I kept driving getting my head bashed because I was wondering how it felt to be so missed that your parents would hunt you down like Jesse James. I stopped the car and made her open the top suitcase. It was full of shoes. If I had to get beaten up by a piece of Samsonite, at least it didn't have to be violently overloaded.

When we stopped at Hayes and Scott to readjust the suitcase, an older black woman stopped her car. It looked like she had double-parked to run an errand, but she stopped to get our attention. She rolled her window down.

"You girls a sight to see," she said, leaning out. "Those African hair-dos are very becoming."

We profiled so she could see us from the side. She asked how long we'd been wearing our hair in Afros. A year for me, three months for Li-an.

"I can't take this wig hat off my head. I'm too old. Like walking round with no clothes on," she shouted. Cars honked; she ignored them. "It do me a world of good to see you young ladies. In my day, this was impossible.

"I'm just as proud as if I got my hair cut that way." She waved fingers swollen with arthritis and drove off.

....

Wish Woodie was standing outside the apartment building looking out of place when we drove up. I introduced them. Li-an started carrying stuff up.

"Here." He gave me a pair of silver earrings. "I made them."

"Wish, they give off sparkles. I love them." I put them on and began to help him unload the Bug. Wish lugged Li-an's boxes up in forty minutes. We were cooling off with soda on boxes. I had taken the earrings off and couldn't find them. I went into the bathroom, where Li-an had been putting up toiletries. She had the earrings up to her face. She put them on and looked in the mirror.

"They look so hip and he's so not hip."

"But he's a good guy."

"Well, I'm going to class and then hanging out." She dangled them from her head.

"You mean you want to wear them now?"

"Please, Gigi." She had nicknamed me already.

I let her wear them. She was off to her class before I could think twice.

....

Wish pulled out a big joint and we lay there, tripping off each other, happy to be high and together. I heard a bird crowing outside.

"Wish, remember when we went to Stimson Beach, and the cock was crowing?"

"Yeah, it's Stinson."

"What's the diff?"

"You sound ignorant if you say Stimson."

"I am ignorant." We lit up and rested on the mattress on the floor surrounded by boxes.

"Put back on the earrings."

I hesitated. "I let Li-an wear them."

"You what?"

"She begged me. I couldn't refuse."

"Geniece, I made them for you. You can't appreciate that?" I didn't appreciate them. In all the moving, I was losing my attachment to stuff.

30

All Li-an and I did was walk outside and people stared and complimented us, even if we didn't have on makeup or earrings. Li-an had a sexy walk and big sloe eyes. I didn't know if it was the naturals or the two of us together, but we attracted attention just going for a walk. Li-an and I one night went outside to the store about 2:00 A.M. Three doors down we saw a green velvet club chair partially covered by a drop cloth. Someone had set it outside a flat being painted. We eyed it the same way; it matched the green sateen drapes from Li-an's bedroom at her parents'.

"If it's here when we get back, it's ours," I told her.

When we got back, we carried it inside, leaving the drop cloth. We didn't think twice about how heavy it was. Just not being caught was enough.

It became our first piece of furniture, and we took turns sitting in it. Li-an said, "That's the first thing I've ever stolen. I can't believe it."

"Not even a piece of candy?"

"Nothing."

"When I first moved out I was broke all the time." Getting paid once a month meant macaroni and Campbell's cheddar cheese soup, a fifty-cent meal that lasted three days. "This one time, I ran out of salt."

"Oh, bad luck."

"At work, I went in the lunchroom on Friday at 4:15, when it was empty, so I could pour salt into a paper bag. That way I could make macky cheese."

She screamed, "You call it that too."

"I was pouring away when the blind guy who did transcribing came in, whistling and poking with his stick; I thought, *Oh no, I can't live the weekend without salt*; I could tell he sensed somebody; he caught me off guard; I wondered if he could smell me or hear me breathing; I stopped pouring; he moved his cane around; I started pouring again; when he heard the pouring sound, he stopped in his tracks and listened to the salt crystals flowing; the look on his face was befuddlement; he couldn't figure it out and I wasn't about to tell him; he left, but not before trying his darndest to figure that sound."

"Geniece, you have no pity."

"My stomach had no pity."

....

We fooled around at night on Haight Street, at the club, the Haight Levels, laughing at hippies getting zonked. We couldn't have been there a month when some guys from the neighborhood started throwing bottles through shopwindows. The cops came, and the boys began taunting them, cat and mouse. We waited to see the boys carted off in a paddy wagon. Then, like out of nowhere, reinforcements appeared, and the street was ringed with SFPD; the police started rushing everybody, the boys, the onlookers. They looked frightening, so bulky torsoed, coming at me, the nightsticks hanging from their waists like long black penises. My body froze. In my head I heard, *I'm wearing a minidress to a miniriot.* Li-an pushed me in the direction of the Panhandle.

"Run, Geniece."

"I can't run fast."

"Run, Gigi, run," she said, and I ran fast. She shouted, "Zigzag, Gigi, zigzag," to get me to break the straight line of fire. But the police fired tear-gas canisters. The crowd dispersed. Li-an and I ran for several blocks before we felt safe enough to slow down.

I felt the same after the riot as I did when I took the VW for its first checkup.

First car from my first real boyfriend, first servicing—I treated myself to a movie, *Bonnie and Clyde.* From the posters outside the Shattuck Cinema in Berkeley, I thought it was a Ma-and-Pa-Kettle type of movie, the kind I used to see on Sundays with my cousins for a quarter and three bottle caps. I should have known from the shoot-outs how it was going to end. I chomped away on popcorn, still not expecting what happened: just purely bullets after bullets after bullets, rounds upon rounds upon rounds, bodies falling everywhere every kind of way— and then dead quiet.

I started crying. *I can die. I can actually die if I keep going this way.* I don't know if I was sobbing. I think I was. I rushed out of the theater and forgot I had a car. My thoughts hovered over the bodies of Bonnie and Clyde spilling out of old-timey cars. I felt the same walking home with Li-an from the riot. *I can die if I keep going this way.* Bonnie and Clyde went out like swatted mosquitoes on the screen. People in Detroit and LA died in the riots. *Could that happen to me? How could it possibly happen to me?* But my curious heart was stronger than any sense of fear or caution.

31

A week later I was excited about attending my first tutorial program meeting. Tutoring primary-grade students off campus would fulfill some Experimental College units. I wanted to meet the program director, whose bearded face was plastered on Freedom Rider posters used to recruit tutors on campus. An Eyewitness News truck was blocking my shortcut to the streetcar. I didn't even bother to find out why. TV and newspaper people were there every other day. Students whooshed past. I didn't want to be late but couldn't avoid the commotion. Next to a poster proclaiming the Sexual Freedom League, a white guy was taking his clothes off in the Commons, as fast as if he was taking a shower. The late-morning chill from Lake Merced had me with a thick sweater on; I felt cold for him. But it was hard to look away from public nudity. Someone yelled, "You need a tan," and someone else said, "Horny Horny." The crowd started chanting and laughing; even students from the top floor of the library were chanting. I felt like the fly on the wall taking it in, but darn, my meeting was calling me. This was my first day at the Tutorial Center in Potrero Hill.

I grabbed a tuna sandwich from the lunch truck to eat on the way to the meeting. Waiting for the M streetcar, I could see the hullabaloo and felt superior to it. I was going to meet with the program director, a man who had been a Freedom Rider, for heaven's sake. Public nudity was frivolous, civil rights profound; the difference was clear. The BSU and the BPP occupied the radical end of the civil rights spectrum, the weighty end.

The sun was breaking out of the clouds over the Hayes Valley District where the program director lived. At the foot of the open door to his flat, boots, leather sandals, platforms, moccasins, and a pair of pilgrim pumps rested. Ahead of me, a guy wearing a tie-dyed tunic and bell-bottoms walked inside the living room and started reading a book. About ten minutes before the meeting was to start, a young white woman walked out of the back and started opening the curtains and blinds. She stretched as if waking and acknowledged us silently, nude as a baby except for a beaded necklace. The director, a spitting image of Che Guevara, came in, naked to the waist. Oblivious to us, they kissed, a postcoital, satisfied smacker, and went in the back. A few minutes later, he started the meeting, and she left the house in a patchwork skirt and a peasant blouse, as quietly as she had stood nude before the two of us early arrivals. As the director introduced himself and the program goals, I drew mental lines between the deep justice, civil rights freedom fighters, the shallow, sexual freedom, barefaced nudity in front of a raucous crowd, and a nude embrace in front of the afternoon sun and strangers. But the lines kept blurring. Individual freedom and hippies and Black Panthers and Blackness with a capital B and Robert Williams and armed struggle and Martin Luther King Jr., and Bull Connor's hoses and snarling dogs and tie-dyed clothes and African art and Aretha Franklin and lava lamps and bell-bottoms, miniskirts, and Fillmore West—it all began to merge. I was beginning to suspend categorization. I couldn't cross people and incidents off the list as casually as I had done before. Right and wrong, good and evil, those categories couldn't hold a candle with what was compelling, educational, eye opening. My eyes were being propped open, wider every day in San Francisco. Sometimes every hour.

32

Tourists came to San Francisco to see panoramic Nob Hill, not Potrero Hill, the site of my tutorial assignment. Nob Hill meant wealth, flamboyance, masked balls, high society, and high rents. Potrero Hill, in southeast San Francisco, contained the projects, the sewage treatment plant, distilleries, factories, warehouses, high infant mortality rates, and my work-study job.

Work-study was a twofer. I could get academic credit through the Experimental College and get paid two dollars an hour. EC 199 was a community service sociology practicum that involved tutoring inner-city kids. The day after the tutorial meeting, I made my way to Army Street on Potrero Hill, down into a basement, which looked dark from outside. The sunlight in the Potrero Hill classroom exposed a collection of empty food boxes and packages. The bright containers played background to a familiar figure standing, one foot in a chair, and three children, black, young, each desperately trying to get his attention, screaming, "Grits . . . grits . . . can't you hear me? . . . call me, it's grits."

"All right, all right, so you know it's grits. Grrrrrrits. Now, how do you spell it." His upper lip trembled and made his mustache shake ferociously as he sounded it out, holding an empty package of hominy grits. I recognized him.

"You look like a bulldog, Bibo." A skinny girl made the other kids laugh.

"Yeah, and the bulldog wants to know, How do you spell grits? Up to the board, Tammy." He extended chalk to the skinny girl with cat eyes and a lone pigtail shooting off the side of her head.

"I know it but I can't spell it," she said, walking to the board.

"Write it, Tammy, just like you see it on the package."

The other kids egged her on. "Go on, Tammy. . . . You know you bad. . . . Spell it, fox. . . . Grrrrrrits . . . spell it with your bad self."

"You eat grits, don't you?" He handed her a longer piece of chalk. "Find me the letter G. Just find me a G, nothing else."

She studied the box and pointed to the G in GRITS on the bright label.

"Miss Fox, Miss Tammy Fox, Miss Stone Cold Fox, you found your G. Now write it," he said.

Screeching the chalk against the blackboard, she wrote a crooked G and gave a dainty smile to Bibo, and a wicked one to a bigger girl behind him.

"Tammy think she done something writing G," the bigger girl said. "Betcha can't spell the rest, Tammy. You so dumb for eight years old."

"I can spell it. Just watch me, Yvette." Tammy looked at the box Bibo held steady and found the G again. She squinted as she sounded out the letters. When she finished, she said to the other girl, "Now!"

"You got, it, little sister. Now write it on the board just like you spelled it." He thumped the board with his knuckles. "Right here on this BLACKboard, dig."

She wrote it slowly, screeching the chalk with every letter.

"Let's dance. Let's listen to records now, Bibo," the older girl spoke in a bored-stiff voice.

"I want my snack," a boy next to her said. "All that screeching made me thirsty." He got up, stretched, and looking in my direction, asked, "What fruit do we got today?"

Bibo pointed me to an open door, putting the empty boxes and packages in order. "In the back room, back there."

"Oranges," I answered when I spotted the crate.

"The first one to spell orange backward gets three instead of two," Bibo said as I put the crate down.

The older girl reeled off the letters before he finished his sentence. "I'm almost eleven. This is baby stuff."

"I finally made Yvette do something," he laughed. He had laughed the same way when he called me quaint at the Black House. I passed out oranges and gave him my work-study slip, which he studied intently.

"What? Does it look counterfeit?"

"I was just trying to think where I had seen the name."

"We met at the Black House." Brother for Real, don't hop off Cool City express and land in Phony Town. "Don't act like you don't know me. The Black House, uh-huh?"

"Yeah," he rubbed his chin. "Allwood's sister, right?"

I shook my head. "I'm a sister, period."

All the oranges were gone in a few minutes.

"Dig, little warriors." Bibo stood erect, his full figure commanding attention. "This place is ours, and we are responsible for keeping it clean. We will take pride in our surroundings, because that indicates pride in ourselves. Everybody picks up their peelings and puts them in the trash can."

The boy threw a peeling at Tammy that twisted around her ponytail like a bright orange ribbon.

"Mufucka, don't be throwing no shit at me." She grabbed the peeling and threw it on the floor.

"Hey, hey," said Bibo. "Is that the way a black princess talks to her black brother?"

"I ain't black. You darker than me." She pushed out her bottom lip at him. "My mama told me ain't nobody black and ain't nobody white. Now!"

"Bibo." I bent beside Tammy to pick up the peeling. "Maybe the little brother should apologize, since he started it."

"All right. Chester, tell Tammy you're sorry." Bibo put his hand on the back of the striped T-shirt Chester was wearing.

The other kids ate their oranges slowly, section by section, looking for a showdown.

"I ain't telling her nothing." Chester was unfazed. "Our teacher at school don't do nothing when I hit Tammy. I wish it woulda hit her in her squinchy eyes."

"Don't make fun of my sister. Want me to knock the stripes off your shirt?" Yvette stepped up to him.

"Hey, you guys are acting like a bunch of Negroes. A bunch of people who hate each other." All eyes went to Bibo.

"How come you always say that?" Yvette demanded. "There's nothing wrong with Negro."

"Negro is a color, not a people. All of us in this room," he gestured, "are black people. That's a word we can use when we need to call ourselves by one name. It means we're not ashamed anymore. We are the darkest people in the entire world, and we're proud of what we are."

"Yvette not dark. She light," Tammy spoke up. "Yvette daddy white, huh, Yvette? You got good hair, huh."

Bibo sat on the edge of a chair and continued, "Probably everybody in this room has some white blood in them."

They all grimaced and made ugly faces. He kept on.

"But it doesn't make any difference. Let's do an experiment. Everybody put your hands in your hair. Feel it. Is it straight? Nappy? Now take your fingers and feel someone else's hair. Let's feel Geniece's hair."

Everyone put their hands in my natural. "Your hair pretty. . . . How come you don't press it? . . . I like the way it feel? . . . Your hair nappy all over. . . . Why we doing this?"

"Now!" Bibo said. "Pull her hair. That's right, pull it hard. Hurt her."

Tammy yanked it the hardest.

"Ouch, Tammy, give me some slack."

Everyone pulled it, looking in my face to see how much it hurt. Even though it hurt, it didn't hurt. It felt good that they were learning from my hard bushy head.

"Now, let's do that to everyone. Feel it and then pull it, me next." Bibo put his head down. The kids were amazed at their power to hurt us. They took turns feeling, pulling, hurting, and being hurt, laughing. Bibo ended the experiment when Chester tried to pull Tammy's twice.

"See, no matter how nappy or straight, nobody's hair protects them from hurt. We're the same no matter who's a little black or a lot black, right?"

They nodded, and I nodded with them.

"It's time to go." Yvette ran out of the basement. "I got the front seat."

"Last one is a Negro," Tammy giggled.

"You might as well go along for the ride." Bibo emptied orange peels into a large garbage can outside the front door. "Work-study. You know you'll end up working more than fifteen hours a week. If it's cool with you, it's cool with me."

In an old station wagon, he drove the kids to the yellowing, brown-trimmed projects on Potrero Hill and saw Chester to a doorway, where he disappeared. The girls went to another building. Bibo hollered out, "Missus Moore!" and a woman came and ushered them inside, waving at Bibo.

"That's the girls' mother. I make sure I see them in, because sometimes she's drunk."

We got back in and Bibo started in the direction of the Fillmore, steering with one hand, pulling the hairs of his mustache with his free hand.

"You think you fine, don't you?" he said. "You think being fine protects you, don't you? It only arms you with a weapon for the time, California girl."

"You say that like you're from someplace else."

"We're all from someplace else."

"I'm a native of Berkeley, baby."

"Nah, you're a native. Period." He laughed. I kept dumping my naïveté, and it kept following me.

"I can read your mind. You trying to decide which man'll be your teacher."

"Nothing could be further from my mind. I'm a student of the planet."

"Nah, you trying to make up your mind as far as who to learn from—the intellectual, the hustlers, or the petty thieves. It's all over your face. And your body."

"Aren't you a hustler?"

"And an intellectual. Don't leave me out of that category."

"Oh? I didn't want to insult you."

"You had Allwood. He broke you in."

"Pullease."

"We thank you, Mr. Allwood. But the good brother's gone, so I understand, and here you are back in the forest with the wolves. And it's getting dark, baby cakes. The wolves is starting to howl, hungry for fresh meat. Present company excluded."

"Oh really?"

"I have a queen at home raising my sons. So they don't have to be tutored by strangers. I would never do anything to mess that up. I'm not a wolf. I'm a disabled vet."

"Vietnam?"

He nodded. "'Nam taught me everything I know."

He pulled at his mustache. "Red Riding Hood, I'm your new guide."

"So you just want to be my protector?"

"We're going to perform an experiment," he said, steering the wagon through the city, past the tall buildings, to the edge of the industrial nub of the city, just blocks from the transbay bus terminal.

"You with me all the way?" His voice matched the dusky light of the street lamps.

I couldn't answer. I had no clue other than having seen him at the Black House where everything was new, intriguing, and dangerously different.

He parked the wagon. We kissed, but it was not romantic, more exploration and curiosity, at least on my part. "Take off your jacket, and pull your belt as tight as you can."

I did. He opened my door and we walked down the street.

"Now, just stand here and, uh, yeah, that's right, you got it; we gonna make us some money tonight."

I threw my head back. Bibo waited in a darkened doorway, silently. A man in a suit with a face that matched the used concrete came down the street. My scent reached him. He slowed. Smiled at me. Stopped. Bibo's knuckles rippled across his chin. He slumped. Bibo found his wallet. Emptied it. Threw it in the gutter. I peed on myself. My father, as big as the bridges adjoining the city, gazed at my hands holding the filthy lucre. *There's not a thief in this family.* I had taken money that didn't belong to me. And I didn't feel guilty, even with his eyes piercing the night sky of my mind. I had ceased being a spectator. I could feel my naïveté sloughing off like snakeskin.

33

Outside of the Admissions Office I noticed a flyer about accelerated matriculation. I thought it might be one more way to help me graduate. I caught the end of the meeting at the Ecumenical Center across the street from the campus. Several guys from the Black Student Union were listening to a short brother in the uniform—SNCC overalls with the deep cuffs and chambray shirt. The cuffs looked a little ridiculous with his height.

"We need more black students admitted to State. These are the last days of this corrupt white world and its hold on people of color," he said. "We're fighting racism, fascism, and imperialism."

I couldn't keep quiet. "Do you know about the two percent rule?" He looked at me like I was high or something.

"Sister, I was on the Freedom Rides." That was supposed to shut me up, like who was I to interrupt a student who had come back from the dead and politicized the whole campus.

"Yeah, and I could be wasting my time playing cards in the cafeteria. But I'm here instead." I wasn't going to be cowed by him, even if he pulled movement rank.

"Oh yeah. Ever been chased down a country road by some shotgun crackers who whipped a cattle prod on your black ass? That's why I'm here."

"I work in Admissions," I said. "Two percent of the total enrollment has to be set aside for applicants who need preferential treatment. I've seen it in action for Dumb Debs and jocks."

He looked at me like I had discovered uranium. I went on. "And no way do they have the grades to get in."

"That's one of the key tasks sisters with skills can take care of—getting information from the man and passing it to the people," he said.

Another brother said, "I suggest we try for forty students through special admit."

I said, "Two percent of 18,000 equals 360, not 40."

They all just sat there for a minute. I said, "Why not round it up to four hundred?"

One of the brothers said, "What it is, what it ain't, what it oughta be." I had to go to class. I left as they were making open admissions for four hundred students a part of a letter to the president of the college.

....

The streetcar was so crowded late that afternoon I found myself pushed up against some doofus white boy from Lowell, the public preppie high school near State. I was looking out the window at the St. Francis Woods mansions, the rumbling of the streetcar wheels vibrating my nipples when the brother who had chaired the meeting approached me.

"Chandro-Imi, what it is," his voice low and cool even with the din. "Your suggestion was very important."

"Oh yeah? I didn't think it was that big a deal."

"You got skills, like the sisters in SNCC." He was cool, with his briefcase between his feet. "I like sisters with moxie."

"Moxie? Like balls between my legs?"

"SNCC sisters teach literacy for voter registration, run the offices, deal with the press, take good care of brothers, and—" He paused for emphasis.

"And they shine your shoes too, right?" I said rolling my eyes. Him being a Rider impressed me big-time. But he wasn't going to lord it over me, like I was a sister-in-training.

"And," he continued with a half smile, "they do all this because they know these are the last days."

"As in the Last Days of Pompeii?"

"Yeah, only niggahs is Vesuvius." He combined street with smart. I saw why he chaired the meeting. We'd gone through the Twin Peaks tunnel and come out at Market and Castro, with the Bank of America building rising angled out of the concrete sidewalk. I liked seeing it there every time I came out of the tunnel.

"Yeah. These are the white man's last days. The bourgies' last days too." He let go of the strap.

"Hey," he said, talking with his hands free. "It's over."

I didn't want any of these things new to me to be over. But I nodded.

"Soon as I saw that you didn't waste your time playing nigger bridge, I knew you were a together sister," he said. So he had been checking me out. I neglected to tell him I didn't play bid whist because I wasn't good at it. When I got off at DuBoce, I had company.

"Chandro-Imi. The name is Chandro-Imi. Rhymes with creamy."

"Oh, not Imi as in gimme," I chucked back.

"You definitely have edge," he said.

Is this about dick? I wondered. When we got to Divisadero, he turned to cross against the light. I thought, *Well, that's that. I'm not interested anyway. He'd probably try to tell me how to wipe my ass.* And he was short.

"You need to join Black Care."

"What's that?" He moved away. I felt pulled in the same direction but resisted.

"The women's auxiliary to the BPP of Northern California."

"Women's auxiliary? Like a Sistahs Junior League? Spare me," I said.

"Don't close your mind so quick. We're talking about a violent revolution getting ready to go down. Sisters have to be prepared to take care of the brothers who get wounded."

"I'm not Florence Nightingale."

"I got something else for you to do then." He stepped off the curb.

"What?" I felt anxious for him in traffic even though no cars were coming.

"Something you'd like." He motioned his head toward the apartment building we had come to.

"Do I have to go up to your place to see it?"

"I'm not trying to hit on you. Hey, if that was the case, I'd be a lot more straightforward. I'm a simple man."

"I don't know about you being simple," I said. "That's not the first thing that comes to mind."

"What does?"

"The cattle prods, for one thing."

"Are you impressed?"

"Isn't that why you tell people?"

"What is this? A game to you?"

"Are we walking somewhere specific?" I countered. He pointed to the building across the street.

"My pad."

I crossed Divisadero. Even though I was following him, I felt like Sacagawea, the Shoshone leading Lewis and Clark across the Rocky Mountains. I felt determined, strong, in control, as if I was taking a test I had studied hard for. We went into his building; he walked bow-legged, like a cowboy. He turned around and caught me sizing him.

"You walk like you have a Stetson on your head," I said.

"Bet you didn't know I'm originally from Texas," he said. "Beaumont." Upstairs, his floors were shined and clean.

"Where's Beaumont?" I asked, passing a bedroom with an iron bed-stead.

"Way back in the past." He walked to a mirror at the end of the hall. "Come here." I stood next to a chest he began rummaging through until he pulled out a sheaf of papers.

He looked at me in the mirror, then at himself. "To get rid of my Southern accent, I stood in front of the mirror when I was fourteen and repeated what I heard on TV."

"TV?"

"Yeah. Everything came from LA except for local programs. I said everything the way I heard it."

"I think Southern accents are beautiful. All the men on my father's side have deep Southern accents." A black cat purred and walked down the hall. He stroked it.

"But you don't," he said. "Your voice stands out."

"Strong lungs."

"I want you to check these out." He handed me the sheaf of papers. "These poems by a sister from LA named Mali are cold."

"I saw her in the Gallery Lounge. She's bad."

"As bad as it gets. She's gonna be as bad as LeRoi." He handed me a stack. "She's calling them *Urban Prescriptive*. I want you to read them."

"And do a book report?" I felt relieved that he wasn't hitting on me, at least not directly.

"Read. In front of a microphone and a crowd. Like tomorrow at school."

"Are you serious?"

"Dead on." That was all he wanted. I walked home, reading the poems out loud against traffic and honking horns. I had recited Rudyard Kipling and Robert Frost in junior high. But these poems were about black people loving and being together, fighting the system. In front of the medicine cabinet mirror, I read out loud. In bed, I read them out loud. I woke up in the middle of the night to read them out loud.

When I got up in the Poetry Center at school the next day to read, I knew I looked odd, with my double-breasted peacoat buttoned up. I had perspired so much I didn't want to raise my arms by mistake. I missed the first part of the program because I had a test in Psych. 151: Abnormal Psych: Minor Variations. Mali's phrases kept going through my head instead of the minor variations. As I approached the podium, Chandro-Imi said, "one of the baddest poets out there." While I read, I tripped on how it would feel if he had said that about me. Everybody perked up, as if Mali's words were crushed ice hitting their faces. I took off the peacoat, because I was burning up. When I was done, the whole place clapped. I was a phantom falling gently out of anonymity.

I walked away glowing.

34

The next week, I read again in the Gallery Lounge, and Chandro-Imi started having me read, at different events, poems that Mali mailed him from LA. He also had his eye on Li-an. After I read, a guy approached me and introduced himself—Dillard. He was older, spare, not dressed in desi boots, khakis.

"Ali doesn't have squat on you. I can't get your voice reading poetry out of my head. It trips me out." He was blasé instead of euphoric over Ali's victory over Ernie Terrell. He wore slacks, musk. Something about him was unconcealed, though I didn't know what it was.

"I liked the *never* poem. Liked you reading it."

"Want me to read it for you right now?"

"You got it memorized?"

"After a few times, it's like the Pledge of Allegiance."

He looked at his watch. "I have to make a run off campus. Keep me company?"

I looked at my watch even though I knew I was going with him. We got in a red '64 Karmann Ghia and drove out of the parking lot and over to Stonestown mall. He went into the post office and mailed a package he'd had on the floor of his car. I recited the poem as he drove back. It sounded entirely different.

you never existed
you never knew truth
you never made history
you never created wonders
you never built a pyramid
you never knew mythology
you never constructed temples
you never took part in civilization

you never conceived philosophies
you never carried your weight
you never were Egyptian
you never were a master
you never even existed
you never prospered
you never conquered
you never were
you never are
you never will
under
stand?

We parked in the same spot; he asked me to say it again while he got high; taking whiffs between stanzas, I said it a second time, swifter; I thought he was going to pull out another joint, for laughs; but he pulled out a bag of white powder; he asked me to take off his horn-rims and hold them; he used a tiny spoon to dip into the powder; he sniffed at the powder and ran it along his gums like snuff; he told me to sniff it too; I said, I hate stuff going up my nose; he said, I'll put it on your gums then; he put it along my gums like snuff; it felt like Novocaine; we started kissing; I was surprised that it was the middle of the day and the parking lot; we finished kissing as if a bell had gone off; we walked back to school; he asked me out; I asked him if the powder was cocaine; he started to laugh; I asked him, How often do you do it?; he said, as often as I want, baby; I gave him a fake number.

I thought not joining a sorority meant I was immune to rituals I didn't believe in. But I kept getting myself snared in initiation rites, even right up under my nose.

35

One ritual I did love: Li-an, Xavi, and me at Xavi's studio late in the day making monster spaghetti and getting bombed. I loved going over Xavi's hashing out why insanity was insane. We pulled up the lines guys were giving us: "Forget every nigger who's ever gotten next to you, baby. They were preparation for the main course." "You will never ever forget me, no matter what." "Is this shit deep enough for your fine black ass? Huh?" Li-an dispensed passion to brothers. She had enough passion to fuel each train that stopped, each puffing locomotive. I envied her, the jubilance she produced when each one came and went, greased by her firm buttocks. *She gitsta fuck i gitsa think about it.* I heard her wide heart fuel their hard cylinders.

"How come they all say the same stuff? Why do they talk so much shit?" Xavi asked.

"Don't they realize some things need to be forgotten?" Li-an said, pointing to the front window. "Like hippie dippies," she said with disgust.

From time to time, hippies walked by. A couple of longhairs stopped to talk about scoring loud enough for us to hear.

"When their money runs out," Li-an said, "they head straight for Western Union."

"Runaways," Xavi said. "They need to stay away."

"Here's Chandro-Imi, Mr. Cool." Li-an stood and gapped her legs, holding an imaginary dick. She made her voice masculine. "I gotta hold on or it might run away from me. Become a hippie dick."

"You can laugh, but Chandro-Imi never tried to get over on me," I said. "He told me I have an unusual voice. I think Chandro-Imi's for real."

Li-an had been stirring chopped olives into the pot but stopped and said, "He told me he liked my eyes. He called them his lighthouses."

"His?" I said.

"He didn't mean personally his. He meant for the people," Li-an said.

Xavi spoke. "He told me I had honest calves. Calves that could move mountains."

"Your calves? I don't believe it," I said. "Is this his come-on? 'I love your wide hip bones. They'll carry a heavy load one day.'"

"It may be corny, but at least he's not dogging around. I mean, did he come on to you, Li-an?" I asked. Li-an kept looking at the pot.

"Li-an," Xavi asked, "are those olives swimming in the spaghetti?"

I went over and moved her jaw from left to right. "Say it, Li-an. Say: 'No, the Negro has not got in my panties.'"

I couldn't make her head shake. Instead she nodded fast. We were stunned.

"How could you keep this a secret?" I said. She shrugged. "So every poem was his chance to get next to you. And I thought he had a purely platonic interest in us."

Li-an spoke. "He does. In you."

"All right, Pussy Galore. You'll pay for this."

Xavi and I took the pot holders and poured the spaghetti into a serving bowl. The steam hit our faces and we locked eyes, got the same thought, and started laughing so hard we had to sit down.

"What's so funny?" Li-an said. "Spaghetti?"

"Not hardly," Xavi said, getting forks and bowls out. "We heard you one night. That night we did our grocery shopping."

"Was he over when we came back?" I asked. Li-an nodded.

"Xavi came in," I said, "because she didn't feel like walking across Golden Gate Park by herself."

Xavi mumbled, "I hate to hear sex. I think I'd rather watch than have to listen." She began to imitate how they sounded.

"Do it, Geniece," she said. "You make the sound better than I can."

"I'm not making those crazy sounds," I said. But Xavi was right. I mimicked the high-pitched damsel-in-distress moans and Xavi pulled up the gruff manly moan, the huff and puff. "And I'll blow your house down," I bellowed, jumping up and down. Li-an didn't get offended. It was so ludicrous and we were loaded. We howled so that we didn't hear the knocking at the door.

Xavi opened the door to her landlady, a prim black woman who stood with a stern look. Xavi invited her in, a mistake; she might get a contact high. She refused, looking at us like we were hyenas. We were emitting little blips.

"Please quiet down. If I can hear you, people on the street must can hear you too." She turned to walk upstairs grumbling out loud for us to hear. "A shame. Young ladies carrying on like hooligans. And where are your young men?"

We calmed down and cleaned out the pot. Xavi looked at the clock, her polite way of saying it was time for us to go home.

When Li-an and I got back home later, I apologized. We were each in bed and our voices floated through our curtain.

"I'm sorry for embarrassing you," I offered.

"No big deal," she said. "I didn't know it sounded so funny."

"It didn't sound funny when we were hearing it. It felt awkward, like if we didn't tiptoe, you'd know we were there. But once we got outside, Xavi started making your sound like Little Red Riding Hood and I made his sounds like the wolf."

I started to fall off to sleep. "Chandro's a good man."

"Are you falling for him?"

"Fell."

"Have a happy landing."

36

We must have been asleep an hour when the bell started ringing off the wall. We woke up; I pressed the buzzer.

"Who is it?"

"Xavi. Let me in."

Xavi came up the stairs, stomping into our hall.

"What is your problem, negro, at this time of night?" I wanted nothing but sleep.

"My landlady kicked me out."

"What?!"

"The old battle-ax thinks we're a bunch of lesbians."

That woke us up. Fully.

"While we were in her crummy studio laughing our asses off, she thought we were having sex. 'Outrageous sex!' Her words exactly."

"That's utterly ridiculous. Does she not know the sound of fun? Is she that decrepit?" Li-an said.

"Maybe it's been so long since she's had fun or sex she forgot both," I said. Xavi's eyes were shiny with tears.

"She kicked me out. My stuff is on the street."

"How could she do that?" It took us a few minutes to dress and walk across the park. It was midnight, but this was the city. The oasis. Hippies, semihippies, dudes, girls walking dogs, a couple strolling. We were not alone.

Sure enough, on the street outside Xavi's building her clothes were strewn on hangers, along with her plants, magazines, bathroom articles, the pot we had eaten spaghetti out of, bowls and utensils, and, of all things, a stethoscope. A powerful energy had seized her landlady.

"I'm a vagrant," Xavi said, crying. "My life is spilled on the street. I've been evicted for something I didn't even do." She started bawling. People stopped and began picking through her things.

"Off-limits," I said. "Get away. This is not a party."

We sat there for a minute. I saw the landlady in the window looking at the three of us. Li-an gave her a dirty look back.

"Where's your key, Xavi?" Li-an said.

"I gave it to her," Xavi said.

"Why?" I asked.

"Because she told me to give it to her."

"And you paid her the rent on time?" I knew she had.

"This is not about money," she said. "Don't you see? She thinks we're an abomination. We have violated nature in her view."

Li-an and I looked at each other. We sighed.

"Come on," Li-an said. "Let's get what we can carry."

Xavi sighed. "How are you going to get everything?"

"We can't," I said. "Get the clothes. Leave the plants. The pots and pans. We have all that. Get your toothbrush."

"Lady," Li-an muttered, "you will pay for this one day."

I shouted up at her face in the window. "What goes around comes around."

We loaded our arms with clothes and belongings.

"We need a wagon," Xavi said, "a little red wagon." She pointed to her stacks of *Glamour, Mademoiselle, Cosmopolitan.*

"How are we going to get those?"

Li-an and I were getting grumpy.

"Fuck the magazines. Let the hippies have them," I said. Li-an's arms were full. She started walking.

"So many good articles in them," Xavi said.

"Give the moo magazines a break," I said. "'How to Be an Intelligent Cow.' 'How to Tape Your Breasts So Your Nipples Won't Show.' 'Heifer Do's and Don'ts.'" I loaded her arms with toiletries.

"Is this yours?" I asked, picking up the stethoscope. She nodded. I plucked it up and hung it from my neck. I was too disgusted to ask her what she used it for, and frankly didn't care. I put her hats on her head and mine, one on top of another. We started walking away single file; I brought up the rear, Xavi the middle. We were silent, balancing, thinking, tired. Xavi turned to talk.

"Don't look back," I said.

Li-an began singing the Tempts' "Don't Look Back."

Xavi kept walking. "What we need is a beauty magazine for sisters."

"Brilliant idea, Xavi. 'How to Be a Chocolate Cow.' 'Moo-moo, I give chocolate milk,'" I said. We were crossing the park. Not that many people were around now.

"Why did she think we're lesbians?" Xavi said.

"Because we spent the day laughing," I said.

"Watch your step," Li-an called back.

"She thinks," I said, "that no ordinary black women would be together that long without bitching and crying over men."

We had traversed the park diagonally. The N streetcar came out of the tunnel headed for downtown. A dog that had been walking placidly with its master started barking at the streetcar.

"It's her loss," Li-an said.

"If she only knew what nice girls she's decided to shun," I said. The dog chose to run right in front of me. I kept my balance but the leash tripped me. When I fell, the hats tumbled, not making a sound. Li-an and Xavi kept on walking. They finally looked around for me.

I hollered, "Weren't you listening? Wasn't I part of the conversation? Did you even miss me?"

Li-an paused at the curb and said, "Geniece, just keep cool and stay on course."

37

I had been in awe of Li-an up to that point. Her half of the room was an infirmary, mine when I was there an observatory of sounds that floated through the curtain. It was like her specialty—sexual resuscitation. When the Panthers came to campus recruiting, just like Uncle Sam looking for recruits, Li-an decided we should sign up. To Panther or not.

"I'm signing. We all should. I got us applications." Li-an laid out mimeo sheets with the ten-point program listed above the signature spaces. No was not an option.

"I don't want to sign anything. My uncle told me, Don't sell my body, my country, or my soul."

Li-an aimed her load at me. "What's the difference between being a highly visible Black Student Union member, reading poetry at the Black House, and being a Black Panther? Your name's already on the list of subversives. What makes you think you aren't already a Panther?"

"I don't carry a gun and I don't wear a black beret." Damn if I joined the Panthers as a group act, like getting baptized in the YMCA pool when I was nine, rubbing chlorine out of my eyes with my cousins. "I have to think about it. They don't look like they're playing hopscotch."

I could hear Boy-Boy in the back of my head: *Niecy, you spent all this energy getting through Oakland City. It took you three years to finish your course work. For what? To become a full-fledged black militant that we see on the six o'clock news? You're going bass ackward.*

They joined. I didn't. But I started reading the *Black Panther Intercommunal News Service.* Nothing like the *Trib* or the *Chron* or what I learned in journalism classes and read in the *Gator* or *The Tower.* Even though I had decided against a journalism major, newspapers still entranced me. I wanted to know what was going on in the world, even if I had to ignore my distrust of so-called objective reporting. I wondered what objective meant when the front page, obits, society columns, ads reflected the World According to the White Man, black bodies in motion only on the sports pages. I'd watched Uncle Boy-Boy and Aunt Ola read the *Trib* front to back, even as they called old Knowland, the owner, a peckerwood. They always supplemented the World According to White Folks with the World of the Black Strivers—the *Post*, the *California Voice*, San Francisco's *Sun-Reporter*, the local versions of the *Pittsburgh Courier* and the *Chicago Daily Defender*. The more I delved into the BPP paper, the more it fascinated me. For the first time in newsprint, somebody else thought some of my thoughts. Out of curiosity, I read Huey's long pieces and Eldridge Cleaver's editorials in the BPP paper. I had read *Soul on Ice* when it first appeared in segments in *Ramparts*, and shuddered at the man/rapist philosophizing, but his editorials pulled me in:

> Later for all of the garbage of the white mother country, later for the mother country and everything in it. When we organize our own Third World institutions, then the honkies will get uptight because they won't be able to relate to what we are into. So let them go their white way and we will go ours—deep off into the beautiful world of Blackness.

And deeper off into the world of Blackness I went, following a trajectory that had begun with Allwood and Oakland City College. Militant. The word was frightful. I had come from being entertained by militants at Oakland City to resisting political indoctrination while falling in some kind of love with a militant to enrolling in a school full of so much militancy I couldn't blink without a rant in my face. Sure, I had fancied myself militant. That fit my naturally rebellious nature. But to *be* a militant was frightful. Yet intriguing.

38

I signed and joined the BPP because the party's indignation and cry for self-determination matched my own. It took me a while to see that. To feel that. When I did, I became a member and went through basic training: PE classes, weapon handling, setting up rallies at different colleges and schools, disseminating important position papers and quotes to the media outlets, both alternative and mainstream. I began seeing the world of the BPP in every utterance around me. It was like a torrent.

Eventually I became an editor at the BPP paper. I thought I'd renounced journalism with my disgust at the *Gator*, but like a persistent ex-lover it kept showing up at my doorstep looking for action. This is how we put out the BPP intercommunal news service: We got documents, position papers, and editorials from Huey, Bobby, Eldridge, who was the minister of information, or George Murray, the minister of education. George, who was a fellow student at State, had handwriting that drove me absolutely nuts. Pages and pages—since he was a genius, of course—of chicken scratching that took me hours to transcribe. There were endorsements, poems, and reports of police brutality and repression from all over the Bay Area, then from all over the United States. Some needed retyping and proofreading, which I did. Many we were able to reproduce directly. Emory the artist did the entire layout and the editorial cartoons. Huey's picture front and center, his eyes above the fold always, glistening with black defiance. Once we were through, we hand carried it to the printer. When we got it back, we sold it, alongside the rank and file, for a quarter. My ears and eyes took in so much.

I heard Huey say: "The panther never attacks first. But once he is attacked, he will respond viciously and wipe out the aggressor thoroughly, wholly, absolutely, and completely."

I heard Ron Dellums, a Berkeley city councilman, say: "White reaction to the Panthers is hung up on words—military, violence, revolution, black. . . . People are so involved with the language they ignore what is being said. . . . The Panthers aren't talking racism or hatred; they're talking change."

Huey P. Newton is the ideological descendant, heir, and successor of Malcolm X, so saith Eldridge.

. . . .

Xavi and I were in the administration building at State when we ran into Eldridge, right on the landing between the first and second floors. He recognized me from PE classes. He was holding the hand of a striking, unusually pretty woman, high yellow, green-eyed, with a puffed brown-sugar natural.

"We just got married," Eldridge told us, pride of ownership all over his face. "This is Kathleen."

Her smile was shy like a bride's, but the eyes spoke their own truth, wired for takeoff. She extended a smile. Eldridge said something about her being secretary to a SNCC field general. I could see her taking care of business, but not small stuff. That's what we were there for. "Be who you is cuz you ain't who you isn't." It was so stark. She was the bride, we were bridesmaids. The bridesmaids of the revolution.

Kathleen talked to me directly: "I understand you're a writer and you're helping with the paper."

She invited us to their flat on Oak Street, if we wanted, that evening. Xavi didn't want. I did. Xavi was still a good girl. I wasn't anymore, and I knew it.

. . . .

When I got there, Kathleen greeted me warmly in the hallway. I saw Eldridge pontificating before two cameramen and two reporters, in a living room overflowing with books, periodicals, and posters of Che,

Fannie Lou Hamer, the Mississippi Freedom Democratic Party, Marx, Fanon, and the table where the paper was being laid out. Kathleen also had Priscilla—a white girl!—as her assistant, typist, and all-around handmaiden. I couldn't believe it. I guess turnabout was fair play. The assistant pulled me into the kitchen.

She whispered, "They're filming an NBC interview." Bright spotlights, like klieg lights, were set in the living room around Eldridge.

The reporter was asking him, "What do you mean by the word *jackanapes*?"

Eldridge, as commanding as a member of Parliament, replied, "These are brothers who only want to off a pig. Adventurists, rogues."

One of the reporters ordered the camera off and conferred with the cameraman. I turned to the kitchen, where Kathleen and the assistant were fixing beef stew. Kathleen moved with the velocity of an open fire hydrant. She stopped abruptly and turned to me.

"This is how the French do it. They don't wash their pots after every meal. They cook in them over and over. The flavor stays and it lets the herbs seep in."

Her assistant put beef cubes, carrots, chunks of potatoes, and chopped onions in the pot and turned on the burner. The cameraman resumed filming Eldridge pontificating. "Huey P. Newton is the ideological descendant, heir, and successor of Malcolm X."

The reporter seemed fixated on getting titles right: Eldridge, minister of information; Bobby, chairman; Huey, minister of defense; Kathleen, communications secretary. I loved the grandiosity of the titles but could see the reporter's half smirk. Which country, what nation? The black nation? The checkered nation?

As a teenager, I had rebelled against church every Sunday because I could see past the stage play of the black church, past the garbled grammar of the country preachers, the big hats and airs and Cadillac flair. Sometimes I caught the preacher misquoting the Bible, which Aunt Ola held in her lap. I said something about it once to my aunt, who shushed me with "Don't countermand the preacher."

This was different. I saw both the grandiloquence in Eldridge and the reporter getting all the titles right so he could make fun of them later, whether slyly on-air or privately with his colleagues. I recognized the arrogance of journalists, of smart people for whom knowledge was a commodity. I knew condescension well and how it is an important part of making broken people feel worthless. Aunt Ola Ray tried to make me feel that way, but Goosey was my homemade antidote. However, Ola's belittling made me fight to see my worth. In the process I came to understand her lack of worth. In a way, Ola made me a freedom fighter. I so wanted not to be what she thought I should be, worthless. She was somebody because her husband had a title in front of his name. Without Boy-Boy and his title, Ola was an ordinary colored person, like the salt of the earth in the streets of Watts, Philly, and Cleveland rioting and fighting oppression. Without the insulation of my uncle's profession, Ola might not have had time to look down her nose at other people. These journalists were looking down their noses at Eldridge and the party. They loved him because he made for a good story. But it was infatuation, not real love. And as soon as a more appealing subject came along, not only would they turn away, they would scorn him. Watching the journalists interview Eldridge, I was seeing why I didn't take any more journalism classes once I transferred. I was also seeing why I saw through the paper panthers, even though I appreciated their breadth of knowledge. They lacked the courage to take on the power structure. What was more powerful than the police, armed and ready to be judge, jury, and executioner in our communities?

The party was taking the powerful tools of oppression and placing them foursquare in the oppressor's face. The guns, loaded, in the state capitol. The power of the press; the war of words. We had been likened to apes and monkeys for centuries. *Off the pig* vomited that garbage in an instant. The power of titles. Every revolutionary coup begins with titling the soldiers, and thus entitling the people. The BPP had appropriated the language of the oppressor, as Jean-Paul Sartre said the colonial subject had to do; use the oppressor's language, use his tools to tear down the master's house.

I knew that oppression was alive and well, and nobody was standing up to it full force but the BPP. Huey Bobby Eldridge Kathleen David D. C. The Fortés. I was getting to know them like neighbors in the same messed-up part of town. Not a jackanape in the bunch. They were brave, which I wasn't. But I was born with more than my share of curiosity, and I knew about being broken.

39

My life didn't shift seismically. All I did was join. I was still a student at State. Shortly after joining I walked down the slope and into the Commons, where William 12X was preaching as usual, no one listening. As usual, the black students had gathered like covered wagons around Marcus, from the bid whist crowd, and Bibo, who was dressed in the Panther black and blue. I muscled my way into the circle. Everyone was staring at two rifles encased in leather so new the buffalo might have been nearby. Marcus unzipped a case. "I got this 30.06 from my uncle. He paid four hundred smackers. It's beautiful."

A student said, "That's a hunting rifle. Where you going with it?"

Marcus said, "Don't know bout you, but I'm going to the rifle range and get in some practice. With my good man, here."

"For what? Deer season?" another student piped up, sarcastic as all get out.

No one was paying our black circle any mind except for a scowling William 12X. "You can't outdevil the devil. You're not evil enough."

Marcus sneered at him. "Old man, this is about a damn good rifle. And marksmanship. I'm not into your race game."

"It's not a game. When you get some wisdom, you'll understand."

I decided to go with Marcus and Bibo and two other students to the range. It was misting lightly on campus and none of us had umbrellas. My hair was getting wilder and nappier by the minute. But it was a glorious feeling, like I was doing something terribly important. We set out for Walnut Creek in two cars, Marcus, the rifles, Bibo driving, me riding shotgun in his wagon, the other students behind us.

"LBJ want a Tet offensive; this our Tet offensive right here," Bibo says.

The road got bumpy and none the wider the farther we went. I fingered a rifle through the canvas; my mind replayed what I'd seen of gunfire: Vietnam bloodied and bombed, Audie Murphy movies, World War II newsreel clips, televised riot scenes, Watts and Detroit. I saw a crowd of faces surrounding the Lincoln monument, the face of Martin Luther King, the word—*dream*—on his forehead.

"Bullshit," Bibo said. He held the wheel, jaw set in a bulldog scowl. The shiny cases with their new-leather smell rested on our laps like children ready to go any minute.

"Bullshit," he repeated.

"What? What, what?" Marcus asked.

"Martin Luther King, that's what. Bullshit."

"You mean nonviolence?" I asked.

Bibo said, "Gonna get somebody killed. He wouldn't pull that shit up here. He couldn't find two flies to drop in front of a bulldozer, let alone two brothers. If someone gets killed down there, King oughta be wiped out. He's dangerous."

Marcus tilted toward Bibo. "How so?"

"He's dangerous to white folks, cuz they don't know how far he'll go. He's dangerous to black folks, cuz they don't know how far he's taking 'em."

"You saying folks ain't ready for King?" Marcus asked.

"Listen! Nobody fights war with limp bodies. We need guns. This is war. White folks ain't playing. We need bombs. That's the next step."

"That's patently ridiculous." Marcus started laughing his ass off.

"You think so?"

Marcus kept laughing.

"You got to put fear in the man's gut. White man don't know hungry, don't know suffering. He ain't bleeding, ain't seen his woman raped. Does he study his kids hanging from trees? I want his neck on the bottom of my foot."

When Marcus finally stopped laughing he talked with pure sarcasm. "Oh, I get it. What we need is a black mafia, hit men, silencers. Right?"

"Yeah, man, people who ain't afraid to kill, cold-blooded black men, women, and children who kill systematically. Oppression is a beast, a monster you can't kill with kindness and a picket sign. We have to crawl up the beast's leg systematically until we reach a vital point, then strike and keep moving. When the beast's hand swats us, we split, approach vital organs close to the heart, we attack en masse, deliver the death blow."

Marcus was making fun of Bibo. "Oh yeah, it's about the killer instinct which unfortunately black folks ain't got. We got the be hip instinct, the feel good instinct, the sho nuff instinct, but we ain't killers."

"That's what we have to become," Bibo said. I didn't believe him. I thought it was bluster. I didn't think of any of these guys as killers. Killers had deranged eyes and choked innocent victims to death. Killers jumped into the abyss and never came back. That wasn't what being black was about. It was about pride and self-awareness, rejecting white dominance, protecting the underdog, and helping poor black people out of misery, poverty, and ignorance.

At the suburban range, thick-skinned, redneck, suburban, and rural white men assembled guns peacefully. Bibo, Marcus, and I fingered bullets, counting them into rounds of thirty. My green army parka, buttoned up cardigan, and long-sleeved blouse were too much. I took my parka off and unbuttoned the sweater. I went back to the car and put them on the seat. Walking from the car back to the range I saw the stalls in front of each, a lane six feet wide marked off in white. At the head of each was an old lumber post, wide enough for paper targets. The others posted theirs. I saw Bibo's wild uncombed Afro, my Nefertiti profile, gold hoops like halos on my ears. Marcus sidled up to me and whispered loudly, "What are we doing here? They could off us. No one would ever know. A band of gun-smoking black students disappear, and the world wouldn't miss a minute off the clock. You know that, don't you, Miss East Oakland?"

Bibo walked to the edge, target in hand. He had bowlegs like Chandro-Imi. Maybe he was a cowboy back a century ago. I watched him post the target. He walked up and unraveled his target. Cocksure he posted it. The rednecks moved fast. When they reached him, they pointed to the target. Our target was different. Theirs was abstract, round circles within a circle, ours a man's torso with a small circle on the heart. Bibo argued with his fingers pointing, head bobbing. The men jabbed at the target. One motioned to the office. Three men, red emblems on their arms, rushed to the post, dressed alike in jump-suits. They argued. Their shoulders jerked. Marcus began taking our target down, neatly rolling it under his arm. He came over and handed it to me.

"I'm just getting my edumacashun, dig? Y'all too East Oakland for me. Fuck this confrontation bullshit." He got in the second car, carrying his uncle's rifle.

Bibo and I left together, the noise of ricocheting bullets behind us. I sat silently. I had never handled a gun. I hadn't grown up with guns or hunters. I knew having a weapon didn't mean you had to use it. For heaven's sakes, the United States had the H-bomb all those years and didn't use it. But the threat of annihilation scared the hell out of Russia.

I didn't figure we were killers, not really, but if we didn't stand up to those who would kill and annihilate us, who would?

I understood the gun as a symbol of defiance.

I understood that at the airport with Betty Shabazz, when the flaky Panthers showed up with empty guns, that was chickenshit. The po-lice hadn't shown up with unloaded guns.

I wasn't at Allwood's side anymore, but I didn't want to kill anyone or be killed. I was still on the fence between all-out revolutionary and curious Geniece. I decided to give the BPP a rest for a while, kind of a hiatus from the deep.

40

I didn't fly into Dillard's arms when I saw him again. But when he asked me out, I gave him my address. That weekend, we popped in on Pharoah Sanders in the Fillmore and ended up at Dillard's place. His pad on Stanyan Street was so luxe I felt underdressed. It had oriental rugs, damask rose upholstery, and velvety footstools. I knew his bed wouldn't be a mattress on the floor. It was an oak four-poster. As soon as I hit the surface of the bed Dillard went to work. He pulled off my panties with the efficiency of a gift wrapper at Christmastime. I was wondering if he'd maneuver my slip over my shoulders or wriggle it past my hips. He didn't need to do either for slip fucking. It felt like a Ferris wheel ride, up, down, all around, but the mattress was lumpy.

"You need a new mattress," I told him afterward.

"Shit, the landlady needs a new mattress. I don't need a new nothing."

"This *is* your place?"

"Renting."

"You're not renting the bed?"

"Bed, linen, furniture. I don't even replace lightbulbs."

I got back in the rented bed while he did some coke. I ran my finger along his nostril. He grabbed my finger, licked it, and kissed it. "I have this girlfriend. She was going with this guy named Joe the Blow man. She's crazy about him."

"And he's crazy about blow, right?"

"Yeah, but he gets stoned off LSD every weekend, it seems."

"He's wired."

"She's always asking, 'How much do you love me, Joe?' She even asks me how much. He tells her you can't measure love."

"Sounds right to me."

"Eventually he calls her to get her stuff. She'd been half expecting it, but you know, this was bad. In tears she gets there, the door's unlocked, she walks in, and he's in the bedroom, fucking an Asian chick. Of course, she runs back out, crying, stunned to the bone.

"He finally answered the question on her mind." He was cracking up.

I saw it as tragic. "Drugs and hallucinations and being high every day make a man cruel?"

"Nah. He was copying *The Carpetbaggers*. The movie with George Peppard."

"I didn't see it."

"When Peppard couldn't get through to his old lady the soft and stupid way, he made it pictorial."

"Why doesn't a guy who wants out just say he's through, good-bye?"

"Guys are cowards."

"Cruel cowards?"

"Give you a clue, though. No man likes to think a woman will ever forget him."

With his index finger he touched my throat. "Even when we get to the bottom of our little soiree, it would hurt to think that you might forget me."

"Would you carpetbag me?"

His face contorted. "Hollywood! That's how the white man sells himself to the world. Paddy boy can't teach me shit about shit. I fall into better heights than he dreams of reaching."

His emotion was blood kin to the defenselessness I hid from the world.

And so I fell into Dillard's arms.

The next time we got together we stopped by his mother's Edwardian just two blocks from the Black House. Her front door closing behind us echoed like the tomb at Gethsemane. I looked through the etched glass oval onto Sutter Street, where a car went by like a windup toy.

"You can't hear the traffic once you get inside," Dillard said. He opened a set of French doors. Our heels clicked across the checkerboard tiles of the foyer. The living room had wainscoting white and gleaming next to walls that were faded red like dusty persimmons.

"This is grand," I said to him in a gilt mirror. "Did you grow up here?"

There was so much to look at. A table with inlaid marble nicked my knee as I edged past; samurai dueled and postured across the dusky blue panels of a screen. Naked from the waist up, Japanese maidens lolled about, their hair elaborately piled.

"Here and next door." As he opened blue-and-white porcelain jars on the mantel, they clinked like chimes.

"What's next door?"

"Pops lives there. Moms here." He sat on a red chintz sofa with curlicue fringe. "Sit. Next to me."

I sunk into the sofa. "This is where you get your love of luxury."

"You call this luxury? You should see Dad's."

"What do they do for a living?"

"Same thing yours do. Work, work, work."

"Not your favorite pastime?"

"Not if that's all there is. Dad's a longshoreman. She teaches. Good enough?"

I shrugged.

"Why ask?"

Why did he deal blow if he came from this—and was smart. "Do they know you deal?"

"Be for real."

I was silent. "They're divorced?"

"No need for that."

So he was a broken-home baby too.

"We have holidays together."

"Do they borrow sugar from each other?"

He nodded. "Thanksgiving here, Christmas there."

A light-skinned woman came in the room with a bearing to stiffen Marie Antoinette's spine.

"What's all this Thanksgiving-Christmas talk?" she said.

Dillard got up. "Mother, this is Geniece." I stood, but it was clear from her nod and look-me-over that I was not to cross over to her. Dillard kept opening jars without putting the tops back on.

"I would appreciate you keeping your sticky fingers off my chinoiserie," she declared.

Dillard, urn top in hand, snorted. "I'm letting the haunts out."

"Nonsense," his mother said. "That's an eighteenth-century French antique."

He peered in an urn. "They love to hide inside. Probably a crowd inside this one. Join us, *s'il vous plaît.*"

"Don't fool with me, Dillard. That box was made from Honduras mahogany, inlaid." She gave me a final scrutiny. "Young lady, I hope you know what you're doing."

She left and Dillard started saying, "Muhammad Ali. Muhammad Ali."

I knew he wanted me to say it again and again. "Now what does Cassius Clay have to do with genies in jars?"

"If you believe in Cassius Clay, who no longer exists, you might as well believe in haunts. What does the man have to do for you to honor his personhood? He's officially declared himself Muhammad Ali."

"I give. Muhammad Ali. Muhammad Ali."

He began replacing the tops. "Now the haunts go back."

41

When Stokely Carmichael came to town again, Chandro-Imi told Li-an and me that we could host the party after his speech. Li-an started list making and Xavi joined in:

- clean spots off kitchen floor
- wax the hall (which we'd been intending to do since we moved in)
- hang our mirror (which we'd left sitting against the wall because we didn't want to break it and get seven years' bad luck)
- buy munchies

Li-an got to "buy" and stopped writing. We looked at Chandro-Imi, who pulled out a ten-dollar bill.

"Peanuts," Li-an said.

"Should we go down to the candy store and buy a few boxes of Jujubes?" Xavi asked.

"This is all I have," he said, pulling out a twenty-dollar bill. Li-an snatched it. I took it from her and waved it at him.

"But money's not the object in this. We're not capitalists," I said, tearing the bill in half. "Are we?" I handed the halves to him.

"Are you off?" Chandro-Imi said.

"Brother-to-the-big-time, we need sixty dollars," I said, pulling a figure out of my head. "We're going to get down on our hands and knees, wax, polish, dust, fix food, and shine up our behinds for thirty dollars? Is his name Saint Stokely?"

He shook his head, like I was pathetic, and I shook my head back at him.

"Okay, I'll get the money out of the student activities budget," he said.

"Today," Li-an said, putting the list down on the table. I gave her the thanks-for-kicking-in eye. She was no stranger to putting her foot down, but she looked up to Chandro-Imi. Yet I knew from Uncle Boy-Boy about money up front, even small bills.

"So what am I supposed to do with this?" Chandro-Imi held the torn twenty-dollar bill up. I went to the kitchen drawer and got some Scotch tape.

"Nothing but filthy lucre, especially by time cullud folks get it," I said, taping it.

....

Unannounced and unattended later that evening, Stokely Carmichael walked in, glittering in the dark of the hall, wearing the SNCC overalls. He looked like himself, sexy as a motherfuck. My mouth fell open.

He smiled. "May I come in?"

I opened the door wide. I couldn't speak, and he wasn't going to cross the threshold until I did. I got my throat unthrottled. "Please. We've been waiting for you. I saw you speak last year at Berkeley."

I almost said I'm a fan. I closed the door and watched him move into the party. Several people gasped. Xavi picked the needle off the record player. The people started to clap and shout, "Black Power, Black Power." All the energy in the Greek Theatre at UC, where I first saw him, filled my apartment. I barely heard the bell buzz again. Two tall black men in the trademark overalls, clunky boots, and serious, biblical beards, not goatees, presented themselves by nodding silently, as if to acknowledge that this was routine: Stokely first, "Black Power" next, and then them. I watched the three of them, distinctly tall and self-assured, as people crowded around. It didn't matter if people couldn't get to Stokely Carmichael all at once with them there. Clusters worked their way up to Stokely.

Li-an sidled up to me. "Are those his lieutenants?"

Chandro-Imi, the overseeing soul, spoke. "They're field organizers. And they're not his."

"Well, what do they do?" she asked.

"Why don't you ask them?" he said, his smile as wide and pleased as

I'd ever seen it. Li-an plunged into a cluster and started working her way up.

"So, you pulled it off?" I said to Chandro-Imi.

"No, we pulled it off. This is a unity thing," he said.

By then, the party was in Stage III. Stage I: warm-up, arrivals. Stage II: main event, Stokely Carmichael. Stage III: hookups, departures. Stage IV: afterset talk for serious folk. Food gone and garbage heaped in the can. I hadn't shaken The Hand yet; we had this big mess to clean up. I left the kitchen mess, rum and Coke in hand, to see Stokely in the center of the room surrounded by a phalanx of worshippers.

". . . cattle prods, racist sheriffs, vicious dogs trained to salivate at the sight of black people, courts whose main activity is injustice, century-old prisons used not only to punish blacks, but to teach them they can never win."

Stokely Carmichael talked for forty-five minutes. No one moved; it would have been obscene. Our unbroken attention didn't faze him. He said he had been speaking before black students at white colleges for the past three months. One of the field marshals took over:

"What amazes us is how similar each group is: You're all well dressed. Have we been away from the bourgeoisie this long? Your common denominators are the Afro, dashikis, and repulsion to anything white. The others, more so than you here at SF State, are unaware of the great avalanche of power emanating from the struggle of the black South. Most of them, unlike you, the vanguard of the black student movement, have never heard of Frantz Fanon. They pay lip service to W. E. B. Du Bois, and the Marx they know best was a frizzy-haired clown with a stogie in his mouth."

It sounded like he had been set to go with a canned speech and then realized we were not kids stuck inside an isolated ivory tower. Somebody hipped him either at the airport or on the way over.

". . . been arrested eighty-six times."

Li-an whispered, "He didn't say eighty-six times. This makes me want to dance. New dance, the eighty-six times, doodoowop."

"I know the South the way you know your campus. The most

important lesson I've learned is how strong black people are. Without black folks, there would be no Mississippi, no Alabama, and no Georgia. We made the South, and from that came the nation. Black people are strong and resilient."

Li-an whispered, "If he moves like that in bed, eighty-six times, doodoowop."

He paused and looked at us, his brown eyes shining. Like an actor he could make his tear ducts work on call.

"Strength, beauty, resilience—our weapons. The fight is just begun. Prepare yourselves to struggle against oppression for the rest of your lives. When and if you have children, prepare them to struggle. When you go home, prepare your mothers and fathers, and especially your younger brothers and sisters to struggle."

The other brother, a mariney-red man with an untrimmed natural, stood close to me in his Big Ben blue-and-white railroad overalls.

"Would you sisters like to meet Stokely?"

"Would we!" Li-an answered.

This field marshal said, "Sisters, no hollow reverence."

I was impressed. "If he's just going to shake my hand and give me his playboy of the Western world smile, I'll check him out from the peanut gallery."

I felt the familiar ridiculous oscillation in my abdominal cavity. I scolded myself: Don't you have any ability to differentiate? He was obviously too old, not chronologically but experientially. "You must be his bodyguard or some other kind of movement veteran, right?"

He stared at me, not unfriendly but completely cool. "Field secretary, movement veteran, worker."

"I'm Geniece. I live here. What does a field secretary do?" I suppressed my urge for flippancy.

"We mobilize the community. Voter reg, union building, farming cooperatives, freedom schools." He folded his long arms and leaned against the wall, at ease.

"And why have you come here? We can vote, join unions, all that."

"We want to expand our operation into the northern cities."

"You mean you're finished with the South?" Li-an asked.

"No, not at all," he said. Li-an, bored, walked off.

"She's going for bigger bait, I see," he said with no animosity. I pulled my eyes off his bony fingers and looked at him to see if he noticed me staring at him. He was observing me just as closely.

"Okay, let's stop playing games," I said. "I can't figure this out."

"Figure what?"

"You and him." I pointed to Stokely and the clamor around him. "And—"

"And what?"

"If you guys are here to score or are about change for oppressed people, which can only mean liberation, a totally new and different system. Right?"

"Right."

"How?"

"Any means necessary."

"No, that's thoroughly nebulous," I said. "What is the method? Guns? Voter registration? Education? Black culture and history? There's got to be a way that's clearly articulated, that the masses can relate to. Right?"

"Wrong," he smiled. I shrugged. Out of his wallet he pulled his driver's license and two other IDs.

"Geniece, hold your hands out," he said.

I held out my hands as I thought, *What's he going to do—spit on me?*

This man, like me yet so different, had me look at his IDs. "See the first one?"

It was his student body card from Morris Brown.

"Your smile's as wide as Texas. You were a freshman."

"You can tell."

"Young and dumb," I said. "And *quo vadis* to the bone."

The second ID was a Mississippi driver's license. The camera caught his hair growing into a bush. "They told you not to smile?"

"Ain't nothing to smile bout in Mississippi."

In the third picture, his Alabama driver's license, a barber somewhere in the Delta had tamed his bush. His smile was a tired older smile. "You changed a lot, didn't you?"

"Not really. Things changed around me. I changed the world around me. I'm still the same person, I only look changed."

"More things change, more they stay the same?" Out of the corner of my eye, I saw Buddy slow dancing, like doing the grind, with Xavi. They were laughing and chatting it up. He in no way looked like a married man.

"No. Listen carefully. I say, 'Things change.'" The field secretary carefully put the pictures back into a wallet like they might fall apart.

"People don't? Why are we doing all of this?" I imagined how it would feel for him to fingerfuck me and let go of that as he refolded his arms.

"People adjust." He paused. "Were you involved in the riots?"

"No. I didn't live here then."

"Were they rioting where you lived?"

"Windows being broken. Small-time looting. Silly. Why go down for a TV set?"

"The television, the petty vandalism—it's all symbolic," he said. "It caused millions of dollars worth of fear. The results of that fear made a difference for those of us who survived."

"I can respect all that. But why burn down our neighborhoods?"

"Are you afraid to break the law?"

"I break the law by being black."

"So what's wrong with burning down a slum?" He was cool as ice.

"You talk about terror, about putting fear in the white man's heart. Listen to this: We've been kicking this around." I moved a little closer and detected Jade East aftershave, which perplexed me, along with the rough washed smell of his denims. Buddy walks over and gives me a kiss on the cheek.

"Niecy, I'm taking Xavi away from this madness," he said. Xavi was putting on her coat. "And she may never come back."

Xavi started giggling and said, "Your cousin is mad. And I love it."

"You two hooked up that quick?" I asked her.

She shot back at me, "If it's right, it don't take all night."

That was one of Buddy and Uncle Boy-Boy's favorite phrases. She had gone mad. All I could do was continue talking to my SNCC guy. I didn't see Xavi until the next day.

"We have these wild visions of the sky lit with fire, of white folks running deranged through the streets."

"Why white folks?"

"Hear me out." He folded his arms. "The suburbs are on fire. Instead of us being devastated, living in ruins, let it be them. We even got a name: the Revolutionary Night Lighting White-frightening Fire Brigade.

"What changes in the inner city? Geniece, let's say your shock brigade sets fire to a suburb, burns down a few houses. Now return to the scene of the original crime, our turf. What's changed?"

"It's called payback. Retribution. Justice."

"No, it's stupid, thrill-seeking adventurism. The revolution is not a tea party. Read your Red Book. It will not be won in a day, sister." He leaned off the wall, placed his hands on my shoulders. I stiffened.

"Relax. I just want to tell you something." He bent close enough to smell my natural hair spray. "If you want to burn something, burn down the ghetto."

"What would that accomplish? Look at the riots."

"Burn this shit down. The man would have to do something for all the displaced victims, most of whom are on one or another kind of welfare. We're the ones in need of new housing."

I picked up an A in Speech 102: Interpersonal Communication for reporting on what it was like to hear Stokely Carmichael in a small personal setting versus hearing him speak at the Greek Theatre.

Then I got "Conversation with a SNCC Field Marshal" published in an Experimental College brochure. Minus my sexual thoughts. I wasn't that out there.

42

Chandro-Imi kept giving me little tasks. He asked me to find LeRoi Jones and his wife, Sylvia, an apartment. The Black Student Union had invited him to teach a class. I spent two weeks walking up and down the hills of the Fillmore and the Haight with $250 from the Associated Students in my purse. I felt mortified at failing the test. Someone else, more on the ball, had to find them a pad. We ended up temporarily putting them up at the Travelodge on Market Street.

Then I saw LeRoi in the flesh, at his vociferous best, at the student body funding debate. I was stone-ass surprised that he was even there. I thought of him as a Big Important Writer From The East Coast In A Tweed Coat With Books Under His Arm, squirreled away from us except for class. And there he was, not in his book-lined study, surrounded by Balzac, Genet, Ionesco, or Brecht, hunched over a Smith-Corona portable as inspiration poured from his fingertips, on the phone long distance with some big bubba-tubba negotiating another run of *Dutchman*. Nope, he had left Beat nihilism for black nationalism. He was with us, giving much lip to the punk-ass white boys who controlled the student body budget and wanted, for some perverse reason that I'm sure would never have occurred to them in their native Stanislaus or Siskiyou counties, to pick a fight with the BSU over our altogether legitimate and defensible hiring of LeRoi. We packed the classroom for the meeting with students—black, white, Hispanic, Asian—and community people. We drowned the white boys, washed over them in a wave of derision. Every time they tried business as usual, we up-against-the-wall-motherfuckered them. They got tired of beating their heads against the united front and grudgingly agreed to give it up. Yea us.

Yea me. Financing LeRoi meant I got financed too—I was the

warm-up act, reading poetry from Gwendolyn Brooks, Don Lee, Kwame Nkrumah, Aimé Césaire, and crowd-pleasers from a new poet named Sonia Sanchez.

LeRoi immediately set us to rehearsing and performing. As the Black Arts and Culture Troupe, we got a van, ran up costumes at the pad, and put on shows. Within a matter of days we were gone, black train down the black track, LeRoi the engine. We had an array of talent in the BSU—actors, singers, modern dancers—to supply motive force. Chandro-Imi, saying I was the quintessential naysayer, even gave me the part of the official naysayer in the play, the last line, which I delivered and even changed if I chose, since the clapping and the *right-ons* started just before it and nobody could hear me say squat. We took the show to colleges, centers, and any place they'd let us in—East Palo Alto, West Oakland, Western Addition, Marin City, Seaside, Hunter's Point. I was a little star.

The play was big fun to perform. No *Romeo and Juliet* here; no boy gets girl, boy loses girl, boy gets her back stuff here. We improvised a riot, more like man gets mad, man gets Molotov, woman throws it. Sometimes I threw in Goosey's old favorite, "Don't let no man drag you down," changing it, if people could hear me, to "Don't let the man drag you down," or the old standby, "You can do bad by yourself." But the point of the naysayer, as LeRoi explained it to us in class, was to show that quality of self-doubt in blacks that would always accompany liberating actions, but which would be drowned out by the exulting of the people at the moment of liberation.

Once, driving back from a show, I stood in the back of the van towering over LeRoi; I held on to the rail and observed him. He had a funny cackle, a little guy who hunched in his finely embroidered dashiki. A compact man. Even a gentle man. He bantered, for heaven's sake. I liked him and not at all in a sexual way. Thank goodness, he didn't give off that vibe. His vibe was *Let's get going, let's do business, let's put on a really good show.* Onstage he became ferocious, harsh, scary.

The one time I saw him mix the two personas was his last night in town, our crowning performance at the Black House in the Fillmore

District. LeRoi ranted, raved, screamed; he also talked soft and tender about his wife and the baby on the way. I got the shock of my life when he pointed her out. LeRoi Jones's wife! She had foreboding eyes and was taller than I was! I had to force myself not to gape. He married up, not down!

But I couldn't help staring. She was pregnant, nearly due. Her belly bloomed out so perfectly pregnant I could see her enlarged belly button sticking out through the African cotton like a pacifier. Her hair surrounded her proudness like so many twisted branches of a tree. Even with the baby blooming, she retained a feminine slim curve to her dancer's figure. And she talked about California like it had a tail. She did not like California, San Francisco, the Bay Area, and, by extension, us. "California niggers are out to lunch," I heard her say loudly several times that night. She insisted on dancing, and did a solo bit. So supple she looked boneless, she rolled over on her bloomy stomach as if it were a bag of raked leaves. When she finished her dance, she went upstairs. I heard her say, "These San Francisco niggers are trifling."

Dillard was there, watching everything with a slit-eyed demeanor. I'd tried to get him to give a few hours at the Tutorial Center; he had laughed me down to the ground. I reminded him he could get credits toward his degree. "It's all a get-over, Geniece, don't you see that? Niggers getting over. Tutorial, BSU, the movement. It's all Get Over City." He had upset me so that I had written something for him. I guess I wrote it at him. It wasn't a poem, like one by Mali. I had taken to reading it, like filler over the din of the stage crew. I read it right at him. Dillard didn't bat an eyelash. Maybe he was high, ethereally out there; he looked like raw meat that I had eaten out of sheer hunger. He seemed to be floating in his galaxy, out of my sphere of need. We went outside to talk. I was hot and didn't want to cool. The icy riffs in the San Francisco air ran up my nostrils and into my ears, carried on little knives.

"Did my poetry insult you tonight?"

"You call that poetry? Sound like somebody babbling. Telling all their business. Putting somebody else's in the streets." He was putting me down.

"I think you're an interesting sociological specimen."

"I think you're full of shit. Naive, innocent shit, but shit just the same."

"At least, Dillard, I'm trying."

"Yeah, you're trying, all right. My patience." Every time I decided to stop seeing him altogether something changed my mind. But now the thought of him, of his hard rubbery dick, turned me off as much as it had turned me on.

"I'm trying to help people," I said. He was stinging me. His ridicule brought up stuff I thought I had left behind. Innocence, naïveté.

"My people, my people, as de monkey said."

"You must need something you can only get here, or else you would be someplace else." I had heard my aunt talking once about some-body's divorce. Her comment so stuck in my brain: When a woman loses her taste for a man, it's gone. "If you're so cynical, why are you even here?"

"I came to see you. To be insulted by you."

"It wasn't an insult. It was a kind of praise."

He shook his head. "You want to convert me, Geniece. This is your church."

"It's not." I had lost my taste for him.

"Yes, it is, and I'm the unrepentant sinner." It was gone.

"Dillard, we should stop seeing each other."

There, I had said it, and it silenced him. He looked at me like I had told him his house burned down.

"I'm into this. You're not," I said, tilting my head toward the Black House. He started coughing, the smoke from his burning house caught in his throat,

"Don't want to be."

"We can still be friends," I said.

"That's what your girlfriends are for."

"Well, it's not going to work out. We're different." Why was he making this hard? He never said I love you, not even in the heat of passion. He belittled me. "Why is this difficult?"

"Ah, difficult. That's what my teachers always called me in grade school." He put good-riddance-to-bad-rubbish high on his shoulders and walked off.

I walked back into the Black House feeling just this way: *I'm so alive.*

43

Xavi, Li-an, and I had outgrown the studio. Our search for a new place was more successful than my search for the Joneses. We found a roomy flat next to a grassy park on Potomac Street, with the N street-car crawling out of the tunnel on its way downtown, and two friendly white girls in the upstairs flat who did tai chi on the grass, their *Vogue* magazines stacked in wicker baskets on the landing.

We had been there barely two weeks when, after I got up late on a Saturday, all these Panthers arrived in a flash of black berets, funk, fe-line stealth, and unshaven jawbones, filling the hall and back room next to the kitchen, legs sprawled, arms grabbing for ashtrays, hats coming off. They locked up their pieces in the cars, and one brother stood outside watching the cars. Bobby Seale, knock-kneed and every step in charge, walked over to Li-an and set her in motion. I kissed my shower good-bye. If you can't beat the funk join the funk. Li-an kept it moving. We set up a little assembly line to pull together tuna sand-wiches. One of the brothers, tall and scrawny with bumpy skin, named Barry, kept coming in the kitchen looking at the bread and me like we were one and the same. I slicked the mayonnaise across the bread as if to say: *Look all you want. That's as far as it goes. Maybe I'm a Panther; that don't mean I have to screw one. Take a bath; maybe I'll think about it. So you think I'm cute. I think I'm cute.* He walked over to where I sat the eggs in cold water. I picked them out, cracking and peeling.

"I bet you break a nigger's heart the same way you break those shells, don't you?" He picked up a peeled egg. I thought he was about to bite it when he popped it in his mouth whole.

"Why can't you wait like everybody else?" I glanced back to see if anyone was looking at us. They were going off about Sacramento and the bust that had gone down. Some thirty brothers and sisters had gone up to the state capitol on May 2, to protest the gun laws.

"Man, the sight of all those brothers carrying loaded shotguns into the State Assembly, pointing them up in the air or straight down at the ground, like Huey had taught them, man!" a brother said.

Another brother said, "We vamped on those pigs in Sacramento. Shit."

The group hadn't been arrested at the capitol. Instead, they got busted on their way back, outside Sacramento, for disturbing the peace. Bail was set at twenty-two hundred dollars for two dozen Panthers.

"You shoulda seen the looks on the pigs' faces when we walked into the chamber." Two brothers slapped hands and laughed. It was like the shot heard round the world. Newspapers, national and international, carried the photos and the story.

Barry wasn't paying that any mind. "Everybody else ain't as hungry as I am, can you dig it?"

"No, I can't, and where are your manners?"

"I ain't got none, can't you tell?" When he laughed I saw between his front bottom teeth a perfectly hollowed out oval of decay.

"You're in my way."

"Yeah, and that's where I'm gonna stay."

Li-an came back in. "You two look cozy, but the sandwiches aren't done." She started to move fast, and I followed. We laid out bread; I began putting the faces together and slicing crosswise. Before I got going good, Li-an stopped me.

"Geniece, don't slice. We're not fixing lunch boxes. That's not how you fix a sandwich for a man."

....

Everything black in the world was tumbling down like snow from a precipice, where it had stood for centuries, for all I knew. There was nothing for me to do but be surrounded. The brothers left the same way they came, with a lot of noise and odor. I opened windows to get a breeze from the park through the house.

"I love me some revolutionary brothers, but they need to get hip to Ivory soap," I said to no one in particular.

"Ain't nobody got to do nothing except fight for this funky system to be overthrown." I recognized the voice but not which room it came from.

"Now who left you here?" I shouted.

"Chairman Bob, that's who. If you don't like it, talk to him." Chairman Bob, my foot. I went to the kitchen where Li-an was picking up. "Why is he still here?"

"You mean Barry? He's staying with us. He needs a place to lay low, you know; he's hot."

"Wait a minute." I cleared the table. "We need a house meeting for something like this."

"Couldn't wait. Bobby needed a place for him today."

"Like what happens if he hadn't found a place to stay?"

"Look." Li-an threw up her palm. "This is the deal. Can you dig it?" Discussion over.

"Well, where? Not in my bedroom."

"We have enough room, Geniece, more than enough. If he tries anything, tell him I will personally kick his ass."

....

Revolutionary sisters, my roomies and I did office work, opened mail, called the press conferences. The brothers from the street put their lives on the line. Street versus bourgies, smart versus rough, intelligentsia versus the lumpen. Barry broke that down as we cleaned his fourteen-shot Browning automatic, the two of us in the tiny windowless room we designated as his.

"Let's get into it," he said. I handed him a rag wrapped around a pencil to clean the chamber. "Let's fuck."

"You're crazy."

"You know you want to." He blew smoke from his cigarette in my face.

"I don't have to sleep with you."

"You know you want me; I can tell."

"Barry, frankly, you're detestable."

"C'mon woman, let me jump on it."

I put my hand on my hip. "Since you can't pay money, pay attention. I am not going to fuck you."

"That's what you think." He put the barrel across his thighs and looked into the chamber. "Baby, here I am working from can't see in the morning till can't see at night, and you gonna refuse me some poontang."

"Barry, staying here is not about free fucking."

"Oh, you charge for your shit? I bet if it was Huey P., you be singing a different song."

"No, I wouldn't."

When I visited Huey in jail he gave me instructions for the paper, always polite, and always specific about the lumpen proletariat, everyday black people, about revolutionary art and the importance of the editorial cartoons, about the manifestos he was working on and where they should go. He alerted me when to expect position papers from Eldridge, which always went in the centerfold, and letters of support from important people, national figures and international ones, like Bertrand Russell. I knew I was a little potato on the way to big stew. Once, behind me, Huey's lady stood waiting patiently, a straighthaired brown-skinned sister who sang opera and towered over Huey. She looked bourgie. But then, I looked revolutionary, though I was afraid to sign my name on a paper the government might see.

That part of me wanted to learn how to fuck someone I held in contempt. Nobody put a gun to my head and made me fuck Barry . . . like I was a member of a Mississippi chain gang: *I was forced to sleep with a fugitive.* Fuck that.

"Yeah, pigs get itchy fingers when they see bros riding around fodeep in black leather. Any nigger they see with black leather on, they want to fuck with." He put the gun on the side of the bed. "Pigs changed up for now. They the ones riding around fo-deep, 'cause you got to bring some to get some."

"Bring some to get some?"

"Yeah, if they want us, they got to come to our neighborhoods, and they ain't coming alone. 'Cause they scared, dig it?"

"Are you scared? Ever?"

"Hell, yeah. But I ain't scared to be scared. Che say, 'Whenever death may surprise us it will be welcome, provided that this, our battle cry, reach some receptive ear.'"

I sat next to him. I saw the dark beard of Che Guevara, the fierce look on Che's face, I saw a picture flash by of the island hemmed in by U.S. Navy battleships, Kennedy and Khrushchev eyeball to eyeball, playing brinkmanship. I saw the whole world tilting on its axis and people falling like dolls off the earth into space, I saw myself sitting next to an unwashed funky guy getting ready to fuck him, whatever we did anticlimactic to what was going on around us. I put the tip of my tongue into the oval of decay and sucked the ashy spit from his tongue. The jagged edge of Barry's teeth tore my tongue. I tasted blood. When he didn't finish reciting Che, I scolded him with the rest of it: "that another hand be extended to pick up our weapons, and that other men come forward." I ran my fingers over his balls. I was trying to fuck him and fuck with him at the same time, but he overpowered me. I looked at his torso, lean and bare. I took a deep breath of funk, cleaning fluid, smoke. Fuck him and get this out of your system. He's fuckable. I went deep off in the funk, all the way in and all the way out.

"Baby, you so dark you ain't even got rim round your fingernails. Damn, that's dark."

"I'm fucking your fugitive ass for free and you're putting me down."

"Don't get me wrong, baby. I like it. Your pussy hair kinked so tight it's stinging me."

When we switched and he went down on me, I came really hard. He gasped as my thighs clapped against his ears.

"Your pussy lips dark as a bulldog's nostrils. I like it."

We came out of the clinch.

"Black as boysenberry."

Good grief, stranger fucking was stranger than fucking. Brides in the revolution didn't stand on ceremony. In the revolution I had signed on to willfully there was no dating, no waiting.

44

I liked the fluidity of the revolution. *yeah baby yeah burn baby burn,* reading ecstatic poetry as an opening and closing act for LeRoi Jones. Up and down the peninsula, arousing cheers and fears—it caught up with me. I flunked two classes at State running with the Panthers and being a little star. I applied to Cal State Hayward for the summer to pull my GPA up to snuff, a common strategy among State students. Li-an said nobody's irreplaceable, and sure enough, another sister, from LA, came in to help with the BPP newspaper. My roomies used my VW to do revolutionary work while a friend from social psychology hooked me up with her ride from the city to Hayward.

Cal State was different from State: modern new spacious empty devoid. Was it too hot to take classes? I became an anthropological specimen. Sisters wore their hair cascading onto their shoulders, black Barbies. My kinky hair was confrontation. Just walking to class minding my own I stirred things up. They looked at me, smiled weakly. One person was halfway hip. This guy, Drummond, was president of the black student group. "Call me Drum." I wanted to tell him, *I'm already there square.* But he wasn't square, just bourgie conceited unctuous full of it. We met in the hall between the buildings by the pool, yeah. *We real cool we meet at the pool.* That's how black we were. That's where he laid down his heaviest rap, me in my swimsuit with the foam rubber cups, him with his stuff hanging out anthropologically. We met surrounded by white folks swimming and sunning, the rest of the world in a snit over Vietnam. San Francisco and the long hot summer of urban riot fears a world away.

Drum said: "Let me take you to the beach. We could get down and around."

"Take me to the beach? Not let's go, let me take you? You a camel with humps?"

"Let's play hooky," he said. I knew this was about nookie. He touched my hair, fascinated by a natural woman. He said the biggest turn-on was seeing me float on my back with no cap on like a white girl. What did this dude want? *Yeah man, got down with a queen, made her holler and scream.* Wouldn't know my name if I plastered it on my forehead. I drew my leg to my chest, extended it to the sky. I was an aquanette. His rap sounded light in the sun, like margarine for butter.

. . . .

I walked home every afternoon from where my ride dropped me off, the hippies shitting in doorways, psychedelic posters plastering the windows, doors, streets, phone poles, windshields, up and down the street. I got high with my roomies. We tripped down Haight Street, zeroed in on brothers with white girls, creeping up on them. Xavi had her lighter; I had the SNCC poem; Xavi lit her fire as I fired off the poem syllable by syllable:

> Bro / ther / we / don't / want / to / harm / you / we / on / ly / want / to / bring / you / home

If the white girl dared open her mouth we threw down with our homemade poetry:

> Shut up hussy / before we burn / your blond
> stringy stuff back into baldness / like a
> baby / !huh!

School was unreal. I ripped off my books. The bookstore was a joke. I bought Rocky Road candy bars, five for fifty-nine cents, and stashed the books in my big straw bag. The more I stole the bigger bag I had the next time. The only cheating, stealing, lying I didn't do was on my own test. *Too smart to cheat,* I thought, but wouldn't say so to my buddies, who suggested we sit in a row at the back of the room and copy from our driver. I used my own answers. I aced the test, sailed out high, took my bag to the campus bookstore, got even higher on the LP collection I had eyeballed for days—Coltrane Miles Pharaoh MJQ Archie Cecil. I was supposed to pass on all that? It was my finest hour, actually two. I stuffed my bag, waited for the bookstore to empty, put in a couple of albums, chatted with the clerk, waited for her to gab on the phone, put in a couple more, kept my eye on the clock so I wouldn't miss my ride. My purse was too heavy to walk itself across the bay. I'd have my roomies gaping at me when I got home. I put my initials on each album, even though my roomies said they were the property of the house.

I passed all my tests, got cockier, went back to the bookstore the next week and outright lifted two chunky textbooks—my straw for gold—figured on thirty bucks. The buyback desk kept me waiting. I saw a student go by I'd known at City College. I felt for him. I wondered if he ever got laid, left his mama's house, got loaded, wondered, wondered, wondered, when a campus cop took me by the hand, escorted me gingerly to the storeroom. Stacks, cartons, piles, reams, shelves, towers of books surrounded us. He questioned me. Where did I get the books? I stonewalled. What do you mean where? Here. When did you buy them? A few weeks ago. Did I know they put them on the shelf today? Today? Yes today. Sign this. I read a sign-on-the-line don't-do-this-dastardly-deed-ever-again-here-or-you're-a-goner form. No arrest. No record. Just a good scare. I signed my name. My hand was shaking. A damn good scare. I got up to leave, didn't want to miss my ride to the city. A brother came in, maybe thirty years old. He looked hipped to it, short, bearded, dark-skinned; the other man left. The brother motioned for me to sit. I sat. He asked questions. I answered the truth: who I was; where I lived; where I went to school. He looked like a black Rumpelstiltskin, a gnome, but we thought the same thing about the campus: scenic, panoramic, breathtaking; students dull, unimaginative, content. I told him about State: big gray buildings, nothing to look at, exciting as hell, overflowing with jam-packed students on the floors and windowsills, ideas, demonstrations, haps. He said this like he'd been waiting to get it off his chest for days: "I'm from Harlem. People don't play this revolution bullshit back there. You Californians are out to lunch." That's all he had to say. I didn't know what he meant, because people were political in Harlem and joining the BPP there too. His words echoed LeRoi Jones's wife Sylvia's rant on California at the Black House. No matter. I was off the hook and about to miss my ride. He shook my hand. What a grip. He held me as if I was falling into an abyss, reminded me three months' grace on the paper I signed, wished me luck. I got out of there, got to the parking lot just in time to see my ride leaving me, the artful dodger, to bite that red-awful Hayward dust and ride the bus back home sweet home.

Senior

....

45

Even though I was doing my work, what was going on outside the classroom was far more compelling. But I finished the year, thanks to Cal State Hayward, with decent grades:

- Psych 196, Theoretical Backgrounds, [B];
- Psych 112, Psych Measurements, [C-];
- Counseling 190: Principles and Practices, [A];
- Educ 177, Miseducation of the Negro, [A];
- Geol 5, Historical Geology, [B];
- English 27, American Literary Eras, 18th century, [B].

....

Dillard was waiting on my steps when I got home one night.

"My Ghia's been stolen," he said. "Let me use the VW for a few days, Gee."

"I can't loan you the car even for the night." I thought, *Little brain, dick brain* when he started talking. It was the first time I put the paper to bed by myself. The biggies were out commanding the troops up and down California.

"Why? Muni runs twenty-four seven."

"Because I work for the people around the clock. That's why."

"Shit."

"Yeah, you wouldn't understand."

"Oh, I understand perfectly. Let me tell you, shit gets old, even good shit, your shit too. Everything gets old."

I screwed up my mouth. He wanted to lord it. He was yesterday.

"So who you screwing in the party?"

"No one." I thought of Bibo.

"That's impossible," he said. As fine and neat as he was, he sounded like an old, broken-down car, not sleek like his Ghia. "What's the diff between screwing for the revolution, Geniece, and servicing the quarterback on the football team? Different team, same position."

He wanted me to feel like him, but I didn't want an angry man. That had thrilled me, the headboard banger—fuck hard, fight the system even harder. No more. The movement had softened my anger at my father for leaving. My father was a victim of the harsh reality of racism and leaving was his way of not being a victim.

"What's the deal?" Dillard said. "You back to jacking yourself off? You think you got a dick down there? I'm here to tell you—you don't."

Later for his bitter ass.

....

Becoming a senior was my dream come true. I thought of Juliegirl off in South America, probably a hippie with long flowing hair instead of the Dutch Boy bob. I had gone my very unorthodox way too, but getting out was still my goal. I didn't know what I could do with a psych degree in the revolution. Draft counseling? It was hard to think beyond my immediate situation. It seemed sacrilegious to think about making money while making revolution. All the same, I signed up for a yearlong seminar or special study that required enrollment in both semesters simultaneously. My faculty adviser, an old leftie with Abraham Lincoln Brigade posters all over his office, signed me off:

- English 199, Exploring Poetry, 6 units—*Fall-Spring*
- Geology 119, Seminar in Geologic Hazards, 6 units—*Fall-Spring*
- Psych 177, Seminar in Community Teaching, 6 units—*Fall-Spring*
- Statistics 2, 6 units—*Fall-Spring*

Geology and Stat were the toughies. I had used up my allowed Experimental College units. But I could handle six units of tough, as long as the other six units required papers or community work. I could finagle anything written. Maybe there would be field trips in Geology. For some reason, I loved geology. That left Statistics to barrel through.

I kept doing my do, working on the paper, managing my classes, going to tutorial. Xavi was more and more pulling a disappearing act. I figured she was involved with somebody who was apolitical. Chandro-Imi wasn't coming around so much, but I wasn't there long enough to figure out his and Li-an's stuff. I saw and heard about drug tripping. It was all around me. Various people in the party took various stuff. I took bennies to meet our deadlines for the printers. We had grown to a circulation of 125,000 after Sacramento. Bennies enabled me to stay up for two or three days at a stretch. I found out why it was called speed. Others took what I considered to be crazy-making drugs. I took pride in staying away from anything psychedelic, just weed, and that only occasionally since I had moved across the bay. Mainly I didn't want to trip out and become irredeemable, wandering through the streets of my emptied mind. A stumbled-into-nothingness spook. Something about people who drank too much made me afraid of drugs. However, I was a sucker for colors, prisms, rainbows, kaleidoscopes, impossible dreams, anything mutable, rain when the sun shines, and serious young men.

Bibo was one of the brothers who was always helping the staff at the paper, all around go-get-it guy, food, supplies, and drugs. He was like my shadow. When school was out and the tutorial program ended for the semester, I met up with him again on Oak Street. I never mentioned or asked him about robbing the man on the street. And he didn't either, like it was a silent initiation rite that I had to do once and never again. Whenever we pulled an all-night watch on Oak Street after putting the paper to bed, Bibo started telling me about mescaline as we were doing a lips-only make out. I liked kissing him and liked that he didn't push for more. He said mescaline was beautiful, mentally purifying, astounding, breathtaking, woodsy green, free meadows, spring blossoming, eye delighting, brain sensitizing, nature phantasmagoria, I fell into the witches' brew, fear, rationality, and semibourgeoisie disdain notwithstanding.

But I had one condition—I did not want to be left alone. Bibo assured me he wouldn't let that happen. I took a half tab. Nothing happened. I didn't trip out. I didn't freak. My soul stayed with me. And I didn't see any fantastic spring or summer, or transeasonally green Elysian fields. When I complained, Bibo said I should take the other half, because his trip was mellow. He said his heart was poised outside his body, where he could see and hear it beating, like a tom-tom. When he lay down it positioned itself.

I was getting unscrewed enough to enjoy his trip, even if mine was a no-show. Then my thighs lifted me farther from him. He was floating about the room, pink and moist, with arteries routing into his ears. *Weird*, I thought, *but harmless*. I couldn't quite deal with his joy, the goofy smile and aura so unlike his regular cool. His show was releasing him from his front. I wanted mine to do likewise, but I didn't want to play with my heart. It would be okay to sit in a meadow.

As I left to go upstairs to get the other tab, it happened, i.e., the consciousness of it, lightness, as if I had taken off ten pounds. The door at the base of the stairs was open. When I closed it behind me, something in me turned liquid, some organ near my stomach dissolving. I clutched my stomach and inside my closed eyelids were the countless diagrams I had seen of ovaries. I was on them, a comic miniature of myself about the nose and face, a white pipe-stem body sitting on a left ovary. *This isn't too bad. Kinda silly, but no scary stuff. Might this be my exit and the end of my mescaline trip?*

I moved up the stairs. Now that I had begun to trip, I wasn't afraid to take the other half tab. I was still Geniece. I felt a swoosh in back of me.

I was downstairs near the door. Had all this ecstasy been a simple walk down a flight of stairs? I looked for Bibo. No Bibo in sight. No matter. It was the end. I got hold of myself and wobbled out the door. The street looked like it had been tarred that morning. The thought of having to walk on it seemed stupid. *Who would want to get that gooey?* I decided to sit on the bottom step of the stairs and wait for Bibo. Or should I wait for someone?

I must have stayed like that for the next hour. Bibo never came. Where did he go? I tried to walk, and this time the street looked navigable if shiny, like patent shoes had melted on it. I walked the six blocks to my place, even though I could have sworn my feet were sinking in poured tar. I vowed to go back to weed exclusively. I love colors, but mescaline was too circuitous a path to get to them.

The next morning, Bibo rang my bell, waking us all up before the crack of dawn.

"Huey got into it with the pigs last night. One pig is dead, the other one's hurt." We hadn't even put robes on.

"What happened to Huey?"

"He's in critical condition." He looked at us like we were totally behind the train. "It's going down. Get yourself together. And stop worrying about being cute."

46

We had to put out a special edition of the paper. We had to get attorneys. We had to mobilize the community. We had to raise money. I crossed the bay to see the only people I knew with money.

Uncle Boy-Boy and Aunt Ola were presiding at their dinner table. I had come for money. Ashamedly. "Neither a borrower nor a beggar be." When I walked in the door, the first thing Ola did was give me a new straw bag. She knew I loved big purses. I hugged and thanked her.

"What costume you got planned for Halloween, Niecy?" Uncle Boy-Boy knew Halloween was my favorite holiday. But Huey had been shot October 28. Boy-Boy was avoiding asking about school. I didn't want to lie about school. And he didn't want lies at the table either.

"You know that Buddy and Andrea are having some problems," Uncle Boy-Boy said. So the mocha couple floated up shit's creek. Too bad, but it was a ways from what I needed right then. I thought about James Baldwin on love—that it doesn't begin or end the way we set it up.

"Uncle Boy-Boy, you know I don't ask for money. But the party needs bail money for the brothers who have been harassed by the police. We need money to pay the printer for the paper. We just need it. So some of us are asking our folks to contribute."

Aunt Ola directed the conversation away from reality. "Niecy, do you know that Hopalong Cassidy waved directly at Buddy, like he was a little hero, during a parade in downtown Oakland in the fifties?"

I nodded. She teared a little. I'd heard this one. What difference does a fake Hopalong Cassidy make? Did money float out of his pockets and land in Buddy's lap? Aunt Ola showed me a picture of Corliss graduating from Lone Mountain, throwing her cap in the air, her hair completely natural.

"Her hair doesn't look like such a bad grade; maybe the Lustrasilk has a residual effect," Aunt Ola remarked.

The meat loaf with its ketchup covering, the au gratin potatoes from scratch, the fresh mustard greens tasted different. Ola's cooking had improved or I was eating on the run in too many crap soul food joints.

Uncle Boy-Boy brought reality back into play. "Cousin Reddy seen your boy in the jailhouse. Reddy say they put Newton in the hole in the county jail. They call it the soul breaker. But I hear your boy is holding up. Reddy say that policeman Huey shot was a badass. Says he was hard on ordinary Negroes but kept his distance from the pimps. Now, you know that ain't right."

"That is the original stimulus for the party. Patrol the ghetto to prevent the police from mistreating us."

Uncle Boy-Boy kept with what he wanted to say. "Reddy also say the OPD the night of the shoot-out looking for two male Negroes riding around. And they knew that your boy had a big fuzzy natural and was light-skinned. Sound like a setup to me."

"Uncle Reddy is the original invisible man, Uncle Boy-Boy."

My uncle leaned back. "My passing-white cuz knows how to keep his mouth shut until he needs to open it."

Ola had left the price tag on the straw bag. "I never gave you a gift proper for graduation."

I pulled the tag off the straw bag and began putting the contents of my worn leather purse in it, including an issue of the *Black Panther Intercommunal News Service*. As I looked at it, I decided to show it to them.

"Here's the very first issue of the paper."

"Did you work on that, Niecy?" Aunt Ola asked, beginning to read the front page.

"No, I wasn't a member yet. I knew about the Panthers but hadn't joined." The banner headline was WHO KILLED DENZIL DOWELL?

"Was this the young man in Richmond?" Uncle Boy-Boy got his reading glasses out.

I nodded. "You know, when the Richmond pigs shot the two others before they gunned down Denzil, the coroner found bullet holes in their armpits."

"My goodness," Aunt Ola said. "Does that mean they had their arms blown off?"

"Ola, the police shot the young brothers while they were holding their arms up over their heads, like they had been asked to do." Uncle Boy-Boy scrutinized the paper. "So the Panthers are going to patrol the community and patrol the pigs."

"Now, dear, don't you start calling policemen that word," Ola admonished Boy-Boy, turning to me. "Why do you use that horrible term anyway?"

Uncle Boy-Boy leaned back from the paper. "Ola, these young people are reminding us that the Gestapo in World War II did the same thing. Those Nazis treated Jews the same way, came into their communities, brutalizing and killed, shipped them off to the camps because they were a different race. Same problem, different time. Prejudice, hatred."

"Aunt Ola," I said. "Bobby Seale says a policeman is a pig when he violates the constitutional rights, and even human rights, of the very people he's sworn to protect."

"All police?"

"Ola, the ones who shoot black boys in the armpits." Boy-Boy placed his finger next to Denzil Dowell's image in the BPP newspaper. Ola picked up the paper and began reading it again.

"But what really frightens me are the guns. Why do you need to fight violence with violence?" she said, getting more stressed with each page she turned. "This is a very dark world, Geniece. And why are there so many cartoons with killing and blood?"

"Aunt Ola, this is what's happening here. Not just down South. Why do you think people are rioting in all the big cities? Chicago, Detroit, LA. The police have taken the power that we have given them and abused it. They think it's all right to trample on black people."

"Answer my question, Niecy."

"About violence?"

"You know it's about the violence. Don't play with me. I'm not as dumb as you like to think."

I sighed. Ola's hackles were up. "Huey P. Newton says that we're

going to defend ourselves against any racist attacks. It's a way of showing the people that they don't have to take all this brutality sitting down.
They need to form neighborhood patrols. They need to put some fear
into the pigs' hearts."

"Are you a parrot for these older men? They prey on younger
women, you know, especially idealistic ones. Have they asked you for
sex, Niecy?"

"No, Ola, actually they're perfect gentlemen."

"What!?" She was astounded. Manners were as important as beliefs
to Ola. I was beginning to feel less shitty about asking for money.

"Yes, they are. I met Huey at Oakland City. His girlfriend's locker
was right next to mine."

"Did he begin indoctrinating you then?"

"Ola," Uncle Boy-Boy busted in. "You know Niecy's too hardheaded
to be indoctrinated. She's just a natural rebel. Who's afraid of cats. She
likes some damn panthers but hates cats."

"Well, do they hate white people?" Ola was beginning to soften up.

"That's a cultural nationalist position. Black pride and wearing the
big Afros."

"Niecy, you've been doing those things since you started college.
Aren't you a cultural nationalist?"

I shook my head. "An Afro doesn't stop bullets. Black pride is not a
weapon against police brutality. And the Panthers have alliances with
white radicals, something Allwood and his group would never do."

"But all this started from those ideas of Allwood, did it not?" Ola
was smarter than I thought.

"I give Allwood credit. He introduced me to many ideas and books.
But he wasn't radical. A radical gets to the root of a problem. Books
alone can't change the problem. Somebody has to take action on the
theories. That's why I became an activist."

Uncle Boy-Boy walked out of the room, raising his voice so I could
hear him.

"Now, Niecy, you all call yourselves black revolutionaries. 'Off
the pig,' you teach the young people, 'Death to this Racist System.'
You're teaching yourselves to bring the system down. 'Kill or be killed.'

'Give me liberty or give me death.' But when the man turns on you because you turned on him, you want to cry foul play. And you want us to give you our hard-earned money for your beloved defense committee, for something you willfully brought on yourselves. Now, I ask you, does it make sense for me to give you my hard cash so you can make a white lawyer rich, the bail bondsmen rich, and the newspapers rich running behind and quoting you on the six o'clock news?"

He came back in the dining room with a small white envelope and shoved it in my purse.

"Uncle Boy-Boy, you know I don't like asking anybody for anything."

"Like your pops. Hardheaded. But you're swimming in catastrophe here."

When I pulled up to the Bay Bridge and opened the straw purse for the toll, I found a note from Uncle Boy-Boy with two hundred dollars in twenties, tens, fives—cash my relatives had paid him bill by sweaty bill. The note said: "Be careful, I don't want to pick you up in a pine box." Pinned on the note was another seventy-five dollars that I knew from the way it was pinned was Aunt Ola's doing.

My people knew the police weren't right.

Every tribe had sent one like me into the BPP, the people's army, to grieve the system. The roots of the BPP lay in the goodwill of the black community and its utter disgust with the occupying army called the police. Our relatives were our invisible members. To cut these roots would have been disastrous.

. . . .

That Sunday, while my aunt and uncle were sitting, I presumed, in church, I joined a platoon of sisters inside DeFremery House, a twenty-four-room house supported by round columns, enclosed by a railing of balusters. Outside in the Oakland sun, with oaks and magnolias shedding late autumn leaves, two thousand Panther supporters, fellow travelers, and sympathizers had gathered to protest police brutality. We gathered for the revolutionary moment at DeFremery Park in West

Oakland. I was a scribe, but I could do sisterly work too. Inside the creaking nineteenth-century Gothic Revival house, we peeled boiled potatoes, cracked shells of boiled eggs, and chopped celery for the potato salad to feed the people.

Elaine Brown walked in. She had set up the party's Free Breakfast for Children program in Los Angeles before moving to Oakland. We had had no contact, but her revolutionary singing moved me with its fervor and aching simplicity.

"Separate the egg yolks from the whites and mash them with the mustard," she instructed us. "This is the way you do this."

"It's already done," I answered. "Peeled, chopped, and mixed in with the mustard."

She yelled at me, not like she was mad, just in charge and hierarchical. A cool anger spurted up and down my body. She didn't know me from Adam. I was an example for the others. In the flesh, she was a high-yellow stalker. I talked to myself: *I'm cool, I'm a worker, I can take it, the people matter.* But it wasn't cool.

I had scoped the set and it was looking like a scene, like a fashion or a trend. A young, healthy, fine, attractive, lively crowd here to see and be seen, to support the party, yes, but to catch and be caught. It was a dating game for young blacks in the Bay Area, a spin-off of the movement. Some of the same guys on the lawn at DeFremery I'd seen at the rifle range comparing prices for 30.06s. Gun as status symbol, metal dick.

The potato salad got made and taken outside. I tasted Elaine's. It was tangier. Hers had bite. I understood why she was moving to the center. I had a sharper taste on my tongue than potato salad, the taste of being relegated. Not to my taste. But injustice was stronger than a bad taste.

47

I had to continually cross the SF–Oakland Bay Bridge to take care of party business. Donations for Huey's defense fund were coming from all over the Bay. Going back to Oakland was like dragging the new-me suitcase across the Bay Bridge, with the new me falling out and refusing to cross the choppy waters. I found myself saying stuff like "I don't have to go back"; "I'm a Bohemian"; "I belong to the world"; "I will not be pulled backward." I still thought in my boxed-up heart I could cut myself neatly from the past.

When I drove back across the bay to go to a special meeting with a renowned jazz singer, I felt all that. I wouldn't have gone to the meeting—for sisters only—at a church, except someone from the BPP needed to pick up a donation. I was too busy to go to the concert but remembered the jazz singer's heart-shaped face and tart tone.

In person, she was even sweeter looking, with her shiny sheath and pumps. I hadn't seen women so dressed up since Aunt Ola's church. The women in the room were dressed in the fashion, dashikis, wraps, bubbas, their naturals cut to a barber's T. They began asking her simple questions, the answers to which they could have gotten from liner notes or magazine articles. *Didn't they read?* They were college-educated women spouting fawning, doelike homage to the esteemed visitor.

After putting the paper to bed and three days on speed, I wasn't in the mood for stargazing. A wave of disgust came over me at the smug demureness, as if a struggle for the life of our people wasn't going on outside to which only the privileged few had been invited. I thought I would be at least interested, not hateful. I turned, ready to hat up, when the great lady asked, "And what about these Panther girls? What do they call themselves? Pantherettes? They dress like men."

Pantherettes? Pantherettes!? As in Ronettes and Marvelettes?

"They're so . . . ," she sputtered. She was reaching for the word *crude*, perfect innocence on her face as her off-base questions poured forth. "Do they have to dress like that? Who makes them do that? Do they carry guns?"

A tremendous anger rose in my body, beating a path to my temples. But my mouth was frozen shut. If I said a word, I would have exploded. I nibbled on butter cookies like everyone else. Michelle Stubbs, who went with Allwood's buddy back at City College, approached me in the vestibule.

"Geniece, you look very uncomfortable. Did the Panther stuff offend you?"

"I'm not a Pantherette."

"How come you didn't speak up and answer her? That's what she was asking."

"I didn't want to sound too strident or bitter, too black."

"What's wrong with that?"

"I'm not on twenty-four hours a day. Do I have to defend the party everywhere?" At home? At school? In bed? I got the donation and left.

Driving back across the bridge, I sorted things out. *Was this concept of black people fighting to be free so damn alien that it couldn't be recognized without binoculars? Who did I have to make understand this? Anybody at all? Why was it so important for famous people to endorse us? What was so great about talking to somebody famous? Or fucking a famous man? Or being famous, like we were collectively? Why was I in this? For the excitement? Was I willing to die for the cause? Like Mx? Or Medgar Evers? Or Nat Turner? Had any black women been martyrs? Would I like to be one? (Chairman Bob said we only die once, so there's no use in thinking about it a thousand times.) Okay, I wouldn't think about it, but I could ask. Who was this person I called myself and why was she doing all this?*

....

The past and present of my life kept colliding. The Sunday after Thanksgiving, I was standing on Sacramento Street in Berkeley in front of Byron Rumford's Pharmacy selling the BPP newspaper. I glanced at the *SF Chronicle*, the right front top part housewives said they didn't read anymore. A Marine had testified in Congress that the new M-16s jammed and killed Americans in 'nam. We had cashed in student council vouchers to the BSU and bought M-1s in Reno for the BPP.

A convertible stopped, young women in their Sunday best, my age. Exactly my age. They knew the BPP logo. They knew the police knocked heads—the heads of sons, brothers, and fathers. They were curious. They wanted to buy the BPP intercommunal newspaper. The women in the convertible called me by name. We had graduated high school together. The driver aimed a fusillade of friendly questions at me.

How long have you been a Panther, Geniece? Less than a year.

Did you quit college? Still in college.

Do you have a boyfriend? Not right now.

What do women do in the party? Run the office, do scheduling, set up rallies, march, we do everything anyone else does.

How come they wear berets? Freedom fighters all over the world wear black berets.

What do my folks think? They just want me to finish college.

Am I going to finish? Definitely.

Do I wear a uniform? Jeans are my uniform.

Am I scared? No time for fear.

Do I carry a gun? I handle guns like everyone else in the party.

Still on the paper like in high school? Once a scribe always a scribe? Yeah.

I opened the paper to explain the ten-point program and put them at ease. They apologized: Geniece, we have to go to church. Like polite tourists they bought all my papers, BPP-intercommunal-paper-as-souvenir. And off they went with their pressed hair, carefully outlined lips, pastel linen dresses, and matching pumps.

....

I made it to my poetry class for the final, a holiday party with the visiting poet Don Lee. I wanted to have been there for more, but the revolution was moving too fast. The poet wore a handmade embroidered dashiki, probably from the motherland. He looked beautiful, irrelevant, and romantic as Huey called cultural nationalists. Surely we had space somewhere for this kind of softness. Nice thought that had no place in the moment. The grand poet from Chicago finished his presentation by reciting the title poem of his book, *Don't Cry, Scream*. He paused at every "scream" in his poem to shriek. Each scream tore at the box inside my chest. I pled silently: *Would you please shut your mouth?* He answered with a long drawn-out scream.

48

After tutorial one evening, Bibo drove to the Army-Navy store on Mission. I thought he was getting stuff for himself. When he insisted I go in, I protested that I had to study for my stat final in the car. I did not want to be buying clothes for some other woman's man.

"Geniece, you need fatigues." He walked me over to a table full of pants for men in green camouflage.

"I know you don't think that's for me. They're not even feminine."

"In combat, you're not trying to look like Twiggy. It's about protecting yourself."

"In the jungle, yes. In San Francisco, I would just look conspicuous. I'm behind the scenes, anyway."

I would not even try them on. "Chanting 'off the pig' is as masculine as I'm getting."

In the car I needed to get things straight. "Don't try to dress me again. Do you think you're my father? And since you've never officially hit on me, you're not my man either."

"I'm just trying to bring you up to speed. I told you I'm married."

"If you were my husband, I wouldn't like you spending so much time with me."

"We're comrades, Geniece. At some point, you gotta get it through your head: This ain't a tea party."

....

So I was taken off guard when we kissed, off drugs, for real, and it felt way beyond comradely. It was Christmas in San Francisco. Over a period of two days right before Christmas, nearly 750 demonstrators protested at the Oakland Army Induction Center. Bibo and I were at the Potrero projects in the city, crossing the grassy area, under the squared arch consecrated with piles of Christmas gift wrapping, cardboard rectangles of discarded bicycle boxes, strands of tinsel all over. There at the doorway to the projects, he kissed me.

"This is yours," he said.

"Mine? On lease? Your mouth, your tongue, your teeth?"

"Whatever you want. It's yours. As long as I have a heart."

"Thanks. When does the lease expire?"

"Who knows?"

Tammy and Yvette, the two little Tutorial Center girls from the projects, told Bibo they had Christmas presents for us. We walked up to the girls' door, and touched lips again. The door opened as we broke apart and saw the girls standing close together, picture pretty. Their mother, Mrs. Moore, had dressed them alike in princess coats and fur hats, Tammy in green and Yvette in red.

"You look like two little women," I told them. The door opened wider and I saw the kitchen first. The table was overturned, its chrome legs at right angles to the floor. Broken dishes covered cracked linoleum. One curtain hung torn from the rod. Drawers had been pulled out of the cabinet, dish towels and pot holders strewn across the floor.

"What happened?" Bibo spoke. I moved behind him. But he grabbed my arm and forced me to stand beside him. The girls stood in the same spot, as close as could be short of adhesion, their eyes glistening. Tammy moved first to my side, where she smothered her face in my coat. Yvette spoke first.

"My mama and her boyfriend, Mr. Johnson, had a fight today." Her voice was strong, her eyes wide open, the first tears yet to spill out. "He beat her because she spent his money on our new clothes."

Tammy spoke, her hands cinching my waist. "Let's go, Bibo. We hungry."

We looked at Bibo, who walked toward the kitchen, where he picked up a pot holder. He found a plastic garbage can that had been thrown across the room, surveying the contents spilled unevenly past the couch. Picking up the can and filling it slowly with the garbage, Bibo talked. "I cooked a turkey at the center last night. Fixed all the trimmings. Even a pecan pie."

He looked at me. "For you guys." I started to question him, then ran my fist over Tammy's fur hat. "That was a nice thing to do."

I tried to soothe Tammy, but my eyes went to Yvette. "Where's your mother? I want to see if she's all right."

"She's drunk." Yvette watched Bibo pick up garbage. When she finally blinked, a line of tears disappeared into her fur collar.

"Is she in her bedroom?" I asked. Bibo began sliding the curtain back on the rod.

I pried Tammy's fingers from my coat. "Let me go see about your mother. Okay, sweets?" I moved past the girls into the hall, which reeked of whiskey. In the bedroom, Mrs. Moore lay slumped, half dressed on her back, her swollen face hanging on her shoulder, a near empty fifth in her left hand.

"Vette, Tam." Just above incoherence, the words stumbled away from her. "Pusha new cose on."

I walked to the foot of the bed. "Mrs. Moore, this is Geniece from the Tutorial Center." I spoke plain and loud, as if that would bring the situation into control. She tried to straighten.

"I shaid, pusha new cose on." Her empty hand jerked, and she yelled. Pain twisted the swollen contours of her jawbone. Then she eased down. "Broke my back . . . weasel."

She pushed her neck back onto the pillow, her grimacing face like Yvette's characteristic scowl. I tiptoed out of the room. In the living room, partially in order, I turned to Bibo.

"We have to call an ambulance."

As he dialed the operator, I turned to the girls and asked Yvette, "When was Mr. Johnson here?"

"He left about an hour ago."

"Were you awake when he was here?"

"Yes." She turned from me, looking at Bibo on the phone.

Tammy spoke up. "Yvette saw him fighting my mama. She was looking through the door. She made me get under the covers, 'cause I was crying."

"Did he hit her?"

"He picked up the broom and hit her across the back. When she fell down, he kicked her, right here." Yvette pointed to her left shoulder blade. "Then he kicked her in the face."

Tammy screamed, "He was gonna kill her."

Yvette continued calmly. "I came outta my room. They always have fights, but he was looking for a knife. That's why he was breaking everything in the kitchen. He was looking for a knife. He said so. He said he was gonna kill my mother. When he turned around and saw me looking, he cussed at me. Then he kicked her. He kicked her over on her stomach and told her to crawl back to bed. He said crawl in front of your little yellow bastard."

Yvette shook as she pushed the last words out. "Then he picked up the garbage and threw it at me." She dropped on the couch, like crumpled velvet.

"The ambulance and the police are on the way over." Bibo's voice shook with rage and distress.

"The police! Why the police?" I asked.

"Ambulances won't come down here without a police escort," he said.

I lost my composure. "Down here! We're up on a hill. Why is it we're always down somewhere?" The minute I lost my calm, the girls started to cry. I had to regain it for them. I sat on the couch between the girls. Bibo moved toward the bedroom.

"Either her back or her shoulder's broken. I don't think we should move her," Bibo said.

"We have to put her clothes on. Come on." I got up to go help him and Tammy pulled at my side.

"Are we still going to eat turkey?"

They still had on their coats, Yvette's hands inside her muffs, two little black porcelain dolls.

"Just wait," I told her.

....

Inside Mrs. Moore's bedroom, she had fallen half out of bed, her bottle propped against the bed, still in her hand. She jerked her head around and moaned as I moved to the bureau to get her some clothing. She pulled her head to the side and looked at Bibo, her eyes surrounded by puffy bruises. She screamed in fright and dropped the bottle on the floor, where it rolled under the bed. She put her left hand beneath her pillow. Bibo stood at the foot of the bed.

"Donchu come near me, fool. I kill you, I swear I point this gun at yo mean-ass heart and kill you." She had a .38 Special in her left hand. Bibo moved to the side of the bed. She was drunk enough to kill him or me. "You beat da shit outta me, in fronna my babies. I don't care thatcha beat on me. Butchu mess with my child you cheap no good sonofabitch."

Bibo moved back toward the door. I feared he would leave me in the room. At that moment, I realized we might die for Mr. Johnson's bad behavior. But Bibo rolled on the floor to the right of the bed. She turned to shoot, pulling the trigger with her left index finger. The bullet passed through the closet door, piercing the air his chest occupied seconds before. Bibo sprung up and knocked the gun out of her hand. It fell to the side of the bed. I watched her as he jumped over the bed. She tried to turn quickly and wrenched the last bit of consciousness from her broken body. As he picked up the gun, she slumped. He took the pulse of her left hand. For a moment in time, we stood frozen.

....

Then the living room was crowded with eight people, seven of them standing, Mrs. Moore on a stretcher carried by the ambulance attendants, the black policeman talking to Bibo and me. We told him she had been beaten severely by a man friend whose address we didn't know. The girls stood mute, with their fur hats and unruffled princess coats and reddened eyes. At the stretcher with their unconscious mother, Tammy touched her mother's hand and calmly turned to the policeman. "Mr. Johnson live at the Winston Street Motel on the third floor. He beat her 'cause she spent his money on our outfits."

Outside, a crowd gathered—children on brand-new bikes, a few adults pulled from holiday dinners by the siren. Teenagers in twos and threes with grim smirks, their stares said: Who got beat? Anybody die? I didn't hear no shot. Did you?

I turned to Bibo. "I'll go with Mrs. Moore. I guess the girls are hungry, even still." I stepped into the ambulance and sat alongside the stretcher. Tammy stepped behind me, but Bibo lifted her up and turned her around.

"Mama's gonna be all right. Come on, let's go get our dinner."

As he led the girls away, the ambulance closed up and night disappeared. The world became vivid white, bright red, barred and piped with steel. The vibrations of the siren pulsed through me like a blood transfusion as the onlookers vanished into the dark.

. . . .

I was drawn into the movement by the idea of freedom for black people and the image from my childhood in East Oakland, riding to church in the backseat of my uncle's Chrysler Newport, seeing black males spread-eagled on the ground at the mercy of hulking white policemen. Cousin Reddy's stories from the dispatcher's booth at the Oakland Police Department also profoundly influenced me.

. . . .

Yet here I was in the emergency room with a drunken mother. And here I was working behind the scenes, laying out a newspaper. Our revolution wouldn't change much for Mrs. Moore, whose life lay at the bottom of a bottle of liquor. I was fighting for Yvette and Tammy to have different lives, different outcomes, and different opportunities. The image that replaced the ugliness of police brutality was of Yvette and Tammy, each walking across a stage, diploma in hand, gainfully employed, living in a clean, well-maintained environment, pretty much what my aunt and uncle wanted for me. It wasn't what I thought the revolution would be, but I could see the connections.

49

In the dark light of the world I had embraced, so much was difficult. Hard sex. Temporary love. Robberies. Murders. Shoot-outs. Emergencies. Revolutionary culture. And idiot bragging from an idiot named George Sams. There was so much to be done in putting the paper out I was able to ignore him at first. *Free Huey or the sky's the limit.* The shootout made the BPP paper must-reading, our face to the world, the radical world, the black community, the Bay Area, the state. The whole world. I read over and over from the Red Book: "We are advocates of the abolition of war; we do not want war; but war can only be abolished through war; and in order to get rid of the gun it is necessary to pick up the gun." I didn't disavow violence, but I hated the violence that George Sams bragged on.

Of everyone I met in the movement he had the thinnest veneer of trust. I disliked him intensely, everything about him, immediately, by instinct. All I ever saw him do was brag.

"I got shot in the neck five times by the pigs in the riots in Detroit. And survived."

He persisted in showing me scarred exit holes of the bullets that went through his neck: "Check this out. Here, right here, this is what it looks like. I wouldn't lie to you. You a queen."

The very next morning, we were about to take the paper to the printer in the Mission. Bibo and I passed through a room where Sams and a BSU brother had gone, supposedly to sleep.

"Put that motherfucking gun down," the brother was telling Sams and turning to us. He looked crazy scared. "This motherfucker been holding a shotgun to my face."

Sams was grinning outrageously.

"I wake up to this fool holding a shotgun to my face," the brother said.

"Wanted you to know what it's like to wake up to the barrel of a gun. Peep that, bro," Sams said.

The BSU brothers called him an agent provocateur and no one expelled him. He reeked of gunpowder, funk, and tobacco. In the middle of the night the special tactical squad of the San Francisco Police Department would break down the door to Eldridge and Kathleen's apartment, ransack it looking for guns. George Sams was always around when shit like that went down. I no longer saw fearlessness. I saw nothing but foolishness when I had to be around idiots like Sams, braggadocio in the name of blackness.

I hated cliques in high school. I hated the black sororities at State with their color lines and Vidal Sassoon geometric hairdos. Shit, my family had cliques. I hated exclusion. I didn't find it any less discomforting being in a Panther clique, even if it was called a cell. I always felt for the outsider and George Sams was a trained insider. The lumpen brother who stood watch on Oak Street as we put the paper to bed was an outsider.

"I was born and raised in the Fillmore," he said proudly. "When my mama bathed me at night, rats hopped in the bathwater." He was the personification of Rule Two of the BPP's three main rules of discipline:

1. Obey orders in all your actions.
2. Do not take a single needle or a piece of thread from the poor and oppressed masses.
3. Turn in everything captured from the attacking enemy.

He carried on his person sliced baloney from the corner market wrapped in wax paper, sometimes hogshead cheese, a ten-cent jar of French's mustard. He made runs to the corner store for a twenty-five-cent half loaf. We nicknamed him Country. He didn't care what we called him, we who ordered takeout and paid from petty cash.

"Hey, Country," shouted a comrade. "Get Hostess Cupcakes, a Rocky Road for the queen, and Laura Scudder's Potato Chips."

I began to see purity in the faces of children, like Tammy and Yvette. It was scarce anywhere else.

50

I finished the first semester of my senior year in good standing, half-way home. February started fine. "All power to the people." We the people, me the people, Renee the people, Renee, a black student I knew from State who worked at Safeway in Berkeley. There was no reason to shop at Safeway's in Berkeley except it was Renee's Safeway. We the people gave it to her. Whoever we knew was the people's proprietor. We the people gave that proprietor license to let us lift whatever we wanted and walk out scot-free. If that sounds cavalier, it wasn't, at least not in my actions or feelings. I was nervous and afraid of getting caught, even if Renee was at the cash register ringing up $100 of groceries at $38.06 or $50.73.

Renee beat me at nervousness. She wasn't revolutionary, didn't wear a natural, didn't have mouth, was still a virgin (so I heard), had just moved from home, couldn't dance, couldn't outtalk the talkers or out-think the thinkers, an ordinary black girl turning into a woman, getting educated, a right-place-wrong-time person. If she were older she'd have gone straight through, graduated, and become a social worker. But we were all so much spaghetti twisted and stuck together.

The last time I saw Renee, the last time I tortured Renee, the last time I ripped off Renee was for chicken, shrimp, and sourdough bread. I was trying a made-up dish, not something from a moo magazine. On my way home from the printer's I picked up seasonings, onions, garlic, bell pepper, something to drink, dinner napkins—who knew who might come by? And waited until Renee's last customer had gone, and I slipped through the register, rang up my bag at nine dollars and something, but I only had a five and needed change to pay the toll on the Bay Bridge.

I waited for Renee to do something; her eyes darted back and forth, more nervous than ever. I had forgotten to be nervous. She started blinking real fast, which I thought was my signal to go, so I grabbed up my bag, left out the automatic door into the bright afternoon, thinking of who might feast with me, when I felt a light touch on my shoulder like a baby's finger, and then a little voice like a boy's saying, "Excuse me, miss," and I turned still walking toward SF.

The light touch clamped down and the voice turned from boy to man: "Did you forget something?" I looked at my groceries, my power from the people, and said in all honesty, "No, I didn't forget anything." He placed me under arrest for shoplifting chicken, shrimp, and sourdough bread, not for a sit-in, bombing, or protest demonstration, not for the movement, the cause, the vote. Handcuffed and led to a police car, I talked amiably with a young white policeman who looked at my student body card and said, "What's a nice girl like you doing shoplifting?" I shrugged my shoulders, because he didn't know the half of it. I was booked, photographed, given my phone call, which I debated making to Xavi but decided against because I was ashamed, so I called Bibo at the flat instead and then sat in an empty modern well-lit cell with no one but myself ("We're not so busy midweek") for an hour and forty-five minutes, until they told me someone had posted my seventeen-dollar bail. I got out of jail and saw Bibo looking scared for me. His face registered my submerged anguish. I was stunned to have been touched on the shoulder by what felt like providence. We got in the car in the Safeway parking lot. I said, "This car feels like my skin; I never want to get out of it." He started stripping gears like he had been arrested. I felt my insides being shoved back and forth, so I drove back not actually trembling until I got home, shut my bedroom door, and saw my face in the mirror, black ink stains under my eyes.

Getting arrested, booked, and fingerprinted wasn't a good feeling. It wasn't even for the revolution. I didn't write it in my diary. What *was* a nice girl like me doing shoplifting? Bull Connor and that young white policeman were two entirely different specimens of cop. I was tutoring black kids from the projects one minute and robbing white businessmen the next, doing good work for the revolution one day and crazy nigger shit the next, stuff I couldn't even tell my roomies.

Sitting in that jail cell all by my lonesome brought it home. I wasn't even brave enough to get arrested in a march. I wasn't Tracy Simms or a woman in Birmingham protesting segregated buses. I wasn't in deep dukey because I was fighting for the people. I was just a female version of the jackanapes that Eldridge talked about. I got caught stealing onions, garlic, bell pepper, and root vegetables from the virgin soil of the revolution. A common thief. My father might have been hardheaded. But he wasn't a thief. My family might have annoyed me. But they weren't thieves. They were workaday people, not a thief in the bunch.

It had taken a long time to get disgusted with myself.

51

But life went on, self-disgust sitting on my boxed heart where things were getting crowded. The buzz at Fell Street, up- and downstairs, and in the world, was about the Tet offensive. It looked like a defeat for the Communists, because they had forty-five thousand casualties. But LBJ lost support in part because of one photo of a general assassinating a soldier in broad daylight. Murder belongs to night, where its cruelty can't be witnessed, where conscience will not prod one to do something, report it, tell somebody, photograph it. That photo said: We're not invincible. We make mistakes. We are an evil country when we act immorally or encourage shameful acts or ally with wicked, corrupt leaders. We are not impervious to evil.

I hadn't talked with anybody about the bust, about what I was going to do. It seemed insignificant in the face of everything else going on. And stupid. I kept getting the court date postponed. First till March, then April.

....

I found when I did tutorial now the faces of the children buoyed me. I brought Tammy and Yvette home with me when I knew the house would be empty. I could raise them, if only for a night. A neighbor they called Grannie had taken them in for the time being. Taking them felt like I was giving them a home, if only for a minute.

Yvette sat on the edge of my bed waiting for Tammy to finish showering.

"I smell funk from you, and it's coming from here, here, and here." I pointed to my armpits and between my legs. "Yvette, your turn to get clean and then to bed."

I had planned to sit and write about all the turmoil inside me as the girls washed. But I could hear them splashing water and suds all over the place. I had to referee.

"Gimme the soap, Yvette." Tammy grabbed Yvette by the head and pulled her under the showerhead. Yvette yanked away.

"Don't get my hair wet, Tammy." She slapped Tammy.

I took the towel and dried Yvette's head. "Do you guys do this at home?"

Yvette grabbed Tammy and held her under the water until she screamed.

"I hate you, I hate you." Tammy turned to me. "She wants my hair to be nappy. When her hair dries she can brush it. My hair gets wet, I'm gonna be ugly."

"Yvette, why did you do that to Tammy?"

"She ugly anyway."

"I ain't ugly. And you ain't pretty. Bastard. You ain't got no daddy."

"Tammy." My voice was stern.

"I'd rather be a bastard than a nigger with squinty eyes."

"Cut it out, calm down." I began undressing. "Come on, I need to wash myself before all the hot water's gone." They got out; I got in and soaped up.

"What happens to your hair when it gets wet?" Tammy asked, her hands around my waist.

"Tammy, let me go, girl. You want my dirt to wash on you?" She dried herself.

"Are you gonna wash your hair?" Tammy asked. "It's gonna get ugly."

After our showers, we sat on the bed as I braided my hair. Yvette tried on my earrings and necklaces.

"Geniece," she said. "What happened to my mother?"

"Your mother's going to be in the hospital for a long, long time."

"What's gonna happen?" Tammy wrapped kente cloth around her pajamas. "I don't want to stay at Grannie's. I sleep with her and she snores. Can't you take us?"

"Don't be stupid, Tammy. She not old enough." I took a delicately carved Nigerian comb and wound Yvette's long, straight hair into a roll.

"I'm old enough. But I can't take care of you. Grannie's is only for a while."

The nature of the promise and the promise of nature, those bonds by which children are born and nurtured—to be somebody, to function independently, to pursue ideas or goals or even people—birthright. Maybe I lost birthright when my father left, but I retrieved it. Maybe it hardened me to struggle for it. "God bless the child who's got his own." I had to fight for everything. I didn't give a damn if everybody till kingdom come said I needed to stop going for it and fuck lumpen brothers instead. I was fighting to get my degree. My tutorial babies had birthright too.

"Then we have to go to juvenile home. Why can't we do it? Momma can stay home and a nurse can come take care of her. I can do the cooking and cleaning and take care of Tammy."

"Honey, welfare won't pay for that."

"But maybe you could look after Momma during the day," Yvette said, talking fast and gesturing, "and then as soon as we get home from school, you can take night classes and me and Tammy can do the rest."

"Sweetie, your mom is too sick to stay at home. She has to stay in the hospital."

"What's gonna happen to us?" Tammy said, alarmed.

"I know what." Yvette jumped up and the comb fell to the floor. "Do you want to hear it, Tammy?" Her voice trembled and she knelt in front of her, avoiding looking at me. "Bibo and Geniece could get married and adopt us. Then everybody would be family."

I picked up the comb and rearranged Yvette's hair without it, setting the comb in Tammy's hand.

"That won't work either."

"Then what's going to happen to us?" Yvette's voice went flat, and she fell on the bed. "Nobody wants us."

I lay on the bed between the girls. "I talked to the lady there, Mrs. Williamson. The juvenile home won't be that bad. She said they definitely wouldn't separate you."

"From each other?" Tammy asked, running her finger on my shoulder.

"It will be bad. The girls at school told me about dykes." Yvette sat up. "She said they put their fingers up your booty until it hurts while somebody holds you down. You have to do what they say. I'll run away before I go there."

"Who's gonna press my hair there?" Tammy got more upset.

"Listen, I know the girls there press their own hair. So somebody must have a hot comb. If somebody tries to do something to you, and I don't think anybody will if you don't hassle anyone, then do this."

I was hearing Goosey. "Hope that can be seen is not hope." I went to the bathroom and came back with Mercurochrome. "Carry this with you, in your case with your Vaseline and bobby pins. Now if it gets to be late, and you think they're going to hurt you, then smear this all over your vagina. It'll scare them off."

"What's a bagina?" Tammy asked Yvette.

Yvette shrugged. "It's vagina, with a v. It's the place where you pee-pee. Dang girl, shut up."

"Yvette," I asked, "how many holes do you have in your body?"

"You mean all of them?"

"Count 'em, go on." She touched ears, nose, mouth, eyes.

"Seven."

"Wrong."

"Two for my nose. Eight."

"Wrong." I pointed toward her crotch.

"Your pee-pee and your poo-poo, what else, dang?"

"Don't get evil with me. Just get that mirror and squat over here by the light."

She squatted.

"Now, put the mirror between your legs."

Yvette held it between her thighs. She hissed, rolled her eyes, and frowned.

"It's nothing to be upset about. We are female and we have to know what's down there. You haven't started your period yet, have you?"

"Nope. Hope I never do. It's silly. How come women bleed every month?"

"Yeah, Geniece, how come?" Tammy looked in the mirror and Yvette slanted it so Tammy couldn't see.

"I can tell you how and show you where. The why is that's how women have babies."

Yvette started to get comfortable and sat.

"Little lady, I ain't finished. Get up." I took the mirror and in one move, bent and spread the lips of my vulva. "Look! Both of you."

They peered into the mirror and drew back.

"Ick, it's funny looking," Tammy said.

"It wasn't put there for looks."

"Why do you have that funny thing?"

"Listen, you have it too."

"Oh, no, I don't. Not that," she said.

"Okay, just wait a minute. Now look at this." I squatted deeper. "Wait a minute, this is crazy."

I put the mirror on the dresser and got on the bed, drawing my knees to the sides of my chest.

"Okay, this is the real thing. You don't have to look in a mirror to see it. Now when I point and say the word, repeat after me." I splayed my hand over my pubic area.

"My genitals . . . Say it."

"My genitals."

I touched my pubic hair.

"Pubic hair."

"I don't have any of that, so I don't have to say it," Tammy said.

"All right, be funny, ladies." I spread the lips surrounding my vagina. "The lips or labia. I think there's four."

"You think? You don't know, Dr. Geniece?" Yvette said, eyes glued to my body.

"Say the lips or the labia."

"Say the lips or the labia."

As I parted the lips, I wiggled my clitoris. "This is the clitoris."

"Clitoris."

"Clitoris."

"What is that for?"

"All of it works together."

"For what?"

"For goodness sake, okay! Let's move along. What're the parts called again?"

Yvette named each one. Tammy stumbled over all of them, calling the clitoris the clickit.

"Look." I contracted my vagina in and out. "Do you see that?"

They stared.

"Make that again," Yvette said.

I contracted again. "That's the vagina."

"How in the hell does a baby get out of that keyhole?" Yvette asked.

"It expands." I sat up. "It's called an act of God. Sometimes, the doctor has to cut it a little."

"I ain't having babies. Ever." Yvette walked to the dresser to comb her hair. "Ain't letting nobody touch me down there either. Ever."

"You'll change your mind."

"No, I won't. Babies are for people who don't want to have fun." Yvette turned around. "I'm right. Babies make people cry."

"Babies bring happiness. But they have to be fed and clothed." I lay back. "We're not finished yet."

"Ooh, no more," Yvette said, but kept looking at my crotch.

"This will only take a minute." I drew my legs up. "This is the urethra, the last opening, the one you forgot to count."

"Where your urine comes out?" Yvette said.

"Yeah, I can hardly feel it myself. Can you see it?" I fingered it.

"It's tiny," Tammy said. "I didn't know there was a hole for my pee-pee."

"Yur-reeth-ra. Say it."

"Yur-reeth-ra!!" They said it.

"All right, all right. Now here is my anus." I parted my buttocks.

"That's your poo-poo hole, and it's wrinkled, Geniece." Tammy frowned.

"Tammy, you're too smart to call it that. It's anus. A-N-U-S. Everybody, male and female, has one." I closed my legs.

We got into bed, where we became a soft purring animal with six legs and six arms.

I cared about these two little creatures more than I cared about the cause. They were my cause. Through them, I was becoming a caring person.

52

Everything changes in an instant.

Martin Luther King Jr. is assassinated in Memphis on April 4, ten days before Easter. Riots break out across the nation in over 120 cities, including Chicago, D.C., and Baltimore, but not Oakland. Bibo and I are in the car the evening after, listening to KPFA-FM's reporting on the riots. The station plays Stokely talking about King:

> White America made its biggest mistake when she killed Dr. King last night. When she killed Dr. King last night, she killed all reasonable hope. When she killed Dr. King last night, she killed the one man of our race, in this country, in the older generation who's a militant and a revolutionary, and the masses of black people would still listen to.

Silent tears are flying down Bibo's cheeks. They make me full-out cry. All in the space of twenty-four hours, the rhetoric, the buzz, the unbelievable back-and-forth—*Burn Oakland down! Huey says riots are no longer revolutionary actions. Fuck that shit! Burn baby burn*—gets to me. Stokely's voice is calm and sad:

> When white America killed Dr. King last night, she declared war on us. There will be no crying, there will be no funerals. The rebellions that have been occurring around the cities of this country are just light stuff for what is about to happen. We have to retaliate for the deaths of our leaders. The execution of those deaths will not be in the courtrooms, they're going to be in the streets of the United States of America. When white America killed Dr. King last night, she made it a whole lot easier for a whole lot of black people today. There no longer

needs to be intellectual discussions. Black people know that they have
to get guns.

Bibo says, "King became a Panther the instant the bullet took him out.
That was a bullet aimed at the people."

"It's a crying shame that he had to give his life for us to respect him.
He wasn't Martin Luther Queen. Remember when you said that?"

"I underestimated him. Feel better?"

"If one more city goes up in flames . . ." I can't finish thoughts, let
alone sentences.

We stop at my place to get something to eat. The front window is
broken. I open the unlocked door. Li-an and Chairman Bob, and Alex
and Elsa, two middle-aged white leftists who support the party, are
sitting in the messy front room, amid a pile of my stinky laundry. I turn
to Li-an and start sputtering, embarrassed that my shit is on display.

"What the fuck happened?" My blood is beginning to boil.

"They had to break in. Everybody was gone and Bobby's on the
run," she says. Bobby, looking strange minus his beard or thick natural, is on the phone talking a mile a minute. I start picking up underwear. Bobby gets off the phone.

"The pigs in Oakland have been planning for weeks to take us out
all at once," he says with finality and calm. "We gotta split. It's not safe
to stay here."

There's no time to change clothes, grab food, or finish picking up.
We leave the city in Alex's car, the six of us crammed together. The
streets in Oakland are deserted and eerie, as if the last days are upon
us and citizens are preparing quietly for disaster. It's quiet inside the
car too, except Bobby says when we get to West Oakland, we have to
split up. Bobby, Li-an, Bibo, and I take to the back streets. Alex and
Elsa, who must be in their late forties, leave in their car. We hop over
fences, scurry down side streets, and dart through backyards. The
chill from the San Francisco Bay sends cold into my bones even
though we keep moving.

"Where are we going?" I ask. Does he even know? Are we going to run all night? I hear sirens far off. Are we running from the police or the FBI? I look to the skies to see if Oakland is up in flames. We run out of breath at intervals, panting like hunted prey. Bobby has the stamina though he's the oldest.

"Just keep up," Bobby barks at us.

After a few blocks, he stops and summons us around. We hunch to hear him. "Huey P. said Oakland ain't going down in flames. The pigs are just itching for a chance to shoot down blacks in the streets. But Huey said this is no longer the time for spontaneous riots."

We get closer and closer to the Berkeley border and cross into South Berkeley, darting through vacant lots until we arrive at an innocuous duplex. Bobby goes around to a back door and we go in.

"Make yourself comfortable. Get something to eat." He points to the fridge. He sits down in the book-filled living room and makes himself at ease. Like an afterthought, he says to Bibo and to me, "If you want to fuck, you can use the bedroom. That's fine."

I couldn't have sex if my life depended on it. *We're comrades not lovers*, I say silently. I'm frightened to death that the FBI is going to kill us. Bobby falls asleep so fast it makes my head spin. Bibo makes calls, I presume to his wife but don't know and don't ask, since it's none of my business. I sleep fitfully on a sofa. When I wake up, Bobby and Bibo are gone. Li-an says Alex came and got them. We sprinkle cold water on our faces and leave the safe house to get back to our unsafe one.

The next night, April 6, Li-an gets a call. There's been a shoot-out in West Oakland between the police and the party. We call and wait for another call, listen to the radio for news, pace the hall, and wonder how bad it was. The radio responds with bits and pieces: Eldridge's shot, several Panthers arrested, no police injured.

Finally, someone from the office calls the house: "The pigs killed Li'l Bobby in cold blood. Eldridge got shot." Li'l Bobby, the youngest of all, shot and killed. Seventeen years old, the first person to join the party. I can't fathom it. I can't match his baby face with a body being plied with bullets in the heat of a fierce gun battle. In the space of the next seventy-two hours, I hear fiftyleven accounts of what happened. From Po-Rob, a brother from State who says he was in a caravan of cars out to get the pigs . . . led by Eldridge, who stopped to pee . . . at which point pigs surrounded them and they vamped. From the *Trib* . . . which relies on pig facts . . . Eldridge and Warren Wells were injured and held, with six brothers, on felony charges, including carrying a concealed weapon and attempted murder. From the party, that says the police ambushed them. From Po-Rob, who said the brothers ran and hid in different homes. . . . Some got caught. . . . Others got away. From brothers who say that Eldridge got naked before surrendering . . . to show that he was completely unarmed. . . . But Li'l Bobby wouldn't strip. From the *Trib* that says Li'l Bobby had a coat on and ran toward the police . . . crouching . . . and they couldn't see his hands. . . . Shot him seven times. From the brothers who say they saw a volley of bullets electrifying Li'l Bobby. The *Trib* says, the brothers say, the *Trib* says, the brothers say . . . The more I hear, the more my insides go bananas. For days, I can't stop crying screaming fainting listening recoiling retching agonizing, which no one hears or sees because it's all inside me. The details are stumbling all over creation, like drunks at an after-hours club, except for one: Li'l Bobby Hutton died.

MLK becomes a Panther the moment the bullet took him out. Li'l Bobby becomes a peer of MLK and Mx the moment the bullets take him out. In this time of martyrs, death joins all the factions of the movement in one grieving line of rock-hard resistance, one long black line twisting around the USA, Caribbean, Great Britain, Africa, Europe. At night I lie in bed by myself, picturing Li'l Bobby, scared in the basement, refusing to take off his clothes, prison-savvy Eldridge stripping naked to save his ass, emerging into the lethal spotlight. Tears and funerals, funerals and tears—we do the BPP layout between the tears and the funerals. Li'l Bobby's funeral comes first. The community turns out full force. As much as we know, it's still unreal. In jail, behind the glass during visiting hours, Eldridge says he wishes Kathleen had an automatic beating machine so she could beat herself while he's gone. Outside the church, after the service for Li'l Bobby, I cry with my roomies. All of a sudden people start rushing past us, whipping past with gale force, talking, pointing, exclaiming. Is something going down? Not here, not now, how much more can we take? A voice shrieks: It's Marlon Brando.

Someone points him out; people are running toward him. I don't believe it. He looks like an ordinary white man, average height, balding hairline, sport coat, no tie, except he jumps up on a flatbed truck.

He vows: I will do as much as I can to inform white people time is running out.

....

Chairman Bob and Li-an travel to Beverly Hills, where they stay with Brando in his mansion, then they fly on to Atlanta for the MLK funeral. I try to glimpse them on TV, think I see them, start getting scared sick every day, hear sirens every few minutes, especially when I sleep or I'm alone. When they return from Atlanta, the chairman says Brando decided to support King's Southern Christian Leadership Conference instead of the party. Money comes in anyway from all over the world. I'm in the movement. The party is the radical end of the whole movement—civil, human, black, urban, dispossessed, whatever you want to call it. I'm in it. But I'm numb and it feels like a machine.

53

Bobby Seale, grubby and whiskered, in full Chairman Bob mode, armed to the teeth with his cigarettes and tape recorder, leads our indigo-bold pack through Mosswood Park at Broadway and Mac Arthur across from Kaiser Permanente Hospital, where I was born. We are trying for a secluded spot where we can listen, safe from the FBI bugs, to a tape that Huey sent us, via his lawyer, Alex. For elusion, we shift from one grassy knoll to another, as if eight or nine black people in a very bad mood aren't cause within itself for alarm or notice. Silence is golden. The tape plays Huey's tight nasal alto. Everyone listens intently. I'm next to Bibo, who fell in with the group at the International House of Pancakes on Telegraph where we met for breakfast, and I wonder: *If we're so afraid of the FBI, how come any Negro that takes a notion can join, and not only call himself a Panther, but end up inside the inside faster than you can say Jack Robinson?* I snap to attention when I hear Huey mention my name. My name comes out of the recorder like a smoke ring. I am to assume Eldridge's duties as editor in chief of the paper.

Huey says, "I trust the sister; I'm familiar with her work from the paper at Oakland City College; she's a good writer; she participated in the struggle there."

....

My life changes in an instant. We leave the park. I leave everything behind and yet take it with me in my head on pages as colorful as a Montgomery Ward's catalog. Bobby and Huey standing like sentinels in the classroom, monitoring the young white Harvard history professor they hired to teach the first black history course at Oakland City College. I receive a salary of $25 a week. I received $67.50 a week from 401 but this $25 comes from the people's pocketbook; it is sacred. We open the BPP mail every day to dollar bills folded in scribbled notes addressed . . . To The Party . . . for my Brothers and Sisters, some anonymous, many containing checks and donations with letters of indignation, pain, relief attached. A telegram from Bertrand Russell excites everyone, and we feature it prominently in the paper. It begins to sink in why big names are so important for the cause. H. Rap Brown, Stokely's SNCC successor, submits an article; my brain hangs on to his words, which read like an epitaph: DO SOMETHING NIGGER IF YOU ONLY SPIT.

. . . .

LBJ's not going to run for a second term and I wake up once more to Dillard. *When is he going to get it? When am I?* He says, "Throw me your keys." My reflexes off, I throw them. He catches. "Let's go to Vegas, let's hit the road, Jack." The way he says Jack leaves me cold. I move toward my keys. He goes out and down the stairs. "Geniece, I gotta make a run to Vegas, use your car?" I look across the street where the FBI twins park. They're on coffee break. Dillard walks toward the VW. I'm in my robe, good grief. For an older guy, he moves fast. He says, "Sorry, Geniece, I have to make this run." I say, "Sorry, Dillard, not on my time." He fiddles with the driver door lock and pops it up. To stop his ass, I jump on the hood of my VW, smiling like a Cheshire. He smiles back. "I want my keys back." He shakes his head and says, "Call the police, sweetheart." He starts up my car. I say, "Motherfucker." He backs out with me sitting on it. I think he's playing some kind of stupid game with me. "Man, I don't owe you one red cent. What the fuck is in your head?" He shifts into neutral, then first. I grab hold of the roof, my fingers on the overhang. I am splayed on the roof as he accelerates. My grip tightens. Dillard says, "I'm going to learn you how not to trifle with my affections." Dillard starts to weave, trying to make me fall off. I imagine my head being crushed under a wheel. Maybe this is the way I'm supposed to go. I think about letting go. Dillard says, "I'll show your trifling ass how it feels to be trifled with." Why isn't anyone around? Out of desperation I call out, "Xavi, Xavi." Dillard says, "No

one's going to save your ass." I shout, "Get out of my car." Dillard turns
the corner and shouts back, "Get off the car." He starts to roll up the
window. "This is my car, don't you roll that window up on me." He
goes in circles to get me to fall off. I hang on. He says, "I'll drive you all
the way to Vegas, you can catch up with your daddy." We have a crowd
now. I keep calling out to Xavi. Dillard begins to slow down. The people stand in the street to stop the car, shouting, "Save her, save her."
They thought I was saying, "Save me, save me." He comes to a stop. I
slide off onto the street. Dillard gets out and throws my keys at me,
and says, "Hussy, find my car." I cry out, "I don't know where your
Ghia is." He says, "Later for your butt." I mutter, "I thought I was so
sweet." He says, "You ain't no more."

....

I come in very late from working the paper. Somebody's been smoking a cigarette on my bed. A taboo. Xavi points to the bathroom where
Li-an is sobbing.

Xavi whispers: "Li-an has broken up with Chandro-Imi. Don't go in
there. She found out that he was screwing around, because she got
vaginitus."

We called it the screwing-around infection. The last straw was when
Chandro paid rent on an apartment across the street and moved in
some other sister. I go into the bathroom to offer comfort to my friend.

Xavi says: "We're being replaced, you know, by a new crop of sisters,
fresh meat."

Li-an's choking wail is awful, but when I move to hold her, she rips
herself away from me. "I played the game, and I lost."

"Li-an, you don't have to be tough all the time. Hurt is hurt."

"Don't pity me. I hate pity. You need to deal with your own dialecti-
cal shit, Geniece. I dealt with mine, but at least he wasn't married.
Contradiction number one, two, and three."

I feel stung. She goes on, "Bibo, always in motion, now you see
him, now you don't. The real nitty-gritty is, you're messing with a
married man."

"I'm not messing with him." I could have added, *Because he's too slippery to catch.* She redoubles her BPP efforts. We all do.

....

3:30 A.M. Berkeley pigs break into Bobby Seale's apartment, on phony allegations of conspiracy to commit murder. My appetite is up, weight down. I blame the bennies. I only take them on deadline. I crave Goosey's sweet potato pie. I see the lonely face of the white girl Viva on one of my Berkeley runs. She lives in a studio off Telegraph, bright red hair and sensitive, almost mournful eyes. Bibo and I drop by Viva's to pick up copy from the Peace and Freedom Party for the paper. One of our jobs is to deal with white people. Eldridge does it with media and white mother country radicals. We have alliances from colleges with whites and other people of color, the Third World Liberation Front, the teachers' union. And hippies from the Peace and Freedom Party. We stand in the middle of the room because her room is junked with papers and books, the bed heaped. There's nowhere else.

She asks: "Why are you the only black people who'll talk to me?"

We laugh, but she isn't kidding. We can't tell her how contemptuously black people regard white people; she's too nice.

I ask what her real name is: It's Viva, as in viva la revolution. Like she was born in the immediate moment. And so it is, for the moment that we stand in her junky place, we are sprung from the top of our own heads.

I stop calling white girls Julie.

....

Bibo and I have come to the flatlands of Berkeley from the city to score a matchbox, though we're already high as hot-air balloons. He pulls the emergency brake on the VW all the way out of the socket. I wait in the car, but he takes so long I go inside the apartment. The guy who lives and deals there is black and has a natural, but right away I feel something different. There are no books, the first place I've been in months without books or bookshelves. Is it the 9 millimeter next to the stash? The conversation strictly centered on pricing the marijuana? *The way the guy passes us a joint, strictly business? Why am I so bothered by his rank opportunism? The People are catching hell, risking lives, dying; some of us are sacrificing school, job, and a future for this?*

Shit.

....

I straggle in one night, see Xavi looking grave, my cousin Buddy in the hall. My mind leaps to catastrophe. Did Uncle Boy-Boy have a heart attack? Goosey die? It has to do with death. Everything does now. I see death every time I open my eyes. Instead of morning there are funerals and court appearances. Evenings bring memorials. Afternoons are dedicated to demonstrations, where some get trampled, others shot to death. TV shows interrupted by news of body counts. Gossip displaced by shoot-out stories. Lynching up North. The Panthers wear indigo and black; the cops wear indigo and black, a brotherhood of measure. Xavi's suitcase is packed; I can't imagine why Buddy is here. Xavi says she is dropping out of school: "I'm going down South with Bud." They stand, a couple. Xavi and Buddy? Buddy talks: "Xavi and I have been seeing each other and we've decided." "To what? Get married? I saw you become somebody's husband in front of 150 people." They look at each other, not in bewilderment, in love. "How did this happen?" I ask. They start smiling. I say, "Does this go as far back as the stethoscope?" They nod. "What about Andrea?" They'll get an annulment. "I thought that was for Catholics or unconsummated unions." They didn't. "Didn't what?" Consummate. "How are Uncle Boy-Boy and Aunt Ola taking this?" My roomie and my mocha cousin in love. I look at the suitcase. "Where are you going?" "Norfolk, Virginia." His residency. "Tonight?" The airport. "Now?" Good grief, in the midst of all the craziness, romance, romance. Eldridge's dictum rolls through my head: "Brothers, get married so you can concentrate on revolution."

I feel like in some way Xavi and Buddy are asking for my okay on running off together. But of course they're not. They're informing me.

They're packed and on the way to the future. We get tearful as they go to the taxi waiting outside. I wave good-bye and sit on the steps in the cool night air.

....

I try to parse it. Andrea was always the old way. Buddy somehow got an injection of the new way when he went into the military. And when he came back, he couldn't just have a sterile marriage and a black bourgeois life. After all, he was the cuz who farted on my pillow if I didn't give him my Popsicle. He never was going to have a sterile life. Yet Xavi is proper enough, I guess. Oh gosh, I can't figure their attraction. Somehow it's romantic.

....

My heart feels like a river overflowing its banks. I want everybody to be happy. I want everybody to be free. My core says if other people are happy, then they'll leave me alone. And that makes me happy, because I need to explore what happiness is. I don't know what it is, but I'm curious. And I will find out what makes me happy. Likewise, if everyone is free and understands what freedom feels like, then they won't want to limit my freedom. And I can freely explore the whole world with my full heart to find what happiness means to me. Being somebody's wife and having to pick up my life and follow his life ain't it for me. But I grant that marriage brings warring clans together and civilizes men. Even Eldridge Cleaver, the great authority on romantic love, favors marriage. And I grant Xavi her freedom to explore what she wants in life and Buddy his. My cuz don't need nobody to grant him freedom. He was born with it. I, however, have had to fight for it. I had to push open a heavy screeching door to get to freedom. I felt that door creak open when I first started college and then met Allwood. It flew open in San Leandro, when I was getting fitted for my bridesmaid dress . . . and then again at Andrea and Buddy's wedding, when I found out why my father left me. And somehow wide open with Tammy and Yvette, my kinfolk out in the world.

54

Kathleen and I have one run-in. She stalks in while the staff is putting the finishing touches on the layout. We promised the printer we'd get it to him that night. Our eyes are bennie red, my eyelids three-days-no-sleep twitching.

She announces: "Because Eldridge is running for president of the United States on the Peace and Freedom Party ticket, we have to change the front page to a banner headline, a proclamation."

I tell her: "Absolutely not."

She looks like I've lost my mind. I repeat myself, even firmer. All hell breaks loose, a Kathleen-style all hell breaking loose. She throws a Marxist shit fit.

She accuses me: "This is a hundred kinds of error, political blasphemy."

I acknowledge it: "Yes, yes, but the paper has been put to bed, and that's that."

She storms out of the Oak Street flat, promising to convene the Central Committee lickety-split. If she could do that, she wouldn't have come here first. Getting decisions made is no snap when one part of the triumvirate, Eldridge, is in prison, another, Huey, in jail, and a third, Bobby Seale, is off somewhere at any given moment, giving speeches, rallying the troops, setting up and overseeing the national-international explosion of sympathy, drinking bitter dog, getting laid, laying waste.

Has she any idea of how much work, how many hours go into this? I don't begrudge all the high-yellow women, over and over and over, picked to sleep in the kings' beds, but give me a break from propping them on the arrowhead of the revolution to speak for the people. As if they had been chosen by the people instead of a brother entranced by the taboo he breaks or the color gulch he crosses. It's high-yellow hegemony. Work is work. Give credit where credit is due. I bet there are thousands like me: able-brown, consistent-brown, dependable-brown, loyal-brown, conscientious-brown, and invaluable-brown.

Don't treat me like a mule. When you do, I balk. I study the Sisters' Section from an early issue. I knew the editor then, also from City, a fair-skinned intelligent sister. How many people held this job before me? How many will hold it after me? Will this go on into perpetuity, one set of contradictions replaced by another? The pamphlet reads:

SISTERS UNITE. The Black Panther Party is where the BLACK MEN are. I know every black woman has to feel proud of black men who finally decided to announce to the world that they were putting an end to police brutality and black genocide. Then they were arrested even though they had not broken a law. The reason they were arrested, Sisters, is the white power structure doesn't want any brave men with guts enough to say, Hell No, to the police force in self defense of their women, themselves and all our children. That's really telling the power structure like it is. Become members of the Black Panther Party for Self Defense. Sisters, we got a good thing going.

It was a good thing, just not for every sister. Some got treated like chess pieces.

....

Wish Woodie comes by to see me. I'm so glad we never ran into him in the Haight when we were threatening white girls with our cigarette lighters for strolling arm in arm with brothers. Wish Woodie would have been disgusted at our bigotry. He listens to music until I finish talking and laughing with my roomies.

Alone, he tears into me: "Why is Li-an still wearing the earrings I made?"

I say: "Earrings, what earrings?"

He recalls them for me.

I say: "Oh, those . . . we share everything."

He says: "But they were personal, one-of-a-kind."

I say: "I'm not into personal possessions like that."

He shrugs.

I tell him: "The programs the party is instituting—free breakfast for children, free medical clinics, these aren't welfare. We have to show the people what a just society should provide its citizens."

He asks: "Guns? What about guns, Geniece?"

I reply: "Can't we defend ourselves? Isn't that a constitutional freedom, the right of the people to bear arms?"

He throws back: "Ten million black people against the whole world. It's numerically impossible."

I say: "The people's spirit is greater than the man's technology, Wish."

He says: "I fear for your life. Not just physically but morally."

I tell him about Eldridge's marriage dictum. But I seem to have protection from having to screw, because I have a very specific skill with words.

Wish asks: "Have you ever heard of the blue laws lecture?"

He explains they were called blue because they were bound in blue paper, a set of forty-five little-enforced laws in a book by Samuel Peters:

- Married couples have to live together or be imprisoned.
- Every male has to have his hair cut, rounded like a cap.
- No one shall cross a river on Sunday except clergy.
- Whoever publishes a lie to the prejudice of his neighbors must sit in the stocks or get fifteen lashes.
- Women can't kiss a child on the Sabbath or on fasting day.

I ask: "So?"

Wish says: "They didn't enforce them."

I say: "If they didn't enforce them, what were they for?"

Wish says: "To scare you into correct behavior. Believe you me, I would never get married because of some group dictum."

············

Wish Woodie's passion touches me. I appreciate his passion for his orphaned life, for his held-up self, even understanding that his passion is not for revolution except as it turns inside an individual. I am dismayed at how the Black Panther Party and some brothers in the Black Student Union treat women as a class and individually. As sexual cannon fodder in the midst of war. As trinkets to pick up and put down. As handmaidens ever at the ready. As souvenirs to show how much sex one has happened upon. As dupes played one against the other. I know all this is centuries old. But it's been a shock to knock my head on it in the movement.

I am happy with my own growth. Because Wish and I share being orphans, I love him for being concerned and for giving me criticism in an intellectual way, like, Geniece, don't let them run over you. I don't love him in any kind of romantic sense, but that may be good too. I've had a good jab at love as lab experiment. I would like to feel more tenderness and mutual respect. Wish and I respect each other. I admire that he survives, like a dandelion sprouting in concrete.

55

Li-an calls me at Oak Street in the city from the BPP office in Oakland. "The pigs just vamped on the Panther church."

St. Augustine's Episcopal Church on the outskirts of downtown Oakland is the Panther church. Thanks to Father Neil, the rector and a survivor of the Mississippi Freedom Summer, we got our Free Breakfast for Children program off the ground. I see him when I cook and serve for the program.

"Twelve OPD carrying twelve-gauge shotguns have invaded Father Neil's church," Li-An yells, and I hear lots of commotion and sirens in the background.

"Are there police at the office too?" I ask, looking for my purse and keys. She hangs up on me. The BPP has become so hip that everybody and their mother turns out for rallies, gauging a better chance of running into people than anytime since high school. The TV cameras put us on the six o'clock news so often, they should pay us. Being a Panther is cool until the shit goes down. Then it's just the pigs and us in our bloody intimacy. The phone rings. I know it's Li-an again.

"Girl, you won't believe it. Father Neil wouldn't let the pigs in the church. He held his ground. And the pigs had to get back in their cars."

"Should I come across the bridge?"

"What for? The shit went down without you or me. Do your job where you are, revolutionary sister."

Another day, another encounter.

. . . .

I haven't had a period since before time. Who knows why? So much stress, so many bennies at deadline, imbalances up the wazoo. Dillard shows up again, waiting for me outside the apartment. He points to a late-model sedan, two white men staring at us, taking notes as we talk.

He says: "I only came to hip you to these pigs keeping tabs on you."

I say: "The FBI is always here. So what?"

Dillard says: "Do you understand how serious this shit is?"

He walks away. I don't care.

....

Bobby Seale said you only die once so don't die a thousand times in your mind. Okay, I get it. Die once; live. I am too busy for sex. When I hit the pillow, I fantasize myself to sleep. I fantasize Bibo kissing my leg. His tongue wets my limbs like rain from a benevolent cloud. I shudder, twist my legs against his fingers, run into my body. I hear the small voice, the one that pops up every now and then when I have forgotten something important. It says: See about your period. I'm so busy on deadline and getting my papers done for school that I go to Planned Parenthood but forget to go back for the results. Between visits I tell Li-an, because I know she's too busy to tell me what to do. She tells me we need to go horseback riding.

....

We go horseback riding on Skyline Boulevard in Oakland. Horseback riding was one of the classy dates at City College. But if you got pregnant, horseback riding was supposed to dislodge the fetus, make you abort. We go early in the day. I ride my horse at a gallop, enough to bounce up and down, enough to bring a period down. It hurts. Li-an rides her horse like it's a mule, poking along. No blood. Planned Parenthood closes on the weekend. I can't wait for a yes or a no. When Li-an goes out, I take Carter's Little Liver Pills by the tens. Maybe I can get sick and have my stomach pumped. I have never been sick. I don't know anything but good health. I take one hundred Carter's Little Liver Pills. I feel a slight nausea, nothing more than I've felt on and off for weeks. I don't go to the hospital, I don't get pumped. I show up at PP bright and early.

They say: "You're expecting."

I say: "I'm not exactly sexually active."

The doctor says: "It's the immaculate conception; we hear about it all the time."

The next two weeks are frantic. Li-an knows, no one else. If I don't tell anyone, then no one else ever has to know. I gather options: Leave the country and have an abortion in Norway (this from another doctor); keep doing bodily damage until I either abort or kill myself; drink quinine; get the coat hanger. I'm afraid. A woman at PP said I could have crippled myself with the liver pills. She gives me a number to call. I'm afraid. Maybe she's the FBI, trying to get me to commit suicide. The men still sit outside the apartment watching us. Maybe she's not the FBI but has contacts with abortionists, dirty-fingered men in bare lightbulb offices.

I break down and tell Li-an, "I can't hurt myself anymore. I just can't."

Li-an says, "All men are dogs; revolutionaries are dogs with rhetoric, but dogs just the same."

I say, "Li-an, I know you're bitter because of Chandro-Imi's screwing other women."

Li-an says, "I'm not bitter, I'm pragmatic. If I was bitter, I would think the revolution starts and ends with my love life. And I would have quit all y'all."

She suggests I see one of the white girls upstairs from us who works at UCSF Hospital. I find our neighbor at UCSF, where she works as a ward clerk.

She says: "You look worried, what's up?"

My voice wavers: "I'm afraid. I'm out of money. I got pregnant. I can't do it."

She goes to another floor, comes back after a while, and shows me a memo. It explains a new law in California permitting abortion to be legal and performed by doctors in hospitals. She's the first white person in the city to show concern for me.

She says: "Here's a number to call. It's an abortion shrink. You have to visit him twice, talk with him."

I frown.

She says: "It's a formality. . . . But when you go talk like it's already driving you nuts, being pregnant. . . . Act a little crazy or paranoid or something. . . . Then he can sign and you can get it done at Kaiser."

. . . .

I go, nearly three months but hardly showing, to a psychiatrist's office in Berkeley. He knows I'm a Panther. He's a big donor to our clinics.

I say: "The sirens in San Francisco, all the sirens in the city drive me nuts."

Then: "The FBI outside my apartment drives me nuts."

I add: "My teacher from high school and his photos of the man cut in half by the train turn up in my dreams now."

I tell him about George Sams: "He makes my skin crawl."

I don't have to exaggerate. I don't have to lie.

He asks: "Anything else?"

I say: "Sometimes I can't take the contradictions."

He says: "You mean of the movement and radicalism?"

I shake my head: "I can't take the fire engines racing through the city incessantly and the dogs howling afterward, the urban symphony."

He says: "That disturbs you?"

I nod: "One night when I was zonked, I sat at the window looking at the park when, lo and behold, like Santa Claus and the reindeers, a fire engine charged through the trees and raced across the park. It was absolutely fascinating, except I thought it was headed my way."

He asks: "You were using drugs?"

I say: "Just weed. I was transfixed by the thought of dying that way instead of being offed by the pigs. But the driver made a turn and rolled on down the street. We found out later we lived across from an emergency shortcut for the fire department."

After a silence I ask: "Is this enough?"

He nods and signs the second trimester abortion form and walks me out to the reception area, where Bibo is waiting. We leave. I see the reflection in the windows of the shrink standing, gaping. I don't know if it's what I told him or that he's seeing two live Panthers.

56

Bibo and I keep our eyes peeled for the University Avenue exit. After the San Francisco airport, we're on our way to Palo Alto on 101 South. "How long is your appointment?"

"Less than an hour."

"A Stanford donor. That's big money."

I'm going to Stanford; he's going to a meat wholesaler in Union City who has donated sausages to the party for our Breakfast for Children program. We take the exit and drive up to the gates that I had gone through last at the school's Black Arts Week. I had performed with LeRoi Jones.

"Take Palm to Arboretum and left on Quarry," the guard says.

The campus is an idyllic leafy suburb with bicyclists and students with Frisbees. If I didn't read the papers or look at TV, the My Lai massacre might seem like it took place on another planet. Or maybe Stanford is a planet, not a university. When we reach the medical school, Bibo gives me instructions. "This is how we work it. I drop you here. Cut over the Dumbarton Bridge, pick up the meat, and come back right here. I'll be waiting, okay?"

I watch him drive away before I check out the students, guessing which came from money and which were on scholarship. I can't figure it out. Appearances, appearances. Everything that's gold doesn't glitter. I go up to the sixth floor, looking for the State alumni and third-year resident I'd talked to on the phone. He finds me.

"Geniece Hightower from State?"

Now he looks like a scholarship student with his beard, jeans, and sneakers. He ushers me into the conference room and we sit across from each other. I pull out my notebook where I keep a record of all contributions given to me. I record his.

"I want you to know I read the Black Panther paper religiously. And follow the party in the news as well."

"Why religiously?" Sounds like FBI. He laughs and pauses and laughs again.

"That's part of why we wanted to talk to you. All the social programs that the Black Panthers are initiating are extremely important to us. The university has pioneered studies of newborn and early childhood mortality risk and early childhood learning, and we see a correlation between child nutrition, early developmental support in child care, health, and education, and the exact kinds of programs you're running."

From our phone call I'd thought this would go in the direction of a donation from some Abe Lincoln Brigade radical, the kind who fought fascism in Spain in the thirties.

"The school of medicine has reserved four slots next fall for black applicants."

The black premed students I knew had graduated State and were taking advanced sciences, hoping to get in UCSF or elsewhere. Stanford? Impossible without family connections.

"The committee has already made three selections. You're our fourth."

I couldn't believe my ears. Was I dreaming awake? "I don't see how I could be a doctor."

"I've followed your work, brilliant writing on social change and women."

"I did one piece in the BPP. That's not a body of work." I was getting paranoid. Was this how the FBI got informants? I thought it would have been more straightforward. "My science grades, ah, I can't even explain them away."

He is beyond eager. "Look, we bring you in. Use the first year to bring you up to snuff. Tutors, counselors, scholarship, housing, and a stipend."

The thought of a doctor's uniform over my jeans is mind-blowing. Dr. Geniece. He keeps on. Would I be interested in pediatrics? Infectious diseases? Ob-gyn? Then the door to the conference room opens and an older white man, who looks like he was born with money dripping from his umbilical cord, comes in.

"Young lady, I've heard that you're our newest humanitarian project."

This is unfathomable. "Why of all the people have I turned up on your radar?"

"It's not so far from the realm of possibility. Your tutorial program's making quite an impact," he says. "We are one of the funders for the program."

"I tutor kids. How does that connect to medical school?"

He sits and says, "There's a tremendous shortage of physicians in urban communities. We're committed to changing that, and you are bright and committed."

He shakes my hand and walks out. The resident beams.

"I still don't understand why my name came up for this."

"It came up three different ways. The chair of your psychology department gave us a list of possible candidates, and your name was on it." I never had a decent conversation with him. Why would he have done that?

"Secondly, we know of your community ethic with both the Panther Party and your work on Potrero Hill. That's huge for us." Not as huge as it was for Tammy and Yvette.

"What's the third?" They know too much about me. At this point he got excited. "I know that you are almost solely responsible for open admissions. The BSU chairman told me about your work in bringing that about."

Chandro-Imi! I'm stupefied.

"There you have it—the future. Help us change the world." He gives me a sheaf of application papers and I leave the building in a haze. I cross a footbridge and my legs give out. I see Bibo waiting for me and crawl into the car.

"What happened? You're shook. Did you have a confrontation?"

"It was crazy, that's all I can say. Crazy." I give Bibo the blow-by-blow. He cracks up so hard he has to stop driving.

"This is exactly what Huey predicted. He said we'd know we

achieved the revolution when black people had all the opportunities and psychoses of white people."

"You better drive this car. Why is this funny? I don't see cause for hysteria."

"It's funny because it's surreal." We get out of Palo Alto and back on 101. "This is a message from the future."

"Oh, I was dreaming this whole thing? They couldn't possibly be serious?"

"No, baby, they were serious. Are you? Do you want to be a doctor?"

"I was a candy striper in high school."

He yells at me so loud it hurts my ears. "Do you want to be a doctor, fool?"

I yell back. "No, I don't want to be a doctor. Dammit."

He finds some R&B on the radio and lights up. I don't want any but get a contact anyway. Back in the city, Bibo drops me at the pad but touches my shoulder to say, "We won't see the results of the revolution. We'll either be dead or in jail. Dig?"

I call the resident and connect him to the black premed students. I don't want to be a doctor. But it was interesting to peer into the future.

57

It's May Day, 1968. Students all over the world demonstrate by cutting classes April 26 to end the war in Vietnam. When I step again into Yvette and Tammy's apartment, which smells of garlic sausages and fried potatoes, they're washing down dinner with grape soda. They mostly stayed at Grannie's next door even after Mrs. Moore came home from the hospital. Whenever I called, they weren't at home but at Grannie's. I look around for Mrs. Moore. I've got free tickets from the tutorial program to see the Harlem Globetrotters in the gymnasium at State. I want to be on time.

Tammy says her mom is back at her boyfriend's apartment, been there since coming from the hospital. We find seats in the middle of the bleachers, canned music from "Sweet Georgia Brown" filling the room. The kids go nuts as the players cakewalk onto the floor. The kids, slurping Popsicles, love Curly, the bald-headed player—even when he stands mute and stares at them.

Tammy says she wants to move up higher. Yvette tells her to shut up.

Tammy begs. I say, "The bogeyman's crawling around up there. You don't want to go up higher."

Tammy asks to go to the bathroom.

Yvette says, "You went already when we came in." Tammy says, "Can't help it."

I say, "A whale mouse waits in there for little girls who drink grape soda. And he'll bite your pee-pee if you go to the bathroom before halftime."

Tammy asks, "What happens at halftime?"

I say, "He gets spooked when he hears all the toilets flush and hides."

Yvette says, "Yeah, Tammy, he'll bite if we go in now."

The Globetrotters irk me; they're a throwback to Stepin Fetchit. It's painful to watch them, minstrels with basketballs. I buy cotton candy,

Crackerjacks. I think of Bert Williams, who had to please the crowd that wanted nothing more, nothing less, than blackface, an object of ridicule. Yet his essential dignity shone through. I attempt to see the Globetrotters' dignity, but it's hard. The children's laughter resounds.

Tammy says, "Yvette still has some Crackerjacks. Make her gimme some."

Yvette says, "I didn't ask for any of your cotton candy."

I say, putting my ear to the box, "The Crackerjacks say, 'If Tammy eats us, we'll turn her into a big ant, big as this room.'"

She giggles, but she's scared off. When we get ready to leave, Tammy won't go in the stall in the ladies' room by herself. I go in with her and use the toilet standing up so she can see the whale mouse isn't there.

Tammy shrieks, "There he is."

I turn around and look. She smiles.

Tammy says he had big orange eyes and a tail like a whip.

One last treat I buy from a vendor inside is a pack of black Jawbreakers, the strongest manifestation of blackness in the show. We suck them to the center, which is a hunk of chewing gum. They take a while to suck. I hate the texture. It feels like gravel rolling around my mouth. Our tongues turn black. We show each other. "My tongue feels like a driveway," I say. The two of us make big bubbles. Yvette teases Tammy for not knowing how to make bubbles.

Back at the apartment, I wait for Mrs. Moore. She wasn't there when we left. She isn't there when we return. The girls begin getting ready for bed as if this is routine.

"Where is your mother?"

"Out," Yvette says. "She does the same thing all the time."

"She prolly went to a bar," Tammy adds.

They want to snuggle on the sofa with me. We talk about the game, school, the foster home, and how they got used to it. I'm getting tired. *Come on, Mrs. Moore, I'm not staying here until the bars close. Or your boyfriend falls asleep.* I yawn.

"Don't go to sleep, Geniece," Tammy says.

"Don't worry, I won't."

"I want to show you what I can do," she says. She pulls a Jawbreaker out of her pajama pocket. I thought we sucked them all. She bounces it on her palm a couple of times, and before I see what she's trying, throws it up. She positions her mouth to catch it, like a flamethrower. It goes in. I jump up. I hear it hit her pharynx. She makes a sound like she's gargling it. I hold my hands out. I expect it to come back out like mouthwash. Yvette peers down Tammy's wide-open mouth.

"It's stuck," she says. She looks up at me. I look at Tammy's blackened tongue. It looks like a blacktop driveway, the Jawbreaker an oversized stone at the end. Gingerly I put my fingers in her mouth.

"She's not going to bite you. She can't move her mouth," Yvette says. I take my fingers out.

"Your hand is smaller than mine, Yvette. Try to get it."

"No, your fingers are longer." She's right, she's always right. Damn. I stick my fingers into Tammy's mouth. I hated cutting up frogs in lab. Yvette's voice goes up with her anxiety. "Hurry up, Geniece, before she can't breathe."

"Go call the operator, Yvette."

I hear her feet against the linoleum. I hear her dial. I edge my thumb and forefinger toward the ball. I hear each click of the dial as it returns. But the bridge between my thumb and pointer finger is too big for Tammy's mouth. When I close the two together, the thumb doesn't reach far down enough. Tammy keeps blinking but stays calm. Scared stiff, I hear Yvette talking. The Jawbreaker turns a little. A sweet-smelling black viscous strand drips off the ball. It goes down her throat. Tammy begins to gag. Yvette comes back.

"They're sending the fire department."

Tammy's eyes close. I have to do something before she chokes on her spit. I edge my forefinger and index finger toward the ball. If only I had talons. I get ahold of one side but not the other. Tammy gags again. The Jawbreaker spins downward and settles on her windpipe. Her body goes slack. We sit her down. Her eyes blink open. She looks at me, fully conscious, silently beseeching me to let her breathe again. I try again, but it is entrenched. A black thing stuck in her windpipe.

"Maybe if we push it back up. Squeeze it out?" Yvette suggests. The sound of the fire engine approaching steels us. Yvette squeezes Tammy but only funny sounds come out. I reach in again but can't do anything for fear of pushing it down more. Tammy lifts her fingers to her throat as if pointing to the candy.

"We see it, Tammy. We can't get at it," Yvette says. Her voice cracks. "We just can't get at it."

Tammy convulses twice, her eyes reach to me, pleading, between waves, and she goes limp. Her eyes close. Then her lips form a horrible rounding over her teeth. Her mouth is still open but like a fish mouth, limp. The firemen knock on the door. Yvette, in tears, goes to the door, lets them in. They rush to the sofa, take over. As we explain, one holds her lifeless body over his knees, as if the Jawbreaker will come out. But it is lodged there. They take her pulse, go through motions, but I can tell by their faces it's no use. One takes me by the shoulder. He explains it's a freak accident. . . . We would have had to crush her throat to get it or break both jaws. . . . She would've died either way. The ambulance attendants come with the stretcher. When they place her body on it and I see that her top is buttoned crooked, I shudder. The attendants lay her hands at her sides; her head looks like it has wilted from its stem. Yvette holds on to me. The firemen ask if I'm the mother. When I tell them I'm not, they say they didn't think so. I have no idea where she is. I tell them that. I want to touch Tammy's head, straighten it out. It lolls to the side as if she is pretending to look silly. I touch her; I feel the pressed edges of her hair at her temple. I align her head with her body. I brush my lips against her warm face and stand up. Yvette touches her forehead. Death, as if it's been sitting in her throat all day, relaxes the muscles and pushes the Jawbreaker out. It rolls off her chin and onto the floor with more liveliness than anyone in the room. It comes to rest underneath the stretcher. They begin to wheel Tammy out. Our eyes turn toward her. One of the front wheels crunches the Jawbreaker to pieces, black to black to black. The wheels flatten the pieces, rolling out the gumminess. I gather our sweaters and, with Yvette in her nightgown, walk out.

All is quiet, even though many people stand around waiting to see who will emerge on the stretcher. When they see Tammy, they gasp.

Each drawn-in breath rips off the box around my heart; people begin wailing and sobbing her name as we get in the ambulance. Yvette holds on to me for dear life. I want the paramedics to explain how they handle this, fresh, young, inexplicable death. Instead, the ambulance rolls down the hill and I hold on, wanting this entire black, blacker, blackest night to be a parable of destruction I imparted to the girls. Only a parable.

Yvette turns to me and says, "Geniece, something moved around in your stomach, I felt it against my cheek."

It hits me as hard as the surface of one of those Jawbreakers. I am still pregnant. I haven't had time to get an abortion. The ambulance rolls on and Yvette puts her ear at different places on my abdomen. My throbbing heart feels as if someone has touched it and it might hemorrhage. I can't take one more blow to this entity called my life.

. . . .

Between finals I go to the funeral home to see Tammy. I recognize some of the girls' neighbors, their social worker, and Grannie, who motions me to sit next to her.

"Why is the casket closed?" I whisper to Grannie.

She whispers back, "They Catholic, but Mrs. Moore don't go to church. So they had it here. Cheaper. Don't have to move the body back and forth."

"How is Mrs. Moore holding up? Is she all right?"

"No, chile, she ailing bad. Back in the hospital. I don't think she'll be out soon."

"And Yvette?"

She raises her eyebrows. "You didn't hear?"

"I've called and the phone is disconnected."

"Yvette sent to live with her great-aunt in Texas, on the white side of her family. Say they got a good home for her."

"What a horrible shock to lose Tammy, her mother, and then to have to move to Texas."

Grannie pats my knee. "Chile, that girl was pulling the whole family on her shoulders. It was too much. Being an orphan not the worst thing. Sometimes you get to start over, if you can only get some kindness shown you."

Maybe Aunt Ola was right. Maybe I was fortunate Family had spread its wings over me until I left the nest, the orphan blackbird.

58

"Here's the lowdown on the paper," Li-an says. She and I are driving out to State. "They're making Eldridge's cell mate the editor."

I nearly ram a Muni streetcar. "In my place?"

"Don't get pushed out of shape," she says, and touches my shoulder. "It's just the way things are. They make promises in prison. . . . You can still contribute articles."

"I never do articles, I edit."

"I'm telling you what I heard, the scuttlebutt."

. . . .

I've rowed to the middle of the deep blue sea in a leaky boat, faced down Scylla and Charybdis, and now I'm being told to take a walk. Nobody's indispensable.

She says, "By the way, Bibo's back in the pen."

"Back?"

"Don't act surprised, Geniece. He got popped robbing a gas station in fucking Fresno. Packing."

"Armed robbery? He'll be expelled for being a jackanape."

"Already happened. And, Geniece, don't visit his nihilist ass. Leave that for his damn wife."

I'm silent for a few blocks, then say: "I fucked my way into this whole crusade. I thought I would have to fuck my way out."

"Somebody else did that for you," Li-an says. "All you have to do is step aside." It felt like a feather had brushed against me. It didn't feel like a blow. It didn't feel like I thought it would. Everything that I had been doing was behind the scenes. Way behind. I hadn't expected to become helpful and caring. I had wanted to be admired and inspired. I wanted men to call me fine and pant after me. I wanted to be pumped up by one rally after another. I thought it was going to be fun and exciting for days on end. Yet here I was taking galleys to printers in the deep of night, delivering sausages, and scrambling eggs for children whose parents either couldn't or didn't know to say thank you, running out to Santa Rita county jail, where problem inmates were taught the skills that would help them survive outside of jail. My life was a race, not to the protests or press conferences or confrontations or the podiums where the speechifiers held sway, but to the printer and the churches where we served kids breakfast and the county jail.

....

Even though Li-an had told me not to visit Bibo, after three visits to Santa Rita to visit other brothers I didn't even know, I visited him. I waited outside the facility for two hours while the long line of mostly women, some pushing strollers, showed their ID and had their purses searched. It took forty-five minutes before I walked past a labyrinth of zones. We were the prisoners here too. The guards led a group of six into a room as big as a hospital waiting room. Other guards stood at the far side as the detainees filed in. I was surprised that there were no barriers. It wasn't like the movies. Bibo spotted me before I spotted him. He looked different. He had shaved his mustache and trimmed his natural way down.

"Ah, my girl revolutionary. You came to see me. My own wife hasn't been out here." We hugged. I looked around to see if the guards were looking, but they weren't. Other couples were kissing and hugging.

Bibo started talking real fast, too fast for me to understand him. "Slow down, I can't understand you."

"You don't know bout the fire. We did it."

"What fire? What're you talking about?"

"The Revolutionary Night Lighting, White-frightening Fire Brigade. Remember that?"

I nodded. I had been working on the paper. "You mean when I talked it up with the SNCC guy with Stokely at our party?"

"Yeah, yeah, yeah. A bunch of us . . . we went out to the suburbs and did it."

He kept on talking while the other people in the room got even busier with the face-to-face and body-to-body jamming. "We did it. We set the night on fire."

"You guys made a fire. Where?"

"You don't need to know where. That's why I'm in here."

"I thought you were in for a robbery in Fresno."

"Do I look like I'm in jail in Fresno? Who told you that?"

"Never mind who told me. What are you in for?"

"Arson, attempted murder, resisting arrest, and carrying a loaded piece in my car. I'm gonna need a whole lot of lawyering."

I buried my head in my hands. We had just printed a long article on why the party retained the services of Charles Garry, a Marxist attorney, instead of a black lawyer. Garry had won cases for radicals and trade unionists.

"Bibo, your stuff is lumpen proletariat shit."

The sound of a man coming right there in the room jolted our conversation. I looked around and saw a woman wiping his cum from her face and hair. The guards were talking to each other like nothing had happened.

"I can't believe this. What kind of prison is this?" I said.

"It's jail, not prison. If you want to, you can do me," Bibo said.

In the open? It had all boiled down to this? Give it up because he was a down brother? In this Niagara Falls of the West, the Alameda County jail, this library of the lumpen, each person, black mostly, a Mexican, a white, fucked for life already, a history of Western civilization in this room.

"Do I have a say in all this?"

They were working class, never-worked class, incarcerated, their lives incinerated in all this heat. It was a strange moment. I didn't feel contempt for Bibo or any of the people around us, not even the guards. I thought about the lump of tissue and soft bone inside me.

"Yes, girl revolutionary, I love you. Do you need to hear that to get down?"

I shook my head. I had two hearts beating inside me. If I had only one, sure, I would give head, perform fellatio ferociously and tenderly, cup my lips and suck dick, stroke it with all the girl revolutionary fervor I could muster, regardless of his being married, regardless of pride, regardless of the inappropriateness of it all. But the girl revolutionary had fallen on the road back there, somewhere, where she had followed the revolution to the last rung of the ladder.

....

I left Santa Rita.

All the way back to San Francisco, I saw the girl revolutionary standing by the side of the road.

Life, my own and new life, was throbbing in my body.

I had done the revolution without regret. I had done what my instincts and rationality had compelled me to do—violating so many rules, breaking hearts, having my own broken. I had done enough rotten deeds to be buried under the jail. But one law had not been violated—I had never lied to myself.

And I couldn't lie now. I wasn't sure which way to turn, but the road did not go further.

When I moved to Vegas to attend grad school, I dropped the old, odd, berzerkeley clothes in the Goodwill bin on San Pablo Avenue, the books on revolution and guerrilla warfare I sold at the flea market (*Das Kapital*, my old doorstop, got the best price), and the guns, mostly the guns, I sold back to Siegel's Guns in Oakland and Traders' in San Leandro. There were more of those guns than I had thought: 30.06s, revolvers, the .22 I carried in my purse with my lip blush and keys, the .357 Magnum with the barrel bigger than my palm. I had enough guns to start a gun shop of my own. But I got rid of the guns—and the bed. I was tired of them both. What did James Brown say? "Money won't change you / But time will take you on."

People kept finding guns after we thought we were done with them. Li-an wrote that when she left the party to go back to school full-time, she found a 9 millimeter wrapped in a shawl in the bottom drawer of my burl wood dresser. Even Xavi wrote me about her metal footlocker that I had shipped to her in Virginia. A .45 was packed inside her Mother Hubbard shoes. We had been in a war sure enough. Burn it down, burn amerikkka down. On strike, shut it down. Thinking is a free country. Resistance, resistance, resistance. Stop the Gestapo. Control your police. Whatever the man supports, we oppose. What were we planning to blow away?

Goosey died, simply put her crocheting needles down and slumped over. When I went to Fouché's funeral home I had to get over family telling me if I looked at the dead while carrying a baby, the child would sleep forever with its eyes half open. In turbulent times, a peaceful death in old age is a blessing.

Because I assisted behind the lines of fire, transcribing the men's story, tutoring the young, making love and potato salad, I was spared death. My shoot for the moon was on a parchment rocket. I took my small step to the moon infinitely closer by carrying to term and one month beyond. The revolution had been the father of my child, but when my water broke, Wish stepped in as my natural birth partner. When I was wheeled into the delivery room, the doctor told me I was going to have a large, healthy baby for sure. When he asked me to push like I was moving my bowels, I did, figuring he was playing—which he wasn't. I felt a train moving through my body and bawled, "I can't go through with this," at which moment the doctor said, "The head's out." I envisioned the shoulders getting stuck. Wish bent to wipe my forehead, and I pierced his poor eardrum. The doctor said, "Mr. and Mrs. Hightower, you have a son," and everyone started laughing and crying over the same and different things, the baby being born, Wish being called Mr. Hightower, Wish's eardrum getting blown out, and the spectacle of young womanhood changing into motherhood.

Geniece, my virgin soul, left at that moment. But a memorial to her vibrant leapfrogging passes through these pages.

Geneva Anniece Hightower

GENEVA ANNIECE HIGHTOWER

*Written Thesis Submitted in Partial Fulfillment
of Requirements for Master of Arts Degree*

UNIVERSITY OF NEVADA, LAS VEGAS, 1973